life as I know it

life as I know it

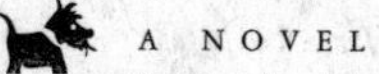

A NOVEL

Melanie Rose

BANTAM BOOKS
TRADE PAPERBACKS
NEW YORK

Life as I Know It *is a work of fiction. Names, characters, places, and incidents are the products of the author's imagination or are used fictitiously. Any resemblance to actual events, locales, or persons, living or dead, is entirely coincidental.*

2010 Bantam Trade Paperback Edition

Published in the United States by Bantam, an imprint of The Random House Publishing Group, a division of Random House, Inc., New York.

BANTAM *is a registered trademark of Random House, Inc., and the colophon is a trademark of Random House, Inc*

Originally published in Great Britain as Being Lauren *by Matador, an imprint of Troubadour Publishing Ltd in 2005 and as* Could It Be Magic? *by Avon, a division of HarperCollins Publishers in 2009.*

LIBRARY OF CONGRESS CATALOGING-IN-PUBLICATION DATA
Rose, Melanie.
{Could it be magic?}
Life as I know it : a novel / Melanie Rose.
p. cm.
Originally published in Great Britain as Being Lauren by Matador in 2005 and, with modifications, as Could it be magic? by Avon in 2009.
ISBN 978-0-385-34399-2
1. Accident victims—Fiction. 2. Life change events—Fiction. 3. Multiple personality—Fiction. I. Title.
PR6118.0845B45 2010
823'.92—dc22 2009037754

Printed in the United States of America

www.bantamdell.com

9 8 7 6 5 4 3 2 1

Book design by Ellen Cipriano

This book is for David, with love.
It is also for all the courageous children
both past and present who have been my inspiration.

life as I know it

prologue

Frankie dragged me gleefully through the dusty parking lot onto the short grass of the Downs, where I paused to inhale the autumn air, grateful to be outdoors at last: away from the gasoline fumes of the nearby road and the confines of my small flat. Bending to unclip the lead from her collar, I straightened to watch my three-year-old terrier streak exuberantly away into the distance. Smiling, I found myself wishing I could run wildly after her with equal glorious abandonment.

Contenting myself with a brisk walk, I caught up with her eventually and we continued in companionable silence along a familiar track on the Epsom Downs, Frankie leading the way on her short, businesslike legs. I allowed my mind to drift while the tensions of the week gradually subsided and my muscles slowly relaxed.

As we climbed a small rise, the sun slid behind a cloud and I glanced up, noticing how still the air had become. The Downs were still there, rolling away on either side of me, but the dry grass and distant trees, which a moment before had been green and brown in the early afternoon sunshine, had been touched by an eerie yellowish hue. Shivering, I pulled my sheepskin coat more closely around me and quickened my stride.

Frankie darted off toward some small trees and I cursed softly under my breath, hoping she wasn't going to vanish just as I was thinking of starting the long walk back to the car. A sudden chill had descended and the sky was turning as purple and black as a bruised plum. The landscape seemed bathed in an unnatural silence. I realized with trepidation that even the birds had stopped singing.

A deep rumble echoed across the distant hills and a few seconds later Frankie came racing back over the cropped turf, her hind legs going so fast with each panicked bound that they seemed almost to be sticking out from under her whiskery nose. She collided with my jean-clad shins and started to whine.

Stooping down, I picked her up and held her against me, ignoring the grubby marks her paws made on my coat. The feel of her warm body and the scent of doggy breath on my face reassured me that I hadn't stepped inadvertently into the stillness of an artist's landscape painting. I stood and stared at the fearsome beauty around me with a feeling of awe. The strange light had brushed the autumnal trees on the far hilltop, tipping them with gold, yet the sky was growing blacker and more ominous by the second.

And then the wind started. It hit with an audible "whoomp," and with such force that I staggered back under the onslaught. It whisked my brown, shoulder-length hair out behind me and clamped its cold hand over my face so that I had to gasp for breath. Frankie wriggled in my arms, but I was afraid to put her down in case she ran off again.

Holding her firmly under one arm, I struggled to clip the end of the lead to her tartan collar, and was lowering her to the ground when I saw a black Labrador rocketing toward us. She was almost upon us when the first streak of lightning split the heavens. The thunderclap that followed seconds later had both dogs cowering against my legs, normal sniffing formalities forgotten. I hunkered down with them, remembering something I'd been told about lightning hitting the tallest point. I didn't want it to be me.

We were still huddled together, heads bowed, my arms thrown protectively around both dogs, when a hand touched my shoulder. My head jerked up to see a man standing over us, dog lead dangling from his hand. "You okay?" he shouted above the roar of the wind.

Embarrassment flooded my neck and cheeks with heat. I struggled to my feet and found myself looking into the blue eyes of a man in his early thirties. I took a deep steadying breath, trying to pull my flapping coat together while keeping my balance against the buffeting gusts and Frankie's insistent pulling.

A second flash of lightning crackled above us and we both flinched instinctively. Disjointed thoughts flickered through my mind, one of which was why did I have to meet every girl's dream guy while huddled in a heap on the Downs with two muddy dogs in the middle of a thunderstorm?

"Is she yours?" I yelled, glancing at the black Lab, which was now bounding around the man in delight.

"Yeah, she ran off. Thanks for stopping her."

His eyes stayed on mine, and I found myself flipping wildly through possible excuses to keep him talking, but my lips seemed obstinately welded together. I watched helplessly as he clipped the lead to his dog's collar, smiled his thanks, and began to move off along the track. That would have been the end of it,

I was sure, except that the rain started then: huge shimmering drops that smacked down, on, and around us like small cannonballs, creating dark splotches on the dry earth where they fell. The man turned back in my direction, pulling up the collar of his jacket and bowing his head against the onslaught. As he drew level with Frankie and me the deluge increased in its ferocity until we couldn't see more than an arm's reach in any direction. It was like standing under a waterfall, and my eyes and mouth and nose were full of it. My sheepskin coat blackened and my hair was almost immediately reduced to stringy tendrils. We looked at each other, this stranger and I, and started to laugh. He had a lovely laugh, deep and throaty, and even with his short hair flattened against his head, and water dripping off the end of his nose, I think I realized he was someone special right then and there.

"My car's parked right over there," he shouted, pointing vaguely in the direction he was heading. "Do you want to make a run for shelter?"

I nodded, and to my complete delight, he took my cold, wet hand in his and pulled me along beside him, the two dogs, tails tucked miserably between their legs, trailing along in our wake.

Our breathing became labored as we ran, increasing with the ferocity of the driving wind and rain. I could feel the blood pounding through my veins, and my fingers, entwined with his, were tingling in an ecstasy that was something akin to pain.

We were almost at the parking lot when the lightning flashed again, illuminating the row of cars hunched in the mist ahead of us. As we drew closer I could see the sheeting rain bouncing off the sleek metal bodies and puddling on the ground beneath. The plunging drops created a misty upward spray, which was beautiful in its way, but not as wonderful as the feeling I had of belonging to this man I hardly knew, whose dripping fingers were burning holes in my palms. There was an electricity between us, something I'd never experienced before, a connection I couldn't begin to put into words.

The rain pummeled our backs, pushing us onward, our steps pounding in perfect unison, and as we neared the car, panting for breath, he looked into my eyes and a tremor of excitement ran through me. He dropped my hand for a moment to reach into his pocket for the car keys, and at that exact point the whole sky lit up with a crackling roar. A shaft of lightning entered my body in a convulsive explosion of white noise.

The euphoria I had been feeling vanished as if someone had flicked off a giant switch. There was a searing pain through my shoulders. I watched, entranced, as the stranger's eyes widened in horror. I could smell the sickening stench of burning flesh and knew with a detached sort of knowledge that it belonged to me. For a split second I felt as if I were hovering above myself, my earthly body engulfed in an aura of red. Then I shuddered and sank down onto the wet ground, closed my eyes, and knew only blackness and nothing.

chapter one

As dreams went, it was a scary one. I snuggled deeper into my pillow, preparing to drift back to sleep, to try to recapture the feeling I'd had with the handsome stranger. But some alien scent or sound roused me, tugging at my consciousness. I opened one bleary eye and turned to look at the bedside clock. It wasn't there. What was there was a stark Formica cabinet topped with a plastic water jug standing next to a white plastic beaker complete with drinking straw.

Pushing myself up on one elbow, I discovered that a needle had been taped in place on the back of my left hand. It appeared to be attached to a clear bag of fluid, which dripped into my veins via a thin line. I stared at it for a few seconds, then peered around at the small windowless room. Apart from the cabinet and the bed, there were various monitors bleeping rhythmically against the wall. Wires led from them toward the bed. Running my hands over the starched white hospital gown in which I found myself, I located the sticky ends of the monitors—they were attached to my chest and sides.

I sat bolt upright and immediately wished I hadn't as stinging pain fizzed across my back and shoulder. Gingerly, I fingered the gauzy material at the back of my neck and across my left shoulder. Bandages. My mind turned back to the lightning strike. It hadn't been a dream, then. For a moment I sat quite still, trying to regain a clear memory of what had happened: the handsome stranger in the storm, the two dogs cowering behind the car, the rain pelting relentlessly down. And what of Frankie? Who was looking after her now?

I lived alone in my basement flat on the outskirts of Epsom. My parents lived miles away, buried in a quiet hamlet in Somerset—a village consisting of a handful of cottages, a pub, and a post office/general store—the sort you could drive through and never notice was there. No one would know to tell them I'd been hurt, or that Frankie was all alone somewhere.

Touching my fingers to the top of my head, which felt tender and tingly, I tried to recall if I'd had any sort of identification on my person when the lightning had struck. My handbag had been in my car, left in a different lot from the one where the stranger's car had been parked. I'd had nothing in my coat pockets except a couple of tissues and a dog biscuit.

Gazing around the whitewashed room, my eyes alighted on a card, partially hidden by the water jug on the bedside cabinet. It had a child's drawing on the front, of a woman surrounded by small children, the heads out of all proportion to the sticklike bodies, the hair bright blue and standing up on end. I flicked it open and read the scrawled message inside.

Dear Mummy. Hope you get better soon, lots of love
from Sophie, Nicole, Toby, and Teddy xxxx.

I wondered vaguely how clean the room was if the previous occupant's belongings were still here, and I had just placed the card back on the side table and leaned back against the pillows when the door opened and a nurse came in carrying a chart. She smiled when she saw me awake and sitting up.

"How are you feeling this morning, Mrs. Richardson? You've had everyone really worried about you, you know."

I frowned and drew my head back slightly to look up at her. "You must have your patients mixed up, nurse. I'm not Mrs. anyone. It's Miss—Miss Jessica Taylor."

The nurse, who was by now leaning over me ready to thrust a digital thermometer into my left ear, straightened up and stared at me oddly. "Do you remember what happened to you, dear?" She pulled up one of my eyelids and peered into first one eye, then the other. Apparently satisfied, she stood back to scrutinize my features and wait for an answer.

I nodded but my throat felt dry. "I was struck by lightning."

"That's right, dear, and you're in the hospital. But do you remember what you were doing when it happened? Who you were with, for example?"

It seemed like a trick question somehow, combined with the speculative look she gave me as she asked it. I didn't see what business it was of hers anyway, so I shrugged evasively, feeling the painful twinge of burned flesh under the bandage.

"I was with someone."

"Who?"

"Why is it important, who I was with?"

She didn't have a chance to answer, for at that moment the door opened again and a group of excited children burst in.

I was so surprised that I sat openmouthed as they bounded

toward me, en masse, shrieking, "Mummy, you're awake!" and "Mum, we've really missed you!" One of the older girls thrust some flowers into my hands. The younger of the two smiled and kissed me. A small boy was shouting, "Let me see her! I can't see!" until the older girl picked him up and deposited him at the foot of my bed. I glanced toward the door where another small boy stood silently, his eyes wide and his bottom lip quivering.

The nurse must have seen my shocked expression, for she lifted the small boy back down off the bed and chivied the children toward the door.

"Mummy is still tired," she said firmly when one of the girls tried to protest. "I think you should wait in the playroom until Daddy has finished talking to the doctor. You can come and see her again later."

The nurse closed the door firmly behind them and turned to face me.

"You don't remember, do you?"

I shook my head in confusion. "There's been a mistake. They're not mine, honestly!"

"It is quite common for people to lose their short-term memories temporarily after a lightning strike," she explained as she smoothly checked my pulse and blood pressure. I watched her jot her findings onto the chart, her face coming closer, minty breath warm on my skin as she peered into my eyes again.

"I'll fetch Dr. Shakir. He can examine you better now that you're awake, and he'll explain what has happened to you. I think he's talking to your husband right now." She smiled encouragingly at me. "Don't worry, Mrs. Richardson. Everything will turn out all right."

"I'm not Mrs. Richardson," I said again to her retreating

back, but this time my voice held less conviction. As the door closed behind her I went to rub my hands over my eyes, forgetting the IV drip, and the movement caused a fresh burst of pain in my left shoulder. Carefully, I lowered my left arm down beside me, then gingerly held my right hand out in front of me and stared at it. The hand was slim, with beautifully manicured nails. Panic spurted somewhere deep inside me. This somehow didn't look like my hand, with its broken nails where my fingertips tapped away daily at my computer keyboard. And where was the small scar that I'd picked up the time I'd cut myself on a tin of Frankie's dog food?

Tears prickled behind my eyes and I blinked them back, determined not to cry, but I had never felt so helpless and confused.

How could they have made such a mistake? It wasn't possible that I had a husband and four children I couldn't remember. I couldn't have forgotten something like that! This had to be a bad dream after all—a very real-seeming dream that would evaporate when I awoke.

I could feel the hands that didn't seem to belong to me shaking, and I tucked the right one alongside the left—firmly under the fold of the sheets. Soon, I told myself sternly, I would wake up and laugh about this nightmare. I'd wonder why I had been so afraid and I'd tell myself how silly I'd been to worry.

Screwing my eyes up tightly, I willed myself to wake up, but when I opened them I was still in the same place and my shoulder still smarted painfully. A little voice deep inside me whispered that something terrible had happened to me, and I shook my head, refusing to believe it.

When I heard the door open again, I sank back down between the hospital sheets and closed my eyes. I didn't think I had the strength to go on with this nightmare. My body hurt and I wanted to go home. Home to my little one-bedroom flat in Epsom, where I could curl up on the sofa with Frankie's head on my lap and watch TV in my pajamas, or call my parents and friends and tell them about what had happened to me while I indulged myself by eating spoonfuls of my favorite pistachio ice cream straight from the carton.

Cool fingers stroked my forehead. The sensation was somehow familiar, yet I couldn't recall anyone ever doing that to me before.

"Lauren? Lauren, sweetheart, are you awake?"

Clenching my eyelids tightly together, I remained obstinately silent. If this was a husband, father to those children, I wanted none of it.

Another voice filled the room, an Indian accent, firm and in control.

"Mr. Richardson, if you would excuse me for just one moment. I need a few words with your wife."

The fingers found my hand and squeezed it. "I'll be right outside the door, sweetheart."

I waited until the door clicked shut before opening my eyes. A tall Asian doctor was gazing down at me, a reassuring smile on his friendly face. "Good morning, Mrs. Richardson." His eyes flicked down to the notes in his hand. "Er—Lauren. The nurse tells me you are experiencing some memory loss?"

"My memory is fine," I answered somewhat belligerently. "It's just that you've got me mixed up with someone else."

The doctor shook his head, still smiling. "I know this must be upsetting for you, Lauren, but I'm afraid that is not the case. There is a good man out there who assures me that you are his wife, and four young children who have been waiting since yesterday for you to wake up. In some cases a high-voltage injury can cause clouded mental status. It's known medically as the Pat Effect, but don't worry, it's usually temporary."

He perched on the edge of the bed and looked at me with dark eyes full of sympathy, and something else I couldn't quite detect.

"Lightning is a formidable force, Lauren, and you are on strong painkillers, which could be causing some of your confusion."

I watched apprehensively as he opened a notebook and scanned its pages. His obvious belief that I was this Lauren Richardson person had me wondering what else he was going to tell me.

"When you were brought in yesterday with burns to your back, shoulder, and the top of your scalp, I did a little research on the effects of lightning strikes. Yours is the first case I've seen personally."

He glanced at me for approval to continue and I nodded, realizing that the underlying gleam in his eyes was professional curiosity.

"Apparently, lightning travels at astonishing speeds of between one hundred and sixty and sixteen hundred kilometers per second on its downward track to the ground. Or, in your case, on its way to you, Lauren," he told me with undisguised awe. "On its return stroke it can reach an amazing hundred and forty thousand kilometers per second, and the enormous spark heats the surrounding air explosively, creating the sonic boom we hear as thunder."

I found myself thinking that he must have made an exceptional—if rather geeky—medical student with his enthusiasm for knowledge, but the facts were sobering when I remembered that the lightning had actually hit *me* at those speeds.

"In some cases this spark can generate a temperature of thirty thousand degrees centigrade, Lauren—about six times hotter than the surface of the sun!" He finished with a flourish.

The look he then bestowed on me was one of thinly disguised fascination, as if, after discovering and recounting how powerful lightning was, he was surprised to find I was still breathing.

"So, you're telling me I'm lucky to be alive," I commented quietly, watching his eyes for confirmation.

Dr. Shakir inclined his head with a small dip that I took to be affirmative.

"Although the scorching to your head appears superficial and the burns to your back and shoulder will heal without skin grafts, we must be careful about infection, which is why you have an antibiotic dressing on your shoulder," he explained. Pulling his notes together he raised his eyes briefly to mine.

I looked at him suspiciously. "What are you trying to tell me?"

"The shock of the lightning bolt stopped your heart for a while. You went into cardiac arrest. We had to shock you again to bring you back. Once we'd got you back with us we concentrated on rehydrating you. That's just normal saline in the intravenous drip you have there. Then we dressed the burns. After that it was just a case of waiting for you to wake up."

"To see if I was brain damaged," I said, shaken that I had actually needed to be resuscitated, and again watching for his reaction.

"I would like to schedule you for a head MRI scan," Dr. Shakir continued smoothly, ignoring my comment and studiously avoiding my gaze. "But in the meantime you will have to trust me that you are the mother of those children and the wife of Mr. Richardson."

I looked at him skeptically. He was hiding something, I was sure, but there didn't seem much else to say. I glanced toward the door and remembered with a sick feeling deep in my stomach that the family out there was waiting to visit me.

"Please, I'm very tired," I pleaded, fighting down the panic that was rising in my chest. "Could I rest before I see . . . anyone?"

The doctor paused as if considering my request, then nodded briefly and left. I lay back against the pillows as the door closed behind him, sifting through my memory for any clue to this unknown family of mine, while the heart and blood-pressure monitors bleeped on beside me. The frustrating thing was that, despite everything the doctor had told me, my memories seemed perfectly intact—they just weren't the ones I was supposed to be remembering. After half an hour of alternately dozing and agonizing over my predicament, I heard my purported husband at the door asking to be let back in. Part of me was curious to see if he still thought I was his wife. I hoped he'd take one look at me and declare that he'd made a terrible mistake, but something deep inside told me that was a vain hope.

To stall for time, I brushed my hair carefully with a brush I was told belonged to me (even though I'd never seen it before in my life), then I sat up rigidly in the narrow bed and waited apprehensively for the stranger to come in.

The man who came toward me was slim and tall, maybe a bit over six foot. He had reddish-brown, slightly wavy hair and freckled skin. He was wearing a black polo-neck shirt under a tweedy jacket, but he didn't look professor-like in it. I wondered vaguely what he did for a living and it occurred to me that it was strange I was supposed to have picked this man for a husband, when redheaded men had never appealed to me in the least.

As he approached, I realized with a sinking heart that the charade was still on. He bent to kiss me, but I turned my head away and he straightened quickly, his face flushing slightly.

"I'm sorry," I said firmly as he pulled out a chair and sat down next to the bed. "But I have no memory of you."

He stared at me, and I could see he appeared to be fighting some internal battle. After a moment he seemed to come to a decision.

"Dr. Shakir told me you've lost your memory, sweetheart. I was hoping he'd got it wrong." He sighed deeply, then forced an uncertain smile and held out his hand formally to shake mine. "I'm Grant," he told me. "Grant Richardson. I'm thirty-seven years old, and we've been married for ten years."

His grip on my fingers was cool and steady, but somehow the smile seemed unsure. I suppose it was a lot to come to terms with, finding his wife had lost all memory of him and their life together. I knew I was certainly finding the whole situation bizarre, and my heart went out to this stranger. If I was struggling to get my head around what was happening, what must it be like for him?

I didn't know what to do. I could hardly say, "I'm Jessica, nice to meet you," so I looked away from him to a point halfway along the wall to where a cart stood stacked with medical supplies, and said nothing while he continued to hold on to my hand.

"Have you got any questions for me?" he asked gently. "Isn't there lots you want to know?"

I had questions all right, but they were more along the lines of "What the hell is happening to me?" than the sort he would be expecting me to ask.

"Lauren?"

Sighing, I realized that I was going to have to play along, if for no other reason than in the hope of getting some answers to this nightmare. I withdrew my hand firmly, then asked, "How old am I then?"

My voice sounded petulant even to my own ears, and his smile wavered momentarily as the depth of the problem came home to him. I shook my head and he sighed and ran his tongue over his lips, somewhat fearfully.

"You're thirty-five, Lauren. We married when you were twenty-five and I was twenty-seven. We were—still are, very much in love."

"When's my birthday?"

"The nineteenth of June."

"No, it's not," I told him firmly. "I was born on the twenty-ninth of April. I wouldn't have forgotten a date as ingrained in me as that!"

Grant avoided my eyes and shrugged. "It's only a small detail, sweetheart."

"Okay, then," I said, taking a deep breath and trying to pull myself together. "How old are these children of ours?"

"Sophie's eight, Nicole is six, and the twins are just four."

We sat in silence while I contemplated the hideous possibility that I was the mother of four children. I'd had very little to do with children in the past. My job as a legal secretary was with a small law firm, where I did far more than just typing reports, legal papers, and documents onto the computer. I also assisted one of the solicitors by researching areas of law for cases he was working on, took dictation, and transcribed records, proofread letters and legal documents, and, more interestingly, went to court, police stations, and client meetings to take notes.

Aspiring to become a solicitor myself in the near future, I had been about to embark on a law degree and didn't have much time to myself, let alone to consider marriage or children.

The memory brought me up short. Perhaps it was time to tell the truth. "It's not that I've lost my memory," I tried to explain to the man beside me. "I have memories—it's just that they're different from the ones you say I should have."

"We should ask Dr. Shakir about it." Grant eyed me suspiciously. "There may be some medical condition that has sparked unreal memories in you."

I remembered the notes I had transcribed the last time I had been in the office, and realized that I could recall them almost word for word. I pictured my boss's diary, where I had entered the times and dates of his appointments with clients and his court appearances for the following week. I could even remember what I'd had for supper on Friday evening after getting in late from work.

"My memories are real to me," I told him.

Grant shook his head tiredly. "I don't know, Lauren. This is hard for me to take in, too. I've been awake all night, waiting for you to come around. And the children are missing you, they're really confused . . ."

He broke off, giving me a sideways glance, and I noticed him anxiously twisting the wedding ring on his finger. I looked down at my own left hand, which because of the pain in my shoulder had been tucked under the covers. While he watched, I peeled away a corner of the white hospital tape that was holding the drip in place, exposing my ring finger. I gasped. A thin gold band gleamed back at me.

This was one hell of a dream, I told myself, hastily covering the ring over again with the tape. But dream or otherwise, I hadn't missed the signs of anxiety in his demeanor when he'd mentioned the children.

"What else?" I queried. "About the children? You were holding something back then."

"I was going to add, 'especially Teddy,' " Grant said quietly.

"Teddy?"

"Edward, the younger of the twin boys," he explained. "There were complications at their birth. Toby was breech, and took a long time coming out. Teddy didn't get enough oxygen to his brain while Toby was being born. He's got . . . learning difficulties."

I pondered this last piece of news with a sinking heart. I might be experiencing a vivid dream, but I was still here, living this life until I awoke, and it seemed to be getting more complicated by the second. How could I be capable of being a mother to all those children? Especially a child with special needs. What sort of wonder woman had this Lauren been? I hoped I would wake up soon, because if Dr. Shakir was right and this was somehow real, I seriously doubted that I would ever be able to match up to her.

I suddenly felt very tired. Something in my face must have alerted Grant, and he stood up quietly. "I'll take the children home," he said, stooping to plant a kiss on my forehead. This time I didn't turn my face away, but he must have seen the flicker of apprehension in my eyes because I saw the sorrow etched upon his face.

"I hope the children won't be upset not to see me," I murmured guiltily.

"They'll cope for now," he answered firmly. "We all will. Look," he added, "can I bring them back this afternoon, when you've rested?"

I nodded, wishing I had the courage to refuse him, but it seemed so petty when the children were obviously missing their mother so much, and anyway, I told myself, I might have woken up by then.

As the door closed behind him, I lay back against the pillows with a groan. "You'd better be wrong, Dr. Shakir," I mumbled to the ceiling. "I'm Jessica, not Lauren. I'll wake up soon and prove I'm still me."

Grant returned later with a huge bunch of flowers that the nurse put in a large vase next to the small vase containing the flowers one of the girls had brought me earlier. Nurse Sally, as she liked to be known, had extracted the flowers from the child before the family had left, promising her I would get them.

"Sunflowers, my favorite!" I exclaimed when Nurse Sally had left us alone together.

Grant looked intently at me, hope lighting his features. "You've always loved them," he whispered, taking my hand. "Do you remember that monthlong vacation we took in Provence, before we had the children? Those fields of towering sunflowers seemed to go on forever and we filled all the jars and vases in the villa with them. "

"I love sunflowers in my real life," I replied stubbornly. "The life where I'm not married and have no children."

"Stop it, Lauren," Grant said, abruptly letting go of my hand. "There is no other life!" He closed his eyes for a moment, as if to contain himself, then opened them again, and even though I hardly knew him I thought he looked drained and weary. "I'm sorry, sweetheart. I'm struggling with this as much as you are. I don't know what to do." He sank down onto the visitor's chair and ran a hand tiredly over his eyes. "I can't bear it that you don't remember us," he said quietly. "All those years, all the experiences we've shared, the loves, the sorrows, the energy we've put into our children. If you don't recall any of it, it's as if it's all gone, it might as well never have happened. I feel like I've lost you." He leaned toward me, but I instinctively pulled back from him and he regarded me with haunted eyes. "I love you, Lauren. When they called to say you'd been rushed in here, and that your heart had stopped, I thought you were dead. Have you any idea how that feels? I thought I'd lost you forever, and I realized I couldn't bear it. When the doctors said you'd live, I was so, so grateful. But you're not really here with us, are you? I've lost you after all."

I stared at him in dismay, not wanting to hurt this stranger, but unable to help him, either. It was bad enough that I'd unwittingly arrived into this nightmare; now I had this man's distress to cope with, too. Why wouldn't I wake up? I'd never dreamed so long and so realistically before. Once, when I'd eaten a particularly hot curry when out with my girlfriends, I had dreamed strange haunting dreams on and off all night, but never anything like this. How long would it last?

I looked into his tortured face, saw the tears not far away, and realized that while I was here I was going to have to deal with the situation as best I could.

"I'm sorry, Grant. I didn't want any of this to happen," I told him quietly. "It isn't anyone's fault. I understand that you want things to be like they were before, but they can't be. I don't remember being your wife. I don't want to be Lauren. There's nothing I can do about it."

He stared at me with tear-filled eyes, then rose from the chair and came to perch on the edge of the bed. He took my hand in his and squeezed it, and it took all my willpower to leave it where it was.

"You'll stay with us, though, won't you?" he asked. "You won't leave us?" I was still desperately contemplating my answer when the door opened and Nurse Sally shepherded the children into the room.

"Mummy!" they shrieked, bounding toward us.

"Careful now," Grant admonished them, rising awkwardly and sniffing back his tears as the children climbed around us on the bed. "Don't forget Mummy's not well."

Feeling as if I were watching myself in a strange play, I let Grant introduce the children to me. The children had been told I'd lost my memory and seemed to find it amusing that I didn't remember who they were.

"Sophie here brought you the flowers," he told me, smiling proudly at his elder daughter.

"Thank you, Sophie," I said, taking in the long chestnut hair so like her father's, the frank green eyes.

"Nicole made you the get-well card."

"It's lovely," I told her with a smile. "You got my hair just right."

"It was what it looked like when the lightning got you," she answered. "It stuck up just like that and sort of glowed."

I felt as if someone had punched me in the stomach.

"You saw it?" I asked in dismay. "You saw the lightning strike me?" Nurse Sally's question about who I'd been with at the time of the accident echoed in my ears.

Nicole nodded. "It was awesome!"

"Nicole!" Grant scolded his daughter. "Don't make it sound as if you enjoyed seeing Mummy getting hurt."

"I saw it, I saw it," cried one of the twins as he jumped at the end of the bed, narrowly missing my feet and causing waves of pain to shoot across my back. "Mummy was on fire!"

Grant looked as if he were about to chastise the boy I assumed was Toby, when a sorrowful little voice from the corner piped up. We all stopped talking as the second twin repeated sadly, "That isn't Mummy. My mummy's gone, and she's here instead!"

chapter two

A hushed silence filled the room. We all turned to where a small redheaded boy stood eyeing us from the doorway, tightly holding a soft, brightly colored ball.

"What did you say?" I asked softly.

"Mummy's gone. She caught fire, and now you's here. I want my mummy!"

And Teddy began to cry.

I realized I was clenching my hands together so tightly that the beautifully manicured fingernails were digging painfully into my palms. My breath, which had left my body in a rush with Nicole's revelation, was having trouble drawing back into my lungs. The fact that it seemed Teddy could see me, Jessica, and not his mother changed everything.

The boy's comment had first filled me with a sick kind of dread that this wasn't just a ghastly dream after all—but in the next heartbeat I felt the beginnings of hope. I wasn't alone anymore in this strange place where everyone insisted one thing while I believed another. This small child saw past the outward appearance of his mother's body and into the person inside. I wanted to hug him for joy.

"Come here, er . . . Teddy." I reached out a hand to him. Some instinct told me to take things very slowly.

He eyed the offered hand suspiciously but I gave him an encouraging smile as he inched a step or two closer before stopping. Realizing he wasn't going to come any nearer, I fixed my eyes on his. Something in his expression warned me to be as honest as possible with him. "You're right, Teddy. I'm not the same mummy as before. I don't know what's happened . . ." I ran my gaze over his confused, tear-stained face and felt a gamut of emotions run through me. I felt a deep sympathy for him, gratitude, and a mixture of relief tinged with fear for myself at his reaction. Struggling to find the right thing to say to comfort and reassure him, I shrugged and ended helplessly, "It'll be all right, Teddy. Everything will sort itself out, you'll see."

Teddy wiped his nose on the cuff of his blue sweatshirt and sniffed loudly.

"Don't be so silly, Teddy," Grant said, going over to the boy and picking him up. "Come and give Mummy a kiss."

Grant lifted the boy onto my lap, and I reached out to pat him awkwardly.

Teddy twisted his shoulder away from my touch and scowled at me.

"Teddy!" Grant admonished him, giving me an apologetic glance.

"I don't mind," I said tiredly, not wanting the boy to have to kiss me any more than he seemed to want to do it. "None of this is his fault, either. This is confusing for all of us."

The other children ignored the interchange and chatted together while Toby jumped on the bed, jarring my burns until

Nurse Sally arrived to change the dressings and suggested to my husband that he take the children home.

"You look about done in," she said when they had gone. She removed one of the pillows and I settled down at last to rest. "Try to sleep. You never know, your memory might come back in the morning."

I was desperate to speak to the doctor again. I had a million questions to ask, but visions of Dr. Shakir's fascinated expression when he'd looked at me set off warning bells in my mind, and I pressed my lips together, nodding obediently. I closed my eyes, realizing how tired I really was after the immense shocks of the day. I lay for a while listening to the sounds of the hospital around me: metal carts being wheeled, doors creaking open and closed, the soft steps and hushed tones of the night staff as they exchanged news, and then I was asleep.

Yet it seemed no time at all before I was being shaken awake. The nurse bending over me was a different girl. Nurse Sally must be off-duty, I realized dozily as I sat up, accepting the drink that was pressed into my hand. Eyes half-closed, I sipped the warm tea gratefully, feeling the heat and sweetness of it seeping into my being. Reaching out to put the empty cup on the hospital cabinet, I felt the empty space with my hand too late, and both cup and saucer fell with a crash to the floor.

Wriggling into a sitting position, I looked in dismay at the mess. The bedside cabinet wasn't where it had been when I dropped off to sleep. It was on the opposite side of the bed and it looked somehow different. The silver light of early morning was creeping into the room from a wide window at one end of the ward. A four-bedded ward. I counted the beds with growing disbelief. Had they moved me from my windowless room in the night?

Alarmed, I found the red buzzer at the head of my hospital bed and buzzed long and hard, my hand shaking with growing confusion.

A male nurse came running.

"What's the problem, Ms. Taylor?"

My mouth dropped open in astonishment.

"You called me Ms. Taylor," I heard myself whisper. "How do you know my name?"

"The man who brought you in found your name and address on your dog's collar," the nurse replied soothingly. "Now don't get yourself all worked up. He said to tell you he's taken the dog home with him for the time being. He said you weren't to worry about Frankie; she's in good hands."

I felt the wetness on my face and knew I was crying, though no sound escaped my lips. The nurse tut-tutted and patted my hand sympathetically.

"That's right, Jessica," he said. "Have a good cry. You're probably still in shock from the lightning strike. You're a very lucky young lady, you know."

I nodded, leaning my head back on the starched hospital pillows, and gave a deep, shuddering sigh. So it had all been a nightmare. I'd been hit by lightning but the rest of it had been a ghastly, unsettling dream caused by nothing more than the shock of what had happened to me. I was still me, still Jessica Taylor. I peered down at my ringless fingers and wanted to sob for joy.

Glancing up, I watched as the nurse made his way back down the ward in search of a dustpan and brush. There were no small children hiding in the shadows, no husband trying to convince me I was his wife. As soon as the nurse was out of sight, I turned my face into the pillow and wept with relief.

I found it disconcerting to realize how my mind had worked

on things while I had slept. In the dream I'd pictured myself much more damaged by the chance lightning strike than it appeared I actually was. In reality, there was no drip in my arm, no heart monitors attached to my chest, and no large bandage round my neck and shoulders. It was as if I had prepared myself for the worst, and now I was pleasantly surprised to find myself almost unscathed. A very young Chinese intern came to see me soon after I'd finished the rather spartan hospital breakfast of cornflakes and toast. He introduced himself as Dr. Chin and assured me I'd gotten off very lightly.

"The burns to your back and shoulder are minimal," he explained. "We have dressed the wounds lightly to prevent infection, but they are superficial and should heal in a few days without leaving permanent scarring."

"No antibiotics required, then?" I asked.

He shook his head, peering at a chart that had been hanging at the foot of the bed. "We only admitted you to the ward because you had not regained consciousness, but your two-hourly observations through the night have proved satisfactory."

"Did my heart stop at any time?" I asked anxiously.

The intern shook his head of sleek black hair. "No, no, nothing like that. You are a very strong woman." He paused before adding, "You sleep very deeply, Ms. Taylor. You have been asleep since yesterday. How do you feel now?"

I thought about this for a moment or two, then grinned at him. "I feel fine. Can I go home then?"

"We will wait for the consultant's ward round," he said, nodding. "But I am sure everything will be okay."

He started to leave, then turned back to me and smiled. "Do you know that once, the Chinese believed lightning to be a very unlucky omen? It was thought that lightning was a sign of God's disapproval. I do not think you are unlucky, though, Ms. Taylor. In fact, I think you had a very lucky escape."

You are not kidding, I thought, watching him scurry off down the ward. I lay back gingerly against the pillows, careful not to snag the light gauze dressing on my left shoulder. In my mind's eye I pictured Grant and the four children. They had seemed so real at the time, and I wondered from where I had conjured up their names and images. It occurred to me as my mind drifted into a light doze that it was strange how I could remember the dream so clearly. I gave an involuntary shudder. It also occurred to me that I had indeed had a very lucky escape.

The ward round consisted of four white-coated doctors hovering around a fifth in ascending order of rank, clustering together at the foot of each bed in turn. It was immediately apparent which was the most senior doctor, and, from the obsequious half bows of Dr. Chin, who stood on the farthest outer ring of the gravitational field of the consultant, I ascertained that my doctor was probably the most lowly figure among them. The realization gave me fresh cause to breathe a sigh of relief. A less experienced doctor must mean that my injuries were minor and little cause for concern.

My mind went back to the dream and Lauren's injuries. She had been far more badly injured than I had been. Of course she wasn't real, just a figment of my imagination, but I wondered why, if I'd invented her, I had also envisaged her as having been struck more severely by the lightning—badly enough, it seemed, for her heart to have stopped beating altogether.

With half my mind still preoccupied by Lauren and the dream, I watched as the consultant, a bald-headed man with a smart pinstripe suit visible inside the flapping white lab coat, looked down his beaklike nose at me as if appraising a joint of meat for his Sunday roast. I tried to dismiss the picture of the buzzard that leapt into my mind as I pulled the bedclothes protectively around my chest.

The buzzard spoke in a rather bored voice that belied the interest in his eyes. "So, what have we here?"

Dr. Chin sprang into action, gripping his notes and reading jerkily, "This is Ms. Taylor. Twenty-eight years of age. She was admitted yesterday with minor burns to the left back and shoulder after being hit by lightning."

"Ah, the lightning girl, eh? Saved by her coat. Jolly lucky escape, Ms. Taylor, if I may say so." The consultant smirked and turned his attention back to the anxious intern. "Any related problems?"

"Ms. Taylor was unconscious on arrival. Two-hourly obs showed everything reading normal. On regaining consciousness, she seemed disoriented, but has since recovered all her faculties."

"So, ready to go home then, Ms. Taylor?"

I nodded.

"Good, good. I think we can discharge her today."

Losing interest quickly, he moved to a bed on the opposite side of the room. I watched as he stared distastefully down at the next unfortunate patient. "And what have we here?" he intoned unemotionally from the other side of the room.

A commotion at the entrance to the ward diverted my attention from the huddle of doctors. The male nurse who had been so kind to me earlier was talking earnestly with a visitor, whose face was barely visible behind a large bunch of flowers.

"You'll have to wait until the ward round is finished," the nurse was saying in hushed tones. "You can wait in the visitors' room. Who is it you've come to see?"

The man lowered the flowers a fraction, and my whole body

tensed with a mixture of excitement and apprehension as I recognized the stranger from the previous day. My first instinct was to slide down under the covers and pull the sheet over my head, but my body seemed to be stuck rigidly in position. He glanced into the room, his eyes searching, coming to rest on my face.

He looked different than how I'd remembered him, his short hair framing a square, masculine face. Behind the flowers he was wearing beige cargo pants with an open-necked polo shirt hanging loose at a slim boyish waist. Thank goodness I wasn't connected to a heart monitor like in the dream, I thought, as I felt the blood pounding through my veins. It would have beeped off the scale!

He waved at me over the flowers, then followed the nurse out into the corridor, presumably to wait until the buzzard had finished his round. As soon as he was out of sight, I bolted upright and ran my fingers through my hair, trying to tease out some of the tangles. Quickly, I rummaged through the bedside cabinet, but this time there was no handy brush, mine or otherwise. I couldn't believe it. Here I was without so much as a hairbrush or lipstick, when the most handsome man I had set eyes on for years was visiting.

By the time the consultant and his followers had left the ward, I was utterly apprehensive. What was I supposed to say to this man whose name I didn't even know? We'd met so briefly, so intensely in the violence of the storm. What must he think of me, a muddy, soaked-to-the-skin girl who was stupid enough to be struck by a bolt of lightning five minutes after we'd met?

My cheeks flushed again at the thought, and I buried my face in my hands with a groan of embarrassment.

"Hi there."

I dropped my hands and looked up. He was standing smiling

at me, as if he knew exactly what I'd been thinking. With calm, measured movements, he handed the flowers to me, pulled up a red vinyl hospital chair, and sat down next to the bed.

"How are you feeling today?"

"Better, thanks," I croaked. "I've just been told I can go home later." Clearing my throat, I tried to gain control of my vocal cords. "I owe you a big thank-you. The nurse told me you brought me in yesterday."

"I couldn't very well leave you lying unconscious in the rain," he said with a smile.

The twinkle in his deep blue eyes was disconcerting. I tried to stop my lips from forming into an indignant pout and forced myself to remember my manners.

"The nurse also said you were minding Frankie for me. I can't thank you enough."

"It's the least I could do," he said, his smile widening broadly.

"You're laughing at me," I accused him in a teasing voice. "I realize I probably don't look much of a picture lying here in a hospital gown, with no makeup, but you could have the decency to at least pretend I'm not a complete mess."

"Are we having our first argument?" he asked with a grin.

I stared at him, momentarily speechless, then burst out laughing. I remembered then how we'd laughed at each other the first moment we'd met.

"I suppose you haven't seen me looking anything other than a mess," I managed to say when the laughter had died down.

"You're really not all that bad," he said quietly. "With or without makeup, soaked to the skin and smoldering in a puddle, or looking palely interesting in a hospital gown."

I gazed up at him, wondering if he was joking, this knight in shining armor who had appeared in my life like a bolt from the blue. Despite the twinkle in his eyes I had the feeling he was being serious. I wanted to say that he was the most gorgeous guy I'd ever seen, but I thought better of it, smiled instead, and asked him his name.

"I'm Daniel Brennan," he said formally, holding out his hand. " 'Dan' to my friends."

"Hello Dan," I replied. "I believe you already found out my name from Frankie's tag."

"Yeah, you had no handbag, nothing in your pockets. Then I realized your dog had a name tag on her collar with your details on the back."

"A regular Sherlock Holmes," I laughed. "Is Frankie okay?"

"She went frantic when the lightning struck," Dan said. "I thought she was going to bury you with mud before I could get to you."

"Poor Frankie."

"It wasn't too great for any of us," he said, his expression finally serious. "At first, I thought you were dead. Your breathing was so shallow I could hardly detect it, and the dogs were going wild. The rain just got worse and worse while I was trying to find a pulse, and you seemed to be getting so cold. In the end I just picked you up, threw you onto the backseat of my car wrapped in the dog blanket, chucked the dogs in the back, and drove like hell to the nearest hospital."

"I'm so sorry. It must have been awful for you."

"Do you know what I was thinking as I drove you here? Not what trouble I'd be in if I turned up with the dead body of an unknown female in my car, but how terrible it would be never to hear you laugh again."

I looked at him askance, and was struggling to think of a suitable reply when he scraped back the chair and sprang to his feet.

"Hey, I'll get you a vase or something for these, shall I?" He grabbed the flowers from my lap and took off down the ward with such speed I thought he was in danger of slipping on the shiny linoleum flooring.

I lay back as a tremor ran through my body that had nothing to do with the lightning strike.

He was gone awhile, and I was beginning to think he had left the hospital when he reappeared with the flowers, still minus a vase.

"I've been talking to the nurse," he said, resting the flowers on top of the cabinet. "He said you can go home as soon as you're ready. He'll be along in a moment to sort you out." He gestured to the flowers. "We may as well take these home with us."

The word *us* sent another tremor down my spine, and I glanced up at him questioningly.

He grinned with his piercing Brad Pitt eyes. "I'm assuming you'll need a lift, as your car is presumably somewhere in a parking lot near the Downs?"

Struggling to keep the excitement out of my voice, I nodded. "That would be very kind of you."

"It won't be the first time you've been in my car, after all," he joked. "Only last time you were unconscious and dripping rainwater all over the upholstery."

The nurse arrived with a bundle of clothing and asked if I wanted Dan on the inside or the outside of the curtain while I changed. I smiled inwardly at the assumption that Dan was my boyfriend. Dan held up his hands as the curtain was pulled around the bed and stepped smartly out into the ward.

The nurse produced a pair of scissors from his short tunic pocket and snipped off my plastic ID bracelet. "The gauze dressing can come off in a few days," he said. "If you have any trouble see your GP, but your burns are minor. You were lucky to be wearing such a thick jacket." He straightened up. "There you are. Free to go. And next time stay indoors during thunderstorms!"

Slipping out of bed, I pulled off the thin hospital gown and laid it on the bed. It felt strange being upright; I was still a little shaky. Sinking down on the bed again I struggled into my underclothes, careful to position my bra strap well away from the sore spot on my shoulder, then pulled the jeans up and fastened them. Someone must have dried them for me overnight because although they were encrusted with mud they were bone dry. It was when I unfolded the sweater that I realized what the nurse had meant about how lucky I'd been. On the back of the left shoulder was a blackened scorch mark about the size of an orange.

Gingerly, I smoothed out the old-fashioned sheepskin coat I used for dog walking. My mother had been about to donate it to a rummage sale years ago but had given it to me when I'd exclaimed how useful it would be for walking Frankie on the Downs in all kinds of weather. I felt the hairs stand up on the back of my neck when I looked at the area around the shoulder where the lightning had struck. It had actually run into a singed mess closely resembling melted plastic.

Tracing the burned area with my finger, I shuddered, realizing how close I must have come to being as badly injured as the Lauren of my dream. Was this ancient coat all that had stood between me and possible death?

A measured Indian accent popped from the recesses of my brain. "In some cases this spark can generate a temperature of thirty thousand degrees centigrade, Lauren—about six times hotter than the surface of the sun."

Oh no, I thought with a sickening jolt. Where had that come from?

I felt queasy suddenly, and was wondering if the hospital would give me a bowl to take with me in Dan's car, when he stuck his head around the curtain.

"You all right?"

Rubbing my face with my hands, I smiled wanly up at him. "I feel a bit sick actually. Is the nurse still around?"

"I'll go look."

He came back quickly with the nurse in tow, who was all kindness and sympathy.

"Do you want to wait here awhile? See if it passes?" The nurse felt my forehead with his hand. "It is possible the lightning has upset your ears, given you a sort of motion sickness. It has been known to cause deafness. Maybe I should fetch the doctor to check that out. Is your hearing okay? Your vision and everything all right?"

I nodded. "I'm fine, honestly, just feeling a bit sick. I was remembering a dream I had while I was unconscious. It made me feel strange, that's all. Could I take a bowl with me, just in case?"

"Of course," the nurse replied soothingly. "But I will also fetch Dr. Chin to have a quick look at you. I'm sure it's nothing to be alarmed about."

Dan came through the curtain a moment after the nurse had left and sat next to me on the unmade bed. "He said I could come in and keep you company. That okay with you?"

I nodded again, swallowing hard to keep the tears of self-pity at bay.

"I feel so stupid," I said between gulps. "I'm sure there's nothing wrong with me, but I keep remembering this dream I had while I was unconscious . . . it seemed so real."

"The nurse said you might feel disoriented for a day or two." He smiled sheepishly. "I think they assume I'm your boyfriend. They've told me to keep an eye on you and treat you gently for a few days."

"Oh," I said lamely, looking down at my hands, which were folded in my lap.

"If you don't feel up to driving, I'll drop you and Frankie at your home, then make myself scarce—if there's someone there to take care of you."

I knew it was a question rather than a statement, and I shook my head again.

"There's no one, not at present. And my parents live miles away." I hesitated. "But a lift to my car will be fine. I can take care of myself."

"I'm sure you can," he replied with a smile. "And I know we're almost strangers. It's just that I feel I've known you for years. And I want to make sure you're okay."

I was saved from having to reply by Dr. Chin pulling the curtains apart and advancing on me with a slim flashlight. He peered into each of my ears in turn, then screwed an attachment onto the flashlight and asked me to look directly into the beam.

"Hmm," he murmured, lifting one lid and then the other. "Everything looks good, Ms. Taylor, but I suggest you have an eye exam at the optician in a week or so. Sometimes sufferers of high-voltage injury develop cataracts at a later date."

"Thank you," I muttered, sliding off the bed. "So I can go?"

He nodded as the nurse arrived with a gray cardboard bowl

loosely wrapped in a paper bag. I took it gratefully, and Dan picked up the flowers, then steadied me by my elbow as we made our way down the ward. "Frankie's waiting in the car," he told me as we took the elevator down to the lobby and walked out into the autumn sunshine. "She'll be pleased to see you back."

We walked to the parking lot to see Frankie and the black Labrador peering out of the back window of a silver Shogun, both seemingly watching for us. Predictably, my precious terrier went mad with joy when we opened the door, and I spent the next five minutes having my face licked as I sat in the passenger seat waiting for her to calm down. Eventually, Dan lifted her off me and carried her around into the back, where she was unable to get to me through the dog barrier. She sat down resignedly next to the Lab with her tongue lolling out.

We drove carefully out of the hospital lot and Dan glanced sideways at me as I sat clutching the bowl on my lap.

"How are you feeling?"

"Relieved," I said. "Glad to be out in the real world again."

"Where am I taking you?"

"My car's parked up by the grandstand," I replied.

I felt in my coat pockets as I spoke, my fingers probing for my car keys, but I looked up as Dan rattled a bunch of keys at me.

"I found them when I was searching your pockets for your identity," he explained. "I didn't think of Frankie's tag right away. I decided they'd be safer with me than in a hospital box with your things. I hope you don't mind."

Taking the keys from him, I thought about what he'd said. Did I mind? Couldn't he have just left them in my coat pocket? I sneaked a sideways glance at him, taking in his handsome features. Was he as harmless as he seemed? My front door key was on the key ring. He'd found out my address from Frankie's tag and he could easily have been around to my flat to snoop since yesterday.

My silence must have alerted him to my discomfort, because he took his eyes off the road momentarily to return my look.

"Hey, don't look so worried," he said lightly. "I'm quite harmless, I promise!"

The Sunday traffic was sparse through the town, and we were soon heading out into the rolling countryside. I stared at the familiar landscape: the green Downs, the trees beginning to turn red, gold, and brown, the imposing white bulk of the grandstand dominating the scene.

"My car's over there," I said, pointing.

Dan navigated the short distance to where my small blue Fiesta was parked unobtrusively among several other cars and drew to a halt nearby.

"Are you sure you don't want me to take you right home?" he said as he turned off the engine and sat looking at me with a concerned expression. "Do you feel well enough to drive?"

"It's very kind of you," I said, returning the look. "You have been great, honestly. But right now I'm feeling fine. I just want to go home with Frankie and lick my wounds, so to speak."

Dan opened his door, walked around the back of the Shogun, and let Frankie out of the cargo space. She came leaping around to see me as I struggled upright, so I grabbed her collar and walked her toward our car. She jumped onto the backseat and sat watching me expectantly as I threw the sick bowl onto the front passenger seat.

Dan came up behind me and handed me the flowers, which I placed next to the bowl.

"They're lovely," I said smiling, and straightened up. "Thank you for everything."

"Here's my telephone number," he said, pressing a piece of paper into my hand. "Please ring if you need anything, or just to let me know you're okay?"

"I will," I said. "Thanks."

Still he hovered, until I went around to the driver's side and climbed into the car.

I started the car and wound down the window.

"Bye," I called, and drove out of the parking lot, leaving Dan standing watching after me, his hand raised in farewell.

Typical, I thought wryly, as I drove carefully onto the road. I hadn't had a proper boyfriend in two years, partly because I'd been telling myself I didn't have the time for romance with my hectic schedule and long hours, and partly because the last man in my life had turned out to be a two-timing cheat and a liar. It was almost as if my heart had been protecting itself from falling in love; every time I met a man who seemed attractive I found a reason not to date him. I didn't have time; he wasn't that good-looking anyway; he was married; or one of my friends liked him, too. I spent evenings in the company of men when my friends and I went clubbing, of course, but none of them had seemed worth the risk of opening my heart to the possibility of finding true love or making a romantic commitment. Not until now.

I pictured Dan as I had seen him on the Downs, and then again at the hospital, and smiled ruefully. At last I had bumped into someone who might actually be worth the time and possible risk of letting my guard down . . . just when my body felt bruised and battered and my mind was churning with confusing images and strange dreams.

Shaking my head in frustration, I turned the car into the parking space outside my flat. Once inside, the place was exactly as I'd left it the day before when I'd set out to give Frankie her extra-long Saturday afternoon walk. No sign of intruders in the sitting room, where several pairs of my shoes lined the wall. Nothing seemed out of place in the small, homey area, with its profusion of potted plants and scattered books. The kitchen was as generally untidy as I had left it, with yesterday's clean dishes still stacked on the drying rack and Frankie's bowl of dog biscuits permeating the small room with the aroma of meat and bone meal.

I put the flowers in a vase, made myself a quick meal of scrambled eggs on toast, then sank down in an armchair to eat it on my lap, after which I realized I felt totally exhausted. Checking the clock, I found it was nearly half past two in the afternoon. I took a minute or two to change out of my jeans and sweater, donning a comfy tracksuit, then returned to my armchair. Frankie was stretched out on the carpet at my feet, snoring gently. I curled up in the chair, my feet up under me, closed my eyes, and nodded off to sleep.

I roused to the feel of someone pulling at my hand, and I stirred slightly.

"It's all right, Lauren," said a voice in my ear. "I'm only disconnecting the drip. The saline's finished."

My eyes flickered open, but there was nothing but a shadowy shape in the darkness. I shivered slightly and curled into a tighter ball, willing the dream to go away.

"There, all done. Go back to sleep, dear," soothed the voice. "See you in the morning."

chapter three

The dream was still with me when I awoke an hour later, disconcerting me. Frankie was curled obediently at my feet. I knew she wasn't asleep, but just being quiet for my sake, and I reached down and patted her head. Getting up, I stretched, then went to the telephone and dialed my parents' number.

Dad answered, and his familiar voice was somehow calming.

"Hello, Jess lovely; how are you?"

I found myself smiling at the warmth in his voice. He'd called me his "lovely" for as long as I could remember, and I was eternally grateful no one was confusing me with a mother of four called Lauren. "I'm fine, Dad."

We chatted for a while about his garden and the village show, where he was hoping to win best marrow competition, and then I said hesitantly, "I had a bit of an accident yesterday."

"What do you mean, 'an accident'?" Are you all right?"

"I'm okay now. Did you and Mum have a storm down in Somerset on Saturday afternoon?"

"We had a bit of rain, not what I'd call a storm. Why?"

"I was walking Frankie on the Downs when a storm came up. There was thunder and lightning and I was caught out in it."

"You are all right, aren't you?" he butted in. "I heard on the forecast that there were going to be pockets of severe storms dotted across the southeast during the weekend. What happened?"

"You're not going to believe this but I was actually hit by a streak of lightning. I'm fine now," I added hastily in response to his exclamation of horror. "I was taken to the hospital but I'm okay now, honestly."

I could hear Mum in the background asking what he was exclaiming about.

"Your mum's trying to take the phone from me. I'll hand you over and you can tell her all the details . . ."

"Jessica? What's this about you being hit by lightning?" My mother's anxious voice came through the receiver loud and clear. It sounded as if she was only in the other room.

"I was walking Frankie yesterday afternoon when a storm blew up," I explained. "The lightning struck me on my shoulder but that old coat of yours took the worst of it, and although I ended up in the hospital I'm virtually unscathed."

" 'Virtually'?" she repeated, picking up on the word immediately. "So why did they take you to the hospital?"

"I blacked out," I confessed. "A dog walker who was caught in the storm with me took me to the hospital in his car. They kept me overnight, but apart from a sore patch on my shoulder, I'm fine. They let me out this afternoon."

"That's it. We're coming up to see you."

"You don't need to, Mum, honestly. I'm okay. The doctors wouldn't have let me out otherwise."

"You always did have that independent streak," my mother tutted. "I suppose you don't want us cluttering up that flat of yours. One day you'll realize you need somebody else in your life, Jessica. You can't always handle everything yourself. Your brother is as bad, going off to New Zealand like that. I don't know why you couldn't both just settle down locally and live quiet, ordinary lives."

I sighed. The last thing I needed was a lecture from my mother about my working-girl lifestyle and what she saw as an inability to commit to a relationship.

There was a short pause at the end of the line, and then, "What about the man who took you to the hospital? I hope you thanked him?"

A picture of Dan popped into my head and I smiled despite myself. "Mum, I'm not a child. Of course I thanked him."

"Well, if you're sure you don't need us . . . I'll put Dad back on to say good-bye to you. Take care, Jessica, and do remember that you're not Superwoman. If you feel at all unwell, then call us."

"Yes, Mum. Bye."

Dad came back on the line, his voice gruff. "If you feel at all poorly, then ring us, lovely, won't you? You know your mother and I would be there like a shot . . ."

"I know, Dad. I promise I'll call if I need you."

"Bye, lovely. Take care."

"Bye, Dad."

I replaced the receiver and went into my little kitchen to put the kettle on for a cup of tea. The conversation with my parents had churned up old feelings of needing to prove myself to them in some way, especially to my mother, who thought I'd failed if I didn't settle down with a nice average guy and have 2.4 children on whom they could both dote. I just wasn't ready for those things. I had a career to forge. I wanted to earn my law degree and be someone in the world; a self-made someone of standing—not just someone's wife or someone's mother. Maybe Mum had been happy with all that, but I wanted something more from life.

The rest of the afternoon passed pleasantly enough. I watered my plants, picked a few deadheads off the still-flowering begonias in the window box, made myself and Frankie some supper, and headed for the bath and an early night. If I felt okay when I woke in the morning, I told myself, I would probably struggle in to work. The office was always busy on Monday mornings and I wouldn't want to let my boss down.

I settled myself as comfortably as I could in bed. It was difficult, since I liked to sleep on my side and the shoulder with the burns was tender, chafing against the soft fabric of my pajamas. I knew I was tired, because my eyes felt gritty and dry, but it seemed my brain was refusing to give in to sleep. I tossed and turned, each time having to allow for the sore area on my shoulder, picturing the images I'd conjured up in my mind the previous night, wondering where and how I'd dreamed up the phantom family. I suppose I must eventually have dropped off, because soon I was waking again and the dream became blurred and faded.

Opening my eyes, I sat up and stared around me in disbelief. The first thing I did was to glance down at my left hand. The thin gold wedding band gleamed back at me, just visible beyond the spaghetti junction of fine hospital tape holding the canula securely in place in the back of my left hand. The drip, I noticed, was no longer connected to the canula, which had some sort of rubber bung on the end, presumably, I thought, to stop my blood from running out of the open vein all over the crisp hospital sheets.

Shock presents itself in different ways, and with me it seemed to manifest itself in a bout of hysterical laughter. I sat and giggled stupidly. The thing was, I tried to tell myself sternly through the shaking sobs, this was just the dream again. And it definitely wasn't funny. Soon I would wake up and this place would disappear. I squeezed my eyes shut and tried to return to sleep, but it seemed my brain was wide awake, and sleep wouldn't come. I opened my eyes again and sat up, the nervous giggling starting again.

The room was quiet apart from the wheezing I was making as my shoulders shook with panicked laughter. I vaguely registered that I was no longer connected to the EKG machine, which now stood silently behind my bed. I stopped laughing with a jolt, realizing that I actually remembered the nurse disconnecting my drip.

Because the room was windowless, I couldn't judge what time it was, but I had a horrible, gnawing feeling I knew exactly what the time was, just as I feared I knew that the drip had been disconnected just after two-thirty in the morning.

Perspiration broke out on my whole body as I thought back. I'd gone to bed early, soon after eight o'clock. I'd tossed and turned for around an hour, which meant I'd probably dropped off soon after that. If it was around 9:15 P.M. at home, did that mean it was the same time in the morning here? Twisting around, I found the buzzer and held my finger down until Nurse Sally appeared, looking flustered. "Thank goodness you're awake at last!" she exclaimed as she bustled around me, plumping the pillows and tidying the sheets. "I was about to beep Dr. Shakir to come take a look at you. I've been trying to wake you for the last two hours. I've never known anyone to sleep so deeply, Lauren."

"What time is it?" I asked.

She glanced down at the watch pinned to her uniform. "It's nine-twenty already. And you haven't even had breakfast yet."

"What time was my drip disconnected?"

"I'm not sure exactly. The night nurse said the last of the saline had run through and she disconnected it sometime in the early hours."

"Could you look it up in my notes?" I persisted. "Please?"

She gave me a searching look, as if wondering what my interest was, but merely nodded and hurried out. As soon as she had gone, I rummaged through the bedside cabinet, which was back where it was supposed to be on the right side of the bed, and found one of the newspapers Grant had brought in for me the previous afternoon. It was a Sunday paper, which meant that yesterday had indeed been Sunday, October 19. It ought to be Monday morning now, unless time had gone as haywire as everything else. Was this a dream? My mouth felt dry and my hands were suddenly sweaty with fear. I breathed as shallowly as I could, hoping to somehow melt into the bed and disappear from this place of nightmares.

Nurse Sally returned with a breakfast tray and the announcement that my drip had finished and been disconnected at 2:30 A.M. by the night staff.

"Your husband is bringing the children in to see you in about half an hour," Sally continued cheerily, unaware of the sickening feeling of inevitability that her words had invoked in me. "I was hoping to have you up and bathed this morning now that your drip is down, but I think we'll have to postpone that until they've gone. You'll be able to get up today and dispense with the monitors and bedpans. That's a step in the right direction, isn't it?"

"Yes," I mumbled unenthusiastically, poking at the dry toast in front of me. I wanted to shout, to tell her that in my other life I'd never been this ill to start with. The real me, Jessica, was at home and recovering. That this was a step in a direction I didn't want to take at all.

Grant arrived while I was still brushing my teeth into a white plastic bowl on the bed table that Sally had brought in for me.

"You were so groggy yesterday, I didn't think you'd need this," she'd explained as she was wheeling the table in.

"And you didn't want anything cluttering the room in case I flatlined again," I'd murmured, thinking of the beeping monitor to which I'd been attached.

She had stared at me, hand on hip. "Well, that too, I suppose."

"Can you fetch me a mirror?" I'd asked, moments before Grant and the children arrived. "I haven't looked at myself since the accident, and I want to make sure I look all right . . . for the family."

In the end, the family arrived before the mirror did, but it appeared Grant had been doing some homework on memory-loss patients. He walked in with a large photo album tucked under his arm. I allowed him to kiss me chastely on the cheek, and I smiled at each of the children in turn. After all, I reasoned, whatever was happening was no fault of theirs. Three of them at least thought I was their mother, and I hadn't the heart to tell them any different—even if I could work out what was going on.

Sophie, the eldest girl, was wearing embroidered hipster trousers and a cropped top that showed her flat eight-year-old stomach. When I caught her eye she stared back almost defiantly and stuck her iPod earphones into her ears, effectively shutting out any kind of conversation. I wondered what sort of relationship she had with her mother.

Nicole, on the other hand, hovered around me anxiously and sat as close to me as she could without actually getting into the bed next to me. If I glanced at her, she smiled hopefully as if silently begging me to remember her, and when I ran my tongue lightly over cracked lips she reached out immediately for the plastic beaker and straw.

Toby seemed like any other four-year-old boy: bored with being stuck in the bland hospital room and ready to make a game out of anything. I watched him lying on the floor opening a paper bag of sterile antiseptic wipes, which he used to scrub his sneakers before trying to cut the laces with a pair of blunt-ended suture scissors.

Teddy, I noticed, was hanging back again, still clutching the squashy ball he'd had with him yesterday. I realized he was watching his brother's experiments with the hospital equipment, but seemed to have no desire to join in.

The girls spread themselves over the bed and snacked on the seedless white grapes they'd brought me, while Grant opened the album.

"I've read that memory loss can be rectified by showing images of the patient's life, listening to your favorite music, or watching your favorite programs," Grant explained. "Here, look, this is a picture of us on our wedding day. I didn't bring in the whole wedding album, since there are some of the best pictures in here, plus vacations with the children . . ."

I had stopped listening to him, my eyes riveted on the photo of the bride and groom smiling outside an old church. Grant didn't look hugely different, maybe a little less lined around the eyes. The bride smiling innocently beside him was about my height and build, with golden blond hair falling in soft curls round her shoulders above the white dress. The eyes staring into the camera were a mesmerizing blue with tiny gray flecks.

"You always liked that close-up one best," he continued when he saw me staring at it. "Of course, your hair isn't quite that blond now, but you're as pretty as ever, isn't she, children?"

"Arms not blue now," Teddy commented from the corner of the room, where until that point he'd been watching us in silence.

"Were my arms blue?" I asked Grant. I snatched at the comment as if, by thinking about that, I wouldn't have to acknowledge the mind-blowing fact that I appeared to be sitting here in someone else's body.

"The doctor said it happens sometimes after a high-voltage injury," Grant said. "There's a huge medical word for it. Apparently your upper and lower extremities were cold and mottled blue when it happened, but it cleared in a few hours." He squeezed my hand. "You look wonderful now."

Nurse Sally chose that moment to appear in the doorway and I glanced up and saw the mirror in her hand. My face must have blanched, because concern suddenly creased her features. I held her gaze imploringly and shook my head. She tactfully backed out of the room again and left me to my supposed family.

"Shouldn't you be at work?" I asked this man, my husband, somehow recovering my voice. "And why aren't the children in school?"

"It's their half-term break, Lauren," Grant told me. "We were going to take a few days off and do some day trips with them."

I looked at the children, who were beginning to fidget in

earnest now. The girls had finished the grapes and Toby had gotten up to inspect the silent EKG machine. Teddy was still glowering at me from the doorway.

"You poor things!" I said with forced cheerfulness, wishing they would all go off and leave me alone. "Fancy having to be here visiting me instead. Grant, why don't you go ahead and take them out to lunch or something? It'll give me a chance to have a bath and sort myself out."

"Lunch?" Sophie repeated, pulling out her earphones and making a "yuk" face. "I want to go to Chessington World of Adventures!"

"Yeah, me too, me too!" cried Toby, rushing over and jumping on the bed again.

"I don't," Teddy muttered from the corner. "I'm goin' to wait here for Mummy to come back again."

"I want to stay here with Mummy too," Nicole said quietly from my side.

Grant looked uncertainly from the children to me, then seemed to come to a reluctant decision.

"Maybe that's not such a bad idea," he said, getting to his feet. "We'll go to Chessington and leave Mummy to have some time on her own." He glanced at Teddy. "You too, Teddy. You'll like it when we get there."

"I won't," Teddy grumbled from the corner. He flashed me a malevolent stare as he was bodily picked up and presented for a kiss good-bye.

I smiled at them all and waved thankfully as they trooped from the room, then, as the door closed behind them, I breathed a sigh of relief and turned my attention to the photo album, which Grant had left open on the bedside table. I stared at the lovely bride for a second or two, then pulled a tuft of my almost-shoulder-length hair in front of my face, peering at it out of the corner of my eye. Blond. Oh no.

Sally reappeared a moment later with the mirror. "I saw the family leaving," she said. "They seemed very excited about something."

"Grant's taking them to Chessington World of Adventures," I told her.

"Lucky them," she said. "Do you want me for anything, or shall I leave you alone for a little while?"

"You can answer me one question, and then leave me alone," I replied, holding the mirror facedown so I couldn't see into it. "Where exactly am I?"

The nurse had the decency to look shocked. It was strange how people took for granted the obvious things, the things that made up their own little universes. They knew I'd lost my memory, but it hadn't occurred to anyone that I might not even know where I was.

"You're in St. Matthew's Hospital, near Little Cranford," she told me. "I'm sorry, Lauren, we haven't been very understanding, have we? I'll leave you to look at the photos and make yourself nice. The bathroom is right next door. You can just pull off the sticky pads from the monitor. Buzz if you need anything. I'm on until two."

I was none the wiser as to my whereabouts. I had never heard of Cranford, Little or otherwise. I stared at the back of the mirror for several minutes once she had gone, willing myself to turn it over. Eventually I plucked up the courage and peeked into the glass. What I saw literally took my breath away. Whether this was a dream or not, it was certainly a nightmare, because despite all my denials, it appeared I really was sitting here in someone else's body. A pretty someone else, with clear English-rose skin and expensively highlighted hair, though I could see if I held the mirror up that the blond locks were singed at the top of my head.

Lauren had a cute snub nose, pouty lips, and cheekbones to die for. But the eyes, which I had expected to be the same clear blue as in the wedding photo, were a grayish green. My eyes, I realized with relief. Hazel eyes belonging to Jessica Taylor.

I remembered the old saying that a person's eyes are the windows to their soul. Well, these windows, despite the fancy dressing, were reflecting my soul. Teddy had been right, I thought with a pang of conscience. His mother had gone, and here was I, stuck in her body, without the first idea what sort of person she was, or how the hell I had gotten here.

In the bathroom, I inspected my new body with a kind of bewildered detachment. I'd always felt my own face wasn't unattractive, with skin that tanned easily and wavy shoulder-length brown hair. But Lauren had full breasts, a solid waist, and long legs. I ran my fingers over the silver stretch marks on her stomach and thighs—my stomach and thighs—remembering that she'd been through three pregnancies, one of which had been with twins. There was bruising to the ribs, which I assumed must be the result of having been given CPR after the cardiac arrest. I winced when I touched the livid purple marks, but at least I was alive.

Groaning, I lowered myself carefully into the bath, taking care not to get the hot water anywhere near my bandaged shoulder, then I soaped the new body wonderingly, surprised that it felt as if it belonged to me. Picking up the shampoo, I began to wash my blond hair until a stinging sensation reminded me about Lauren's head burns. Would I feel such discomfort if this was just a dream, I asked myself with a grimace? I felt so real. Surely this wasn't simply some medicine-induced hallucination?

I rinsed my hair with great difficulty using a plastic container that Nurse Sally had given me. I had to tilt my head awkwardly to one side so the water wouldn't run down onto the bandage. When I returned to the room, wearing one of Lauren's clean nighties with a towel wrapped turbanlike around my wet hair, I climbed back into bed and closed my eyes, exhausted.

Despite my tiredness, I knew I had to methodically process all the information I had if I wasn't going to go stark raving mad. I knew I had been given painkilling drugs, but couldn't believe they were strong enough to have caused me to conjure up a whole new identity for myself. There was no floaty haziness to what I was experiencing. It was just too real, too solid, and so I felt I must try to put these strange events in order.

Fact: I had been struck by the lightning at around two on Saturday afternoon. I didn't yet know much about the details of Lauren's strike except that it appeared to have been more violent than mine, and she seemed to be more badly injured than I was. We had both been unconscious for the remainder of Saturday and into Sunday morning. Lauren had suffered a cardiac arrest, but apparently I had not.

Lauren had woken up first, or rather I had woken up in her body. But she had slept again since then, and I was still here. I glanced at the newspaper Grant had brought in along with the photo album. It was Monday's paper, with a piece about the royal family on the front page. I pushed it away bad-temperedly. If I was really here, then the obvious question had to be, where was Lauren now? I knew she wasn't in my body, because I'd woken up there, too, although if my suspicions were right, what appeared to be night here was day there, and vice versa.

My first inclination was that I should ask Dr. Shakir about what might have happened. Perhaps this sort of thing had been documented before about victims of lightning strikes. I recalled reading an article once about how a lightning-strike victim had tried to kill herself after being struck. She'd been reported as saying she couldn't live with herself after the incident, that she'd felt differently about everything. She'd even been afraid to leave her own house.

I lay and chewed my lip pensively. Could she have experienced something similar to what I was going through now? Could she have come back into a stranger's body?

On second thought, telling anyone about what was happening was probably not such a good idea. I didn't want to spend the rest of my days locked in a lunatic asylum, that was for sure. I imagined myself trying to explain that I was trapped in the wrong body, and how the medical profession would react to such a confession.

Sitting up, I towel-dried my hair, shaking out the damp locks and turning to rummage in my locker for Lauren's hairbrush. No, I thought as I stroked the brush carefully through my hair, I would have to be much subtler in my quest for an answer to my present predicament.

An hour later an orderly came with a wheelchair and took me for a head MRI scan, and I'd not been back on the ward more than ten minutes when Dr. Shakir himself came to see me. He perched on the side of the bed and asked how I was feeling.

"I still feel rather . . . unsettled," I told him carefully.

He nodded, patting my hand in a fatherly fashion. "You have been through a great deal, Lauren," he said. "When part of your memories are lost, your identity seems lost with it. It's quite understandable you should be feeling disoriented."

"Is it usual for patients to lose all their memories?"

He hesitated and I guessed he didn't really want to confound me with the hard medical facts, but then he continued, "Well, it's more usual for victims of lightning strikes to suffer anterograde amnesia, losing memories of the incident and suffering problems with memory afterward. In your case you seem to be experiencing retrograde amnesia, a loss of memories before the incident."

"I think it would help if you could answer some questions I have been worrying about," I said carefully.

He nodded, smiling benignly at me.

"When I suffered the cardiac arrest, how long was I 'dead' for?"

He looked taken aback by the bluntness of my question, but answered anyway.

"We were working on you for almost forty minutes from the time you came in to when we got a sinus rhythm going. I believe the ambulance crew had been doing CPR for at least twenty minutes before that."

"Is it unusual for someone to be 'gone' for that long and have no serious aftereffects?"

He smiled rather patronizingly before answering. "I don't think you need to worry about that, Lauren. Apart from the memory loss, you seem to be recovering well."

"But is it unusual?" I persisted, wanting desperately to know if this body should clinically be dead.

He shook his head. "People respond differently. I suppose, to be frank, I was a little concerned there may have been some brain damage after so long without oxygen to the brain, but as soon as you woke up my doubts were allayed."

"When you were working on me," I continued, "did you contemplate giving up on me?"

Dr. Shakir fidgeted uncomfortably and refused to meet my gaze. Instead of answering immediately he got up, lifted my notes from the foot of my bed and began leafing through them.

"At one point," he said quietly. "I confess I thought we were struggling to resuscitate you in vain. I contemplated calling time of death. I thought you might be too badly injured to survive. But then I heard your children outside the emergency room crying for you, begging us to save their mother. One of the little boys was chanting, 'Mummy, come back; Mummy, come back!' We shocked you one last time, and here you are."

Indeed, I thought wryly. Here I was. But not Lauren. Not the children's mother.

He put down the notes and smiled at me, less disconcerted now that I wasn't asking awkward questions and forcing him to justify his actions, which, let's face it, could have gone badly if Lauren had woken up brain-damaged and needing permanent care. How would Grant and the children have coped then? I wondered. From what I had seen so far, Lauren was the strong one, the one who held that fragile family together. The knowledge transfixed me. Could I possibly step into her shoes? Was I strong enough? Did I even want to try?

I shook my head, realizing that I was straying into padded-cell territory again. Thinking too deeply at this point wouldn't help anyone, least of all me.

"Dr. Shakir?" I asked, in what I perceived to be a deceptively innocent voice—Lauren's voice, not mine, I had realized, since I was using her vocal cords and facial bone structure. "When you came to see me yesterday you said you'd looked up some stuff about lightning strikes?"

"Yes," he said, his eyes narrowing with just a smidgen of suspicion.

"Did you find anything about victims having new memories? Or people recollecting events they couldn't account for?"

The doctor came and sat down on the bed again, trying to look concerned, though I could see the interest gleaming in his eyes.

"There's often confusion, due to the Pat Effect I mentioned to you before, but new memories?" He shook his head. "I've not heard of it." He fixed his gaze on my face. "You're not experiencing anything like that, are you, Lauren?"

"Good heavens no!" I replied hastily with a forced laugh. "I was just wondering what you'd found out, that's all."

"There are many documented cases of lightning-strike victims becoming disoriented, changed in character, for example," he replied, the gleam in his eyes evaporating as quickly as it had arrived.

"Go on."

"The effect of lightning on the human brain is similar to that of patients who have undergone electroconvulsive therapy," he continued. "As I said, the vast majority who survive a lightning strike are confused and suffer anterograde amnesia for several days after the strike. Loss of consciousness for varying periods is common, as are neurological complications and difficulty with memory."

He looked at me intensely as if to check that I was keeping up with him, then he pressed on more boldly. "You have to understand that the cognitive and neurological damage caused to the brain by a lightning strike to the skull is similar to a blunt injury trauma."

"Like being hit over the head?" I asked.

He nodded. "Exactly. You were a very lucky woman, Lauren. According to your children, the lightning hit you directly on the head, back, and shoulders. Your hair, I hear, stood on end and actually caught fire, and there are burns consistent with this."

"The burns aren't deep, though, considering how hot you said lightning can get?" I probed, twisting the unaccustomed wedding band on my finger as I spoke. "Would you have expected the burns to be worse?"

Dr. Shakir smiled. "You are an inquisitive woman, Lauren. Yes, I was surprised there wasn't more burning to your head, but in the case of your shoulder, then no, I wasn't surprised. Skin is the primary resistor to the flow of current into the body, causing the appearance of surface burns, but preventing deep tissue damage. With lightning the current is present in the body for a very brief time, causing short-circuiting of the body's electrical systems: cardiac arrest such as in your case, vascular spasm, neurological damage, and autonomic instability."

"So there was nothing about my case that was out of the ordinary?"

He paused and broke eye contact before shaking his head. "No."

I stared at him, realizing that what he had been holding back all along was the very thing I had been desperate to discover. Had Lauren's injuries actually killed her? From what he had told me, and from the fascinated way he looked at me, I got the very clear impression that all Dr. Shakir's medical experience indicated that I should not be here. My living, breathing presence belied his gut instincts, confounding his diagnosis. No wonder he wouldn't look me in the eye, I thought grimly.

I remembered suddenly what Dr. Chin had said about possible deafness and the chance of developing cataracts at a later date, and put the question to Dr. Shakir.

"You are remarkably well informed about your condition," he said.

He seemed happier now that we were back in safe medical territory. I watched as his shoulders visibly relaxed. "This is accurate information regarding high-voltage injury, but I have checked you thoroughly, and you appear at present to be in the clear." He paused. "In fact, when we have had the results of the MRI scan, providing everything is normal you can probably go home."

"Today?" I asked him apprehensively.

He shook his head. "I will come and see you again tomorrow. If your scan results are available then, and you are feeling generally in good health, we may be able to let you out tomorrow. If you are still experiencing memory loss at that time we could arrange an outpatient appointment for you at our psychiatric unit. Meanwhile, I suggest you get some rest. I'm sure it will be very difficult for you to get much peace and quiet once you are home."

Grant came to visit me alone that evening. He said the children were exhausted after their day out. He'd put them to bed early and asked a neighbor to come in and keep an eye on them for an hour or two.

"How is Teddy bearing up?" I asked him, partly to show an interest in his children's well-being and partly because, despite my denials, I was deeply affected by Teddy's situation.

Grant shrugged. "He's upset, obviously. He doesn't really understand what's happening, Lauren. He keeps crying for his mummy."

I avoided his gaze, thinking that Teddy seemed to have a better grasp of what was happening than anyone else did.

"Have they said when you can come home?" he asked.

"Maybe tomorrow," I said, trying to keep my mind off the hideous possibility of such a thing.

Home. Another unknown step into the dark. A place where, unless I woke up as Jessica again soon, I would be expected to play a role I would have to guess at as I went along; to live a life that simply wasn't mine. I wanted to go home all right, but I wanted to continue with my own life, to be in control of my own destiny. I thought of my mother's comments about not trying to be Superwoman and fought back tears of frustration. I had always been my own woman—fiercely independent and determined to do things my own way. My life might not have been perfect, but it had been mine. And now I found I wasn't in control of anything at all. I was being swept along; a mere passenger on a roller-coaster ride that was more terrifying than anything the children could possibly have experienced at Chessington.

I yawned widely, covering my mouth. Sleep was what I needed now and what I hoped was the key to the door between these two worlds.

Grant got the message. I thought how tired he looked himself as he kissed me lightly on the forehead before heading for the door.

"Good night, sweetheart," he whispered as he closed the door behind him. "I'll be back tomorrow."

"Good night, Grant." I sank back against the pillows, realizing with a pang of guilt as I watched his retreating back that I was fervently hoping it might be the last I ever saw of him.

chapter four

When I awoke snuggled in the double duvet in my own bed, the feeling of relief was immense. I still wasn't convinced that my experience as Lauren was simply a normal dream—there were too many abnormalities, too many questions left unanswered—but I was awake now, I was Jessica again; my body felt physically rested and my mind relaxed as if I had merely been deeply asleep and dreaming. Yawning, I luxuriated in the knowledge that I was home and safe in my own world.

I sat up and hugged Frankie tightly. "You will never believe where I've been," I told her as I slid out of bed and padded barefoot to the high window. I flung open the curtains to another glorious autumn day. "What would you say if I told you I was somewhere else all night while you were lying here keeping my feet warm for me?"

Frankie tilted her head to one side and gave a short bark.

I ran myself a hot bath, and while it was running I gave Frankie her breakfast of dry mix, put the kettle on for my morning tea, and went to the front door in my pajamas to look for the mail.

Nothing but circulars. It should have been sad, really, that few people ever wrote to me. The only mail I received on a regular basis usually came in brown envelopes, with the exception of occasional airmail letters from my brother, Simon, but I supposed that was because I was what some people might call a bit of a loner. I smiled to myself as I sifted through the junk mail. I preferred my own character description of self-sufficient, work-oriented, and perhaps a little wary of commitment. But either way, today I didn't care. All that mattered was that I was here, back in my own body where I should be, flaws and all.

As I lay in the bath looking down at my youthful body, I smiled at the lack of stretch marks and bruises, the dark body hair in all the right places. I wondered if blondes had to shave their legs. I hoped I would never have to find out.

The thought sobered me, robbing me of the joy I'd been experiencing since I'd woken up. Grabbing the soap, I worked it to a rich lather and began to wash vigorously. I might be home now, but the nightmare clung, refusing to simply rinse away with the soapsuds. At some point this body would need to sleep, and while it was resting, the nightmare might return. I had only dreamed the dream twice, but the fact that the second dream had seemed to continue on so smoothly from the first was dreadfully worrying. Suppose I found myself struggling with that other life again?

Lying back in the warm water, my mind dwelled on the possibilities. Dream or not, while I was being Lauren, her life had seemed as real to me as my own.

And what if I had to experience going home to that family? The thought brought a rush of terror. Yesterday, when I'd been dozing, I'd been aware of Lauren having her drip disconnected. Did that mean that every time I slept, I ran the risk of returning to continue the dream? If that were the case then I'd be constantly on the go, flitting from dream to reality without respite.

Watching a tiny bubble drift up to the ceiling, I was filled with the dreadful certainty that the real Lauren was dead. After listening to Dr. Shakir's account of her injuries I was sure he felt Lauren should be dead or irreparably brain-damaged, despite his outward claim that her quick recovery was nothing unusual.

The thought that the children's mother had probably died not only shook me to the core, it brought a lump to my throat. She had been a stranger to me, of course, and possibly a figment of my imagination, but in my dream I had been there in her body and I felt an overwhelming grief for this woman I had never known. My heart went out to her husband and children. They had lost the wife and mother they loved, and didn't even know they should be mourning her loss.

My lips trembled and I pressed them firmly together. There was nothing I could do for her now, I told myself. The best I could do while I was there was to try to keep her body from further harm, and I found myself wondering what another chapter of the dream might hold for me. Meanwhile, I rather guiltily thanked my lucky stars it had been Lauren who had died and not me.

I lay back in the warm water for a moment or two, pondering why I had survived and Lauren obviously hadn't, when the whole situation suddenly seemed absurd. I sat up abruptly, slopping water over the edges of the tub onto the green bathroom carpet. What was I doing, allowing this incredible situation to take over my thoughts? I asked myself angrily. Why was I accepting this living nightmare as if it were a normal, everyday occurrence? I knew that what was frightening me most was the possibility that it wasn't a dream at all. Not in the normal sense, anyway. And if it wasn't a dream, then what?

Sitting in the rapidly cooling water, I gazed into space, wondering. What other explanation could there be, other than the shadowy fear that when I was awake I was Jessica, and when Lauren was awake I was her . . .

I groaned loudly, putting my hands over my ears as if I could shut out the clamoring of my own thoughts, thoughts that sounded as if they had come straight from watching the sci-fi channel. I had to believe that the dream was over now, or I'd be afraid to sleep ever again.

Frankie had heard the groan and was whining at the bathroom door.

"It's okay, Frankie," I called through the door. "I'll be out in a minute."

Still sitting up, I shampooed my dark brown hair, thanking God for the lack of burns to my scalp as I massaged it to a lather. The lightning hadn't hit my head at all.

Perhaps, I thought, as I ran Saturday's events through my mind for the umpteenth time, my lucky escape hadn't been solely due to the protection afforded by my thick sheepskin coat. It might well have been partly due to the way I'd been hunched forward against the downpour, ready to dive into the passenger seat of Dan's car, so that the force had missed my head.

Ducking under the water to wash the shampoo away and then wriggling upright, I stepped out of the bath, squeezed the excess water out of my hair, and wrapped myself in my bathrobe. I glanced at the clock. Damn! I'd been so caught up in what was happening to me, I was going to be late for work if I didn't hurry. I dressed quickly, shoved a piece of toast into my mouth, and ran up the steps with Frankie at my heels. We walked for ten minutes while Frankie sniffed at lampposts and did her business, which I picked up in my scooper. We headed home at a brisk trot.

"See you at lunchtime," I called as I closed the door to my flat behind me and, biting a chunk out of a juicy red apple, headed out onto the pavement for the quick walk to work.

The legal firm I worked for, Chisleworth & Partners, was housed in a drab-looking building on a side street. I took the steps two at a time, and arrived at my desk about half a minute before my boss, Stephen Armitage.

Stephen was a good-looking man in his early forties and had been my boss for the last ten years, ever since I'd left secretarial school at the age of eighteen. He'd overseen most of my training to become a legal secretary and had encouraged me to work toward gaining extra qualifications in the legal field, taking me under his wing as his assistant and protégé. Stephen had been kind and attentive and we spent much of our working hours together, sometimes working late into the night when the office was quiet and we were gathering documents and files for court.

As I shrugged out of my coat in the narrow confines of the outer office, I was reminded of how our working proximity had led one night to a gentle coming together, and while I had never been totally sure of my feelings for him, a relationship with him had seemed easy and inevitable. It had seemed sensible after a while to move into a flat he owned, though I retained my independence by paying him rent and splitting our everyday expenses. Although we had both known I wasn't ready or willing to settle down properly, we had remained lovers for nearly six years.

Walking back to my desk, I flicked on my computer, unable

to keep my mind from dwelling on past actions and decisions I had made. I knew my experience as Lauren was making me question my life here as Jessica, and it suddenly became clear that my doubts about Stephen had probably been obvious to him all along. That doubt was possibly the reason that he'd kept his own flat close to the office, and had influenced our joint decision to see each other socially several times a week rather than living permanently together. I realized now that I had thought of him as more of a friend with whom I was having a relationship than as a partner, and cringed when I remembered I had even introduced him to my parents as such.

I stared blankly at the computer screen as it flickered into life before me, recalling how we'd muddled along in that unsatisfactory fashion until rumors reached me that he was seeing a female barrister on a regular basis. I knew it wasn't so much the lies or the fact that he was cheating on me that prompted me to move out and put a down payment on a flat of my own, but rather the fact that the news hadn't bothered me anywhere near as much as I knew it ought to have if I'd really cared for him.

It seemed that Stephen had felt much the same way, and somehow we'd made the difficult transition from lovers to friends, because I loved my job, even if I had to admit I had never really loved him.

Glancing at the clock on the wall, I knew how fortunate I was that the working day began late at Chisleworth & Partners. Stephen never put in an appearance until after ten o'clock, and as long as I was in the office slightly before him he didn't seem to mind what time I arrived.

This morning he squeezed my shoulder affectionately as he passed my desk, which was unfortunate since the high-voltage burn was still pretty tender. I winced with pain, and he was instantly contrite, asking what on earth was the matter. I told him about the lightning strike and he was suitably horrified.

Not as horrified as he would have been if he'd known I'd spent my sleeping hours since Saturday in the body of another woman, I thought to myself, as he asked me solicitously if I was well enough to be working. The nightmare seemed unreal, even laughable now, in the familiar surroundings of the shabby office, with the coffee machine gurgling away in the corner and the computer blinking up at me.

I assured him I was fine, and he vanished into his office with the undisguised relief of a man who had thought I might have wanted him to do something about it.

There were two other girls working with me: Clara, who was secretary to Rory Chisleworth himself, and Delores, who answered the telephone, made coffee for clients, and spent the rest of the day bitching about her boyfriend to anyone who would listen. As soon as the office door closed behind Stephen's smart but rather dated blue pinstripe suit, I got up and grabbed the newspaper from Clara's desk, my eyes flicking straight to the date. Monday, October 20. And there was the article about the royal family. How could I possibly have dreamed that?

"Help yourself," Clara smiled, with a touch of friendly sarcasm, handing me a cup of coffee before I'd even had time to assimilate all that the date meant.

I sat down at my desk and sipped the hot drink thoughtfully. Monday again, and with the same news. I'd already lived through Monday as Lauren. So what kind of a dream had this sort of continuity? The thoughts that had plagued me earlier returned, reducing my legs to jelly. I'd certainly never heard of anyone picking up a dream from where they'd left off the previous night and living it as if it were an alternate life.

There was that other possibility, I told myself uneasily. It was even more frightening than the dream theory. It might explain why when I was here I was Jessica, and when I was asleep I became Lauren. I knew I couldn't keep blocking out the awful dawning suspicion forever. Sooner or later I would have to face the inconceivable . . . Could it be that somehow my life force—my soul—had been split by the simultaneous lightning strike, so that it now inhabited both bodies alternately?

The outlandish idea caused me to suck in a quick breath, which in turn caused a coughing fit as the coffee slid down the wrong way. Clara, who I believe had been talking to me, came and held out a tissue, which I took gratefully. I wiped my eyes and then gave my nose a good blow, which seemed to calm everything down.

"Are you sure you're okay to be working?" she asked, perching on the corner of my desk. "You look very pale."

"I'm fine, honestly," I assured her.

She'd heard me telling Stephen about the lightning strike and wanted to know the details. I told her about meeting Dan and how he'd given me a lift back to my car the next day. She grinned at me and looked as if she was about to interrogate me further when Delores appeared from reception.

"Mr. Chisleworth's ten-thirty is here," she announced. Clara returned to her desk with a knowing glance at me, and there was no more opportunity for small talk as the working day began.

Today, unfortunately, Stephen was preparing a case for court. That meant I would be working closely with him, getting the files together, and would probably not leave the office until after six o'clock, except for my hour-long lunch break when I walked the ten minutes home again to see Frankie.

As it happened, Stephen wanted to work right through lunch, but he knew I walked Frankie in my break and begrudgingly allowed me half an hour to hurry home. I let Frankie out and sat on the wall that surrounded my little courtyard, eating the egg and cress sandwich I'd bought from the sandwich girl at the office before I left.

Everything was so familiar, so normal. I began to think that my experiences as Lauren must simply have been a very real-seeming dream after all.

Back in the office, Stephen was panicking over some mislaid notes, and I hardly had time to grab a cup of afternoon tea, let alone dwell on the workings of the sleeping brain, or the outlandish theory of shared souls. By the time I returned to my flat after Frankie's evening walk, it was after seven o'clock. I kicked my shoes off in the hallway and walked in stockinged feet into the kitchen to throw a TV dinner into the oven, then flopped down in my armchair with a glass of orange juice.

I glanced anxiously at the clock, allowing my thoughts to return to the forbidden territory of "what if?" So far, if I assumed the worst—that Lauren and I both really coexisted in some way—then it had worked quite well logistically until now because Lauren and I had been keeping strange hours, due to the fact that we'd both been in the hospital. What would happen, I wondered—providing she was real—if she were ready to wake up before I was ready to go to bed? Could both of us be awake at the same time? I couldn't see that it was possible, given that there was only one me, one consciousness—even if I had started flitting between two bodies like something out of a horror movie.

After eating the cardboard-flavored shepherd's pie and giving Frankie her supper, I curled up in my chair to see what was on the television, flicking through the channels without much success. I was about to give up and see if there was any ice cream in the freezer when the phone rang.

It was Dan.

"How are you today?"he asked solicitously."Feeling better?"

Adrenaline flooded my body at the sound of his voice. There was a discernible tightening in my chest and my palms became so clammy I thought the phone was going to slip right out of my grasp. My voice sounded strained when I tried to use it, so I cleared my throat and tried again.

"I'm much better, thank you. I went in to work today. I've only been home just over an hour."

"Do you feel well enough to come out for a drink this evening?"

I was about to say I'd love to, when I glanced again at the clock. Eight-thirty might not be late in evening terms, but it was getting late to be sleeping in the morning.

Then I remembered Nurse Sally's voice speaking to me as I'd woken as Lauren the previous morning. She'd complained that I was an incredibly heavy sleeper, and that she hadn't been able to rouse me. Did that mean that Lauren couldn't wake until I went to sleep?

"That would be great," I heard myself saying. "Where should we go?"

He suggested a friendly little pub not more than ten minutes' drive away. I agreed to meet him there in half an hour. However, once the phone was hung up and the feeling of euphoria I had felt at the sound of his voice had started to wear off, I was assailed by feelings of guilt. Poor Lauren—or, rather, poor

Lauren's family, I thought. Suppose my theory was right and this wasn't a dream? Her children would be waiting to visit her and wondering why their mummy wouldn't wake up. On the other hand, I had no wish to jump back into her shoes any sooner than I had to. Apart from the children, there was Grant of course. He seemed like a nice caring husband, but I was not his wife and I could see that things could get very complicated there.

If I could postpone the moment when I was back in her body by an hour or two, then that suited me just fine, especially if she was going to be allowed to go home today. I wasn't looking forward to stepping into that minefield one little bit.

Anyway, I reasoned, as I brushed mascara onto my eyelashes and finished smoothing on lip gloss, this was all simply a wild theory. I would probably tumble into bed tonight and dream about something completely different. And even if I was somehow right, then I didn't owe them anything. If their mother was dead, then that was very sad, but why was it my responsibility? I'd never asked for any of this, had I?

The pub was noisy and crowded when I pushed through the front door, and I was beginning to wonder how I would find Dan when he appeared at my side. "Shall we go through to the other bar?" he shouted over the din, and I nodded, following him into the much quieter lounge bar, where he grabbed us a couple of seats at a small round table.

"What would you like to drink?" he asked.

"I'd like a still mineral water, please."

His eyebrow went up, but he didn't try to change my mind, as happened frequently when I was out with friends. I'd stopped drinking alcohol in any quantity a few months previously, not for any highbrow reasons, but because I didn't like the feeling of being out of control. Now, with the lightning strike and my present state of confusion, I decided it might be more sensible, for the present at least, to abstain from drinking altogether.

Dan returned with my water and a pint of lager for himself, and we sat looking at each other warily across the small divide afforded by the table, sipping nervously at our drinks.

"You're very pretty when you're clean and dry," he said at last, sitting back and licking a mustache of froth off his top lip.

"You brush up quite well yourself," I replied with a smile.

We sat in silence for a moment, contemplating each other over our glasses.

"I'd really like to get to know you better." He blurted it out as if he'd been unable to prevent his thoughts escaping him.

I must have looked rather startled, because he grinned widely and took my hand in his.

"I mean, I'll tell you something about my life, and you can tell me something about yourself."

"You start then," I said, trying not to show that it felt as though his touch was setting my hand on fire.

"Okay. Well, for a start I'm not married," he said, answering the question I'd been itching to know. "I was engaged to a girl for a while a year or so ago, but she ran off with a friend of mine." He took a swig of his lager and looked me in the eye. "Your turn."

"I lived with a guy for a while, but it didn't work out. I moved out and got a place of my own two years ago. I live alone now, apart from Frankie of course."

"My elderly father lives with me," he said. "He's an old rogue, but his heart's in the right place. You'd like him."

"I'm sure I would." I yawned suddenly and clamped my hand

over my mouth, embarrassed. "I'm sorry. It's been a long day, especially after what happened . . ."

"Come on," he said, downing his pint and pulling me to my feet. "I shouldn't have asked you out this evening, especially as you struggled into work today. You would have been perfectly within your rights to have stayed in bed all day."

I longed to tell him that bed was the last place I wanted to be. That was the place where I was thrown into a bizarre alternate world, but that information wasn't something I thought would go down particularly well on our first date.

He walked me to my car, and I apologized again for having to leave almost before our evening had begun.

"I'll ring again in a few days, when you've had a chance to recover properly," he said, giving me a chaste peck on the cheek. "Go on, get yourself home. What you need is a good night's sleep."

It was past ten o'clock when I clambered at last into bed and snuggled down with Frankie on the floor beside me in her basket. I was so tired, I didn't even have time to fret about what possibly lay ahead of me. My last thought was that the nightmare might all be over by now. Perhaps the lightning had, after all, induced hallucinatory dreams, and that being the case, maybe I would never have to be Lauren again.

As it turned out, there was no such luck.

I felt myself being shaken awake by Dr. Shakir, who was standing over me looking extremely concerned.

"How do you feel, Lauren?" he asked as I opened my eyes.

"Fine," I replied groggily. My head felt as if I was waking from the deepest of sleeps, my eyes were having difficulty opening, and I was sure my lids were puffed up like a pig's.

"We have been worried about you. Do you remember who you are?"

I contemplated for the briefest of seconds telling him that I was Jessica Taylor, but decided against it almost immediately. What was happening to me was the result of no medical condition Dr. Shakir would ever have encountered. There seemed no point in doing anything other than playing along with this strange game in which I found myself once again.

"I'm Lauren Richardson," I said. "I'm married with four children."

"Lauren, sweetheart!" came a voice from the other side of the room. "You've got your memory back!"

I turned my head to see Grant advancing on me, eyes bright. "We—the doctors and I—thought you'd gone into a coma! We thought we were losing you all over again." And, to my horror, my husband gathered me in his arms and began to sob uncontrollably.

Dr. Shakir snapped his fingers at Nurse Sally. "Fetch Mr. Richardson a cup of hot sweet tea, would you, Nurse?"

"Grant," I said from somewhere beneath his shirt, "you're suffocating me."

"Don't do that again, my love," he said, releasing me, but taking hold of both my hands as he perched on the edge of the bedside chair. "I couldn't bear it if you left us."

I stared with some embarrassment into the tear-stained face of this man who was gazing at me with such love. I told myself to think of him as if he were the husband of a good friend. I knew that if I were an onlooker and not the object of his love I might have been moved by his obvious devotion. The knowledge quelled my instinctive feelings of alarm and I found a small spark of compassion. Grant was not a strong man.

"I've only been asleep," I told him gently. "I've felt so tired since this all happened."

His eyes darted to Dr. Shakir, who shook his dark head as if my condition was a new one on him.

"The nurses have been trying to rouse you since seven o'clock this morning, Lauren," Dr. Shakir said. "In the end I was called, because they feared you had fallen into a coma. We ran tests, but although they showed your metabolism had slowed considerably, your vital signs have remained steady. We simply couldn't wake you up."

"I think," I said slowly, realizing that my worst fears had been justified, "that I might be needing a lot of sleep from now on. I'm sure there's no need to worry about me, though."

"Lauren!" Grant exclaimed, undisguised exasperation overlying his earlier tone of abject misery. "They've been trying to wake you for the last three hours. That's not normal, sweetheart."

"Wouldn't you rather have me back for a few hours a day than not at all?" I asked him shortly.

Grant looked affronted, but I plowed on regardless.

"What I'm trying to tell you is that if you let me wake when I'm ready, I'll probably recover a lot quicker."

Grant nodded eventually and went out into the corridor. I heard him calling the children and I closed my eyes again, mentally preparing myself to try to be suitably motherly.

"Lauren," Dr. Shakir's voice murmured softly, "is there something you aren't telling us?"

"Like what?" I asked, frightened suddenly that he knew my secret.

"I don't know. Maybe your memory has returned more than you are willing to admit?"

"Why should I say I don't remember things if it's not true?" I asked. I was unsure what he was getting at, but he was looking at me strangely, and I didn't like it.

"You have a very demanding home life," he said with a shrug. "Everyone seems to depend on you. It can't be easy to cope with four children under the age of eight, especially as one of your twins has special needs."

I stared back at him, relieved that he thought I was shamming. It was a lot better than the prospect of him discovering the truth. I had no intention of spending the rest of my days in a laboratory, being hooked up to monitors while I slept, and having my life examined in minute detail.

"If you're insinuating that I'm delaying my recovery on purpose, then I can assure you, you couldn't be further from the truth."

"You haven't seemed too eager to see your children since you've been in the hospital," he pointed out. "No one's blaming you, Lauren. Everyone deserves a rest sometimes."

"Perhaps I should share my secret for a peaceful life with other harassed mothers," I retorted. "Get yourselves struck by lightning, girls; it works wonders in the sympathy stakes."

Before the doctor had a chance to respond, Grant appeared with the children in tow, and I sat up and pecked them each on the cheek in turn. Teddy tried to twist his face away at the last moment, but I managed to kiss the side of his ear. I felt it was the least I could do for Lauren.

"Did you all enjoy Chessington World of Adventures yesterday?" I asked them.

"We went on some really cool rides," Nicole said. "Daddy wouldn't let us go on the really big ones, but Sophie and me went on the Vampire Ride!"

"Toby and Teddy were too small," Sophie put in with a twinge of disappointment. "They only wanted to go into the Bubbleworks and to Beanoland."

"I drove Daddy in a Tiny Truck," Toby put in excitedly, "and in Beanoland we fired foam balls and went on the Bash Street Bus."

"Did Daddy go on it?" I asked with a smile.

"I had to go on all sorts of things," Grant said with a playful grimace. "Most of the rides require a parent to accompany young children, and it wasn't easy with the twins being too small for a lot of the bigger rides." He gave me a wan look. "It would have been easier and more fun if you'd been well enough to come, Lauren. We missed you."

I turned my attention to Teddy. "Did you have a nice time, too?"

He twisted the toe of his shoe into the floor and wouldn't answer.

"You know he finds those sorts of places a challenge," Grant said with a sigh. "Remember when we took the children to the local fair last year and he spent the whole time with his head hidden under my jacket?"

I stared at him blankly and there was a short silence as everyone realized they'd forgotten I didn't remember anything about anything at all.

"Is Mum coming home today?" Sophie asked into the silence.

"It may be possible, depending on the result of the MRI scan and as long as there will be someone at home to look after her for the next few days," Dr. Shakir said.

"I've taken the week off work anyway," Grant said. "And Lauren's sister Karen has said she'll come to stay for a couple of days next week."

Dr. Shakir looked at me. "What do you think, Lauren? Are you ready to go home, even though your memory has not yet returned?"

I didn't like to say that if the return of my memory was the criterion for going home with the Richardsons, then I'd be in the hospital forever. Lauren's memories were not available to me. I would have to start fresh from here, or else I'd have to persuade them to keep her sedated in the hospital for the rest of her life in the hope that under the influence of a drug-induced sleep I never had to return here.

Studying each of her children in turn, I decided I'd give it a go, for their sake. A heavily sedated mother was really no mother at all, and I felt they needed a mother desperately, each in their own special way.

Dear God, I thought, as I watched Toby bouncing on the end of the bed and the girls chatting animatedly about yesterday's outing, is that why I'm here?

Grant brought in a fresh change of clothes for me that afternoon, when he returned with the children for a second visit. He told me he'd gotten rid of the ones I'd been wearing when the lightning struck.

"They were all burned, Mummy," Nicole told me, her eyes as large as saucers as she remembered the incident.

"And your shoes were melted," Toby added. "I carried them to the ambulance for you, but they were squished."

I didn't want to dwell on the horrible reality of Lauren's burns, which I now believed had actually killed her.

"Don't forget I still haven't been given the all-clear from Dr. Shakir," I reminded them gently.

He arrived at that moment looking flustered, and asked Nurse Sally to take the children to the playroom for a few minutes. Grant paled as he looked at the doctor's expression and took my hand in his.

"We've had the results of the MRI scan. It has shown scarring to the surface of the brain." Dr. Shakir came straight to the point. "We have also discovered a weakness in your skull, Lauren. It seems you suffer from a congenital defect that might never have been picked up, and probably wouldn't have been a problem if it hadn't been for the lightning strike."

I stared at him. "What does this mean?"

"It means that the lightning strike, which might otherwise have been deflected by your skull and the skin of your scalp, has penetrated the temporal lobes where memory is stored."

"And . . . ?"

"From the damage we have seen, we are not sure that your memories will ever come back. I'm sorry."

There was a short silence as we each contemplated the enormity of the diagnosis.

"You must be able to do something!" Grant spluttered. "In this day and age you're supposed to be able to fix people!"

"Grant," I said quietly, "I think I knew already that the memories weren't coming back. It's not the doctor's fault."

"I don't understand how this can be happening." Grant put his head in his hands and groaned. He looked shocked, as if this were the first time since the accident that he'd really understood that his life was changed forever.

"The temporal lobes are vulnerable to interruptions in oxygen supply to the brain," Dr. Shakir went on, as if explaining the medical facts would enable us to cope with the reality of the problem more easily. "These in turn wreak havoc with the brain's electrical signaling system. But the miracle is that Lauren doesn't seem to be suffering from any other symptoms, Mr. Richardson. I am hopeful she will be able to lead a normal life." He turned to me. "I have made an appointment for you with our psychiatric counselor for early next week. It may help you to come to terms with your condition to talk to someone trained in such things."

I took the card with my appointment time from Dr. Shakir, then squeezed Grant's hand reassuringly. "It's not the end of the world, Grant," I told him. "If you'll give me the chance, I'm prepared to do my best."

He nodded, biting his lip, and then he went to wait with the children while I got ready to go to wherever it was they called home.

I dressed quickly, being careful to avoid snagging the fresh antibiotic dressing that Nurse Sally had fixed over my burns. When I was done, I looked down at my alternate body attired in what to me were new clothes. Lauren certainly had a flare for style, I thought. Not for her the plain skirts and trouser suits in neutral shades that I wore each day to the office, or the casual jeans and sweaters I wore at home. I was wearing a pair of her soft black jersey trousers, elegantly cut, with a matching black T-shirt worn under an open suede shirt in pale tan. To finish off the outfit, Grant had brought some of Lauren's jewelry: a gold rope chain with matching bracelet and clip earrings, a beautiful gold watch, and what I assumed must be Lauren's engagement ring, all flashy diamonds and sapphires set on a gold band, which Grant had slipped onto my finger before following the children out of the door.

I winced as I clipped on the earrings. Lauren was going to have to have her ears pierced at the first opportunity, I thought with a grimace.

Gathering up Lauren's few belongings one-handed from the bedside locker, I thanked Nurse Sally for everything, and asked her to thank Dr. Shakir for me. I noticed he had made himself scarce after delivering the depressing news of my condition to Grant, almost as if he felt he had failed us in some way and couldn't bear to look either of us in the eye.

I wondered if the good doctor regretted suggesting I had been faking, now that it had been proved without a doubt that Lauren's memories had been irretrievably wiped out.

Grant smiled wanly as I approached the playroom. He was sitting with Toby on his lap. They were looking at a book, but I could see Grant's heart wasn't in it. Sophie was watching Nicole dress a doll, telling her rather bossily that she was doing it all wrong, and Teddy was sitting hunched in a corner hugging his ball to his chest and crooning tunelessly to himself.

"You look wonderful," Grant said with a catch in his voice.

The children's heads shot up simultaneously.

"Are you coming home with us, Mummy?" asked Sophie.

Toby leapt off his father's lap and raced at me, reaching me seconds before Nicole, who threw her arms round my waist.

Taking a deep breath, I looked at them and forced a smile. "Yes, I do believe I am."

chapter five

Home turned out to be a large six-bedroom house on a select road of evenly spaced, elegant houses, each with a manicured half-acre garden.

As Grant parked the silver Ford Galaxy in one side of the double garage and switched off the engine, I stared around me with a mixture of apprehension and interest. The first thing I noticed was how tidy the garage was. My parents' garage at home had always been a jumble of old mowers, strewn tools, and junk that my mother had wanted out of the house but wouldn't actually throw away.

The Richardsons' garage had a board running the length of the back wall with fixtures for every imaginable kind of tool, each of which seemed to be in its proper place. As the children piled out of the car, I followed more slowly, noticing the neatly painted floor, whitewashed walls, and a gleamingly clean silver Mercedes convertible parked in the next bay.

Nicole took my hand and half-dragged me toward a side door, which apparently led into the house. I followed her and found myself in a spacious playroom where a doll's carriage stood tidily against the far wall and a road map covered a section of the floor complete with several miniature cars and trucks. I noticed a couple of beanbags in front of an old television set and an open cupboard full of jigsaw puzzles in one corner.

"My goodness," I exclaimed. "Have you been cleaning up especially for me?"

Sophie ran over and closed the cupboard door. "Daddy says we mustn't make a mess," she said importantly.

The kitchen was futuristic, all white and sterile, the only color coming from a glass fruit bowl full of red apples, early satsumas, and small bananas. I ran my finger absently over a work surface as I followed Grant through the room, feeling the smooth coldness beneath my touch.

"Do we have a cleaning lady?" I asked him.

He turned and looked at me, and I could see that the innocent question had unsettled him. His facial muscles contorted, but then he forced a smile and nodded abruptly.

"She comes in for two hours every morning."

I followed him meekly out into the hall, where blue and white Willow Pattern plates stood on a high, narrow shelf just below the ceiling and matching vases stood on plinths on either side of an oak front door. The hall carpet was a lovely powder blue and I pictured it covered with Frankie's muddy paw marks and dog hairs and the thought made me want to giggle.

I must have made a small snorting noise, because Grant turned and stared at me suspiciously.

Making my expression as bland as possible, I followed him into a beautiful lounge. The powder-blue carpet was in here too and matched the chintz furniture perfectly. Lauren obviously had an eye for interior design, but I couldn't help but wonder how it stayed so pristine with four children in the house.

It was then that I realized they hadn't followed us into the rest of the house.

"Where are the children?" I inquired.

"They're in the playroom, of course," Grant replied.

"Do they spend all their time in there?" I asked, ignoring his mood.

"You don't like them to spread themselves into the rest of the house; they make such a devil of a mess," he replied shortly.

Standing awkwardly with one hand resting on the back of one of the two sofas, I tried to think whether any of my friends' children were kept out of the main living area like this. I hadn't ever had a lot to do with children, but I couldn't help thinking this wasn't quite normal. It occurred to me as I gazed around at the immaculate living room that the Richardsons were somewhat obsessed with tidiness.

"Where does . . . do I . . . keep my things?" I asked.

"What sort of things?" Grant asked, obviously puzzled by the question.

"Handbag, books, hobbies, correspondence, that sort of thing," I said, thinking of my flat with its jumble of unopened junk mail, a half-written letter to my brother Simon in New Zealand, and an open bag of potting compost slung in a corner of the kitchen.

"You keep your things in your dressing room. Come." He stepped past me into the hall. "I'll show you."

From the hall I could hear the children fighting in the playroom.

"Are they all right?" I asked as Grant, seemingly oblivious

to his children's shouts and yells, walked up the staircase ahead of me.

"Maybe we should send them out into the garden in a minute," he suggested. "They're used to being organized during school vacations."

"What sort of things do they normally do?" I asked.

"I don't know. I'm usually at work by the time they're up and about. I work very long hours at the practice and leave the care of the children to you and the nanny."

"Nanny?" I repeated.

He nodded. "We had a nanny until recently. She left a few weeks ago, said the children were too unruly. She used to take them out shopping, swimming, to the park, that sort of thing I think. You prefer them to be out of the house."

This information came as a surprise. I'd been thinking of Lauren as a devoted earth-mother type.

I waited while Grant opened a door at the end of the landing. Sunlight flooded out into the corridor and I followed him into a light and spacious bedroom dominated by a four-poster bed with opulent cream and blue drapes. Ignoring the bed, I walked across to the huge window and stared down into the garden below. Like the house, it was tidy and organized, with a square lawn ending at a tall conifer hedge, side borders brimming with a riot of colorful flowers and a child's playhouse tucked away in one corner.

"Don't they have a swing or anything?" I asked, wondering what they would do when Grant herded them outside.

"We don't like the garden cluttered with their toys," Grant said. "There's always the park around the corner if they want play equipment."

He opened one of the doors off the main room and waved me over.

"Your dressing room," he said.

The room was the size of my bedroom at home, with a bureau on one side and rows and rows of clothes hung on the other. My first thought was that that was how Grant had managed to bring a complete outfit for Lauren to wear home from the hospital. No man I had ever met would know what to choose for his wife to wear in the way of a matching outfit and accessories, and I'd been fairly puzzled by this uncommon ability of my supposed husband.

Now, staring at the hangers full of complete outfits, I realized that Lauren had been obsessed by her appearance. Everything was stored in color sequence from mauves and blues, through to browns and blacks. A large jewelry box stood in one corner, and under the clothes were rows and rows of shoes in all colors and styles.

Imelda Marcos sprang to my mind, quickly followed by an image of my own closet with the smart, if unadventurous work clothes on one side, my jeans and casual attire on the other, along with a few slightly more daring outfits for outings with my friends, and a jumble of shoes strewn on the floor underneath.

Running my hands over the clothes, feeling as though I were in some wonderful expensive boutique, I wondered if I could somehow transport some of Lauren's things into my flat. Strange, though, how that felt so dishonest. Here I was being Lauren, owning these clothes, yet if I were to somehow get hold of them as Jessica it would feel like stealing.

It didn't stop me, however, from taking down one of her dresses and holding it against me. Turning to look in the full-length mirror, I did a little twirl, letting the floaty fabric swirl around my body. It looked and felt expensive and I wondered how many hours I would have had to work at the solicitors' office to be able to afford such a thing. I took down a second outfit and pictured myself wearing the elegant, pale cream two-piece suit with its nipped-in waist, long skirt, and matching shoes. I was itching to try it on, but somehow to do so felt like betraying my true self. Rummaging through the box filled with costume jewelry, I held a color-coordinated shell and bead necklace up to my throat with my other hand and narrowed my eyes, imagining my own slightly younger self as Jessica wearing these fancy baubles. One day I might be able to afford such things, but it would be me, Jessica, who would achieve it for myself by sheer hard work and determination. I shimmied from side to side, letting the skirt sweep softly against my shins. Frankie would soon have it covered in mud anyway, I thought, as I replaced it with a rueful smile.

"Your good jewelry is in the safe," Grant was saying from behind me. "I'll let you have the combination later."

I thought of the safe at work and reeled the numbers of the combination off in my head. How could I remember details like that if that other life wasn't real, I asked myself defiantly? Furrowing my brow, I pictured the appointments diary on my desk at Chisleworth & Partners. Everything about that life was so clear; I could recall not only the layout of the office with its desks and chairs and the coffee machine in the corner, but the dates and times of my boss's client interviews, contract deadlines, and court appearances. That other life—my life—simply had to be more than a confused dream caused by the short-circuiting of this woman's brain.

Grant disappeared from the doorway and I heard him opening another door next to the one belonging to the dressing room.

"The en suite bathroom," he said as I appeared at his shoulder. "It's your bathroom actually. I use the guest-room bathroom at the end of the landing; then we don't bump into each other in the mornings when we're getting ready for work."

"We?" I repeated stupidly. "Do I work? Apart from looking after the children, I mean?"

"You come into the practice every so often," he explained. "When the receptionist is on vacation or out sick. Since it's my own practice, we save money on temps that way, and I don't have the bother of trying to train them when I'm with a patient."

"Are you a doctor?" I asked, surprised. I'd thought I was quite adept at working out what people were good at. Grant didn't strike me as being a particularly patient person or especially sympathetic. If anything he seemed rather highly strung, but then I'd only met him in testing circumstances.

"I'm a dentist," he said wearily. "I specialize in orthodontic treatment, private of course," he added.

Of course, I thought. Now that made sense: He still needed a good chairside manner, but didn't see his patients often enough to have to build up a rapport with them.

I stared into the luxurious bathroom with its cream-colored whirlpool bath and matching sink, toilet, and bidet. The carpet here was a deep cornflower blue, and Lauren had added matching soaps, candles, and vases of silk flowers. It was beautiful. I wondered when Lauren had found the time to use it, with four young children to bring up and a part-time job as well.

A crash from downstairs had us both hurrying out onto the landing. Grant leapt down the stairs two at a time and bent to pick up a broken plate that had fallen from the high shelf onto the varnished telephone table in the hall. The twins were cowering in the corner, Teddy still clutching his rubber ball and Toby looking terrified.

"What happened here?" Grant demanded. "Who did this?"

"He taked my ball," Teddy said in a quiet voice.

Grant rounded on Toby. "You know you mustn't touch Teddy's ball," he admonished his son. "You must not tease your brother. We have told you before. Now look what you've done, you've broken one of Mummy's plates, and she's only just come home."

I took the pieces from Grant's hand and fitted the two halves together. "I'm sure it can be mended," I offered. "Do we have any superglue?"

"Lauren," said Grant, barely keeping the exasperation from his voice. "It's antique, worth hundreds. There's no point in gluing the thing back together. It's broken. What's the point of keeping anything if it isn't perfect? All it's good for is the rubbish bin."

I saw the light go out of Teddy's eyes and guessed what he was thinking. He hung his head as if knowing he was also broken, imperfect, and therefore not worth anything in his father's view, either. My heart went out to him and I held out my hand. "Why don't you show me where you keep your toys?" I asked.

"Teddy doesn't have toys, Mummy," Toby blurted out as Teddy eyed my hand suspiciously. "You know he only likes his stupid ball."

"Well, show me your toys," I said to Toby. "And Teddy can come and watch."

Grant touched my arm and I turned back to him.

"Look, I'm sorry about that. I'm not myself at the moment. This is all going to take some getting used to. Will you be all right if I pop up into my study to catch up on some paperwork?" he asked.

I nodded, already feeling exhausted. The burns to Lauren's

shoulder were beginning to chafe. "I'm sure the children will tell me where everything is," I said, finding myself immensely relieved he wasn't intending to be at my side every second of the day. "It's not as if I'm really ill or anything."

He looked hesitant, but I assured him we'd be fine so he strode off into another part of the house and disappeared from my thoughts. As soon as he'd gone I followed the twins into the playroom. Sophie and Nicole were watching a game show on the old television set, lounging on the beanbags in the middle of the room. Sophie pretended she hadn't seen me, but Nicole sprang to her feet and came to hold my hand as I stood there wondering what to do.

It felt odd to be home in the middle of the afternoon on a weekday, even if I ignored the strangeness of the rest of my situation. With my hand still imprisoned in Nicole's, I walked with her to the window and looked out at the front garden and the road. Outside, the October sunshine beamed down and I thought how lovely it would be to walk Frankie on a day like this. The feeling that I was trapped descended like a cloud over me. I was used to being my own person and I needed my space.

Toby had already started zooming his cars around the road map on the floor, crashing every so often into the white-painted baseboard so that white flakes dropped off onto the carpet. He held up a yellow dump truck. "This is my best toy," he said. "This and the digger."

Nicole was looking at me anxiously. She seemed like a sensitive little girl who was desperate for my attention and I didn't want to disappoint her. I squeezed her hand reassuringly, then turned reluctantly from the window and made a show of inspecting her brother's toys closely.

"They're very realistic," I said. "Do you ever take them outside and dig real mud or sand with them?"

Toby's mouth dropped open slightly and he shook his head. "You said toys aren't allowed in the garden," he replied.

"Well, I've changed my mind," I said firmly, straightening up carefully. I put my shoulder discomfort to the back of my mind. "Come on all of you. Nicole, Sophie, you can show me the garden. And Toby, bring your digger and truck."

I flicked off the television set, ignoring indignant moans from Sophie, and followed a grinning Toby out through a utility room into the back garden. There was a wide paved patio area, which hadn't been visible from above, with a wooden table and matching chairs clustered round it. The patio steps led down onto the grassed lawn.

"What's behind those fir trees?" I asked them, staring down the garden.

Sophie and Nicole exchanged looks as if to say "How can she be so stupid?" and Sophie said, rather condescendingly, "That's where Jim puts the grass cuttings and stuff."

"Jim's the gardener, Mummy," Nicole explained, more kindly than her sister. She took my hand again, rather as if I were the child and she the adult, and led me down toward the trees with the others following. "Do you want to see?"

"I do indeed," I said, glad to be out from the stifling blandness of the house. It occurred to me, as I stood and sucked in the fresh air, that as I was stuck here in this life I might as well try and make a go of this weird thing I was committed to. And if I was going to play the game I might as well do it properly. "I want to remember everything so I can be a good mummy again."

"You can't," said a little voice from behind us. " 'Cause you're not Mummy."

I stopped walking and turned to Teddy.

"I'm sorry, Teddy," I said, hunkering down in front of him. "This is hard for all of us. But I'd be very happy if you'd give me a chance to try."

It seemed as if he were going to object further, but obviously thought better of it because he looked right into my eyes and then nodded abruptly.

"Right," I said, straightening up. "To the compost heap!"

We squeezed through a gap in the conifer trees and, to my surprise, found a large area of unkempt garden on the other side. The grass here was long and brown. To one side of a crazy-paved pathway stood a huge pile of leaves, grass cuttings, and trimmed-off branches. On the other side was a small shed, presumably where Jim kept the mower and tools.

I tried the shed door, using my right hand to avoid pulling the damaged skin under the dressing on my left shoulder, but it was locked, so I shaded my eyes and peered through a side window. I had been right. The shed housed all the implements a gardener would need.

"Do you know where Jim keeps the key?" I asked the children.

They looked blankly back at me, then Teddy said conspiratorially, "I knowd where Jim put it."

He disappeared behind the shed and returned holding a key. I quickly unlocked the door and stood hands on hips, surveying the contents of the shed with satisfaction. "Right," I said, grabbing a spade with my good arm and handing it to Toby. "You'd better get digging, and then you can move the mud away from that area there with the dump truck. It's very important to make a really big hole, because Daddy and I are going to get you a sandbox to put in it."

Toby's eyes shone as he banged the spade into a depression of loose earth. I saw Teddy watching with interest.

"Would you like to help, Teddy?" I said encouragingly, sitting myself down on an upturned wooden crate. "You've already been a big help by finding the key. Do you think you can help Toby by digging out the other side of the hole with a trowel?"

He nodded enthusiastically, his eyes glowing with the unaccustomed praise. I turned to look at the girls, who were watching the boys rather disapprovingly.

"What would you like to do if I told you a little bit of this secret garden was yours?" I asked them. "Would you like to help with the sandbox, or make your own flower beds? Or maybe we could buy one of those swing things with two seats, you know, like a boat swing."

Sophie looked at her toes, then flicked her eyes up to meet mine. I could see she was struggling between the idea of being cool and confessing what she really wanted to do.

"Could we have a rabbit hutch, with real rabbits in it?" she said at last. "I know you don't like animals, Mummy, but we'd look after them all by ourselves, wouldn't we, Nicole?"

The younger girl nodded, her eyes gleaming. "Can I have a guinea pig, too?"

I laughed, surprised at how much I was suddenly enjoying the children's company. Anything was better than staying in that oppressively immaculate house with their Captain Von Trapp of a father, I told myself.

"One thing at a time, I think. And we've got to ask Daddy, of course." I glanced at my watch, realizing that I was not only getting tired, but hungry. None of us had eaten for several hours.

"I'll tell you what," I said, brushing aside the fatigue that was threatening to engulf me. "I'll go and find Daddy and, if he agrees, we can go to a pet shop to look at hutches. After that we could get pizza for tea. How does that sound?"

The girls screeched with glee and Nicole actually jumped up and down with excitement. I looked back at the two boys: Toby was making *brrrrming* noises as he made his digger work, and Teddy concentrated silently on digging out the muddy hole, his ball still clutched in his free hand.

"Carry on with the good work here, boys," I said. "The girls are going to show me where Daddy's study is, then I'll give you a shout when it's time to go."

Grant was astounded when I told him about the rabbits.

"It isn't a good idea," he said, advancing on me from around his wide mahogany desk. "Neither of us likes animals. They're messy, smelly, and unhygienic. We discussed this a couple of years ago when Sophie wanted that hamster. You said you hated the things."

"The children have had an awful shock," I said carefully. "They thought they were going to lose me. I hoped having a couple of pets might give them something else to think about. And of course," I added quickly, "they'd be down the garden, right out of sight of the house."

Grant pursed his lips but then nodded. "Well, if you really think they're old enough to look after them . . ."

"We are, Daddy, we promise," Sophie and Nicole said, bouncing in from the hallway. "Please, Daddy, we'll be really good."

Grant glanced at the paperwork strewn across his desk, then down at his watch.

"I know you've only just come home, but what are we going to do about the children's tea? It's getting on for four o'clock."

"Mummy said we could go out for a pizza, after we've looked at hutches," Nicole said helpfully.

I almost laughed at the expression on Grant's face as he digested this piece of information. In the short while I'd known him I'd already discovered he was rather stuck in his ways, but at least he seemed to be trying.

"Is that okay with you?" I prompted.

He nodded slowly.

"You don't seem very sure."

"It's just that you don't like animals and you detest pizza," he replied in a bewildered voice. "Are you sure you wouldn't rather lie down while I make the children a sandwich or something?"

"I am tired," I confessed. "But I've promised them now."

"Will you be all right?"

It was my turn to be taken aback. "Aren't you going to come with us?"

"I thought I'd done the school vacation chore by taking them to Chessington yesterday," Grant commented.

"I don't know where the shops are from here, or even where we keep the car keys," I reminded him. "The children will be safer if you show me the way."

"Okay, fetch the boys," he said resignedly. "I'll give you a guided tour of the area while we're out so you can manage when I go back to work. I suppose I'd better show you where their schools are as well."

The boys needed a bath when they eventually straggled back to the house, and I managed to get the worst of the mud off them while Grant tidied away his paperwork. Just after four-fifteen we were all back in the Galaxy, with the boys fighting over who was going to sit where, and the girls bickering over which CD we should play.

The commotion lasted until Grant turned to me and asked me to tell the children to shut up.

"Be quiet, children, please, or we won't be going anywhere," I said crisply, in the voice I used sometimes to quell difficult clients. They fell silent immediately, and Grant shot me a sideways glance that left me in no doubt that this wasn't how Lauren usually handled the children.

Little Cranford turned out to be no more than a small village with a church, a pub, and a handful of shops. Grant drove past a boys' preparatory school, explaining it was where the twins went to nursery class every day. We carried on through the village and out onto a larger road with signposts to places I didn't recognize.

"How far are we from London?" I asked.

"Around thirty-five miles," Grant said. "The nearest big town is Cranbourne."

"Oh," I replied, disconcerted at being so far from anywhere I knew.

I sat in silence for the next few minutes, looking out of the window at the beautiful countryside flashing past the window. It occurred to me how unlucky I had been to be in the wrong place at the wrong time. It worried me that not only had I been caught out in the thunderstorm that had raged all those miles away over the Epsom Downs, but that for this to have happened, Lauren had to have been struck at precisely the same time by a second lightning storm that had flashed simultaneously through this small hamlet. I shivered as I tried to block out thoughts of probability and fate and tried to turn my mind to more mundane matters.

"We don't have to go all the way into Cranbourne to get a pizza, do we?"

Sophie and Nicole giggled behind me as Grant explained

that there was a garden center and a pet shop in a complex not far away.

"And there's an Italian pizza place a bit farther along the road," he added, "which seems to be open all hours." He glanced at his watch. "We'll only just make the pet shop. I think it closes at five."

We did indeed catch the pet shop just before it closed, but the proprietor didn't seem in too much of a hurry to shut up shop once he sensed the opportunity for a big sale. The girls, skinny-looking in their baggy hipster jeans and sparkly pink T-shirts, cuddled each of the rabbits in turn, trying to decide which they liked the best, their long hair falling over the rabbits' fluffy backs. Grant begrudgingly took the twins off to the garden center to buy a plastic sandbox and a couple of bags of silver sand. Meanwhile, I inspected the hutches and runs and decided on a good-sized hutch with a separate run.

"Why don't we have the sort where the rabbits can get into the run themselves?" Sophie asked when she saw what I was looking at.

"Because then you won't need to handle them every day and they won't be so friendly," I told her. "I had a rabbit as a child and I know it's too tempting to throw food into the sort of hutch that leads into a run and not have to get the animals in and out every day. If you're going to have these pets, you will have to see to them every single day. Even in the rain," I added.

Sophie was cuddling a dwarf Dutch rabbit. I watched as she held her face against its soft black fur.

"You said you hated rabbits," she said, looking at me accusingly over the rabbit's back. "I didn't know you'd had rabbits of your own."

I felt myself blush. I had kept rabbits, but Lauren obviously hadn't.

"Do you want that one?" I asked, changing the subject quickly.

"Yes please," she said dreamily. "I love her so much."

"What about you, Nicole?" I asked.

Nicole was holding a small multicolored guinea pig with a reddish-brown forelock sticking out just above its eyes.

"Can I have this, instead of a rabbit?" she asked.

"Of course you can," I smiled. "Have you thought of a name?"

"Ginny," she said, smiling to herself. "Like Ginny Weasley in Harry Potter. She'll be my Ginny pig."

I laughed at the joke. Nicole might be quiet, but she had a quirky sense of humor. I realized that there was a possibility I could grow to like these children. The thought was sobering. So far my first day with them had been a heady mixture of new discoveries about the family unit and how it ticked. I'd seen my part of it as a bit of an adventure, rather like I imagined a visiting auntie might feel. Although I believed their mother was dead and I had resigned myself to playing her part, at least for the time being, that was all it had been to me, a role, like I was an actress committed to performing a part in a new play. The Richardsons had meant no more to me than a dreamlike fantasy family, the result of a fluke of time and the elements.

Now, as I watched Sophie stroking her rabbit and Nicole snuggling the guinea pig under her chin, I felt a twinge of some unidentified emotion. After only a few hours in their company I felt a responsibility to them that I hadn't expected to feel, certainly not so quickly anyway.

"Don't forget we can't take the animals with us today," I

cautioned. "It's getting late and we have to find a good safe place for the hutch, fill it with sawdust and hay, and put the food and water in. Tomorrow, as soon as . . . er . . . I'm awake, we'll get it all sorted out and come back for the animals."

"I want to take mine now," Sophie said, giving me a measured glance.

Shaking my head, I told her firmly no. We would fetch the animals tomorrow.

"You'll change your mind tomorrow and you won't let us have them!" she cried. "You said we couldn't ever have pets. I knew it!"

I watched in dismay as she snatched up the rabbit and flounced off to the other end of the shop.

After a few seconds, I followed her and found her staring fixedly at some bird feeders, the rabbit nestled in her arms.

"Sophie?"

She didn't answer at first, so I stooped down to her level and spoke gently but firmly.

"This rabbit is very lucky," I told her. "She's going to belong to a sensible girl who knows that she wouldn't be happy sitting in a box all night. She wouldn't, would she, Sophie?"

Sophie shrugged her shoulders and I plowed on. "We're going to come back for her, I promise. But it is going to take time to prepare her new home properly."

Sophie stuck out her bottom lip and dragged the toe of one of her pretty pink and white shoes across the floor, and for a moment I thought she was going to argue further.

But then she nodded and handed the creature back to the pet shop man, who was hovering nearby, waiting to carry the hutch out to the car.

Nicole meekly handed her guinea pig over, too, then came and slipped her hand into mine as we walked to the exit. It was a strange feeling having her small warm hand in mine, and I squeezed it reassuringly, though whether the reassurance was for her or for myself, I wasn't sure.

We had just closed the rear door of the car on the large hutch, a run, a bag of sawdust, hay, and rabbit food, when Grant appeared with the twins. He was lugging a huge bag of silver sand on his shoulder.

I opened the door again quickly and he threw the heavy sack into the back, eyeing the pet equipment as he did so.

"Good grief, Lauren," he said, straightening up and wiping his forehead with a handkerchief. "Have you bought the whole shop?"

"Actually, it's not exactly bought yet," I grinned. "I said you'd be in to pay for everything in a minute. He's waiting to close up."

Grant turned and went grumbling into the shop, while Toby jumped up and down with excitement. "Daddy says we can come back tomorrow and pick up the sandbox," he cried. "It's green and plastic and it's really big. I'll have to work very hard with my digger tomorrow to make the hole big enough!"

"That's splendid, Toby," I said, opening a back door so he and Teddy could squeeze themselves into their seats among the bags of hay. "This is going to be an exciting half-term break, isn't it?"

Helping Teddy with his safety belt, I glanced into his troubled eyes and gave him a reassuring smile. "You'll love having the sandbox, Teddy. It's going to be yours, too."

He was staring at the animal paraphernalia all around him,

his hands squeezing rhythmically at the ball that seemed to go everywhere with him.

"Mummy'll be cross wiv you," he said quietly. "When she comes home and sees all this mess. She'll make you take it all away again."

chapter six

It felt strange waking as Jessica on Tuesday morning. As I fed Frankie and gulped down a cup of weak tea, I realized I missed the children.

We'd had a great time in the pizza parlor the previous evening, despite the gnawing ache across my injured back and shoulder. Even Grant seemed to have been caught up in the children's excitement as the girls told him about the pets they'd chosen, and Toby rattled on about how his digger was going to make roads and bridges in the sandbox. Only Teddy had sat quietly, slouching and staring into space with strings of melted cheese dangling between his chin and his plate, until Grant had wiped his mouth with his napkin and told him to sit up properly.

I felt bad about Teddy, I realized, as I walked around the block with Frankie and waited while she did her morning business. He knew I was an impostor, and I was pretending otherwise, making him feel he was in the wrong. But what was I supposed to do? If I told anyone the truth, they would have me committed; and if I told Teddy he was right, I risked him telling someone else, and then they'd think he was crazy, too.

By the time I'd been back to the flat to drop off Frankie and had walked to the office it was nearly eleven o'clock.

Clara was busy typing when I slid quietly into my chair and began opening Stephen's mail.

"You're okay," she called across the room. "He's already left for court. Heavy night last night, was it?"

I laughed. "You'd never believe me if I told you, Clara."

As it happened, I'd claimed tiredness and gone up to bed shortly after tucking the children in. And I hadn't needed to fake it. Bedtime for four children had turned out to be an exhausting military operation. The twins had needed help bathing and drying themselves and brushing their teeth, then Grant had told me Teddy still wet the bed at night and needed to be put into a nappy. The girls had wanted bedtime stories and Nicole had begged me to brush her hair for her. I was happy to do it all, but Lauren's burns had really started to hurt under the dressings, and the challenges of the day had finally caught up with me.

When Grant had offered to come up and share my "early night" I'd told him firmly that I was truly exhausted, and he'd looked crestfallen. I reminded him rather shortly that he was still a stranger to me unless my memories returned, which it didn't look like they were going to, and suggested I should sleep in another room. He'd shaken his head adamantly at the idea and promised he'd stay on his side of the big bed.

Too tired to argue, I had flopped into Lauren's bed at nine-thirty, wearing one of her silky nighties, and had fallen asleep the minute my head touched the pillow.

Getting up at nine-thirty wouldn't do, I told myself, as Clara thrust a cup of coffee under my nose. I'd lose my job if I came to work as late as this on a regular basis. Now that I knew my fantastic theory about occupying both bodies alternately seemed to be actually true, I realized that somehow I was going to have to work out the timings better.

It was just that I wasn't sure how on earth I was going to manage it. Lauren couldn't go to bed before nine every night, and next week it was going to be worse because she was going to have to be up by seven to get the children to school without ruining my—Jessica's—social life. How could I possibly be in bed by seven o'clock every evening?

"This has to be one special kind of guy," Clara commented. "You were miles away, Jess. Are you going to tell me all about him?"

An image of Dan popped into my head. She was right, he seemed like a really nice guy. I liked him. Throwing down the mail, I groaned and put my head in my hands. I knew that there was something more than friendship brewing between us, but what was the point in pursuing it when my whole life had just been turned upside down?

"Girl," Clara said, her fingers pausing on the keyboard as she studied me across the room. "You and I are going to have a serious chat at lunchtime. This I want to hear."

By lunchtime I had caught up with the typing of various notes I had taken for Stephen the day before, and leaned back in my chair, flexing my shoulders after a morning spent bent at the computer. Clara pushed back her chair and reached for her coat.

"I know you're about to scurry off to walk that dog of yours," she said as she handed me my jacket. "So I thought I'd walk with you."

I was about to protest, when I realized I was being selfish. I had wanted the time I walked back and forth to the flat to think about what was happening to me, but Clara was a good friend and I didn't want to upset her.

We grabbed the sandwiches we'd bought earlier from the girl who did the rounds of the local offices with her sandwich basket, and headed out of the office just as Stephen strode up the steps unbuttoning his overcoat. "Going out, ladies?" he commented. "I hope you won't be too long. I've got some injunction statements I need to dictate."

"We'll be back within the hour, Mr. Armitage," Clara replied sweetly.

Stephen scowled and I thought he was going to protest, but he seemed to change his mind and he opened the front door and disappeared inside, leaving Clara flashing me sympathetic glances.

"He's never really gotten over you moving out after you found out about the barrister lady he was wining and dining, has he?" She looked at me sideways from under long, dark lashes.

"I think he thought I'd forgive him and go crawling back after spending a few months on my own," I agreed, quickening my pace. "Come on, Clara. We've got to walk all the way back to my place and still have time to eat."

"Is the barrister still on the scene?" she asked as she hurried along beside me.

"As far as I know, it never did blossom into a relationship. I think Stephen was testing the water with her and she wasn't as interested as he'd hoped."

"Did you never consider going back to him?"

"Clara, his two-timing was the best thing that could have happened to our relationship. It wasn't going anywhere."

"I think he might have wanted more from you, you know. He seemed really keen. I thought you two might even get married."

"I didn't want to get married, Clara. Maybe that was the problem; that Stephen wanted more than I was prepared to give." I turned to face her as we hurried along, conscious that after meeting Dan my protestations of independence might no longer be quite as vehement as they had been previously, but I forced out the old adage anyway. "I want a career, not a husband. I want to be able to afford nice things, not settle down and have babies. Not yet anyway," I allowed.

"Stephen would have been able to give you nice things. He must earn plenty of money."

My mind went to Lauren's extravagant wardrobe, her jewelry, shoes, and bags. "I don't want to settle for being a kept woman," I explained. "I want to achieve a good job and a top salary for myself."

"Maybe he just wasn't the right guy for you, then. But there are plenty more of them out there, you know; you don't have to live your life alone."

I thought of Dan again and felt a shiver run through me. Clara might have a point there, I thought, but I pushed the notion away and shook my head.

"My strategy has been not to let anyone get close enough for me to find out, and it has worked pretty well up until now," I told her.

Clara shook her head, but refrained from talking anymore since I was setting a fast pace and she was having trouble catching her breath. We arrived at the flat in less than ten minutes to be greeted by Frankie's ecstatic barks the moment she heard the key in the lock.

As I pushed the door open, Frankie leapt up at me and tried to lick my face.

"This is one happy dog," Clara commented as Frankie turned

her attentions to my friend and began to bound in circles around her.

"Sit down, Frankie!" I called from the kitchen as I poured tap water into the kettle. "And you too, Clara, please take a seat."

We ate our sandwiches while the kettle boiled and then I made us both a cup of coffee.

"So tell me all about him," Clara said, eyeing me over her mug as she sipped at the coffee. "I assume that it's Lightning Man who's been hogging your thoughts?"

I grinned at her.

"Clara, you are so unsubtle. And yes, I have been thinking about Dan, and yes, he is rather gorgeous. We went out for a drink last night."

"Drink? You? I'm surprised you didn't put the poor guy off—I bet you ordered water!" She narrowed her eyes at me. "So what did you do after the drink that left you so exhausted you were late this morning?"

I stood up and took the empty coffee mug out of her hand, depositing it in the kitchen. The activity gave me a moment to gather my thoughts. I couldn't very well tell Clara the truth; she'd think I was crazy. I fetched Frankie's lead and attached it to the dog's collar before answering.

"I came home early and went to bed—alone. I think the lightning strike on Saturday wiped me out more than I realized. I've been feeling very tired."

Clara narrowed her eyes, considering this information. She obviously chose to believe me, though, because she got to her feet, pulling on her coat as she did so.

"You poor thing. Are you going to contact him again?"

"He said he'd call in a day or two."

"Let me know if he does. I'm dying to know more about him."

We walked Frankie for the next twenty minutes, then returned to work with about a minute to spare. Stephen had obviously been waiting for me. He called me into his office before I'd even had a chance to take my jacket off.

"How did it go in court?" I asked, peeling off my coat and taking the seat opposite his desk.

"Oh, you know, the usual."

He stared at me intently, then seemed to make up his mind about something.

"Jess, I've got tickets to a concert in the Albert Hall on Saturday. I was wondering if you might like to come with me?"

I stared at him blankly. This was the first time in two years he had asked me to go anywhere with him. I'd thought we'd made the transition from lovers to work colleagues remarkably smoothly, and I was happy with the arrangement as it stood.

"I'm sorry, Stephen," I spluttered. "I'm not sure that would be a good idea."

"For goodness' sake! I'm only asking you to a concert. There doesn't have to be strings attached. I just thought you might enjoy a night out."

He started banging piles of papers around on his desk and I felt myself tensing up. The room seemed very warm suddenly and my head began to swim. I put it down to the fact that I'd just rushed in from the cold outside, and ran a hand over my eyes.

"You don't have to make a big deal out of it," Stephen was saying indignantly. "If you don't want to go, then that's fine by me . . ."

His voice tailed off and grew muffled, as if he were walking away from me down a long tunnel. I felt the heat rushing up the back of my neck and my senses grew woolly, then I felt myself pitch sideways and everything went black.

Hands were shaking me, calling my name.

"Wake up! What's the matter with you?"

I tried to stir, forcing my senses to function.

"I'm sorry . . . I don't know what . . ."

"Wake up, Lauren. For goodness' sake!"

"What?"

I stared around me at the dark bedroom, my thoughts in total disarray. Grant was standing by the bed, shaking me roughly by my undamaged shoulder, his hands warm on my bare skin where the slinky nightie straps had fallen sideways.

Pulling myself into a sitting position, I registered the hysterical wailing that was emanating from somewhere along the landing. The children!

"What's the matter?" I croaked, swinging my legs out of bed, feeling the deep pile of the carpet soft between my toes.

"Teddy's having one of his nightmares, Lauren! He's been sick everywhere. Now he's set Toby off and he's crying, too. I can't cope with them on my own."

Bewildered and disorientated, I set off down the landing, pulling Lauren's satin negligee around me as I went. The boys' bedroom light was on, both boys sitting up in bed howling loudly. Teddy was covered in vomit. It was on his pajamas, in his hair, all over his space-rocket duvet cover and even on his precious ball.

Sizing up the situation and glancing at Grant's ashen face, I realized I was going to have to take charge.

"Could you run him a bath, Grant?" I instructed as I shushed Toby and gathered Teddy gingerly onto my lap.

Grant disappeared in the direction of the bathroom and I could hear the water running in the distance as I rocked the frightened little boy back and forth in my arms.

"I wa . . . want . . . Mu . . . Mummy," he sobbed.

"I know, I know," I crooned, trying to ignore the smell. "You're all right now, Teddy, I've got you."

He tried to push me away, but I kept him locked in a bearlike embrace, and after a moment I felt his little body relax and fold into me.

"Mummy was on fire," he mumbled through his sobs. "I want Mummy back."

"I know, Teddy," I whispered. "Believe me, I know."

I cuddled him for a long time while his breathing grew steadier and his body stopped trembling. As Teddy's sobs subsided, Toby also stopped crying and rested his head back down on his pillow, sticking his thumb into his mouth and watching us quietly.

"Bath's run," Grant said from the doorway.

"Come on," I said to the sleepy form in my lap. "You're going to have a night bath! That will be exciting, won't it?"

By the time Teddy was bathed, and I'd put a clean sheet and duvet onto his bed, Toby was fast asleep. Kissing them both on the tops of their heads, I gathered up the soiled bedding and trooped downstairs to load it into the washing machine. I wasn't sure how this particular model worked, but I found detergent under the sink in the utility room and turned the machine on to what I hoped was the right cycle.

Grant was back in bed when I returned to our bedroom. I looked at him sitting propped against the pillows with his bare chest showing above striped pajama trousers and felt a flush of embarrassment that I was expected to get back into bed next to this complete stranger.

At least with Stephen, I thought, I had chosen to be there, even if he hadn't been terribly exciting as a lover.

"Are they settled now?" Grant asked.

"Yes, they're both asleep." I found I couldn't look at him and averted my eyes as I continued, "I checked on the girls and they don't seem to have been disturbed by it."

"They're used to it. Teddy does that when anything's bothering him."

"Does L— I mean, do I always sort him out?" I queried as I went through to the dressing room to find another nightdress, then popped into the en suite bathroom and threw Lauren's stained nightie into the bath. After slipping the clean one over my head and making sure I was suitably covered, I washed my hands and ventured back toward the bed.

"You or the nanny; though he's not usually as sick as that. I expect it was the pizza. The children aren't used to rich food so close to bedtime."

I registered the mild accusation in his voice as I climbed discreetly under the covers and turned my back on him. Pulling the duvet up around my shoulders, I felt him settle down next to me as he turned out the bedside light.

A moment later, Grant's hand arrived on my thigh, stroking me gently through the flimsy fabric of the nightdress.

"Stop it, Grant!" Alarmed, I yanked my leg away. "We talked about this earlier. I've got to get to know you all over again, and it will take time. Do you want me to move to the spare room?"

He grunted "No," made a snorting noise, and rolled over in bed. With our backs turned firmly to each other, we fell asleep again.

I awoke to find a bright light being shone into one of my

eyes, and sat up with a start. Dr. Chin let go of my eyelid and jumped back in surprise.

"Where am I?" I asked, staring round at my unfamiliar surroundings.

The smell of antiseptic coupled with the sight of the surrounding curtained cubicles, blue-uniformed nurses, and shiny linoleum floors reflecting overhead fluorescent lighting brought the truth home to me before a familiar voice beside me answered, "You're in the emergency room, Jessica. You've been unconscious for ages!"

Clara was sitting on a hard-backed hospital chair, her face pale even under her smooth Caribbean complexion.

"How long have I been here?"

Clara glanced at her watch.

"About an hour and a half, I suppose. Girl, you gave us such a fright! When Mr. Armitage called out that you'd fainted in his office, I went running in there to find you out cold on the floor. We tried sitting you up, Mr. Armitage even slapped your face, but you wouldn't come around. In the end we called an ambulance and they brought you here."

"How do you feel?" Dr. Chin asked, taking my pulse and scribbling something on a chart. "You had us worried, Ms. Taylor."

"I'm fine now, honestly. I just felt a bit faint, that's all."

"You have been unconscious for nearly an hour and three-quarters, Ms. Taylor. Has anything like this ever happened to you before?"

"Do you mean before the lightning strike? No."

"I think we should keep you in for observation. I would like to monitor your vital signs for at least twenty-four hours."

I became aware that I was attached to a heart monitor, which was beeping rhythmically beside the bed, the sticky ends adhering to my chest and left side.

"I don't want to waste your time," I said, looking beseechingly at the doctor, then at Clara. "You must have more urgent cases who need this bed. I'm feeling fine now."

"She said she was feeling very tired earlier," Clara volunteered helpfully. "She shouldn't have come back to work so soon if you ask me."

"I did tell you to rest," Dr. Chin admonished, wagging a finger at me. "Lightning strike is a very unpredictable thing."

"Have any of my vital signs been unstable while I've been unconscious?" I asked.

Dr. Chin stared at the chart.

"You appear to have been in a state of stasis. Very low heartbeat, low blood pressure, and low body temperature. Like a very deep, dreamless sleep. No abnormalities."

"I really do feel fine now," I said persuasively. "Couldn't I just go home?"

"If you go home, you must take a day off work, maybe two."

"I will."

"Okay, I will talk to the consultant. If he agrees, I can let you go home later."

"Thank you."

"Well, I don't think you should go home," Clara said as Dr. Chin moved away. "They called him down from the ward specially when I told them you'd been in here on Saturday. I thought he was going to keep you in. He was really attentive while you were unconscious, coming to check you every twenty minutes or so himself. I can't understand why they're thinking of letting you out. You're not yourself at all, Jess."

I nearly laughed at Clara's choice of words. I certainly wasn't myself, at least for half the time anyway.

"I'm not discharged yet," I cautioned her. "They might still change their minds."

"I'm going to telephone the office," she said, pushing back her chair. "And tell them you're awake and okay. Mr. Armitage was beside himself when you wouldn't come around."

"Not concerned enough to come with me in the ambulance, though," I pointed out.

"He had a client coming in at two-thirty, or I think he would have. I said I'd go with you, and he seemed very relieved. I followed the ambulance in my car."

As soon as Clara had gone to find a phone, I tried to organize my thoughts. What had happened this afternoon was hugely worrying. It seemed to mean that not only was I inhabiting Lauren's body during my night, but that if the need was urgent enough, she could draw me there even when I should be awake here. Where did that leave me? What about my own life? How could I ever contemplate a relationship of any kind with Dan, or anyone else for that matter, if there was a chance I might disappear at any time to be Lauren?

"What's the time, Clara?" I asked when she returned from making her phone call.

She consulted her watch again.

"It's nearly four o'clock. I could murder a cup of something hot. Shall I go and see if the hospital shop is still open?"

"I suppose you'd better check with a nurse or something before bringing coffee or tea into the accident and emergency department. But if they say it's okay, I'd love a cup of tea."

Clara took herself off again and I lay back against the pillows, fighting off despair. For a couple of days this had all seemed like some strange adventure, a frightening game that had to be played for a while. But if this went on forever . . . it didn't bear thinking about.

Clara and I had only just finished drinking the rather strong stewed tea from plastic cups when Dr. Chin poked his head round the half-pulled curtain.

"The consultant has looked at your readout, Ms. Taylor, and says you can go home. But you must rest. Lots of rest please."

A young nurse came and detached the heart-rate monitor and brought me my clothes, then I followed Clara to where she had parked her car. I sat staring out of the window as she drove me to my flat. The leaves on the trees lining the road were turning from gold and brown to russet and crimson. The long, wet summer had resulted in the most glorious outburst of nature's colors, and the weekend's thunderstorm had uncurled the wilting leaves and filled them with fresh vigor.

Soon Clara was turning her bright yellow Honda into the parking space in front of the flats.

"Do you want me to come in with you?"

"No, but thanks anyway, you've been great."

She handed me my bag, which she'd had the foresight to grab off my chair in the office when she'd left to follow the ambulance. "You take care of yourself, girl. Don't you come in to work for the rest of the week, do you hear?"

I leaned over and gave her a hug.

"You're a good friend, Clara."

I watched as she maneuvered her car around until it was facing the way we'd come, then she headed off down the road, leaving me with a strange feeling of emptiness. I turned and made my way down the steps into my paved courtyard and unlocked the front door to rapturous barks of greeting from Frankie.

After Frankie's evening walk, I wandered around my flat, running my fingers over the dusty furniture and watering my indoor plants. I felt a need to reconnect somehow to my real life, the one I'd always known. I needed to be surrounded by my things, doing familiar chores and savoring the sights and sounds of home. I nearly rang Mum again, but decided she'd panic if she thought I needed her. I didn't want her and Dad to trek all the way up from Somerset. And if they stayed over, how would I explain my early nights and fainting fits to them?

A sharp morning frost had made the begonias wilt in the courtyard, so I pulled them out of the pots, dug in a trowelful of compost, and popped in a handful of spring bulbs. I made myself a plate of pasta, but I couldn't keep my eyes from straying to the clock on the sitting room wall. It was seven-thirty. I knew that by now Grant would be waking up on Wednesday morning and that Lauren would have to wake soon to deal with the children, but I wasn't tired enough to go to bed.

Lauren would be exhausted, I reckoned, after being up in the night. Her body would only have had a few hours' sleep since she'd been disturbed by the boys. Maybe I could let her lie in a bit longer.

I called Frankie to come and sit on my lap, and flicked through the channels on the TV while I stroked her silky ears, but I couldn't concentrate on the programs. By eight-thirty I decided to get ready for bed, and went into the bathroom to run a bath. I was about to climb into the steaming water when the phone rang.

It was Dan.

"Hi, how are you this evening?" he asked.

The sound of his voice sent shivers of excitement down my spine. Clutching the phone as if it were a lifeline, I forced my voice to sound nonchalant.

"I'm fine. How are you?"

"Better for hearing your voice. I've been worried about you. Are you sure you're okay?"

"I did have a bit of a setback today," I told him. "I fainted at work and they took me back to the hospital."

"You should have phoned me!" he said. "Did they say what the problem was?"

"I saw the Chinese doctor again. He said it was probably a result of the lightning strike. I've been signed off work for a couple of days." I hesitated, then added, "He said lightning strikes could cause strange effects sometimes."

"But you're all right now?"

"I think so."

"Shall I come over?"

My eyes flicked to the clock again.

"No!"

I knew I'd sounded harsh, and I regretted it immediately. Dan had the potential to be really special, I knew, but it would be unfair to encourage him while I was going through whatever it was that was happening to me. I wished I could tell him about it. I imagined him holding me in his arms, stopping my soul from leaping to Lauren's body, forcibly keeping me here, in Jessica, where I belonged.

"Right then," he was saying at the other end of the line. "I'll be in touch."

"Wait!"

"What, Jessica?"

"I . . . something happened to me when the lightning struck me. I haven't felt . . . myself . . . since."

"What do you mean?"

"I mean I really like you, Dan. The timing isn't good, that's all."

"So do you want me to call you again? Or shall I wait for you to call me, or what?"

"I don't know," I said lamely. "Well, yes, call me. Maybe."

He laughed suddenly at the other end of the line. "Don't you go making your mind up too quickly, now," he said.

"I do want to see you again, Dan."

"Good. Now that we've sorted that out, I'll let you go and deal with whatever problem it is you've got there."

"Thanks, Dan. Bye."

As soon as I'd replaced the receiver, I burst into tears. Dan was the first guy in ages that I'd actually considered allowing into my life, and now I didn't see how it could possibly work. Frankie came and rested her head on my knee, looking up at me in concern, and I hunkered down on the shiny wooden floor and held her tightly in my arms.

"Oh, Frankie," I wept, burying my face in her doggy-smelling coat. "What on earth am I going to do?"

I woke to find Toby jumping on the foot of my bed. "Mummy, get up," he cried as he bounced up and down. "Daddy says he's fed up waiting for you to wake up. He wants to go to work."

I peered blearily at the bedside clock. Nine-thirty. Not so bad for a school vacation day, I told myself.

"I thought he was taking the week off?"

Toby grinned, his face pink and contorted with the effort of jumping.

"Daddy's going to work, he's going to work, he's going to work."

"Yes, all right, Toby, I've got the message, thank you." I climbed out of bed and walked past him to the bathroom, somewhat disgruntled by the rude awakening. At home I liked to surface peacefully for a few minutes before puttering into the kitchen to make tea and feed Frankie in the quiet calm of my flat.

I realized halfway to the bathroom door, however, that despite my busy day yesterday, the disturbed night, and Toby's incessant chattering, my shoulder felt a lot less painful this morning.

"Why don't you go and tell Daddy I'm awake, while I have my shower?"

To my relief he went off on his errand while I stared into the bath at the soiled nightdress I'd tossed there the previous night, before dropping it into the laundry bin. It stank of vomit, reminding me about Teddy's nightmare. Poor kid, I thought. This whole business must be terribly unsettling for him.

I turned on the water and stood under the hot jet, twisting sideways so the majority of the water missed the injured area of my back and shoulder. Despite my efforts the dressings became somewhat soggy. As soon as I stepped out of the shower I peeled up one corner of the fine adhesive tape from my shoulder and peered at the injury in the bathroom mirror. Lauren's burn seemed to be healing remarkably quickly, but I knew I ought to make time to see the nurse and have it checked out.

Sticking the tape back down, I returned to contemplating how best to handle Teddy. It was strange that out of all the children only Teddy had realized I wasn't his real mother. I knew I was going to have to talk to him about it, but I wasn't sure where to begin.

Grant was waiting for me in the kitchen when I arrived

downstairs dressed in one of Lauren's outfits. I'd picked out some cream trousers with an apricot top, complete with matching two-tone scarf. I'd come to the conclusion that Lauren needed to go shopping to buy some sensible clothing. She didn't seem to own a tracksuit or even a pair of jeans, and I felt overdressed and uncomfortable in her expensive gear.

"You're up then," Grant commented. He looked at me appraisingly, then got off the stool and came toward me to give me a peck on the cheek. "You look lovely, Lauren."

"Thank you."

"I gather Toby told you I'm thinking of popping in to work for a couple of hours?"

I walked over to the kettle and turned it on.

"He did."

"That's okay then, is it?"

"Aren't you coming with us to collect the sandbox and the animals?"

"I'm still not convinced they are a good idea, Lauren. You don't like the children getting dirty, and they'll be constantly trekking sand and animal bedding into the house. It'll make so much extra work for you."

"Grant, they have nothing to play with. It's hardly surprising the last nanny left, if there was nothing to do but take them out all day long."

I paused as I dunked a tea bag into a china cup. "Would you like one?"

He shook his head. "That's a disgusting habit, Lauren. Can't you just make a pot? Loose tea bags are so messy."

I stared at him indignantly. "For someone who dislikes mess so much, I'm surprised you . . . we . . . had four children. The house shouldn't be as tidy as this!"

"I'm not going to get into a discussion about why we had the boys. If your memory ever comes back you'll know that it wasn't my idea." He stopped as if realizing he'd said too much. He took my hand and searched my eyes with his own. "Look, I know this is difficult for you, sweetheart. It's not easy for me, either, but I want it to work. You know I love you, but we've got to get to know each other's little ways again. Let's take it a day at a time, okay?"

Staring into his eyes I felt a rush of warmth toward him. He might be rather persnickety and a bit of a perfectionist, but it seemed his heart was in the right place. After all, none of this was his fault, and he was doing his best in very difficult circumstances. I knew I had overstepped the mark by criticizing the unnatural tidiness of the house—after all, it was his home, not mine.

I nodded, and when he leaned in to kiss me again I didn't turn my head away but let his lips brush mine. His skin felt cool and smelled faintly of cinnamon, and I wondered what would happen between us if I stayed here indefinitely as his wife. A picture of Dan swam before my eyes and a surge of guilt flooded through me. I felt as if I was betraying both of them, and yet there wasn't much I could do about it.

"Are you sure you'll be all right if I go to the surgery?"

"Of course. I'll be fine."

I stood watching as he picked up his jacket and made his way out of the house. I heard the engine start up in the garage, then the sound of the overhead doors grating open and closed, the screech of tires on the road outside, then silence.

Sitting down heavily on the stool he'd vacated, I wrapped my hands around the hot cup and sipped the weak tea, trying not to think about the future.

"Where has Dad gone?" demanded Sophie, shaking me out of my reverie. She was glaring at me from the playroom doorway.

"He's gone to work for a while."

"I suppose I'm not having my rabbit now, then," she said. "I knew you wouldn't really let me have a rabbit. And you've made Daddy cross and he's gone back to work. I hate you!"

She slammed the door behind her, making me jump, and the fine bone-china cup rattled in its saucer, almost slipping from my fingers.

How much had she heard of what her father had said? I wondered as I put the cup down on the sterile work surface and rubbed my eyes wearily. I hoped she hadn't overheard what he'd said about the boys not being his idea. There was so much about this family I didn't know, so much I would have to learn. Suddenly the enormity of it seemed almost overwhelming.

I wandered despondently into the utility room, where I noticed someone had already taken the sheets out of the washing machine and transferred them to the dryer. Grant did have some uses then.

"Everything all right, Mrs. Richardson?"

I turned to find an elderly lady standing behind me, duster in one hand, can of polish in the other.

"Ah, you must be . . ."

"Elsie, dear. Mr. Richardson said you were having trouble with your memory. I hope you don't mind but I've emptied the washing machine. Was young Teddy ill again?"

Ah, I thought . . . the cleaning lady, of course. "I'm afraid he was," I told her.

She stared at me closely, then made a clucking noise with her tongue. "You look exhausted, dear. Shall I make you a nice cup of tea?"

Smiling, I shook my head. Elsie's idea of therapy was close to my own. Whenever I needed time to think or was upset, I put the kettle on. "I've just had one, thank you, Elsie. But tell me about Teddy. Is he often sick?"

"I gather he often has nightmares. But he's only sick with it when he's really upset."

"Thank you for putting his bedding in the dryer—I thought Grant had done it."

Elsie smiled. "I don't think Mr. Richardson even knows where the dryer is, do you, dear?"

I smiled in return. "Probably not."

"Now, I'm going to clean upstairs while you have some breakfast. Mr. Richardson said the doctor told you you've got to rest, so I'll give you a shout when I've made the bed and you can come up and have a nice nap."

She grimaced as screams and shouts erupted from the play-room. "Thank you, Elsie, but I'm going to take the children out in a minute," I said. "You get on, and I'll see you later."

Hurrying to open the playroom door, I was in time to see Sophie hitting Nicole on the head with the television remote control. Nicole was screaming, Sophie was yelling, and Toby and Teddy had taken the opportunity of the distraction to throw the doll's carriage upside down so that all the dolls had spilled out onto the floor. The TV was blaring at full volume and Toby was jumping up and down on one of the dolls' heads, making Nicole scream even louder.

Without a word, I marched over to the girls and took the remote from Sophie's flailing hand, pointed it at the TV, and turned it off. I yanked Toby bodily off the dolls, propped the doll's carriage upright, then stood facing them, hands on hips.

They all stopped shouting and stared at me.

"Right. Go and put on your shoes, go to the toilet, and get into the car. We're going to the pet shop."

Sophie's face lit up with surprise, and I realized she had truly believed that her father's comments about the mess the animals would make had made me change my mind. I smiled at her and she grinned back.

While they were all excitedly scrambling about obeying my instructions, I went into the kitchen and grabbed a banana from the fruit bowl, peeling it as I hurried upstairs to find some shoes and a coat. By the time I came down again, the children were all in the car except Teddy, who was sitting on the playroom floor with his shoes on the wrong feet.

"I think your feet are on the wrong way around," I said as I passed him. "Try them the other way."

Teddy stared at me, then at his feet, and a wide smile lit his face. He took the shoes off and swapped them over.

"It was shoes, not feet," he said in his slow, deliberate way. "I got it right now."

"Well done, Teddy," I said, holding out my hand. "Come on, let's go."

Teddy eyed my hand suspiciously, then seemed to come to a decision. He slipped his small one inside mine and accompanied me to the garage, his ball clutched protectively against his chest.

We spent the morning looking at the animals and filling the car with the sandbox and small-animal accessories, then I bought the children an early lunch in the garden center restaurant. When it was time to pay the bill for the food, I looked at Lauren's checkbook and decided I would have to practice forging her signature at home. In the meantime, she had plenty of cash in her purse, so I paid quickly and ushered the children out, feeling as if I had just committed fraud.

On the way home, Sophie and Nicole sat nursing boxes on their laps, with the rabbit and guinea pig inside them. Toby held a selection of plastic sand toys, including a large new plastic digger. Teddy sat quietly, holding his ball. To my disappointment he hadn't seemed excited about the animals or the sandbox, and I wondered if he felt left out.

The children spent the afternoon digging out the hole for the sandbox and setting up the hutch for the animals. Sophie, to my delight, had come and kissed me on the cheek when we'd gotten home, and I accepted this as her apology for her earlier outburst.

Grant was not yet back, so I decided to go and make the children's tea. Sophie had assured me they all liked breaded chicken fillets and oven fries; something I knew how to make. According to Nicole, however, the nanny used to make the meal with mashed potatoes, vegetables, and gravy, which I had to agree sounded slightly more nutritious.

Leaving the girls feeding the animals and the twins watching children's TV, I ventured into Lauren's kitchen and poked about in the big freezer for a family-size pack of the chicken. It took me a while to work out all the knobs and settings on the space-age stove, but I soon had an enormous pan of water bubbling for the potatoes, another for the broccoli I'd found in the vegetable section of the fridge, and the chicken fillets grilling in the oven.

The quantities I needed for six people had me flummoxed. I'd decided to make the breaded chicken for myself and for Grant, since I didn't know what he'd want or what time he was coming in, and I didn't want to have to cook twice.

Starting dubiously with a pile of dirty potatoes, I washed and peeled a good quantity, assuming two or three per person, cut them, and filled the pan to the brim. As soon as the water came back to the boil, it bubbled up and over the edge of the pan, and although I turned the heat down, Lauren's cooker ran on electricity and didn't respond right away. Brownish-yellow goo streaked down the outside of the pan, pooled on the stove, and charred to a stinking black mess.

"Yuck, what's burning?" Toby asked as he came into the kitchen for a drink.

"Your dinner," I told him sourly as I tried to wipe around the edge of the pan with paper towel, which grew hotter and stickier as more starchy water cascaded down in little bursts.

"I don't mean that, I mean that." Toby was pointing to the oven, where a thin wisp of dark gray smoke was belching from the grill pan.

"Oh no!" Searching through the drawers, I eventually found a pair of oven gloves and whipped the smoldering remains of the shriveled chicken strips out from under the grill and deposited them in the sink. Standing against the counter with the oven gloves dangling from one hand, I wiped the other over my perspiring face and blew out my cheeks as I surveyed the ruined meal.

Toby looked at the blackened food, gave me a sideways look, and slunk from the kitchen, just as Sophie and Nicole hurried in from feeding the animals.

"What's that smell?" Sophie asked as she came around the corner.

"I've burnt the chicken," I told her shortly.

She rolled her eyes with a "you are so useless" look and took off, while Nicole stood and chewed her lip thoughtfully.

"We could have fish sticks," she suggested.

"What, with potatoes and broccoli?"

"I said we should have fries!" Sophie called from the playroom.

"The nanny used to make us fish sticks with mashed potato," Nicole confirmed, ignoring her sister. She went to the freezer and took out a large bag. "Me, Sophie, and the boys have four each," she said kindly, as if speaking to a child.

I took the fish sticks, reckoning that if the children had four each, Grant would probably want six. With four for me, that was twenty-six fish sticks—six months' supply for me at home, since I didn't eat them very often. Tipping them onto a baking tray, I put them under the oven grill while I turned to scrape off the burnt chicken and scrub out the blackened grill pan. The potatoes had settled down now and were simmering in the pan, so I dropped the broccoli into the second pan and scurried off to find plates and cutlery.

By the time the fish sticks were done, I had mashed the potato and dished it up onto six plates alongside hunks of broccoli.

Nicole crept back into the kitchen and eyed the enormous piles of gray mash and overcooked broccoli on each plate, dwarfing the fish sticks.

"It's too much, isn't it?" I asked her anxiously.

"Never mind, Mummy," she said. "Trudy the nanny made horrible food, too."

At six o'clock the bedtime routine started all over again, and I didn't surface for air until nearly seven-thirty. I had just settled at Lauren's desk with her handbag in front of me, with the intention of practicing her signature and memorizing her pin numbers, when the bedroom door opened.

Looking up I saw Grant framed in the doorway.

"Hello," I said neutrally. "I wasn't sure what time you were coming home, so I've saved some dinner for you."

"I'm not hungry," he said, his voice slurred. "I need you, Lauren, I want you back."

"Grant, I'm busy," I said, my voice rising in alarm. "And I told you last night, we've got to take time to get to know each other all over again."

"You don't want me anymore," he said, eyeing me forlornly.

"It's not a case of not wanting you, I just don't know you. And this isn't helping."

"But you're my wife." He advanced on me, pulling me toward him and nestling his face in my neck. "You've got to love me."

"You've been drinking," I said, turning my face away as he tried to plant a slobbery kiss on my lips. "Stop it, Grant, I'm saying no."

For a second he pinned me up against the desk, the wooden edge digging painfully into the back of my thighs. I stood rigid before him, feeling the hardness of him pressing against me, and I reached behind me for anything I could find to ward him off. My hand brushed against a glass paperweight and I grabbed it, but he saw it before I could swing it at him and knocked it out of my hand.

"Bloody hell, Lauren," he grunted as he stared at the heavy weight now lying on the thickly carpeted floor. "You weren't really going to hit me with that, were you?" He pulled away from me, his face white. He crumpled to his knees at my feet and held his head in his hands.

"Grant," I rasped, my voice husky and breathless from fright and heavy with emotion. "I think for the time being we should definitely sleep in different rooms. I don't mind going to the guest room if you'd rather stay here."

"I knew you didn't love me anymore," he groaned. "I've known it for months." He looked up at me with red-rimmed eyes. "There's someone else, isn't there?"

"If there is, I know nothing about it," I told him. "You have to believe me when I tell you I've forgotten everything I ever knew."

"Truly?"

"Really truly."

He seemed to calm slightly and staggered unsteadily to his feet.

"I'll sleep in the guest room. My things are there anyway."

"Come on, I'll help you," I said, relieved that the fight had gone out of him. I put his arm round my good shoulder and supported him as he swayed out onto the landing.

When we reached the guest bedroom, he dropped heavily onto the bed. I stared down at his crumpled form. My hands were shaking uncontrollably, but I slipped his shoes off his feet, pulled the duvet over him, and crept out again, quietly closing the door behind me.

Once back on the landing I held on to the wall and took several deep, steadying breaths. What the hell, I asked myself self-pityingly, had I gotten myself into?

"Is Daddy all right, Mummy?" asked a small voice.

I looked down to see Sophie watching me from her bedroom door, her long chestnut hair falling over the shoulders of her pale blue pajamas, eyes wide. I nodded.

"He wasn't feeling too well, but I've put him to bed and he'll be fine in the morning."

"Why is he in the guest bedroom?"

"He felt sick and didn't want to disturb me. Come on," I said, taking her hand. "Back to bed, young lady."

I bent to tuck her in, and as I did so she wound an arm up around my neck.

"I'm sorry I was mean to you, Mummy," she said. "I'm so happy you bought me my rabbit. I'm glad you're not dead. I'm really glad you're here."

I kissed her and gently brushed a wisp of her silky hair from her forehead, feeling ridiculously pleased that she seemed to have accepted me, for the moment at least.

"I'm glad I'm here, too," I said.

As I dimmed the light and walked back down the landing to Lauren's bedroom, I smiled to myself.

Maybe, just maybe—well, some of the time at least, I thought—I was glad to be here.

It occurred to me while I was lying curled up in bed with Frankie the next morning that I was about to live through Wednesday again. I closed my eyes and ran through all sorts of illegal scams in my head, like finding out the lottery numbers as Lauren and filling in the winning ticket the next day as Jessica. Or maybe I should find out which horses came in first at the races and put my savings on the winners. The trouble was, I thought with a grimace, not only was I basically an honest person, which is why even spending Grant's money while being Lauren was causing me pangs of guilt, but I was worried that until I understood more clearly what was happening to me, I couldn't risk changing fate in any way. If I cheated my way into millions, I thought, as I sipped at my morning cup of tea, maybe that dishonesty would come back to haunt me in ways I couldn't imagine, and I might never be free of this predicament.

I lay there listening to the sounds of my neighbors getting ready for work. One or two car engines started up and faded into the distance. Front doors slammed. I stared at the ceiling and pondered why the flat seemed so quiet this morning. I wasn't sure if it was because I was usually only here at this time on weekends, or whether I was actually missing the children.

The phone rang, startling me. I looked at it suspiciously, then put out a hand and picked it up.

"Hello?"

"Hi, Jessica, it's Clara. How are you doing?"

"I'm lounging in bed wondering why it's so quiet," I confessed with a rueful smile. "I wish I was at work."

"Mr. Armitage came in early this morning. He said he might pop around to see you at lunchtime. I thought I'd warn you."

"In case I had Dan here?" I asked with a giggle. "I should be so lucky."

"You never know," Clara said. "You seem smitten with him. Love at first sight can happen, you know."

"It's early days yet, but you're right, Clara. I'm ever hopeful."

"Got to go," Clara said, dropping her voice to a whisper. "Boss has just come in."

"Bye, Clara. Thanks for the warning."

I replaced the handset and slipped out of bed. I wasn't ill, of course, and felt rather guilty that everyone was so worried about me collapsing in the middle of the day when I knew I had merely skipped over to Lauren's place for a while. Hard work though the Richardson family had been, I really didn't require a day in bed to recover from them.

I decided to stop feeling sorry for myself and enjoy my day off. The summer had continued into a glorious autumn, though the temperature had plummeted dramatically. I walked Frankie for an hour, scuffing through the first fallen leaves, and stopped off at the local mini market for some groceries. I then went home and cleaned the flat, loaded the washing machine, and settled down with a book I'd been meaning to read since last Christmas.

I'd only gotten past the second page when the doorbell rang. I glanced at the clock. It was after one o'clock. Stephen, of course, stopping by on his lunch break.

Throwing the book onto the coffee table, I went to the front door, running my fingers through my hair to tidy it. Frankie was barking wildly. Opening the door, I found it wasn't Stephen, but Dan standing there.

"Oh! Hello."

"Hi there. Not interrupting anything, am I?"

"No, of course not. Come in."

I held Frankie's collar to stop her jumping up and stood back to let him pass, noticing the softness of his leather jacket, the cut of his cargo pants, the faint scent of his aftershave. It was as if all my senses were on red alert.

"What are you doing here?"

"I was passing by, thought I'd see how you're doing."

We stood looking at each other awkwardly. I wondered if the intense feelings he aroused in me were visible on my face. The thought made me blush.

Closing the door, I let go of Frankie and she leapt up at Dan as if he were her long-lost friend.

"Frankie, get down!" I ordered, using the dog as an excuse to cover my nervousness.

I stooped to grab her collar again just as Dan bent to pat her head, and I unwittingly found my face a fraction from his, his hair almost touching my lips as we straightened and stared hungrily into each other's eyes. We were standing so close I could feel his breath on my face. Mesmerized, I simply stood there, unable to break away.

His lips were suddenly upon mine, and I melted into him, returning the kiss with an intensity that took my breath away. It was as though I'd waited for this moment all my life. Nothing else mattered except him and me.

And then the doorbell rang again, and I froze in Dan's arms.

"Are you expecting someone?" Dan whispered into my hair.

"My boss," I said, pulling away from him, my cheeks burning. "My friend Clara rang earlier to say he might pop over."

Dan held me at arm's length, regarding me steadily as the doorbell rang again.

"Do you want me to leave?"

"No, I'd like you to stay."

I went to the door with Frankie leaping around my legs and found Stephen standing on the doorstep clutching a bunch of roses.

"How are you feeling?" He leaned toward me and kissed me chastely on the cheek.

Before I could think of what to say he had pushed past me into the living room. He stopped dead when he saw Dan standing there.

"Oh, I didn't realize you already had company."

"This is Dan," I said hoarsely. My breath was tight in my throat and I didn't know if it was because my heart was still pounding from the kiss, or because my ex-lover was about to meet the man I hoped might become my new one.

"Dan took me to the hospital on Saturday after the accident. Dan, this is Stephen Armitage, my boss."

Dan stuck out his hand, but Stephen hesitated, and for an awful moment I thought he might refuse to return the gesture. Fortunately it seemed his good manners won the day, and he shook hands briefly, his expression carefully blank.

"Er, do sit down," I said to both men. "I'll go and put the kettle on."

Escaping into the kitchen with Frankie at my heels, I had just begun filling the kettle with water when I felt a hand slide around my waist. Twisting, I found Stephen standing closely behind me.

"How are you feeling, Jessica?" he whispered in my ear. "I've been worried about you."

"Stephen! What do you think you're doing?"

Pulling away from him, I plugged the kettle in and pushed the button down with a click.

Stephen took a step closer.

Frankie began to growl.

"I've missed you," he murmured, ignoring the dog. "When I heard you'd been in the hospital I realized how much you meant to me. I've been stupid, Jess. I want you back."

"It's too late," I told him. "I'm a different person now."

I felt the hair on the back of my neck stand up at the unintended connotation of my words. Suppressing a shiver, I composed my expression into what I hoped was a mixture of firm intention and sympathy.

"It's very kind of you to bring me flowers, but I think you should go. I'm sorry, Stephen, but we had this out two years ago. It didn't work then and there's no reason to think it would work now."

He stared at me, his eyes flashing with anger, or hurt, I wasn't sure which. What I was sure about was that I didn't want Dan getting the wrong idea.

"You'll regret this, Jessica."

Looking at Stephen's disgruntled face, the beginnings of light lines etched into his forehead, the hair just starting to show gray around the edges, I realized for the first time just how much older than me he seemed. I'd been eighteen when I'd first started working for him and had seen him as a mature, attractive man. Thirty-two had seemed rather exciting and I'd admired and looked up to him. I suppose I'd been flattered that he had been interested in me, and I had to admit it had been convenient to forge a relationship with someone with whom I spent so much time. Now, in his early forties, he suddenly seemed old and tired.

Maybe it was the late hours he kept or the stress of the job, but I understood with sudden clarity that I felt nothing at all for him. And I wanted him out of my flat.

"I think you should leave," I said shortly. Shutting the still-growling Frankie into the kitchen, I walked purposefully ahead of Stephen, showing him with no uncertainty to the front door, trying not to meet Dan's speculative gaze on the way.

"Thank you for the flowers," I said as I started to close the door behind him.

He paused on the threshold and tried to take my hand, but I pulled it away.

"Your loss," he said, shaking his head. "Don't say I didn't warn you."

"I'll see you in the office on Monday morning. Bye, Stephen."

I walked back to where Dan was perched on the edge of the sofa and sank down next to him, avoiding his eyes.

"Don't tell me," Dan said. "He was the guy you lived with for a while."

"I don't understand it," I said, shaking my head. "It was over. We've worked together ever since and there's been no problem. I don't know what's gotten into him."

"He sensed a change in you, maybe," Dan commented. "Perhaps he's been perfectly happy seeing you every day, knowing you're on your own, not having to make an effort with you. Maybe he thought he still owned you, but without having the bother of commitment and an actual relationship."

"Are you a shrink or something?" I asked with a laugh.

"No, but I can tell a jealous man when I see one. When he followed you into the kitchen he was marking his territory, making sure I knew he was something more than just your boss."

"But you stayed."

"I wasn't going to give up on you that easily."

"The weird thing is, we've only just met, you and I. You could easily have thought he meant something to me."

"After that kiss? I don't think so, Jessica. There's something between us that I sensed the first time I saw you up on the Downs. You feel it too, don't you?"

"Yes."

He rested a hand lightly on top of both of mine, which were twisted together in my lap. His thumb strayed onto my knee, and I felt the heat begin to rise up in me again. I'd never experienced anything quite like the effect his touch had on me, and I turned sideways to face him as he sat beside me, my skin burning.

I knew he was going to kiss me again, and I closed my eyes in anticipation.

The touch of his lips was so light it was almost like experiencing a tiny electric shock. His lips moved softly over my face, hardly brushing my skin, moving from the corners of my mouth, across my cheekbones to the outer edges of my eyes. He kissed my forehead and my hair, until I thought my chest would explode with desire.

I opened my eyes and looked at him, and he smiled at me with a look of such desire that it simply took my breath away.

One hand still holding mine securely in my lap, he raised his free hand to my mouth and traced the outline of my lips with his fingertip, before traveling down my neck and coming to rest at the zipper of my jogging top. His eyes looked questioningly into mine, and I nodded infinitesimally, paralyzed by the glorious sensation of his touch.

Slowly, the zipper traveled downward, revealing my white lace bra, breasts rising and falling within as I struggled to catch my breath. He lowered his head to my cleavage and I felt his tongue flicker across my skin, sending prickles of delight up and down my spine.

He let go of my hands then, and used both his to ease the silver-gray top from my shoulders and down my arms, until it slipped away behind me. When he paused to shrug off his own jacket I reached across and unbuttoned his shirt, thrilling at the sight of his suntanned, well-muscled chest.

I reached back and unfastened my bra, and he slid it off deftly, lowering his face to my breasts as he did so. I closed my eyes and arched my back against the softness of his warm mouth.

I found the belt buckle of his trousers and undid it quickly, then I wriggled out of the rest of my clothing and dropped it to the floor. I could hardly believe what was happening to me. It had been more than two years since I'd slept with anyone, and it had never, ever been like this.

"Dan," I gasped as he pressed me to him. I felt the warm skin of his chest, bare against my naked breasts as he lowered himself onto me. He was so hard and warm and strong, I thought I was going to burst with happiness. His lips found mine, firm this time, his tongue probing, searching. I opened myself to him and felt him inside me and I moved against him, rocking gently, our mingled perspiration glistening on his face and neck.

I clung to him as passion overtook us, and at some point later we made our way to the bedroom, where we lay giggling in each other's arms before beginning all over again.

The afternoon light began to fade, casting a gray sheen over the room, and I risked a quick glance at the bedside clock. It was five o'clock. Teddy had thankfully slept through most of the night without disturbing me, and I was eternally grateful for small mercies.

We drew the covers up around us as the air began to cool, and as we lay entwined in the snug warmth of the duvet I stroked his shoulder and smiled into his eyes. "I'm glad I didn't go to work today."

"So am I," he replied with a grin. "I think I can honestly say this is the best afternoon I have ever had."

I leaned up on one elbow and studied him closely. "Really?"

"Well, it beats work any day," he said, and I hit him over the head with my pillow as we fell back laughing.

chapter seven

I was lying comfortably in the crook of Dan's arm when I heard Frankie whine from the kitchen. She'd obviously gotten fed up with snoozing in her basket.

"Poor Frankie! She's been shut up in there for hours."

Grabbing up the duvet, I wrapped it around me and headed for the door, looking back at Dan's naked form stretched out on my bed.

"I'd better let her in."

"Yeah," he said, swinging himself to the edge of the bed and getting to his feet. "And I'd better put some clothes on before I freeze to death."

We had a quick meal of smoked salmon I took from the freezer together with some scrambled eggs, then sat on the sofa drinking tea, with Frankie lying across our legs.

"Frankie didn't seem to care much for your boss," Dan commented as he stroked the terrier's ears.

"She doesn't really know him. I bought her from a shelter

when I moved in here after moving out of Stephen's flat. I thought she'd be good company, and I was right."

"She's a good girl. She behaved impeccably while she was staying with me on Saturday night."

"Did your dog mind her being there?"

"Bessie? No, she loved the company. The two of them curled up in Bessie's basket as if they were sisters."

"Is Bessie a young dog?"

"She's only two. Dad bought her for me, he thought she'd be company for me when I'm out and about on my travels."

"What do you do for a living?"

"I own a company called 'Brennan's Bandits.' I hire out slot machines to pubs and clubs. I have people working for me who service and empty them and that leaves me free to drum up new business. You could say I'm a kind of salesman, as I drive all over the country, though I'm hiring the machines out, of course, not actually selling them."

"So you spend a lot of your time in the pub," I said with a giggle. "And you're with a girl who doesn't drink."

"Yeah, I noticed that," he said, snuggling closer to me and nuzzling my neck. "You'll be nice and cheap to date."

I was about to exclaim indignantly when my eyes flickered over to the clock. Oh, no! It was half past seven already.

I looked at him anxiously, not sure what to say or do. It was obvious he was expecting to stay for the evening, if not the whole night, but soon I'd be needed elsewhere. I wondered how Grant was feeling this morning, or even if he was awake yet. The thought dawned on me that he might be in a bad way after the condition he'd been in the previous night. Suppose the children were awake with no one to supervise them?

I pictured the twins running amok while Nicole and Sophie tried to rouse first their father and then their mother without success.

"I'm really sorry, Dan, but there's something I've got to do this evening."

He stared at me in surprise. "Really?"

"Yes, I, er . . . I said I'd meet my friend Clara. We go to, um . . . a class in the evenings."

"What sort of class is it?"

I glanced around the flat trying to think of a subject I might be interested enough in to do as an evening class. My eyes alighted on the row of potted plants on the high sill.

"It's a gardening class. You know, learning when to put in spring bulbs, what to feed them with, that sort of thing."

"Oh, right."

He shifted Frankie's weight off his legs and stood up, flexing his shoulders.

"Can I see you again tomorrow?"

"I'll be out tomorrow evening as well."

"I meant during the day."

"Shouldn't you be at work?"

"That's the glory of owning the company," he said with a shrug. "I can choose my own hours." He looked at me with the faint stirrings of suspicion. "How often do you go to this class?"

"Er . . . it's a bit flexible. It's in someone's house, so we go when it suits the teacher, usually late in the evening."

Dan frowned, and I could see he didn't entirely believe me. He shrugged again and picked up his jacket.

"If you're sure you want to see me, I'll come around again tomorrow lunchtime then. I assume you're definitely not going to work?"

I knew he'd heard me tell Stephen I'd be back to work on Monday morning. He must be checking that I wasn't just making excuses in case I didn't want to see him again.

I stood up and went to him, putting my arms around his waist and resting my head on his shoulder.

"I had a wonderful day today," I told him sincerely. "I'm at home again tomorrow on doctor's orders, and I can't think of anywhere I'd rather spend the afternoon than here with you."

He smiled, presumably reassured, and kissed me, then headed to the door. He paused there and looked back. "I'll see you tomorrow then. Enjoy your class."

As soon as he had gone, I fetched Frankie's lead and gave her a half-hour walk around the block. Back at the flat, I gave her supper, took a quick shower, brushed my teeth, and climbed back into the rumpled bed. It still smelled of Dan and me, and I smiled contentedly as I closed my eyes. I had been right about Dan from the moment I'd first set eyes on him. He was definitely something special.

Grant was being sick in the en suite bathroom when I hurried past the guest room door. I'd leapt out of bed the moment I'd opened my eyes, afraid of what the children might be getting up to, and had run down the long landing to look into their bedrooms.

All four of the children's beds were empty. I stopped at the guest room door, listening to Lauren's husband retching, and decided that at this moment he probably didn't know or care where the children were.

Wrapping the silk negligee closely around my waist, I hurried downstairs, noticing how quiet the house was. The kitchen door was open, dirty cereal bowls lying on the countertop. Sophie must have given the boys their breakfast, I thought, as I crossed quickly to the playroom.

Nicole and Toby were slumped on the couch watching morning TV. Teddy was lounging on a beanbag holding his ball and staring into space, mouthing silently to himself. He was still in his pajamas, the trousers drooping with the weight of the large nappy he had to wear to bed.

"Where's Sophie?" I asked from the doorway.

Nicole and Toby both glanced up, slowly registering my presence. Teddy continued to stare into space and chant wordlessly.

"She went to see her rabbit," Nicole replied. "I wanted to go see Ginny, but bossy-boots Sophie said it was too cold out there."

"Did she take a coat?"

Nicole shrugged, her attention returning to the television set.

Hurrying back upstairs, I peered out of my bedroom window, where a light frost had powdered the grass and bushes white, but as I had promised Grant, the animals weren't visible from the house. Worrying that Sophie had gone out alone and that she might be cold, I grabbed a casual tan overcoat from Lauren's wardrobe, slipped it over the negligee, being careful not to snag my bandaged shoulder, and went back downstairs.

The utility room door was ajar, letting in an icy blast, and I closed it behind me as I set off briskly down the garden in a pair of ankle boots. To my relief I found Sophie sitting in the gardener's shed, wrapped in a thick sweater with her rabbit nestled in her arms. She looked up as I opened the door and I perched on the upturned crate next to her.

"How is she?" I asked, reaching out and stroking the rabbit's silky back.

"I thought she might be cold," Sophie explained. "Do you think we could move the hutch in here?"

I nodded. "I think that's an excellent idea. I hadn't realized it was going to get so cold so quickly. We could shift all the tools to this side then I think the hutch would fit along that wall. Maybe we could get some sort of table or bench to stand it on to keep it off the floor."

Sophie was looking at me strangely.

"What?"

"You're different," she said simply. "Before you got struck by the lightning you hated animals. Now you're being really nice."

I felt myself blush as if I'd been caught with my hand in the proverbial cookie jar.

"You're lucky I don't remember I hate animals," I said with a smile. I made a mental note to be more careful in the way I acted in front of the children. The trouble was, I reminded myself, I didn't know Lauren at all. All I could do was be myself.

Sophie smiled back, then shivered, holding the rabbit closer to her chest for warmth.

"Come on, she'll be okay in her hutch now," I said, standing up. "The sun's coming out and melting the frost, and there's loads of straw in there. She can snuggle up with Ginny while we get things sorted out indoors. We'll come down later to see her again."

Sophie nodded and put the rabbit back in her hutch before skipping up the garden ahead of me. I watched her feet dancing across the brittle grass and felt something stir in my heart. I was happy for her, of course, I reasoned, but it was something more than that. Could it be that I was experiencing some sort of awakening maternal instinct?

Any ideas I'd had about the joys of motherhood were quickly banished as I walked back into the warmth of the playroom to be assaulted by the most horrible smell.

"Teddy's pooped in his pants, Teddy's pooped in his pants!" Toby chanted, in a voice muffled by the fact that his face was hidden inside the collar of his dressing gown. Nicole had her hand clamped over her nose and was pretending to gag.

My gaze rested on Teddy, who was sitting where I'd left him on the beanbag, appearing completely unperturbed by the commotion he had caused. I looked to Sophie for guidance and she shrugged.

"You have to take the nappy off as soon as he wakes up," she explained. "When it's on, he thinks he doesn't need to use the toilet."

So it was my fault. I ran a hand over my face while I contemplated the awfulness of the task ahead of me. It was almost ten o'clock, I wasn't even dressed yet, and now I had to deal with this.

"Stay there," I ordered Teddy. "Don't move. I'm going to run you a bath."

While the bath was running, I rummaged in Lauren's wardrobe for something casual to wear.

"You must have an old pair of jeans or something," I murmured, searching through the racks of glamorous designer clothing despairingly. "What do you wear for doing jobs like this, for heaven's sake?"

A movement behind me made me jump. I turned around to find Grant standing in the doorway.

"Talking to yourself?" he commented dryly.

I felt myself blush again. I would have to be more careful or I'd wake up one morning and find myself in that padded cell.

"You can talk," I countered. "After the state you were in last night."

He had the decency to look abashed. "I'm really sorry, sweetheart. I think I had a bit too much to drink."

"You frightened me."

An anguished look passed across his face and he came toward me, his hands held up as if in apology. "I said I'm sorry. I just want us to be close again. I miss you, Lauren."

He looked so forlorn that my heart went out to him, but my sense of reason prevailed and I kept the distance between us while giving him what I hoped was a sympathetic smile.

"I've got to go turn off the bath, or we'll have a flood," I said, walking past him.

He followed me along the landing to the family bathroom and watched while I turned off the faucets in the nick of time and let some of the water out of the drain.

"Have you really lost all your memories, Lauren?"

He was leaning against the frame of the door, contemplating me speculatively. The question startled me, and I felt my mouth drop open slightly.

"You heard what Dr. Shakir said about my temporal lobes being damaged," I said, straightening up. "It's hardly something I could make up."

He eyed me doubtfully. "You muttered something in the hospital about having other memories. And the nurse told me you thought you were someone else when you first woke up."

"I was confused," I lied. "Don't forget I almost died, Grant. Maybe I'd been dreaming or something." I shrugged. "I don't know."

He was still staring at me speculatively and I began to wonder if he knew something. Had he sensed that I wasn't really Lauren after all?

"I've got to go and fetch Teddy," I said, ending the discussion. "While I was sleeping in and you were sleeping it off, Teddy stayed too long in his night nappy, and now he's messed himself. Fine parents we've been."

We were saved further recriminations by the arrival of Sophie, who announced that Teddy was downstairs crying. I left Grant leaning against the bathroom door and hurried downstairs to find Elsie standing over a distressed Teddy.

"Just look at him!" she was saying, her voice raised in indignation. "He's not fit to be in a nice house like this. Look what he's done."

"It's all right, Elsie, I'll deal with it."

The cleaning lady turned to stare at me with disapproval written all over her face, and I realized I still hadn't found the time to get dressed.

"I'm sorry, Mrs. Richardson, but the smell is intolerable. And it's not just him, either. There's straw tramped all over the utility room floor, and dirty breakfast bowls dumped in the kitchen . . ."

"Elsie," I said in a placating voice. "This is exactly why we need someone as experienced and professional as you. As you know, the nanny has left, and I've just come out of hospital. Mr. Richardson isn't feeling well this morning, either. Now, I'll deal with Teddy here, if you could help with the other things as best you can. We really appreciate everything you do. You know we simply couldn't manage without you."

I watched as Elsie pursed her lips and nodded her head, obviously appeased by the praise.

"I'll go and start in the kitchen then," she announced, with one last disgusted glance at Teddy. "Don't you worry about a thing, Mrs. Richardson."

She waddled off and I went at last to deal with Teddy.

"Sshh, don't cry. It wasn't your fault. Daddy wasn't feeling well and I was still asleep. Come on, it's bath time again, and you can have your favorite ball in there if you like."

I turned to the others as I led Teddy from the room.

"While I'm getting Teddy cleaned up I want you each to draw a picture of the thing you like most in all the world. I don't mind if it's a place or a person, or a toy, but it must be colored in and as neat as you can do it. I'd like to remember what you like best. And then we'll go out to see the animals and play in the sandbox, okay?"

Sophie and Nicole nodded enthusiastically and went to the toy cupboard, where I assumed they had paper and crayons.

"You too, Toby. I'm sure you're good at drawing. I'll be down later to see what you've done."

Cleaning Teddy up was no mean feat, but with the help of almost an entire toilet paper roll and the bath to finish off, he was soon respectable again.

"There," I said as I finished dressing him. "Does that feel better?"

He nodded and I gave him a hug, despite the fact that he remained rigid and unbending in my arms.

"Will you go downstairs by yourself while I get dressed?"

He nodded solemnly.

"And draw me a picture, Teddy. Draw a picture of what you like best in all the world. Your ball, maybe?"

Grant was nowhere to be seen as I scrubbed the lingering smell off my hands, selected an outfit, and dressed quickly. I wondered how Lauren had coped with Teddy or whether she had left it all to the nanny. I began to feel an affinity with the poor woman, whoever she had been. This was certainly parenting at its most challenging, and I couldn't say that anything in my own life had prepared me for it.

Standing and surveying Lauren's reflection in her full-length mirror, I groaned inwardly. It was almost lunchtime, and all I'd managed so far today was to get myself and Teddy dressed. Goodness knew when I was going to find time to make the children any lunch, especially as I felt I should spend quality time with them during their half-term break, rather than leave them watching television while I cooked and cleared away.

I longed suddenly for the simplicity of my other life. Even though Stephen was a demanding boss and I often worked late into the evenings preparing depositions for court or searching out legal documents that could make or break a case, I enjoyed the challenge of the work. And when I went home at the end of the day I could forget all about it for a while and concentrate on my own needs, puttering around the flat, taking Frankie for a walk, or spending what was left of an evening out with Clara and our other friends.

Smoothing the cream linen trousers I'd selected over my hips, I stood rooted before the mirror. It was still a surprise to see Lauren's reflection looking back at me whenever I caught a glimpse of myself, and I found it hard to resist striking poses and pulling faces just to prove to myself that the image I could see had some correlation to the person I was inside.

As I stared, fascinated, at my still very alien appearance, I thought of my own life and the dwindling group of girlfriends in my other existence. One by one they were marrying or producing babies and, apart from Clara, most of them only came on an evening out now and again. I thought back to our last night out on the town, when only three out of a group of six friends from college and work had made it, and how I'd thought their excuses of not being able to leave the new baby or get babysitters for their toddlers were a bit lame.

Adjusting the shoulders of the lightweight sweater, I smiled ruefully at myself. I certainly understood something of those ties and obligations now. With four children waiting for me downstairs and a husband who had hardly appeared this morning, I felt almost overwhelmed by what I was starting to understand was a full-blown twenty-four-hour, seven-days-a-week task. This parenting business was totally consuming. The routine of the household never let up. If I wanted to steal a moment to myself, even to have a bath or get dressed, then the children would be bored and get into mischief, the animals would go hungry, and my husband—Lauren's husband—might feel neglected. Worse still was the knowledge that in the course of a normal day my actions could affect the children for the rest of their lives.

"You can do it," I told my reflection in the mirror. "You owe it to Lauren."

I went downstairs to find Teddy crying again.

"What's the matter with him now?" I asked Sophie.

"He tried to take the coloring pencils," Nicole answered. "Sophie wouldn't let him have them."

"Why not?" I asked, surprised.

"He's not allowed," Sophie said sullenly. "You said he makes too much mess."

"Last time he got felt-tip pen all over the carpet," Nicole put in. "It took Elsie ages to get it out."

"For goodness' sake, this is a playroom, isn't it?" I asked of no one in particular. I immediately forgot my intention to try to act more like I thought Lauren would and marched over to the toy cupboard, grabbed a handful of pens and a sheet of paper, and set them down in front of Teddy.

"Here, Teddy. Draw me a picture."

The others looked on disapprovingly as Teddy tentatively took a pen and touched it to the paper. A look of satisfaction crossed his face, and his tongue soon protruded between his lips as he began to concentrate on the line he was making.

I turned to the others. "Are you going to show me your pictures?"

Toby thrust his effort into my hands and I held it up to admire it. He'd drawn a picture of his new sandbox complete with a yellow blob on wheels that I took to be his digger.

"That's lovely!" I said, ruffling his hair. "Would you like to go down and play with the real thing now?"

He nodded.

"Go and get dressed then, and put on your boots and jacket, then you can go down to the garden and play."

Toby scampered off and I looked at Nicole's drawing. She'd made a picture of a creature I assumed was her guinea pig, complete with ginger forelock. It was sitting in front of a box hutch.

"It's great," I told her. "I love it. You can go down with Toby and play with Ginny if you want. Don't forget to hold her how I showed you."

I turned to look at Sophie's drawing, expecting to see a black rabbit, but she'd drawn a person instead, with a big heart on the front of a blond-haired figure.

"Who's this?" I asked.

"It's you, Mum," she said. "It's the you after the lightning strike. The different Mummy."

I looked over my shoulder to check that Grant wasn't standing there. This was just the sort of thing that might show him I was irreparably changed in some way by the accident. I forced a smile. "It's lovely, Sophie. I really like it. In fact, all the pictures are so good, I think we should put them on the wall."

Sophie's eyes grew wide.

"But . . . it'll make a mess."

I was about to say "hang the mess, you are children and this is a playroom," but I caught myself in time.

"You are absolutely right, Sophie. We won't put them on the wall itself. I was thinking we could buy a board and pin them up on that."

She nodded, accepting the compromise.

"Can I go and see Blackie now?"

"Of course. And Sophie . . . ?"

"Yes?"

"What sort of thing do you all like to eat for lunch?"

I remembered the disaster of yesterday's tea and hoped it would be something simple.

She tilted her head to one side as if weighing me up, and a small smile flickered at the corner of her lips.

"Fries with ketchup—and ice cream," she said with a grin. "It's our favorite."

While I cooked oven fries and found a bottle of ketchup to go with them, I forgot about Teddy and his picture. When I eventually wandered back into the playroom, my mouth must have actually dropped open in astonishment.

Teddy was stretched out on the floor, his picture in front of him. As I looked at the picture from over his shoulder, I could hardly believe what I was seeing. It was a work of art.

Kneeling down beside him, I asked him where he'd gotten the idea for his picture, but he just shrugged and kept drawing.

I watched entranced as he put the finishing touches to it, then sat up and studied it critically, his head to one side.

It was a picture of the garden. The proportions seemed perfectly correct, with the patio, lawn, and scrub area all included. He'd used a pencil as well as the pens to shade and color the picture. It was incredible that a four-year-old had produced such a masterpiece of perspective and accuracy. I sat next to him and grinned.

"You are a talented boy, Teddy. I can see you are going to go far in this world."

"What nonsense are you filling his head with?" Grant asked from the doorway.

I held the picture up so he could see it.

"Look what Teddy has done!" I exclaimed. "It's brilliant."

"I suppose it is quite good," Grant agreed. "Did he copy it?"

I shook my head.

"I think it's all his own work, just from what he's observed."

"He shouldn't be drawing on the floor, though, he'll get felt-tip on the carpet again."

"The children should have a table in here where they can draw and paint and do messy things," I countered.

Grant recoiled at the word *messy* and I rolled my eyes skyward in exasperation.

"What do they normally do all day, for heaven's sake?"

"I told you, the nanny takes them out. In fact, it's time we started interviewing for a new one. The children are obviously too much for you while you're ill."

"They'll be back at school next week. Is it worth getting a nanny now?"

"How are you going to get up in time to take them to school,

Lauren?" he asked bluntly. "You haven't managed to get up until after nine for the last two mornings. They have to be at school by a quarter to nine and you're going to have to get up at seven o'clock to get them all ready."

"We wouldn't have a nanny in time for next week even if we advertised right now," I pointed out. "Couldn't you take them to school next week?"

"I'm afraid that's not possible. My first appointment arrives at eight in the morning."

"Didn't you say something about my sister coming to stay?" I remembered suddenly. "Does she drive?"

"Good Lord, I'd forgotten Karen was coming. I telephoned her when you were first taken into the hospital. She said she could take time off work next week to come and help out." He rubbed his chin thoughtfully. "She might do the school run for a few days if we ask her nicely. Give you a bit longer to recover your senses."

"What's she like, my sister? Do we get along?"

Grant let out an exasperated sigh, and I knew he was still struggling with the enormity of the fact that I couldn't remember anything.

The doorbell rang as we were contemplating each other, and I got to my feet, glad of an excuse to be out of his presence. I opened the door to find a plump woman standing on the porch. She had a very short, spiky haircut and large dangly earrings. But it was her clothes that made me stare rather rudely at her. She was wearing a pair of loose-fitting silk trousers under an enormous purple blouse, which stretched over her very ample bosom like a mini marquee.

"Hello, sister dear," she said, offering me her cheek. "Grant said you were at death's door, but here you are alive and looking well. I thought I'd come and help out with the children while you were sick, but if you'd rather I went . . ."

"Karen?"

"That's me, little sis. So you're out of the hospital then?"

"This is really weird—we were just talking about you." I looked at her speculatively and she returned my gaze as I nodded. "Yes, I came out the day before yesterday, and no, I don't want you to go."

"You look in remarkable health for someone who was dying a few days ago. Look, can I come in then? I've had a pig of a journey and I'm exhausted."

"Of course, I'm sorry, Karen. Come on in. You're in time for lunch if you don't mind oven fries and ice cream." She stared at me incredulously, as if I'd made a huge joke, but the smile faded as she looked into my eyes.

"You look . . . different," she said, pushing past me while I closed the door. "There's something about you . . . I can't put my finger on it."

I was saved from my sister realizing that my eye color was slightly different by Grant's arrival behind me. He took one look at his sister-in-law standing there and hurried over to give her a perfunctory peck on the cheek.

"Well, speak of the devil! I thought you couldn't get away until next week?"

"You made it sound bloody important," Karen said, dumping an overnight bag in the middle of the hall. "When you rang from the hospital I thought Lauren was about to meet her maker. I requested compassionate leave, and here I am."

I smiled at her, liking her already.

"I'm so glad you're here," I told her. "I don't know if Grant told you, but I've lost my memory. I can't remember anything at all about who I am or what my life is like. I'm hoping you can fill me in."

Karen stared at me, her eyes almost popping from her round, friendly face.

"Well, bugger me," she said.

chapter eight

Grant took advantage of Karen's arrival to escape with somewhat indecent haste, saying he'd take his account books into the practice to work on them there. He kissed us both, collected his briefcase and vanished to the garage.

"No change there then," Karen commented as she followed me into the kitchen. She stopped and sniffed the air. "Hmm, something smells good."

I opened the oven to see how the fries were coming along, and realized they were almost ready.

"I'm going to call the children in for lunch," I said, slipping on the ankle boots. "Teddy is in the playroom; you'll never believe what he's just drawn, Karen. He's really talented."

I was aware of my sister's astonished gaze following me as I hurried out through the utility room to the garden. I realized Karen, as her sister, must know Lauren better than anyone. They had grown up together, they would know each other's strengths and weaknesses. And I could tell she was an intelligent woman, not someone who could be easily hogwashed.

As I rounded the row of conifers, I stopped and caught my breath. The two girls were sitting opposite each other on the grass, their legs stretched out, feet meeting at the ankles to form a small diamond-shaped arena between their legs. In the middle, Blackie was hopping around nibbling here and there at the brown grass, and Ginny was trying to climb onto Nicole's lap. Toby was making *brrmming* noises with his digger in the nearby sandbox, now filled with fine silver sand.

Nicole glanced up and saw me watching. "Mummy! Ginny knows her name! She makes little chatting noises when I call her, watch!"

I came and squatted down beside them while Nicole spoke to her new pet. The furry creature was trying to stick its head into her sweater.

"They're both lovely, and very clever," I agreed, stroking Ginny and smiling. "But I've got another surprise for you. Auntie Karen is here. She's come to visit for a few days."

Their eyes lit up and they both grabbed their pets and scrambled to their feet. I could tell from their reaction that Auntie Karen was a favorite relative. I checked that the hutch door was properly closed once the animals were inside, then called Toby and followed the girls up to the house.

Karen was sitting on a beanbag on the floor of the playroom, looking at Teddy's picture. She struggled to her feet when she saw the other children and held out her arms, folding them into her with a bearlike embrace.

I decided to leave them to their reunion and hurried into the kitchen to check the fries, which were turning dark brown around the edges. After extracting clean forks from the drawer and plates from the cupboard, I peeled some carrots and chopped them into thin fingers. Locating the oven gloves where I'd hurriedly stowed them the day before, I piled fries liberally onto the plates, then called the children in to lunch. "Don't forget to wash your hands," I reminded them.

The girls and Toby climbed onto stools at the central breakfast bar, while Karen followed holding Teddy by the hand.

"You're right, Teddy is talented," she commented as she helped him up onto a stool. "I can't think how no one ever noticed before."

"Mummy doesn't usually let Teddy have the crayons," Nicole said, spitting fries as she spoke with her mouth full. "He makes too much mess."

Karen's eyes met mine and I glanced away, embarrassed at Lauren's shortsightedness.

"Well, he can have them whenever he wants from now on." I went to the fridge and extracted a packet of ready-cooked chicken portions. "And we're going to buy a board so we can display all your pictures, aren't we, Sophie?"

Sophie nodded through a mouthful of carrot and fries. I was cutting pieces of chicken and handing them to the children, who grabbed them eagerly, stuffing them into their mouths.

"I'm sorry this is a bit of a thrown-together lunch," I said to Karen, offering her a plate of cold chicken. "I'm all at sea after the accident. I can't seem to get things flowing smoothly yet. It's the lack of memories, I don't know how the household ticks; I can't remember how to cater for five or six and I can't seem to wake up in the mornings to get going."

"You appear to be getting the important things right," she said, eyeing me with interest. "Sophie was just telling me you've bought them pets."

"The children didn't have anything to do," I replied, chopping salad and putting the bowl on the breakfast bar in front of her. "I'm not surprised the nanny found them a handful if she wasn't allowed to play with them."

Karen helped herself to a large portion of salad, which she piled next to the chicken, and then she took a heap of fries from the remainder on the baking tray.

"I want to hear all about this accident of yours," she said as she squeezed tomato ketchup all over the fries and stuck her fork in the resulting mountain of food. "And I want to hear exactly what the doctors had to say about it. I'm surprised they let you home so soon; you're obviously not yourself at all."

I told her about the burns to my shoulder and back, but added that they were healing remarkably quickly. "I've been given an appointment at the psychiatric clinic next week to help me come to terms with the memory loss, but I don't really want to go," I confessed. "Being here with the children is all the therapy I need."

Karen stared at me as if weighing things up.

"You ought to take care of that burn, at least. I'll take a look at it later."

After lunch, I sat still while she peeled away a corner of the antibiotic dressing.

"It's not bad at all," she said, surprise in her voice. "I thought it would be much worse."

"I told you, it's healing really quickly."

We cleared away the lunch things while the children vanished into the garden again.

"I thought we might go out this afternoon and pick up some bits and pieces for the children," I said as I finished loading the dishwasher.

"As long as you feel up to it."

"I'd rather be out of the house," I told her. "It's all so sterile and neat indoors."

She stared at me again without speaking, and I hoped she had put my dislike of my own house down to the memory loss.

After lunch we all piled into the minivan and headed into town. The children fidgeted and fought over where they would sit, until I told them we wouldn't go if they didn't settle down.

"Don't forget, we're going in especially to buy a new play-room table, proper paints, and a board to put your paintings on. If you'd rather stay home and bicker while Auntie Karen and I drink coffee that's fine by me."

The sudden silence in the van was almost tangible, and Karen chuckled under her breath.

"Now," she said, settling her not insubstantial bulk into the soft seat as I started the engine and nosed out into the road, "you've told me all the medical stuff but not what actually happened. Do you remember anything about it at all?"

I was shaking my head when Sophie piped up from the back seat.

"Mummy had to take us to the park, because Trudy left. She said we were horrible uncontr . . . ble—something, anyway—brats."

"Your mother said that?" Karen exclaimed in horror.

Sophie giggled. "No, Trudy did. The nasty nanny."

"I didn't like her because she smacked Teddy all the time," Nicole put in.

"She smacked me, too," said Toby, not to be outdone.

"So what happened in the park?" Karen asked hastily, before the debate could turn into a full-blown argument.

"It started to rain," Sophie said. "The sky went really black. Mummy said we must go back to the car, but Toby had thrown Teddy's ball in the bushes when Mummy wasn't looking and Teddy wouldn't go."

"Mummy shouted and went after him," Nicole added. "And then the lightning came down, right on top of her, and her hair went up in the air and went all blue and crackly."

Even though while I had been in the hospital I had heard something of the children's account of how Lauren had looked when the lightning had hit her, my hand went automatically to the top of my head, where Lauren's blond hair was still brittle and singed, and I gave a heartfelt shudder.

"Good grief," Karen exclaimed. "What did you do then?"

"There was a man in the park, he'd been talking to Mummy, and he phoned up the hospital on Mummy's mobile phone." Sophie took up the story again. "The man waited until the ambulance came and took her away."

"Yeah, he was crying, yuck," Toby said from the back.

I stiffened in the driving seat, and felt Karen's eyes upon me. Fortunately, we were on the edge of town and I had to concentrate on the traffic and where we were going to park.

The conversation was put on hold until much later, when we were home again and Karen and I were trying to work out the assembly instructions for the vinyl-topped table in the utility room while the children watched the late-afternoon children's programs on TV.

"What does Grant make of all this?" Karen asked, holding a table leg in place while I applied glue.

"He seems to be very insecure about the whole thing. He actually asked me if I had really lost my memory."

"And have you?"

I stared at Karen, nervous that she should ask such a thing. "I'd hardly make something like that up."

She eyed me skeptically and I felt myself flush under her steady gaze. "You always did like to be the center of attention."

I felt myself bridle at the dig, but then I relaxed. Of course she couldn't have suspected I wasn't really Lauren. I decided to take the opportunity to find out a little more about the woman whose body I was occupying. "Remind me about our childhood, would you? The doctor at the hospital—Dr. Shakir—told me I have a congenital weakness to my skull, which is why the high-voltage charge from the lightning caused such damage to my temporal lobes. Apparently that is where memory is stored. Was there any sign of it when I was a child?"

"I've always thought you were pretty thick skulled," Karen said with a short laugh. She glanced at my crestfallen face and softened her tone slightly. "There was no sign of anything untoward about you as a child that I can recall. I'm sorry if I sound harsh, Lauren, but our mother used to tell us to try and put ourselves in other people's shoes, to see the world from their perspectives, but you were never very good at that. Even as a child you seemed to think the world revolved around you and that everyone in it was there for your benefit."

"I get the feeling we weren't exactly the best of friends."

"You could say that. You were such a prissy, stuck-up little cow, Lauren. As a teenager you always wanted new things, even though Mum and Dad couldn't afford it. They worked all hours to keep us clothed and fed and you accepted everything as if it was your due. You chose your so-called friends for what they could do for you; as if by surrounding yourself with people who you perceived to be higher up the social ladder, they would give you a leg up too." She tested the table leg and moved on to fit the next one in place. "I could never understand why it mattered so much to you how you looked and who you associated yourself with. Mum used to tell us that all souls are of equal importance, each with our own tasks to fulfill in this life. She believed in karma and reincarnation and would give everything she had, not only to us, but to friends, acquaintances, and even complete strangers. You never understood that, did you?"

I fixed my attention on the table leg as she forged on. "I'm not surprised you married Grant when he came along with his fat wallet and the expensive sports car he drove then, filling your head about his private practice and extravagant lifestyle."

Pausing with the oozing tube of glue in midair, I raised my eyes to hers. "Well, I'm surprised you came here to help when Grant asked you to. It doesn't sound as if you liked me very much at all."

She smiled suddenly with such warmth that it was like looking at another person. "For all your faults, you are still my sister," she said. "And I was worried sick when Grant told me you'd nearly died. It made me realize that maybe we don't have time to bicker any longer and that perhaps it's time to put aside our differences."

"I'm glad you came," I said, returning the smile with some relief. "I want us to get along very much."

"Well, maybe you are starting to try to put yourself in other people's shoes at last," Karen went on, oblivious to the irony of her words. "You certainly seem to understand for the first time why you haven't been able to hang on to a nanny for more than a month or two at a time. You used to treat the poor girls as commodities, like a washing machine or a vacuum cleaner; here to perform a service, with no concern for their feelings or needs at all."

"It doesn't sound as if I was very happy."

"No, I don't think you were." She peered into my eyes and I looked away, afraid she'd see someone else there. "You were restless and always looking for something more. The strange thing is, you seem happier now than you've ever been."

"It is hard, though," I admitted as I squeezed glue onto the last leg. "Everything about this life is a blank. It's really awkward with Grant. He wants me to love him, but I don't know him, so how can I? He's like a stranger to me. And I can't understand why he doesn't believe I've lost my memory when he was there with me when Dr. Shakir explained what had happened."

"I'm beginning to think you really don't remember anything." She stared at me intently again while I risked a guarded look back. "Good grief, you truly don't, do you?"

"Not a thing."

"Bloody hell; how awful." She appeared momentarily sympathetic, but then she roused herself and grinned, obviously realizing the implications of me having no memories of our childhood together. "Wow! It lets me off the hook for all the times I beat you up when we were kids, doesn't it? It's fantastic really; until your memories return it's as if we've been given a clean slate. We can leave all our childhood baggage behind us and get to know each other afresh."

"I'd like that."

"Let's just hope that when your memory does come back you don't remember how embarrassed you are to have a sister like me."

"Dr. Shakir doesn't think I ever will get it back properly," I told her. "And I'm sure I'd never be embarrassed by you. I'm not the same person I was before. Give me a chance to prove I've changed."

Karen pulled at the table leg, testing its strength. Apparently satisfied, she helped me stand the table upright.

"From what I've seen so far, you are a different person. I can see why Grant is skeptical. It's quite spooky really."

"Tell me about the rest of our family," I said, steering the conversation away from such dangerous territory. "Where do our parents live?"

Karen's face paled. "Shit, Lauren. You don't even know that, do you?"

"What?"

"They died two years ago, in a terrible car crash. It's just you and me now, kid."

I digested this piece of information, realizing I should feel sorry or something. From what Karen had told me I felt I would have liked Lauren's parents very much. I knew Karen must be hurting and I put my arms around her.

"I'm so sorry, Karen. But we've got each other, and the children."

She hugged me back and we stood there for a moment, gaining comfort from each other's arms. I quite liked the idea of having a sister. I pictured us shopping together, sharing gardening tips and secrets, choosing gifts for each other at Christmas and birthdays and phoning each other with detailed accounts of our daily lives when we couldn't be together in person. I thought what fun it would be for the two of us to walk Frankie, until I realized the impossibility of such a thing, but then I consoled myself with the thought that we could take the children for shared days out and laugh and joke together as one big happy family.

I'd never had anyone to run my thoughts by before. If I mentioned any silly little worries to my parents they would worry for me, and I had never wanted to bother them with my doubts and fears. Even Clara, though a good friend, had a habit of offering unwanted opinions. But a sister might be able to listen without judging or feeling the need to interfere, and I could listen and commiserate when she had worries of her own. I thought how much I would enjoy getting to know Karen better.

"You're not married, are you?" I asked, glancing at her empty ring finger.

She broke away from me and looked at me long and hard before seeming to come to a decision.

"I'm living with someone," she said guardedly.

"Have I met him?"

"It's not a him. It's a her."

"Oh." I paused, then said quickly, "Then have I met her?"

"Bloody hell. What's happened to my sister? I feel like she's been beamed up by aliens, leaving you occupying her body or something!"

I laughed uneasily. "I think you must watch too much *Star Trek*."

"I keep an open mind where these things are concerned," she replied with a laugh. "It would be nice if the 'new you' does too. And no, you have not met her. Her existence is a bone of contention between us. You do not—perhaps I should say did not—approve."

"How long have you two been an item?"

"About eighteen months."

"Have the children met her?"

"You must be joking! You wouldn't allow her near the house."

"When I'm a bit more settled here myself, I'd very much

like to meet her. First, though, I want to reacquaint myself with you."

We went out to the kitchen to put the kettle on. "What are you doing about their dinner?" she asked as I poured boiling water into the pot.

"I can't get used to this constant feeding the kids and clearing up, then cleaning them and feeding them again," I said with a sigh. "I don't know how Laur—I ever did it."

She gave me that look again and I knew my slip of the tongue hadn't gone unnoticed. "There are probably some sausages in the freezer," she said. "You usually keep it well stocked. Shall I look?"

We ended up defrosting sausages in the microwave, then we transferred them to the conventional oven, and while they cooked we chopped and peeled potatoes and vegetables and laid the table in the dining room for tea.

"Will Grant eat sausages?" I asked anxiously. "I haven't cooked for the poor man since I came out of the hospital."

"Poor man my arse," Karen said, tipping the potato peels in the bin. "He should have been cooking for you. Didn't you tell me the doctor recommended plenty of rest?"

"Well, yes."

"So, he eats sausages or he orders takeout. His choice."

I giggled. "I can't believe we didn't get along before. You're so—down-to-earth."

"Have to be, in my job. Can't let the buggers get you down."

"What exactly is your job?"

"Probation officer. You should see some of the cases I have to deal with on a daily basis. You simply wouldn't believe some of the people who are out there walking the streets. I've been threatened with glass bottles, called all the names under the sun, but I love the job, Lauren. I feel I'm making a difference."

After the meal, I sent the children up to get ready for bed. I read stories to both the boys, with Toby sitting snuggled on my lap in his pajamas and Teddy leaning tentatively against me hugging his ball. The ball, I reminded myself with a shudder, that had caused his mother to linger in the storm that had killed her.

Karen had read something to the girls, and I'd heard laughter coming from down the landing before she went downstairs. The phone rang in the distance and Karen answered it. She appeared at the boys' door a moment later.

"It's for you. What shall I tell them?"

"Would you ask who it is and take a number?" I whispered over the boys' heads. "I'll call them back in ten minutes."

The name and number were, of course, unknown to me. Karen had written "Cassandra" on the paper, with a number. I wondered what I was going to say if I rang her back. I wasn't sure if Grant had told anyone outside the family about my memory loss.

Eventually I plucked up the courage to ring Cassandra back, and a cultured voice answered on the second ring.

"Lauren, darling, how are you? We heard you'd been struck by lightning, is it true?"

"Yes, I'm afraid so."

"Do you still want to do lunch tomorrow? Are you up to it?"

"It's the half-term break. I can't leave the children to come out to lunch."

There was a pause at the other end of the line, then Cassandra laughed. "Leaving the children has never bothered you before, Lauren. Where's the nanny?"

"She left."

"Oh, how ghastly for you. What about your sister, the one who answered the phone? Can't you park them with her?"

"I don't want to park them, Cassandra. It's their vacation and I want to spend some time with them."

"Good grief, darling. I heard you'd been hit on the head by lightning but I didn't think you were going to be gaga." Her voice dropped an octave and she said quietly, "I was looking forward to hearing the news."

"What news was that?"

"You know, darling, about him."

I felt myself bridling. I didn't know this woman from Adam, but already I didn't like her one bit.

"There's no news, Cassandra. I have to be going. Bye."

As I replaced the receiver I realized my hands were trembling. I'd already had my suspicions aroused about the possibility of Lauren having had extramarital relations when the children mentioned the man who had been with their mother in the park. I remembered Grant asking me about the possibility, too. Now it seemed everyone knew about Lauren's indiscretions, and I was angry with her for risking the children's happiness in this way.

"Trouble?" Karen asked softly at my shoulder.

I jumped, startled.

"I think I might have been having an affair," I told her bluntly. "It might explain why Grant is so insecure and wanting me to prove I love him."

Karen steered me toward the living room, flicked on the lights, and drew the curtains.

"Come and tell me all about it."

"There's really nothing to tell," I said, sitting beside her on the sofa. "This friend of . . . mine seemed to think I had some news for her about a man, that's all. Coupled with what the children said about the man in the park, I'm worried I might have done something stupid."

"The fact that the idea doesn't appeal to you is good news," she said, patting my hand. "Whatever happened before, you don't have to go on with it now, you know."

"The thing is, I don't know if I can love Grant," I confessed. "I'm not sure I can be a proper wife to him, and if the marriage fails, what will happen to the children? They are so special, so fragile. I wouldn't do anything that might hurt them."

Karen stared at me, nodding that she understood.

"I always thought you married Grant for all the wrong reasons. You were very immature and I was never convinced he was the right man for you. I don't know if it was because Mum and Dad did everything for you, but at twenty-five you were really still a spoiled little girl. He thought you were pretty and delicate, someone he could dominate and control, but he's a weak man and you didn't see that until you'd grown up yourself. I have to confess I'm not entirely surprised you might have strayed."

"What am I going to do?"

"About Grant? I don't know. About this other man, absolutely nothing. Unless he makes contact, it will be all over anyway. I would just ignore the whole thing and hope it goes away."

I yawned widely and apologized. "I think I'll turn in if you don't mind. I assume you know your way to the guest room?"

"I've put my things in the spare bedroom, Lauren. From the look of the guest room I'd say Grant has been sleeping in there."

"Oh, I'm sorry. I forgot."

"Don't worry about it. And don't get up early tomorrow if you want to sleep in. I'll deal with the children . . . and Grant."

I kissed Karen good night and hurried upstairs to get ready for bed. I wanted a long, hot soak in the bath, but it was already half past nine and I pictured Frankie begging to be let out. She was normally very good, but even she had to do her duty after being kept indoors all night.

I fell asleep almost immediately, which was surprising as I'd slept in so late this morning as well. My last thought as Lauren was that both she and Jessica were getting around twelve hours' sleep at a time, and then I was stirring and stretching in Jessica's bed, ready to have Thursday all over again.

Frankie was standing patiently at the bedroom door and I padded over to let her out.

"You poor girl," I told her as she rushed out into the courtyard and up the stone steps to the lawn, where she relieved herself on the grass while looking over at me reproachfully. "I'll make it up to you with a nice long walk."

After a late breakfast I fetched Frankie's leash and we set off at a brisk pace into town. I knew exactly where I was going, and we soon arrived at the smart new building that housed the town's library. After tying Frankie's leash to the leg of a bench outside, I went through the automatic doors and up the escalator, then headed straight for the nonfiction section. There were several books about extreme weather conditions and I soon found a section about lightning. I flicked through the pages looking at amazing pictures of forked lightning, and I nearly allowed myself to become sidetracked reading personal accounts from various victims of lightning strikes. They were truly fascinating, but nothing quite echoed my own experience. I verified what Dr. Shakir had told me about the heat involved in a strike and the related medical issues, but nowhere was there any mention of a time slip or the splitting of a soul into two bodies.

I noted with interest that not only were lightning bolts well-known for their destructive power, it was also thought that some of the essential building blocks of living matter were originally formed by the electrical energy of lightning. If lightning could create life, I thought, then why couldn't it divide life, like the splitting of two cells?

The next thing I looked for was a section on dreams and their meanings. When I'd first woken as Lauren in the hospital I'd been convinced that I was experiencing a complicated and very realistic dream, and I couldn't rule out that possibility now. Just because Lauren's life seemed so real, didn't mean it definitely was real. I wondered whether the lightning strike had sparked some part of my brain into this vivid dreaming pattern. It was certainly no more bizarre than thinking my soul was being shared by two very different people.

I found a book and took it to the reading table where I leafed through it avidly. I read with interest that dreaming sleep is thought to be primarily a period of mental restoration during which the mind may sort and store information acquired during the day. But if that was the case, where had I conjured up Lauren's entire family from?

Of course, there was always the possibility I'd seen the characters from that other life in a film, a TV show, or created them from people I knew, but I had no memory of having seen them anywhere except in this particular dream.

Worse still, I thought to myself grimly as I turned the pages, what if it turned out that I really was Lauren, and the damage caused to Lauren's brain had invented Jessica's existence to fill the void in her own memory? In which case, I thought with a shudder, my worst fears had been justified; I was dreaming now, and Frankie and Dan were all part of Lauren's subconscious imagination.

I shoved the books back into their places on the shelves and tried to calm my nerves. The last thing I needed was to have a panic attack in the public library. I closed my eyes and took several deep breaths, and when I opened them again, my gaze came to rest on a book about the works of Albert Einstein. I knew nothing about the famous man's work apart from my schoolgirl knowledge that he had written about the theory of relativity.

I ran my fingers down the book's spine. Could the possibility of being in two places at the same time be explained in here? I wondered anxiously. Scanning through the pages I paused at one particularly interesting item. It was a summarized version of the theory of relativity. I read it through once and then took it to a nearby table so that I could read it again more slowly.

According to the book, by using extremely sophisticated mathematics, Einstein had apparently shown that the universe was not like clockwork, as Newton had previously theorized. He'd discovered that neither time nor space was an absolute quantity, the dimensions of things were not fixed, and that time and space were intimately connected, even down to the behaviour of the tiny particles inside atoms as well as on the astronomical scale. It was possible—if I believed what I was reading—that the appearance of an event or object would change entirely if the circumstances in which it was observed were altered radically enough. I ran a hand across my face and tried to think. Could a lightning strike, which was, according to the previous book, a force powerful enough to form the building blocks of new life, create the catalyst by which time and space could have been radically altered? I liked the idea a lot better than the possibility my whole life might be someone else's dream.

Standing up, I put the book away and made my way down and outside into the crisp morning air. Frankie rubbed her warm body against my legs as I untied her leash, and I inhaled deeply, feeling the cold air filling my lungs. I gazed about me at the reds and golds of the changing leaves on the ornamental trees in front of the building and up at the clear blue of the sky. A mother with three small children and a stroller passed by, and I listened to their chatter as they went into the library behind me, with a joy building in my heart that I hadn't felt for a long time. It was the wonder of simply being alive.

I took a circuitous route home, much to Frankie's delight, and we arrived at the flat as Dan was climbing out of his car. He grinned when he saw us and I realized he was probably echoing the joy he saw in my face as I looked at him. He had Bessie with him, and the two dogs greeted each other with lots of sniffing and tail wagging. It crossed my mind that I would have liked to have greeted Dan the same way if convention had allowed. The thought made me smile even more widely, and Dan swooped at me and encompassed me in his arms until I gasped out that he was squashing me.

We walked to a nearby pub for lunch and sat outside in the cold sunshine with the dogs lying companionably by our feet. We ate steaming steak and kidney pies washed down with beer in his case, and water followed by coffee in mine.

We walked back to my flat holding hands, the dogs trotting along on either side of us, then we left the two of them with the run of the kitchen and living room while I led Dan into the bedroom and closed the door.

As soon as the door closed behind us Dan pulled me into his arms. Our lips met gently at first, as if finding their way, and then more passionately as our bodies warmed to each other's touch.

We staggered toward the bed, holding the delicious kiss, our bodies pressed closely together, when something about him caused me to hesitate. The intoxicating smell of his breath and body altered somehow and my head began to swim even as I tried to pull away. The memory of Grant touching me the night Teddy had been ill filled my head, and although I could hear Dan calling me in the distance, I discovered that I couldn't move.

I awoke to find Grant pulling up my nightdress. His hand was rough on my thighs and he was slurring drunkenly in my face. Shocked and disoriented, I twisted my head away from his whiskey-scented breath and shouted at him to stop. He took no notice and continued to press himself against me, one hand caressing my face while he fumbled at my nightdress with the other.

Flapping and wriggling beneath him like a flailing fish, I managed to dislodge him for a moment, throwing him off balance, but he was too drunk and too strong for me to hold off for long. I bit down hard on his fingers and he let go of my face with a yelp of pain.

"Get off me! Get off!" I cried, pummeling his face and shoulders. "You're hurting me, Grant, stop it!"

"I love you," he slurred, leaning over me then, sucking at his injured finger. In the thin light seeping from the landing through the crack in the partly open door, I watched as his expression turned from puzzlement to annoyance. He regained his hold on me, straddling me. "Stay still. You're my wife, you're supposed to love me, stay still!"

"I'm not!" I cried in terror as he lowered himself onto me. "I'm not Lauren. Leave me alone!"

The bedroom light snapped on, and Grant went still.

"You heard, get off her," Karen said from the doorway.

"Go away!" Grant snapped, turning his attention back to me.

In a few short strides Karen had crossed the room and yanked at his shirt.

"Get off her, or I'll call the police."

Grant stared at her, the words finally penetrating his alcohol-befuddled brain. He rolled off me and got unsteadily to his feet.

"There's no need for that, Karen. Lauren is my wife, you know."

"She doesn't want you in here," Karen said firmly. "You're drunk, go back to your room."

I thought he was going to protest, but he simply nodded in a rather abashed way, threw me an accusing stare, and lurched from the room. Karen sat on the edge of the bed and put her arm around me.

"It's all right, he's gone now," she crooned as I wept. "Lock your door so he doesn't bother you again tonight."

After she had gone back to her room it took me a while to force myself to move, but the fear of Grant returning eventually unparalyzed my limbs enough for me to stagger across and lock the bedroom door. After climbing unsteadily back into Lauren's bed, I closed my eyes but sleep wouldn't come. Tossing and turning, I dwelled upon what had just happened and the more I worried about that and what Dan must be going through at the flat, the more awake I became. I glanced at the bedside clock and felt another rush of panic surge through me. It had been about three in the afternoon when I'd been snatched from Jessica and thrust into Lauren, but it was now past four in the morning.

At home I would have been unconscious for more than an hour, and Dan must be worried sick. I hoped he hadn't called an ambulance. The last thing I wanted was to end up in the hospital again. The more often it happened, the more the doctors would run tests and dig into my medical history, until in the end they'd probably put my collapses down to mental stress or emotional problems.

I wondered fearfully what would happen if one of these fainting attacks happened while I was in court or at an important corporate event. If it happened more than once it might not only put my job in jeopardy but would reflect badly on Chisleworth & Partners in general. And it wasn't as if I was only unconscious for a few moments; I could be "gone" for as long as the Richardson family needed me. How would I explain that to a roomful of legal personnel? I thought, with a shiver of foreboding.

I was back to the straitjacket scenario again, it was clear. And I buried my head miserably under the pillow.

chapter nine

I must have dropped off eventually, because I woke to hear whispering coming from somewhere nearby. For a moment I wasn't sure where I was. Had I woken as Lauren or was I Jessica?

I opened my eyes and saw Clara sitting in a corner of my bedroom with Dan crouching next to her. Their heads were bent together and they were murmuring conspiratorially.

"We'll give her another few minutes," Clara was saying. "I know it looks bad, but when she did it the day before yesterday in the office she was as right as rain when she woke up in the hospital. I really don't think she'd want to go to the emergency room again."

Dan glanced over at me. His face was gray and his eyes heavy with concern. When he saw me looking at him, his features lit up as if a ray of sunshine had come out from behind a cloud.

"Jessica!" he exclaimed, hurrying to the bed and taking me in his arms. "What happened?"

"I'm so sorry!" I cried, burying my face in his shoulder. "I should have warned you this might happen again. It's something to do with the lightning strike. I'm so, so sorry."

He held me close as I burst into tears of relief. After a moment I looked up, feeling all wet-faced and runny-nosed.

"I don't suppose you'll want anything to do with me now," I murmured.

"Don't be silly," he said. "You won't get rid of me that easily. I'm hooked, can't you tell?"

I glanced over to where Clara was watching us rather uncomfortably.

"How did you get to be here?" I asked her.

"This man of yours went through your address book," she said, wagging her finger at him in mock disapproval. "He remembered you telling him about your friend Clara, and, fortunately for him, you'd filed me under my Christian name."

"Weren't you at work?"

"I certainly was. But I had my mobile switched on, and I came right over. It was nearly home time anyway." She glanced meaningfully from Dan, then back to me again. "I can see you are making good use of your sick leave, girl."

"Thank you so much for not taking me to the hospital," I said, ignoring her comment and wiping my nose on a tissue. "I'm not usually gone for long."

"You make it sound like you just popped out to the shops," Dan exclaimed. "How often does this happen?"

"It's only happened twice out of the blue like this," I said truthfully.

"This is ridiculous," Dan said, getting to his feet and starting to pace up and down beside the bed. "Is it like some form of epilepsy?"

"It didn't look like any sort of fit to me," Clara said. "She just goes to sleep, and nothing and no one can wake her until she's ready to come back."

"And it never happened before Saturday?"

I shook my head. Saturday. Only five days had passed since then, but it felt like a lifetime ago.

"Do you think I should stay with you tonight?"

I hesitated, not knowing what to say. Much as I was tempted to have Dan stay with me, I knew he would simply be lying next to my comatose body all night long.

"No, I'll be all right," I said at last, shaking my head.

"Hey, you can always come over to my place if she doesn't want you," Clara joked flirtatiously to Dan.

Dan smiled, then glanced at the clock. Clara seemed to get the message and picked up her coat, which was hanging over the back of the chair.

"I'll leave you two lovebirds together then, if you're sure you're all right, Jess?"

"I'm fine now. Thanks so much for coming over, Clara. You did the right thing. I really didn't want to end up in the hospital again."

"Just be careful!" she admonished, waving a long, red-varnished fingernail in my face. "You're supposed to be resting, remember."

As the front door closed behind her, we calmed the dogs and went through to the kitchen, where I turned the kettle on and stood facing Dan anxiously. As far as he was concerned we'd been about to make love when I'd collapsed. I, however, had just experienced what felt like a near rape and had no desire to continue where we'd left off.

He came to stand close to me and, taking my hand in his,

studied my face with a concerned expression. It was almost as though he sensed the change in me and was being considerate and cautious.

"You're not all right, are you?" he said slowly. "Something's different about you."

I pulled my hand away and turned to pour water over the tea bags.

"I need a while to recover after . . . what happened."

"You should see a doctor, Jessica. It can't be normal to fall unconscious like that without reason."

The boiling water missed the mugs and slopped over the counter, splashing my hand. I felt tears prickling not far away again. The memory of Grant's probing fingers made me feel sick. I knew it had been Lauren's body he had been molesting, not mine, but I'd been there, experiencing everything he'd been doing, and I felt violated.

Dan reached out to touch me and I stiffened. He stepped back at once and stood looking at me, confusion in his eyes.

"I'm so sorry, Dan," I whispered. "It's not you."

"Maybe I should go."

I nodded, hardly able to raise my eyes to his face. He turned and called Bessie to him, then he gathered up his jacket and car keys and headed for the front door. He stopped and looked back, his hand resting on the door handle.

"Will you be all right?"

I nodded. "I'll be fine now, honestly."

"Can I see you tomorrow?"

"I'd like that."

He gave me a half smile, and then he was gone.

After clearing up the slopped tea, I took Frankie for another stroll around the block, relishing the chilly freshness of the evening air. As soon as we returned I made us both an early supper and went back to bed with my book. After about fifteen minutes I threw the book down and ran myself a hot bath. It was impossible to concentrate on anything when all I could see in my mind's eye was Grant's red-rimmed eyes, the smell of drink on his breath, and the pressure of his hands on my thighs.

I sat in the hot soapy water, glad to be away not only from Grant but also from the children. Here I had no one to worry about but myself, and at the moment I needed to concentrate on me. I scrubbed at my body until my skin was red and stinging. But I knew it wasn't my body that needed healing, it was my soul.

I wondered if there was somewhere people went to have their soul cleansed, then remembered that was what church was supposed to be for. Church. I lay back in the bubbles, remembering the church my parents had taken me to as a child. It had smelled stale and musty inside, the vicar had been busy and distant, and it had been so cold I'd been able to see my breath when I exhaled. I'd had to sit quietly until my fingers and toes were frozen. As soon as I'd been old enough to make my own decisions I'd refused to go back.

Recalling those Sunday mornings spent in communal prayer and exultation, I wondered if perhaps I should give worship another try. Maybe, I thought desperately, if I prayed hard enough, my soul might be made whole again. The trouble was, I realized ruefully, while I believed in God, I imagined Him as some huge, powerful force, an energy source so great that everything came from it and was a constant part of it. I wasn't sure my views would be welcome in a regular church.

I remembered the vicar of my childhood telling us that Jesus was in every one of us. Okay, I reasoned, blowing a pile of bubbles gently to one side. If Jesus was part of that force, then maybe the vicar had been right. If all living things were part of it, returning to the main collective energy source when they died, to be reborn as the life force of another living being, we were all connected, all part of the same energy, all part of one another and God. But according to some intricate, sublime design or accident that I didn't understand, I was now not only a part of Lauren, I actually was Lauren.

"I don't want to be her!" I shouted defiantly, closing my eyes as I slid down under the bubbles. "Lauren's dead. I don't want to do this anymore!"

Even from under the water I could hear Frankie whining and pawing at the bathroom door. She didn't understand why she wasn't allowed in, and she seemed to have sensed my despairing mood. I felt a deep warmth rush through my body and I pushed myself upward, the water streaming from my hair. This wasn't something I could run away from, I told myself severely. I was made of stronger stuff than this. The flow of time and space might be fluid, but that didn't mean there was no pattern to our earthly lives.

Suppose somewhere in the electrical crackling of the universe, the Almighty had wanted Lauren's children saved from the anguish of losing her? Who was I to question why she had died and why I was there instead? The children needed a mother, and I was beginning to think that maybe, just maybe, I might need them.

Climbing out of the bath, I wrapped myself in a soft towel hot from the radiator and opened the door to Frankie, who bounded in sniffing at my clean legs and whining as the water growled down the drain. I patted her silky head and felt much more positive about things. I didn't feel quite so alone. Not only had I reminded myself that I was part of a much bigger picture, but I could see that on a practical level I had a newfound ally in Karen. Between us, we would handle Grant and I would learn how to be a mother to his children, if not his wife. It seemed to me that this was to be my destiny.

Sleep came more easily to me that evening than I had imagined, and soon I was waking in Lauren's bed to the sound of Elsie vacuuming the carpet outside the bedroom door on Friday morning.

A quick, invigorating shower washed every trace of Grant's touch from Lauren's body. I peeled off the wet bandages and decided to forget the doctor's appointment I'd promised myself because, as Karen had noticed yesterday, the injury seemed to have healed miraculously quickly on its own. All that was left of the burn was a patch of inflamed, angry-looking skin, and there was no sign of blisters or infection.

I dressed and made my way downstairs to find Karen and the children in the kitchen making pancakes.

"Mummy!" Nicole cried, flinging her arms around me and burying her head against the soft material of my skirt. "Can we take down the table thing you bought for Ginny and Blackie's hutch? Can we put them in the shed today?"

"I'm sure we can," I laughed, bending to kiss the top of her shining head.

"Auntie Karen has put up the board you bought yesterday for our pictures," Sophie told me with a smile. "Come and see." I gave her my hand and allowed her to drag me into the playroom, where the large board now hung on the center of the wall.

"Can we put our pictures on it?" she asked, watching me as if she thought I might suddenly change my mind.

"Of course. What happened to the pins we bought? Ah, thank you, Toby. Right, Teddy's picture first, I think!"

I soon had the children's drawings pinned up and immediately the playroom took on a more cheerful air. "Now, let's finish those pancakes," I said, chasing the girls and Toby back to the kitchen.

Teddy was already sitting at the breakfast bar pouring syrup on his pancake. He looked up when I ruffled his hair and grinned lopsidedly at me. I noticed that his ball was on the floor beside him rather than on his lap. It was the first time I'd seen it out of his grasp.

Karen had noticed, too, and we smiled at each other, acknowledging the change.

I was feeling happy and more comfortable being Lauren this morning, despite what had happened last night, and was about to suggest that we set up the new playroom table with the paints when Grant appeared in the kitchen doorway.

"Lauren, would you come here a minute?"

I must have looked frightened, because he was immediately contrite.

"I'm not going to hurt you, for goodness' sake!"

I glanced at Karen and she nodded, so I followed him reluctantly out into the hallway.

"I had a chat with your sister this morning," he began hesitantly. I noticed he was cracking his knuckles nervously, but he saw me watching and thrust his hands into the pockets of his trousers. "She has explained to me what it must be like for you, losing your memory and everything. I don't think I realized how difficult it has been for you. To me, you're just the wife I've been married to for the last ten years. And I've been reluctant to believe you've really lost all your memories . . ."

"You've made that patently clear," I retorted before I could stop myself.

He held up his hand. "But Karen has made me understand that I really am like a complete stranger to you, and that we need to get to know each other all over again."

He stared at one of the paintings on the wall as if he'd never seen it before, then dragged his gaze back to me. "What I'm trying to say is, I'm sorry for the way I've behaved. I drank much too much, which was inexcusable, and I've been clumsy and insensitive. Can you find it in your heart to forgive me? I want you to know that until your memory comes back, or we get to know each other again, I won't be bothering you . . . in that way."

"Well, it's a start," I said woodenly, trying to keep the relief out of my voice.

"I thought, maybe, we could try again. Perhaps we could go somewhere today, just the two of us?"

I reminded myself I had resolved to make a commitment to this family for the sake of the children and decided not to throw the olive branch back in his face. "It would be good for the children if we spent the day as a family," I said carefully.

He swallowed hard, his Adam's apple working up and down.

"That wasn't really what I had in mind. I mean, where could we go that the whole family would be happy with?"

"What about a farm, you know, one that's open to the public? The girls seem to like animals and these places usually have play equipment and things."

Grant paled.

"I'm not sure I can cope with animals, Lauren. They're so dirty and smelly."

"What do you suggest then?"

"I hadn't thought that far. I thought it might be just the two of us."

"I want to go to a farm," Sophie said from the kitchen doorway.

Grant turned to look at his daughter and raised an eyebrow. "Someone's been eavesdropping, I think."

"I want to go where Mummy said," Sophie replied stubbornly.

"I think we should let Daddy decide," I said.

Sophie scowled at her father, turned her back, and flounced away into the kitchen.

"Look, you and Karen can take them to the farm," Grant said wearily, turning away as if it were all too much for him. "I've got work to catch up on."

"I think we should all have that day out," I said, warming to the notion. "It was a good idea, Grant. And it doesn't have to be a farm. Sophie can't always have her own way, and she shouldn't have been eavesdropping anyway."

Grant appeared somewhat surprised and mildly pleased by my support. But then he looked pointedly at his watch. "I said I might pop into the practice again today anyway. The locum isn't working out too well. You and Karen go ahead and take them to the farm."

He leaned over to kiss me, and I forced myself to stand my ground and accept the peck on my cheek despite the feelings of panic I felt at his closeness. He was a good-looking man, and in different circumstances I might have been attracted to him. I quelled a pang of guilt about not having accepted the offer of a day out with him. I knew he had been trying to make amends for his behavior the previous night, but the thought of being alone with him filled me with trepidation.

I leaned against the wall when he had gone, drained by all the emotional upheaval. What he'd done the night before was unforgivable, but then he had thought I was his wife, after all. And he was the father of the children. Closing my eyes, I allowed my mind to touch on the question of how far I would be prepared to go to make this family work. Could Grant ever mean anything to me in the romantic sense? At the moment I certainly didn't think so, but these were early days. Perhaps I had hardly given him a fair chance.

There wasn't much time to dwell on my shortcomings as a wife, however, as Karen was calling from the kitchen and I was sucked swiftly back into the daily whirlwind that had been Lauren's life. At home all I had to think about were Frankie and myself, I thought ruefully, as I wiped syrup off the counters and loaded the dishwasher. As Jessica I cooked simple meals for one, did my washing once a week, and visited my parents once a month. And I went to the cinema or the theater with Clara or clubbing with the rest of our group of friends whenever I wanted, whereas as Lauren I'd have to fit any sort of social life around the children's bath and bedtime story.

I thought again of how intolerant I'd been of some of my friends' domestic problems and groaned. I supposed now I'd be at the mercy of babysitters who might or might not show up. I fell to wondering how Lauren had ever helped out at Grant's dental practice, when one of the children might be ill, or couldn't go to school for any reason. If I stayed here as Lauren indefinitely, and refused to employ a full-time nanny, I didn't see how I could ever leave this house again.

My working hours at Chisleworth & Partners suddenly seemed very tame, I thought half an hour later, as I stepped around Elsie's vacuum cleaner with an armload of dirty laundry and hurried down to load the washing machine. Elsie had changed the children's bedding and piled the dirty sheets and duvet covers onto the clothes I'd gathered off their bedroom floors. At a rough guess I reckoned there were at least five loads of washing to get through today alone.

"Mummy, when are we going to move the hutches to the shed?" Nicole asked as I passed her, dropping socks and vests from the pile as I hurried to the utility room.

"As soon as the washing is in."

"I want to play in the sandbox," Toby whined, jumping up and down. "Can I go out now?"

"Yes, go on, Toby. Close the door behind you."

"I thought we were going to the farm," Sophie reminded me.

"We'll go at lunchtime and get something to eat there," I told her as I shoved sheets into the machine and closed the door.

I looked around as I hurried into the playroom and saw Teddy sitting on one of the beanbags. He was rocking to and fro, talking silently to himself again. I went and crouched down beside him, noticing that he still had pancake syrup on his chin.

"Would you like to draw again, Teddy?"

He gazed up at me as if only just registering my presence, so I stood up and fetched the drawing pencils and paints and put them on the new table.

"Come and draw something," I coaxed. "You did such a lovely picture yesterday. Look, Teddy, I've put it up on the wall."

His gaze wandered to the peg board and stopped at his picture. His eyes widened slightly and I thought I detected a faint smile.

"Come on. We need lots of lovely pictures to make the room look colorful."

Teddy got up and shambled over to the table, then sat down

on one of the blue plastic chairs I'd bought and put his ball on the table next to him. I watched as he picked up a crayon and bent his head over the paper, then I slipped quietly back to the kitchen to find Nicole standing impatiently with her hands on her hips.

"Can we go and move the hutch now, Mummy?"

I groaned. I'd thought Stephen's demands on my time at Chisleworth & Partners could be exhausting, but trying to balance the needs of this family was like organizing a military operation. Putting things into perspective, however, I realized that although I felt I was being run ragged, each child was only requiring a reasonable amount of my time. It was when everyone's needs had to be considered simultaneously, while I was also planning ahead for the next meal, the next event, the next day, that I felt completely overwhelmed.

I took a deep breath and looked out the window at the thin autumn sunshine. You can do this, I told myself firmly as I hurried off to find a jacket. Returning a moment later, I squared my shoulders and gave a bright smile. "Okay, Nicole, let's go."

Karen pulled on a shaggy cream and gray jacket above a black ankle-length skirt that had metal rings hanging on it and clumpy Doc Martens–style boots. She lifted the other end of the new wooden folding table and followed us outside.

"There were two phone calls while you were asleep," she informed me as we walked down the garden behind Nicole, who was jumping around like an excited colt. "One was from a woman reminding you that Sophie is supposed to be sleeping over at her daughter's house this evening."

"Did you take a name and directions?" I asked anxiously over my shoulder.

She nodded. "Yes, it sounded easy enough, and Sophie seems happy to go."

I could hear the hesitation in her voice and glanced around at her anxiously.

"And the other one?"

"Was from a man. He wouldn't give his name. He just asked if you were okay, and when I told him you were recovering, but asleep, he hung up."

I grimaced.

"Sounds like it might be the man from the park."

She nodded again. "That's what I thought."

We'd arrived at the gap in the conifers, and Karen gasped, staring round her. "I didn't know this section of the garden existed! It's almost as big as the back lawn."

I grinned as I let the table down. "I know. Wonderful, isn't it?"

"Look at my digger, Auntie Karen," Toby called. "I'm making roads and a tunnel."

I left Karen bending over the sandbox and went to the toolshed. I was about to open the door when it opened of its own accord and an elderly man came out with a rake in his gnarled hands.

"Mornin', Mrs. Richardson," he said. "Looks like someone's been having fun and games down here."

"The children needed something to do," I said with a smile. "I hope you don't mind if you have to share the toolshed with the rabbit hutch. It's getting rather cold at night to keep them outside."

"It's your shed, missus," he said, walking off through the conifers.

The next two hours passed in a blur of hutch moving, pegging washing on the clothesline, reloading the machine, and dispensing drinks and cookies to the children and coffee for Karen, myself, and Jim. Teddy spilled some of the newly purchased children's paint on the playroom floor and went into a fit of hysteria, apparently thinking he was going to be smacked, but I cleaned it all up and assured him that accidents were bound to happen.

At twelve o'clock, despite the fact that my shoulder was beginning to feel quite sore again, we all bundled into the car and Karen and the children guided me on the twenty-minute journey to an open farm. Once there, we started our visit by trooping into the old barn restaurant for filled jacket potatoes and cola drinks. The afternoon passed in a pleasant haze of feeding animals with paper bags full of sheep nuts, petting the small animals, watching the children play on the hay bales and pushing Teddy endlessly on the swing in the children's playground.

"Do you know, Karen," I commented as I swung Teddy back and forth, being careful to use only my good right arm," I think we ought to have a swing at home. I mentioned it to Sophie when I first saw the size of the back garden. Teddy obviously loves it, and if we get one of those big contraptions with more than one swing and a glider thing, they won't have to fight for a turn."

Karen turned to check on where the other children had gotten to, and seeing they were out of earshot, she said quietly, "You know, sis, I can understand that your memory was wiped by that lightning strike, but the strange thing is that your whole personality seems to have changed. All these years and you wouldn't let them have a swing in the garden, and now you're suggesting it like it's the most natural thing in the world. I'm not criticizing, believe me. I like the new you. But, I mean, didn't you say the hospital had referred you for some therapy? Don't you think you should go and talk to someone? They can't have intended for you to just walk out of there so completely changed, with no backup or anything."

"Yeah, I've got that appointment for next week," I replied, shoving the swing high into the air with Teddy hanging on tightly. "I'm to talk to someone in the psychiatric clinic. I've got the details somewhere." I took a deep breath and kept up the rhythmic pushing of the swing. "The thing is, I don't want to go. I'm happy as I am, Karen, and I think the children are happy, too."

"Last night," Karen continued in a low voice, "when Grant was trying . . . you know. You told him you weren't Lauren. I heard you."

"I meant I can't remember being Lauren," I said, keeping my eyes firmly on the back of Teddy's Wellington boots as they came and went.

"What I don't understand," she went on, "is why you have changed so dramatically. Just because you lost your memories of who you were before, it doesn't mean you're not actually still the person you were before. I mean, how come you suddenly don't mind handling animals? You hated them before, Lauren. What has changed that? And what about your newfound attentiveness to the children? I don't mean to be unkind, but the Lauren I grew up with was selfish and vain. As long as she looked good and did what she wanted when she wanted, she was happy. How can you have altered so much?"

I fell silent, not knowing what to say. I'd been right in thinking it was going to be difficult keeping the truth from Karen. Her sister was dead. I was not Lauren. Perhaps I should sound her out—maybe try to prepare her a little for the eventual revelation that I was not her sister.

"Do you believe that everyone has a soul?" I asked her tentatively as Teddy swung to and fro in front of us. I was thinking of what she'd said about her mother telling her that everyone's soul was of equal importance, and of her belief in reincarnation and karma.

Karen nodded, frowning.

"And do you think our souls make us the kind of people we are?"

I glanced sideways and saw her studying me.

"Is it because you nearly died?" she asked softly. "Did you have some kind of out-of-body experience?"

I nodded, surprised how easily she was following to the place I was leading her.

"I've heard it can happen to people when they're near death," she continued in hushed tones. "Did your life flash in front of you or something? Did you realize the error of your ways and what your family meant to you?"

"It wasn't exactly like that," I said carefully, not looking at her. "The thing is . . ."

I stopped, not knowing how to put it. I couldn't very well blurt out, "Well, the thing is, I think my soul was divided into two when I was struck by the lightning." I stared at Teddy's back for a long moment, then shrugged.

"Something did happen before I was brought back by the doctors. I think the lightning strike caused something drastic to happen to me."

"What are you saying?"

"I'm not sure, Karen. But I think that when I suffered the heart failure, I did actually die."

I glanced sideways to see that Karen's mouth had dropped open.

"So you did have an out-of-body experience then? Can you remember being 'dead,' is that it?"

I decided to take the plunge and tell her the truth as far as I knew. "What if I told you two people were struck by the lightning, in two different places, and at exactly the same time?"

"Two?" I could see her mind churning, trying to work out what I was getting at. "Who was the other one?"

"A twenty-eight-year-old woman from Epsom, called Jessica Taylor."

"And . . . ?"

"What if both victims had what you call 'out-of-body experiences' at the same time? And suppose one of them actually died?"

Karen's face had paled and she dropped her voice so Teddy wouldn't be able to catch her words.

"You're frightening me, Lauren! What are you getting at?"

"What if the one who died shouldn't have? Suppose for a moment she was still needed too much by her family for them to lose her like that?"

Karen put her hand over her mouth, her eyes wide. "You're not saying the soul of one woman went into the body of the other?"

I stopped pushing the swing and turned to face her. "I'm saying exactly that. Only Jessica Taylor wasn't intended to die, either. In fact her injuries were far less severe than Lauren's."

"You're talking about Lauren as if you're not her again," Karen wailed. "I knew you should have seen someone in the psychiatric clinic earlier than next bloody week! It's ridiculous the way they've just let you out of hospital like this with no immediate support!"

I grabbed her wrist and stared into her eyes. "Look at me, Karen. I'm not Lauren. Look into my eyes. Can you see Lauren there?"

I watched as her eyes gazed into mine, searching for something familiar. I saw her own eyes widen with a flicker of fear and she pulled away from my grasp.

I plowed ahead. "Lauren died. But for whatever reason, some of Jessica's life force—my life force—went into her."

"I'm not listening to this," Karen said, pulling Teddy from the swing and looking around for the others.

I touched her beseechingly on the arm and she stopped and stared at me.

"You're not well," she said.

"I am well," I replied firmly. "In fact my injuries are healing incredibly quickly. You said yourself how well the burns were looking."

"That's not what I meant and you know it."

"Humor me," I said, with the beginnings of a hopeful smile.

Karen's expression relaxed and she looked quizzically into my face.

"You're asking a hell of a lot, little sister."

chapter ten

We walked slowly along beside the sheep field with Teddy swinging his feet between us. The other children were still playing in the play area but we could see them from where we were.

"Let me get this straight," Karen whispered after a while. "You're saying your soul's in the wrong body?"

I nodded.

"Shit, Lauren! They'll cart you off to the funny farm if you come out with this sort of claptrap at the hospital!" Karen exclaimed. "Maybe it's just as well you haven't been to see the shrink. They'd tie you to the couch and write a bloody thesis on you."

"That's why I didn't say anything to the doctors."

"So you're telling me you've got this other woman's life force keeping you here with us?"

"Yes—only, as I was trying to tell you, Jessica Taylor isn't dead, either. I'm both of them, Karen."

Karen stared at me in silence for what seemed like several minutes, then shrugged.

"That must be a bit complicated."

I stopped walking and faced her. "You don't believe me."

Karen sank down onto a nearby bench and continued to stare at me.

"What the bloody hell do you expect? It's all so far-fetched, so incredible. And anyway, if I believed you it would mean that my sister is dead."

"I'm so sorry, Karen," I whispered. "I believe that Lauren died when the lightning bolt hit her. I understand from what the doctors said that medically speaking her injuries would have killed her. I was struck in the same instant, only time has shifted slightly and both bodies have survived simultaneously."

"Now I know you're joking."

"I wish I was."

The silence hung in the air between us, and Karen edged slightly away from me.

"We had our differences, Lauren and I," she said at last. "But she was still my sister. I loved her. I don't want her to be dead."

"Believe me, I don't want her to be dead. I want to be who I was before."

I gazed at the panoramic views of the countryside rolling away on either side of us, at the cows, sheep, and horses in their fields; I heard the sound of laughter from children playing on the old tractors and hay bales, and realized that what I had said wasn't entirely true. I enjoyed being Lauren some of the time. It made parts of Jessica's life seem empty and meaningless.

For a moment I wondered why I chose to spend the best part of my week closeted in that dingy solicitors' office. I knew I wanted to get those extra qualifications; to strive for an improvement in how people perceived me and also in my standard of living, but without someone to share it with—someone to love—what was the point? My relationship with Stephen hadn't worked out, and no one since had come close to stirring my heart—not until Dan, anyway, and the prospect of trying to form a new relationship with everything that was going on seemed so terribly daunting.

Shading my eyes with my hand, I glanced down at Teddy's tousled head, then stared back toward the play area and felt a lump rise in my throat. The children loved their mother so fiercely, so unconditionally. What must it be like to love and be loved like that? I envied Lauren that joy, and the prospect of Karen taking away that gift left me unaccountably desolate.

"What are you going to do?" I asked her anxiously. "Will you tell anyone?"

"Oh yeah. That would go down well on my CV," she muttered. "Miss Harper, age thirty-seven. Committed for believing her sister's dead body is being possessed by another soul. I can see it now." She turned toward me, a wan smile on her face.

"You do believe me then?"

"Let's just say I believe you believe it, and therefore I'll go along with it. For now."

"I want you to carry on being my sister," I told her earnestly, hugely relieved that she was at least keeping an open mind. "I've never had a sister, and I really like you. I like the children, too," I added, looking down at Teddy, who was staring at a sheep that had come up to the fence for food.

"It's bloody weird all the same," Karen commented, handing Teddy a paper bag full of sheep nuts.

"I didn't believe it myself to begin with," I told her. "But here I am."

I watched as the sheep snatched at the bag through the wire fence and Teddy drew back in alarm. Karen bent to retrieve the spilled animal food.

"Have you ever had a dream that seemed so real that when you woke up you couldn't believe it wasn't your actual life?" I asked as she straightened up. "It's been like that for me every day since Saturday. Every time Jessica goes to sleep, I wake up as Lauren. When Lauren's body needs rest, I go back to being Jessica."

"Bloody hell."

"I want to swing more," Teddy announced suddenly.

"Okay, let's go back to the play area."

We walked back to where Toby was sitting on an ancient farm tractor. The girls had disappeared inside a play tunnel. Teddy stuffed his ball under his sweatshirt so he had his hands free to hold on and pulled himself onto the only free swing.

"You like the swing, don't you, Teddy?" I asked as I commenced pushing. "I was just saying to Auntie Karen that we should have one at home. Then you can swing while Toby digs in the sandbox. Would you like that?"

He nodded solemnly. "But Mummy won't let me," he said in his slow, ponderous voice. "She'll make you take it away."

"What do you mean, Teddy?" Karen asked quickly. "If Mummy says you can have one, she won't take it away, will she?"

"Not this mummy," Teddy said, twisting on the seat so he could look at me."The other mummy will take it away when she comes back."

Karen remained silent as I pushed Teddy back and forth. I didn't know what she was thinking, but I decided not to say anything. There wasn't really very much I could say, in the circumstances.

After a minute or two I looked at my watch. "I suppose we'd better round up Toby and the girls," I said, giving Teddy one last big push. "We've still got to go and get Sophie packed up for her sleepover."

Karen remained quiet and aloof in the car on the way home, and I didn't feel I should press her. I wasn't sure if she was going to keep this thing a secret, or what would happen to me if she decided to tell someone. It wasn't as if I could pack my bags and go back to being Jessica. I was here, and it seemed I had no choice in the matter whatsoever.

The children were hungry again by the time we arrived home, and I put a large pan of pasta to simmer on the stove. Meanwhile, I brought in the washing from the line, sent the girls down the garden to feed their pets, and collected up their discarded straw-filled coats and boots from the car.

Karen volunteered to help Sophie pack up her few bits and pieces and her sleeping bag and drop her off at the friend's house. They went off together while I finished preparing the meal. I felt that Karen probably needed time to be alone. After all, she'd just been told that her only sister had died, not to mention the rest of it.

Half an hour later she came back looking slightly better. I noticed some of the color had returned to her cheeks. She walked into the kitchen, where I was dishing pasta onto plates, and gave me a weak half smile.

"I've been talking to Sophie," she said hesitantly as she helped Teddy up onto his stool. "She's been chattering away to me about how delighted she is that you've allowed them to have pets at last. She says . . . she thinks you love her more . . . since the accident."

She stopped talking as a harsh sob erupted from her throat. The children stopped sucking pasta into their mouths and stared at her, their eyes wide and round.

"I'm sorry," she said, holding a hand over her face and rushing out of the kitchen.

"I don't think Auntie Karen is feeling very well," I said as calmly as I could to the children. "Carry on with your dinner while I see if she's all right."

I found Karen sitting on the wide bottom stair, leaning her head weakly against the wall, a tissue clasped to her mouth.

"I just can't believe it," she sobbed as I squeezed onto the stair next to her and put an arm around her shaking shoulders. "This is all so ridiculous! But I knew something was strange about you from the minute I walked into the house and found you cooking bloody oven fries." She sniffed and blew her nose loudly. "What Teddy said at the farm about the 'other Mummy,' and what Sophie said today . . . it's frightening, Lauren. Or should I say Jessica?" She took a deep breath and gazed at me through red-rimmed lids. "Lauren always put herself first, but she did love the children in her own way."

"I'm sure she did," I murmured. "Everyone has their own way of doing things. Maybe I shouldn't have tried to change so much so quickly. It makes it seem as if I disapproved of the way she did things, but that isn't true. I haven't judged her, Karen. I'm simply doing the best I can in the situation I've landed in."

"I know, I can see that," Karen said, smiling through her tears. "And you've done a good job. The children are happier than I've ever seen them. They never liked having a succession of nannies. I don't think Lauren was cut out to be a mother of four."

"Grant said something about the twins not being his idea. Is it true?"

"Sophie and Nicole were planned babies," Karen explained, dabbing her eyes as she spoke. "Lauren was delighted to have the two girls—she never liked boys. She wanted to have the requisite two children, dress them up, and show them off. The girls were very well behaved when they were tiny. But then she got pregnant again. It wasn't planned, and she wanted to end the pregnancy. Grant certainly wanted her to terminate it. She was booked into the clinic and everything, but then she got cold feet. I don't know if you realize, but Lauren is . . . was, very religious. The family attends church every Sunday. Someone there put pressure on her to keep the baby. So Lauren decided to go ahead with the pregnancy, even though she didn't want another baby, and then further scans revealed that she was carrying two babies, not one, and they were both boys. It was too late to terminate the pregnancy by then."

"Poor Lauren," I said, thinking that she must have been feeling as much out of her depth then as I had done when I'd first come to in the hospital and discovered I was to be responsible for her children. The boys were a particular handful, especially for someone with little tolerance for small children. If she hadn't been a particularly maternal person, she must have been as daunted by the prospect of them as I was. In the short time I'd been living in her footsteps, I could see from her glamorous clothes, her stylish possessions, and the personal glimpses I'd had into her life that she was a real girly girl. I could quite see that the idea of boys—and two of them at once—had very possibly terrified her.

I thought of Grant and his knowledge of his wife's shortcomings. What had he made of her deciding to keep the twins? I wondered. It must have been a terribly difficult decision for them to make.

"Grant seems quite besotted with her," I said, "and it must have been hard to see his wife going ahead with something he knew she didn't want and probably couldn't cope with."

"And he was right, as it turned out. I think she felt out of her depth when the boys were born," Karen continued. "And when it was discovered that Teddy was brain-damaged, it was as if she stopped trying to be a good mother. She hired the first in a succession of nannies, refused to allow any sign of the children to interrupt her precious house or beautifully manicured garden, and escaped with her friends at every opportunity. And I don't mean just for the day. She had long weekends and even weeks away with her girlfriends, leaving the nanny and Grant at home to cope with the children."

"Why did Grant allow her to go off so much?"

"I told you, he's a weak man. He adored Lauren and I think that deep down he believed he wasn't good enough for her. He wanted to control her, but she was growing up, growing away from him. I think he let her go off to keep her happy, but the fact that she wanted to leave him so often made him feel even more inadequate. Then he began to suspect she was having an affair."

"Did he actually tell you that?"

"This morning, when I was giving him a piece of my mind for what he tried to do last night, he confessed he'd thought for a while that she might be seeing someone else." She looked at me and laughed tearfully. "I can't believe I'm talking to you about my sister in the third person. You look exactly like her. This is so unreal!"

We were still sitting huddled together when Nicole poked her head around the kitchen door.

"Teddy has tipped his pasta into his lap," she told us. "Toby is laughing at him, and Teddy's getting cross."

We rose to our feet in unison and headed toward the kitchen, the conversation over.

An hour and a half later, when the children were in bed after the usual routine of bathing, toothbrushing, and storytelling, Karen and I went into the lounge together to continue the conversation. However, before either of us could broach the subject that was uppermost in our minds, we heard Grant's car turning into the drive, and I stood up again, drawing the curtains and turning on the lights.

He stuck his head through the lounge door a few minutes later, and I hung back, waiting to see what kind of mood he was in. He flicked a nervous glance in my direction and I wondered if he was doing the same thing with me. Deciding to be magnanimous, I went to him, feeling sorry for him after what Karen had told me about Lauren's careless treatment of him, I asked how his day had been.

"My nurse phoned a couple of days ago to tell me that the locum dentist wasn't much good," he said, crossing to the sideboard and pouring himself a whiskey. "She was right. I've had patients coming back today complaining of tooth pain and loose crowns; it's been a complete nightmare."

"I'm sorry. Would you like something to eat? I've made a pasta dish."

He looked at me over the rim of his glass and nodded. "Yes, I am rather hungry. Thank you, Lauren."

He was no longer treating me with casual familiarity, but rather with the formality of one talking to a guest. Presuming Karen's chat with him in the early hours must have done some good, I felt a wave of relief wash over me. If he was prepared to behave properly, then I would find a little charity in my heart for this man, who must be feeling almost as confused by the change in his wife as I was in myself.

He followed me to the kitchen, which Karen and I had cleared up after the meal, and settled himself at the breakfast bar while I placed a dish of food in front of him.

"This looks good," he said, taking a mouthful and chewing thoughtfully.

"Thank you. The children liked it, too."

"I can't get used to this new you," he said, washing down a mouthful of food with the remains of his whisky. "You seem very attentive toward the children."

"I suppose after my brush with death I feel I should make the most of them," I said evasively. "You never know what's around the corner."

"No indeed," he said, considering me closely. "The thing is, though, as I said this morning, I was hoping it might stretch as far as you and me. I know you wanted to include the children today, but would you like to come out with me this evening, just the two of us? Karen would babysit if we asked her, I'm sure."

I wondered if my newfound forgiveness would stretch as far as spending some time with him and reckoned I could maybe give him a chance to redeem himself. I glanced at the kitchen clock. It was eight o'clock. Frankie needed to be let out soon. Tonight was out of the question.

"I'm really tired, Grant," I said, watching his face fall. "But as tomorrow is Saturday, I could have a long nap and then maybe we could go out somewhere later?"

Grant beamed at me, and I felt a pang of guilt about how easily I could please him. I suspected that all he wanted was a partner who showed she cared enough to spend time with him; someone to make his life easier and make him happy.

"Where would you like to go?"

"I don't know. What do you like doing?"

He held out his hand and I had no option but to take it. It was cool, dry, and steady, but there was no electric current running between our connected fingers, as there had been with Dan.

"This is very strange, Lauren, trying to remember you don't know anything about me. How about the cinema. Would you like to see a film?"

"I don't really mind."

"What about a meal? We could try that new Italian place in the village?"

"Yes," I said. "I suppose we could."

I went up to bed shortly after, making sure I locked the bedroom door before climbing in between the clean sheets that Elsie had put on that morning. Despite the early hour I was genuinely exhausted. Looking after four children was certainly no easy thing.

It seemed no time before I was opening my eyes and sitting up in bed as Jessica. Frankie was delighted to see me up, and ran in circles around me barking as I opened the front door, letting in a blast of cold air while she shot out into the garden to sniff around and do her business.

I brought in my pint of semiskimmed milk, smiling as I thought of the five pints a day that was ordered in the Richardson household. Even my refrigerator suddenly looked tiny compared to the large American model in Lauren's home, which dispensed ice cubes at the touch of a button and ice-cold water from a filter.

Calling Frankie back indoors, I put the kettle on while looking through the meager pile of mail. There was an advertisement for cheap pizzas; two letters from charities I had already supported this month; and a hand-addressed envelope I recognized immediately as being in Mum's writing.

Tearing open the envelope, I found a get-well card inside with a note from Mum saying she hoped I was keeping warm and eating properly. We had never been a particularly close family, but her long-distance fussing was a way of making me feel she cared. I wondered vaguely whether if she knew I was the mother of four children she'd still treat me like a child myself.

The cupboard was looking particularly bare, and I made a mental note that I must go shopping for supplies. Just because I was Jessica only half the time didn't mean I should starve myself. Each of the bodies I was occupying needed feeding and grooming properly in the time I was in them, because they were both having to live simultaneously full and active lives. It was only my consciousness they were sharing between them. It would be all too easy to neglect one or the other of my selves because I had only just eaten or bathed in my other life. I just hoped that the normal physical prompts of a rumbling stomach or the unclean feeling of needing to bathe or brush my teeth would override any mental perception that those tasks had recently been performed and therefore didn't need doing again.

I breakfasted on muesli and part of my pint of milk, fed Frankie, and watered my indoor plants. As I was pulling on a pair of comfy jeans, I wondered how I could get some of my wardrobe to Lauren. I knew that her choice in clothes was not helping me to settle into her role. I needed casual, comfortable clothing for her at least some of the time. I reckoned she and I were similar in size, because although she was older than me and had had four children, she'd made much more effort to keep in shape. If I was being totally honest with myself, I knew I wanted the comfort of having some of my own possessions in that other life, and I also wanted an excuse to try a little experiment.

After rummaging in one of the kitchen drawers, I came up with the spare front-door key to my flat. Then, taking some Blu-Tack, I went outside and attached the key to the back of the rain gutter in the paved courtyard. When I'd completed the task to my satisfaction, happy that no one would come across it by mistake and that it couldn't fall off, I went and fetched Frankie's lead and took her for a long walk.

On the way home I bought some baguettes, cold meats, and salad from the local shop, then sat in my favorite chair and tried to read my book. Frankie was dozing by my feet, and the sound of her even breathing and the ticking of the sitting room clock echoed loudly in the quiet of the room. I was enjoying the lack of activity and quiet afforded by my single life and wondered if Lauren ever found the time to read.

I jumped when the doorbell rang, dropping the book on Frankie's head as she scrambled to her feet and raced to the front door. Following more slowly, I tried to quell my racing heart. I stood inside the door, smoothing my jeans down my thighs and running trembling fingers through my hair, before plucking up the courage to open it.

Dan stood there, smiling hesitantly as if not sure of his welcome. I smiled widely in return, not to put him at his ease but because I couldn't help myself.

"Am I forgiven?" I asked as he stepped over the threshold and took me into his arms.

He nuzzled my neck and breathed deeply as if drowning in the scent of my skin. I reached out a foot and kicked the door closed as we tumbled toward the couch, Frankie bounding madly beside us. Everything about Dan excited me. I loved the way his hand held mine while we made love, the smell of the shampoo in his hair, the look in his eyes as he called out my name. My earlier uncertainties about the wisdom of Jessica having a relationship while everything else was going on were soon soothed away by Dan, and I knew without a doubt that I had fallen head over heels in love with him.

Later, when we were eating the filled baguettes and drinking hot sweet tea to refuel our exhausted and tingling bodies, he asked me how I was feeling.

"Right now, I feel more alive than I've ever felt in my life," I replied, still unable to stop smiling when I looked at him.

"I meant, have you had any more of those turns?" he said, returning my smile with a grin.

I contemplated telling him the truth. If I loved this man, perhaps I should trust him. But how could he be expected to believe such a story? Surely he'd simply put me down as a weirdo and keep his distance. What normal man in his right mind would want to continue a relationship with a woman who claimed to have been split apart by lightning and to be currently inhabiting two different bodies at almost the same time? Not to mention the small matter of a time-shift being involved.

"No."

"Let's hope yesterday was an end to them," he said, licking mayonnaise off my fingertips.

I thought of Teddy and his nightmares and grimaced. Somehow I had the feeling that the "turns" might not yet be completely gone.

"I was wondering," he said, staring searchingly into my face with his penetratingly blue eyes, "if you'd like to come back to my place to meet my father? The old boy has sussed something major is happening in my life and has been asking me questions."

"I'd like that," I told him. "When did you have in mind?"

"What about this evening?"

I thought of the Saturday-morning late sleep. Karen would be there to see to Teddy and the other children and Grant would be around to collect Sophie from her sleepover. I needn't surface until midmorning if necessary, which meant I could stay up as late as eleven o'clock if I wanted.

"That sounds great."

We drove to a beauty spot in the afternoon and walked hand in hand in the sunshine with Frankie at our heels. Before last weekend's thunderstorm it had been a wet but sunny summer, and now the trees were turning glorious shades of red, amber, and gold. We wandered through a beech wood, the ground carpeted in orange, the gray of the beech trunks twisting and turning upward through the amber canopy and into the clear blue sky.

"It's hard to believe we're in late October," I murmured as I scuffed through the fallen leaves with my boots.

"Clocks go back on Sunday."

"Oh no!"

Dan gave me a sharp look. "What's so bad about that?"

I thought of trying to calculate what time I'd need to go to bed on Saturday evening to be up at the right time on Sunday for the children with the added complication of an hour's time change.

"Nothing really, it always throws me off, that's all. I don't know why."

"You are a strange person sometimes, Jessica Taylor," he said, squeezing my hand. "But I wouldn't want you any other way."

I squeezed his back, but the joy had gone out of my day. I didn't want to dwell too much on my other life when I was with Dan. It seemed dishonest somehow, almost as if I were cheating on him. I was lying, after all; I had another life he didn't know about, and although this was my immediate reality, I couldn't forget about Grant and the children completely.

"Bessie would have enjoyed this walk," I said, kicking at a couple of fallen beechnuts still encased in their brown shells. "Why didn't you bring her along?"

"Dad gets lonely if I take her out with me every day. Yesterday he went to the Day Center, but today he would have been on his own all day. He gets depressed if he's alone for too long."

"How old is your father?"

"He'll be seventy-five next week."

"You were a late baby," I commented, doing the sums in my head.

"He married four times," Dan explained. "I have numerous half sisters and brothers scattered across England and Ireland. I'm his youngest child."

"What about your mother? Did he leave her?"

"You could say she left us. She died of cancer when I was only four. Dad left a lot of angry family behind in Ireland when he married my mother, a sweet young English girl from Surrey. Mum's family didn't think much of Dad, either, so there was no family to park me with when she died. Dad stayed here and brought me up by himself."

I thought of Toby and Teddy and how awful it was for a four-year-old to lose his mother.

"I'm sorry, Dan."

"Don't be. Dad and I have always gotten by just fine."

We were almost back to the car when Dan pulled me to him

and kissed me hard on the mouth. "Don't let Dad put you off by telling you what a Jack the Lad I've been in the past. I swear there's never been anyone like you, Jessica."

We drove straight to Dan's house, which wasn't far outside Epsom, probably only fifteen or so minutes from my own flat. The house was a typical mock-Tudor residence in a quiet residential road full of three-bedroom properties.

Dan pulled his car up in the gravel driveway and unlocked the front door, calling to his father as he did so. "Dad! I'm home. I've brought someone to meet you."

Bessie bounded out of the front room, nearly bowling me over in her excitement, and I was glad we'd left Frankie in the car, giving Bessie a chance to calm down.

"I'm in here, lad," came a broad Irish accent from the front room. "Did you say you've brought someone with you now?"

I followed Dan into the front room to find an elderly man ensconced in a large armchair watching the television. His rheumy eyes lit up when he saw me, and he tried to get to his feet.

"Please, don't get up, Mr. Brennan," I said hurriedly. I went toward him, holding out my hand. "I'm Jessica Taylor."

"So you're the bit o' stuff that's kept my lad from his work," he said, his eyes twinkling at me from under bushy gray eyebrows. "The business won't run itself, but I can see why Dan might want it to try."

He looked up to where Dan was hovering in the doorway. "Did you bring my beer?"

"I'll fetch it later, Dad. I thought we might have a cup of tea. Jessica doesn't drink."

"The saints preserve us! You've chosen a wee lass that doesn't like the hard stuff? What were you thinking of, boy? She'll have you on the wagon before you can say 'Jack Daniel's.' "

"I've no objection to anyone else having a drink," I told him firmly. "I'm just trying to keep a clear head at the moment."

"Is it a control freak you are, not liking to be under the influence?"

I contemplated this remark, wondering if it might not be rather too near the truth.

"I'll go and put the kettle on," Dan muttered, and he escaped into the kitchen, where I could hear him clattering about with the tea-making things.

The old man turned to me and grinned. "You've got the boy all in a dither and no mistake, lass. I hope you'll let him down gently when the time comes."

"I hope I won't have to let him down at all, Mr. Brennan," I said. "And if he's anything like his father I'm sure he can look after himself."

The old man stared at me for a moment then started to laugh. "You can call me Pat, lassie. To be sure, I think you and I might get along just fine."

By the time Dan returned, balancing three mugs, I was sitting on the couch and Pat and I were getting along like old friends. Bessie had come to sit by my feet, and we must have painted a picture of sheer amicability because Dan grinned happily when he saw us and took the seat at my side.

"Pat has been telling me how you're a magnet to women," I said with a look of mock disapproval.

"Dad, I told you not to tell stories," Dan said, placing a mug in his father's hand and handing another to me. "You know I haven't had a serious girlfriend in two years."

"That's not for the want of them throwing themselves at your feet, now," Pat said. "It's just you didn't fancy picking any of them up."

"I was waiting for the right one," Dan said, giving me a sideways look.

"As long as she doesn't end up breaking your heart, lad," Pat said, returning his attention to the television set.

While the old man watched the TV, Dan gave me a guided tour of the house. Two of the upstairs rooms were obviously the bedrooms of Dan and his father, but Dan had turned the third one into an office. There was a black-and-white photograph of a pretty young woman in a silver frame on Dan's desk.

"Is that your mother?"

"Yes. Dad doesn't like to be reminded of her, so I keep it in here."

"Why doesn't he want to remember her? I thought he loved her."

"It was a terrible situation for all of us," Dan said, gazing sadly at the picture of his lost mother. "She had a tumor in her brain. For the last six months of her life she didn't know who or where she was. Some days she'd talk wildly about being in the wrong body and at other times she'd sit silently for hours at a time. Dad can't bear to remember her like that, so he tries not to remember her at all."

"That's awful, Dan. I'm so sorry."

I stared at the picture above Dan's desk with a sinking heart. Now I knew I would never be able to tell Dan about my situation. If I tried to tell him what was happening to me he'd assume I was going mad, like his mother. My secret would have to stay hidden from him forever if I wanted Dan to be a part of my life.

chapter eleven

For me, the pleasure had gone out of the evening after Dan's revelation about his mother. We ordered takeout and rented a DVD. Dan didn't want to leave Pat on his own for the evening and I could see that he was devoted to his father. The three of us ate together in the front room while Patrick made derisive comments about our choice of film.

My thoughts were in turmoil as I tried to concentrate on the screen. After my reluctance to make a commitment in my previous relationship with Stephen, or with anyone since, it seemed so unfair that now I wanted to throw myself body and soul into this relationship with Dan but there were so many obstacles stacking up against us. Just when I'd decided to trust Dan with my secret, the knowledge of his mother's illness loomed between us like an impossible stumbling block.

It seemed incongruous that it was the parent who was no longer alive who presented the biggest hurdle, I thought, as my eyes stared unseeingly at the TV screen. Patrick himself wasn't a problem. Although he was dependent on his son, he seemed to like me and I him, and I felt we could get along reasonably comfortably together. I chewed on the rather rubbery chicken madras, my eyes still fixed on the screen, and hoped that nothing would happen in the early hours of the Richardson household that might endanger this fragile new relationship. If I collapsed in front of Patrick he would probably immediately think of what had happened with his own young wife, and my copybook would be well and truly blotted.

At a quarter to eleven the film finished and I asked Dan to take me home. He'd obviously sensed the change in my demeanor, because he sat quietly in the car, hardly speaking unless I spoke first.

When he drew the Shogun up in the space outside my flat, I had a favor to ask him, but wasn't sure how to broach the subject when we had been so distant with each other on the way home.

I turned to face him in the dark interior of the car. "I was wondering," I started hesitantly, "if you would take Frankie home for the night. I don't feel brilliant and I wouldn't like her to be neglected in the morning if I have to stay in bed."

Dan was immediately contrite. "Why didn't you say you weren't well? I . . . I thought you didn't like my father, or the food, or the film . . ."

"Your father's great, Dan, a real character. It's just I'm still not myself after what happened on Saturday, that's all. It took a lot out of me and I seem to get tired very easily. I've got a bit of a headache."

"Of course I'll take Frankie." He leaned over and kissed me. "Are you sure you'll be all right on your own? You're not still having those turns, are you?"

"No, I'll be fine. I'm going to have a very long sleep and I'm sure I'll be much better in the morning."

I watched as Dan nosed the car out of the turnaround, Frankie's whiskery face peering back at me forlornly from the rear seat. As soon as they were out of sight I rummaged in my bag for my house keys and walked the short distance in the darkness across the grass, down the steps, and into my courtyard. Before unlocking the door, I went to the gutter and checked for the spare key. It was exactly where I'd left it. Without further ado, I opened the door and walked into the silence of my empty flat.

I awoke to pandemonium. Someone was banging on my bedroom door and I could hear shrieking coming from the garden below my window. Bounding out of bed, I unlocked the door to find Toby standing on the landing jumping up and down excitedly.

"Mummy, Blackie and Ginny are loose in the garden! Nicole went to feed them 'cos Sophie was still at the sleepover and they fell out of the hutch. The shed door was open and they ran away!"

"Is someone trying to catch them?"

"Auntie Karen is running around but she's huffing and puffing. She can't get them."

I went into the dressing room and pulled on a pair of jersey trousers and an angora sweater, then followed Toby downstairs and out into the garden. Karen was trying to shoo the rabbit into a corner by the shed, but every time she thought she had it cornered it slipped from her grasp and bolted away down the garden.

Grant must have fetched Sophie home during the morning, because she was back now and tearing around after her pet. Meanwhile, Nicole was lying on the grass near the shed, peering into the gap underneath and calling Ginny loudly, with rising hysteria in her voice.

"Having fun?" I asked Karen as she threw her hands up in despair.

"You've decided to join us then," she panted sarcastically, pushing a damp spike of her brown hair from her forehead.

I grinned. "I'll tell you what. Sophie can head Blackie off and send her back this way, then you and I can corner her between us."

Sophie ran behind the frightened rabbit and shooed her toward us. I told Karen to stay very still. I crouched down, and as soon as Blackie was within reach I made a dive for her, scooping her up in my arms. I held her for a moment until her heart had stopped pounding wildly beneath her soft fur, then handed her to Sophie, who cuddled the rabbit to her chest.

"I assume Ginny has gone under the shed?"

Nicole nodded, her face tearstained. "She'll get eaten if we don't get her out. I saw a fox this morning, sitting by the shed."

"She'll come out when it's quiet. Look, we'll put a box right by the shed with some greens and carrot in it. She'll come out to nibble and then you can catch her."

I went indoors to fetch some greens from the kitchen and found Grant standing at the window.

"Are you beginning to wish you hadn't let them have the animals?" he asked, giving me an I-told-you-so look.

"No, I still think it's a good idea. It gives them some responsibility, instead of being stuck in front of the TV whenever they're not out."

He stared at me as if he was going to say something else, but apparently thought better of it.

"I might leave the children with Karen and do a bit of shopping this afternoon," I said as I pulled greens and carrots out of the vegetable rack and headed toward the utility room. "I need some casual clothes."

Grant's eyes narrowed suspiciously. "It didn't take long for the 'new you' to go sloping off leaving me and the children, did it?"

"I'm only popping out to the shops, Grant. I won't be gone more than a couple of hours."

"You haven't forgotten our dinner together tonight, have you?"

"No, of course not." I turned to look at him before going out of the back door. "I thought we might take the children to the four o'clock showing of the new Disney film, then leave them with Karen while we go out for our meal on our own."

I watched him struggle with himself. It was obvious he wanted to object, but in the end he merely shrugged.

"Whatever you want, Lauren."

It took another half an hour to catch Ginny, who predictably stuck her head out to inspect the food when everyone except Nicole and me had returned to the house. I swooped on her before she had a chance to retreat, and handed her to Nicole, who sniffled into the guinea pig's tan, black, and white fur with relief. I thought again what a gentle child Nicole was, and I stroked her hair affectionately as she cuddled her pet. She gazed up at me and smiled, and I found myself smiling back and thinking that all these children needed was for someone to love them.

Back indoors, Karen was sitting with the other children in the playroom, watching Teddy as he hunched, completely absorbed, over another masterpiece. Toby was scribbling on a piece of paper and Sophie was trying to plait her own hair.

"Alice has her hair in braids," she said, glancing up at me. "Can't I have beads in mine?"

"I take it you had a fun sleepover last night," I said with a smile. "Were there many girls there?"

"Four of us, including Alice. Her mum lets Alice paint her nails with sparkly varnish, and she's got new shoes."

"Your shoes look quite new to me. How long have you had them?"

"I've had these since last vacation. But they aren't the new sort. Alice has got the very latest ones."

"It can't have been more than six weeks since summer vacation ended," I reminded her. "And you can't wear those on a school day, so I'll tell you what. We'll go shopping in the Christmas holidays for ordinary shoes, and if there's anything special that you see, we'll buy them for you for Christmas."

"That's ages away! How comes Alice doesn't have to wait until Christmas?"

"She probably had hers for her birthday."

"She did not."

"I'll go into town this afternoon and fetch a catalog from the shoe shop. Then you can look through it and choose what you'd like ready for when you can have them. That's my best offer."

Sophie pouted, but didn't argue further.

I beckoned Karen into the kitchen and asked her if she minded watching the children while I popped out.

Karen eyed me suspiciously. "You're not really going out just to pick up a catalog on shoes, are you? Can't it wait? I really wanted to talk to you this morning but it's already nearly twelve. After what you told me yesterday I couldn't sleep last night."

I busied myself making coffee while considering my answer. I'd leapt out of bed so quickly earlier that I hadn't even had a drink yet. I lowered my voice so we wouldn't be overheard.

"Actually, I'm going to drive to Epsom and see what happens if I turn up at Jessica's flat."

"Bloody hell, Lauren. Do you think that's a good idea?" she exclaimed. "How can you do that? I mean, suppose you come face-to-face with her?"

"I don't think that can happen. I can only be Lauren or Jessica, not both at the same time."

Clearly agitated, Karen grabbed the cup I handed to her, took a big gulp, and spat half of it back out.

"Ah! That's hot!"

I sipped at my own coffee more cautiously, watching as Karen wiped up what she'd spilled onto the pristine white counter when she'd jumped.

"The thing is, I want to know that Jessica and I really are both real," I whispered. "I know that sounds ridiculous, but what if this is simply a dream I'm having after all?"

"Or maybe there are two alternate universes or something, and Jessica isn't even sharing the same planet with Lauren?" Karen suggested grimly.

I stared at her, thinking she was making fun of me, but she raised an eyebrow and I realized her "open mind" had been working overtime through the night.

"Don't!" I hissed. "It's too scary to even contemplate."

"I want to know what's going on as much as you do," she said. "Can't I come with you?"

"I need to go by myself first. I want to see if Jessica is still there while I'm being Lauren. The problem is the time difference. I don't want to put you in any danger, and anyway, I need you to watch the children."

"This is madness," Karen murmured weakly, rubbing a hand over her face. "Please tell me that this isn't happening."

"Okay, it isn't happening. I'm popping out to do a bit of shopping and I'll bring back some information on shoes for Sophie. Is that better?"

She stared at me anxiously, ignoring my glib lie. "What if you get stuck somewhere between the two times or two places? What will happen to Grant and the children if you don't come back?"

I felt my face drain of color. I hadn't thought of that.

"I'll be careful. I won't change anything of Jessica's that might affect Lauren."

"How can you possibly know? You don't know anything about what you're getting into." She put out a hand and squeezed my arm. "Please, Lauren. If you're right, I've lost one sister already. I don't want to lose you, too."

"I can't just live out Lauren's life not knowing if there's a way back. I need to go, Karen. It's something I've got to do. I'm only going to look."

"I think you're being selfish," Karen said, dropping her hand and surveying me angrily. "Perhaps you're more like the old Lauren than you think. You didn't arrive here by accident. I've been thinking about it all night, and I believe that if you do exist in two places it's because some greater power put you with this family. Because you were needed here. Are needed here. Don't meddle, please, Lauren."

"I'm sorry," I said, finishing the last of my coffee. "Can you get the children's lunch for me? I simply have to go and look."

It took me over half an hour of driving in what I assumed was the general right direction before I came to any signs I remotely recognized. Eventually I joined the busy A3, passing signs to Guildford and Woking, then continued along the M25 until I saw the sign for Leatherhead, where I took the exit and continued on toward Epsom. I had been pleasantly surprised at the lack of traffic on the M25, a road I had always avoided if possible in the past. As I left the main road the sky grew darker, and I wondered if there was going to be a storm. There seemed to be hardly any other cars on the road. I switched on my running lights and then my headlights, until, as I came into Epsom itself, at about one-thirty, I noticed the day had grown so dark that the streetlights had come on.

As I turned the Galaxy into the space outside the flat and killed the engine, I realized that although my car clock was still reading 1:40, it must be 1:40 in the early hours of the morning here. Quietly, so as not to disturb my neighbors' sleep, I climbed out of the car and pressed the driver's door closed behind me, passing my own little blue car parked in its usual spot.

As stealthily as I could, I tiptoed across the grass and down the steps into my courtyard, where I found the key stuck exactly where I'd left it behind the gutter. Turning the key in the lock, I pushed the door open and stepped inside.

The house was dark and silent, and I was thankful that I'd had the foresight to ask Dan to take Frankie home with him. Whether she would have recognized me in Lauren I didn't know, but it certainly would have confused the poor animal, and she might have woken the neighbors if she'd barked at me.

I let out a long, slow breath, closed the door behind me, and snapped on the living room lights. My little home was exactly as I'd left it the previous night when I'd gone to bed. I walked softly into the bedroom and stared at the sleeping figure in the bed. I didn't turn the light on in the bedroom, but stood silently in the shadows staring at the still form of Jessica, listening to her shallow but steady breathing.

After a moment, I crept over to the bed and perched on the edge of the duvet. Tentatively, I reached out a trembling hand and touched her cool cheek. It was strange, looking at myself as others must see me. Gently lifting a lock of her brown hair, I felt an odd, almost familial sort of love toward this person who was really me.

Reluctantly withdrawing my hand, I stood up and went to the wardrobe that stood in the corner of the room and removed a pair of jeans, a hooded sweatshirt, and a pair of jogging bottoms. Then, laying them over my arm, I took a last look around the slumbering flat before letting myself out.

On the way home, the sky grew gradually lighter as I went from one time frame to another. By the time I was passing Guildford again it was just past two-thirty in the afternoon. Being familiar with these shops, I headed for the town center, parked the car in a handy spot near the bus station, and hurried to the nearest shoe shop, where a harassed assistant gave me a brochure packed full of the latest preteen shoes. I stopped off in Marks & Spencer to grab a sandwich and a bottle of water, which I ate and drank in the car while another driver apparently waiting to park in my space threw disgusted looks at me.

I arrived home just after 3:45 and sat in the driveway while the car clicked and cooled around me, collecting my thoughts and digesting the Richardson residence in my mind. Home. It was a sobering thought. The age-old adage "home is where the heart is" flickered through my mind. I thought of Sophie, Nicole, Toby, and Teddy, and then of Dan and Frankie, and felt the now familiar hot prickle of tears beneath my eyelids.

I heard the front door open and blinked rapidly, clearing my vision as Karen stuck her head out and called to me.

"Lauren?"

I climbed out of the car and straightened up as Karen descended on me, hugging me to her ample bosom.

"What happened?" she hissed in a loud whisper as we stood in a huddle in the driveway. "Are you all right?"

"It was weird." I raised my face and tried to hold back the tears again. "I saw myself asleep. I mean, I knew this was happening to me, but to actually see myself from someone else's perspective, well, it's really difficult to come to terms with."

"So your theory was right then?"

I nodded.

She let go of me and glanced at the armful of clothing.

"Are those what I think they are?"

"Lauren has no casual clothes," I said, shrugging." I thought these might fit since we're pretty much the same size."

"I'm not sure it's healthy," she said as I followed her into the house. "Mixing her clothing with yours. Quite apart from the fact that the whole business is decidedly odd, how will you survive as two separate identities if you start merging the two lives together?"

"I wish I could merge them," I muttered to her back. "Then I could have the best of both worlds."

Grant stepped out from the kitchen into the hall, making us both start.

"Where have you been all this time, sweetheart?" I turned to face him, startled by his sudden appearance. "You've been gone ages. I thought something had happened to you."

"I told you," I said, holding up the clothing and trying not to look as guilty as I felt. "I went shopping."

"Where's your shopping bag then?"

"It's, er, in the car," I said quickly. I wasn't sure why Grant was acting so strangely. It was almost as if he knew I hadn't been where I said I had. I remembered him drunkenly accusing me of seeing another man the other night.

"So what's this about wanting the best of both worlds?" he said, as if he were trying to make a joke of it. "What's this secret life you'd like to indulge?"

"I don't know what you mean."

He poked at the clothing in my arms and made a face. "You wouldn't normally be seen dead in stuff like that."

"I needed something for when I'm playing with the children," I replied. "I can hardly catch rabbits in Jaeger or Chanel, now, can I?"

"You're so different," he said, spinning me around and holding me at arm's length. "You look like Lauren, but you're just not the same person you were before."

I stared down at my feet, unable to look him in the eye.

"Do you think you'll ever be able to love me again?" he asked quietly.

I heard the kitchen door close and realized that Karen had made herself scarce. Grant reached out a hand and lightly touched my hair. "Well?"

"I don't know," I said miserably. "Everything seems so complicated."

"You loved me once," he said. "Can't you find it in your heart to try to recapture those feelings? I'm not an ogre, you know."

"I don't dislike you," I ventured. "Maybe in time . . ."

He brightened visibly at the half promise. "Really?"

"Maybe . . . in time," I repeated. "Now, if you are all ready, we were going to take the children to the cinema, I believe, and we're going to be late."

The children seemed as pleased to see me as I was to see them. Nicole threw her arms around me and told me that she had been playing with Ginny most of the day, but now both the animals were fed, watered, and back in the hutch in the shed. Toby announced he wanted a guinea pig, too, but added that he would make it sit in the cab of his truck or drive his digger. I said I thought he should wait another year until he was a bit better able to look after it.

I hurriedly emptied the contents of the washing machine into the dryer, realizing that the washing pile was mounting, while Grant was putting on his shoes and Karen was collecting the children's coats. I felt a tug at my trousers and glanced down to see Teddy grinning up at me. I realized I'd only seen him smile a couple of times before and the sight warmed my heart.

"We're going to the cinema," I told him. "Are you excited?"

He shrugged and pulled at my trousers more urgently, his ball clutched in his other hand.

"Do you want to show me something?"

He nodded.

I turned the dryer on and followed Teddy into the playroom.

He dragged me over to the new table and pointed to the picture that he'd drawn. I stared at it and gasped in astonishment.

"Why, Teddy, is that me?"

The likeness was uncanny. The picture was unmistakably Lauren, with her features cleverly caught in pencil. The hair had been drawn in yellow and the eyes in green. But they weren't Lauren's eyes, they were Jessica's. My eyes, as I'd first seen them staring out of Lauren's face in the hospital a week ago.

Glancing over my shoulder, I checked to see that Grant wasn't in the room. He might seem unobservant of his wife's eye color—in fact I wondered how many men, if asked, could say with any certainty the exact color of their wife's or girlfriend's eyes—but seeing Teddy's picture accentuating the greenness might jog some forgotten memory. Grant would almost certainly get a shock if he compared it to the blue of his wife's eyes in their wedding photo.

Perhaps I could say I was wearing colored contacts if he challenged me, I thought. I dismissed the idea immediately. Why would I do that? I wondered if there was any documented evidence of people's eye color changing naturally, maybe even a case of it happening to a lightning-strike victim.

Teddy was scrutinizing me closely. His grin had faded, replaced by a look of puzzlement.

"It's wonderful, Teddy," I managed rather belatedly. "Really, really good. You are a clever boy."

He continued to watch me. I could hear Grant calling us from the hall. Then, very slowly and carefully, Teddy picked up a blue crayon and colored over the portrait's eyes so that the green was barely visible beneath a sea of blue.

"Mummy," he said, pointing at the amended picture.

"Thank you, Teddy," I replied. He had drawn a picture of his real mother and not me at all. I took his hand in mine. "That's much better."

The film was a huge success. The children talked excitedly about it and even Grant seemed reasonably content as he drove the packed car homeward.

"I'll get the children's supper and put them to bed if you want to get ready to go out," Karen volunteered as we sped along.

"They probably won't want any supper," Grant said. "I don't know why you and Lauren encouraged them to have all that popcorn."

"I want Mummy to read the bedtime story when we get home," Toby announced.

"Of course I will," I promised. "We'll all get ready then I'll read to you before Daddy and I go out."

"Mummy," Teddy said slowly from the backseat. "Mummy."

It sounded as if he were trying the word out, rolling it around his tongue, and I braced myself for what unfortunate revelation might follow.

"Yes, Teddy?"

"I like you read my story."

I breathed a sigh of relief and rested my head back on the front passenger seat's headrest.

"I will read to both of you before I go out, I promise."

Once home, I wallowed in Lauren's Jacuzzi while Karen gave the children tea. After that, I tried on one or two of Lauren's fabulous outfits, twirling in front of the mirror in each before selecting a smart pair of black trousers with a clingy long-sleeved top. Next, I sat in front of Lauren's dressing table and surveyed her cosmetic collection. Her makeup was vastly superior to anything I owned, and I experimented with her foundation and blusher, which were both in shades chosen to complement her English-rose complexion. At home I bought cheaper brands and I needed less foundation on my more youthful skin. Lauren's Dior eye shadows were in blues and grays, and they looked odd against my eyes. I did my best, however, even though I felt like a small child who had sneaked a try with her mother's makeup, and the result was far from a disaster. Finishing with blue-tinted mascara and soft pink lipstick, I sat back to scrutinize my face, wishing I'd had more time to play with it all.

I picked out some pretty costume jewelry, wishing once again that Lauren had pierced ears as I fixed the rather painful clips into place, then I pirouetted in front of her full-length mirror to admire the full ensemble. Lauren's reflection smiled back at me, and I felt a moment of unease that I had indulged myself so flagrantly at her expense, but there wasn't time to feel too guilty. Toby was calling for his and Teddy's bedtime story.

I read "The Three Billy Goats Gruff" to the boys, then tucked them into their beds. I went to kiss the girls good night and then I presented myself to Grant, who smiled appreciatively.

"You look great, sweetheart."

"Thank you. You look very smart yourself." He was wearing black trousers, a yellow shirt with a black and gold tie, and a black blazer.

We climbed into his Mercedes and waved to Karen, who closed the door as we turned out of the driveway.

"Is it far?"

He glanced sideways at me. "No. It's only about fifteen minutes away."

I felt sure from Grant's demeanor that he still wasn't convinced that I'd lost my entire memory bank. Either that, I decided, or he simply didn't like to be reminded, each time I asked an innocent question, of the fact that I didn't remember anything about him.

We arrived at the restaurant at nine o'clock, and I was thankful for the second time that day that Dan had taken Frankie home with him. By now, I thought, she would have been desperate to be let out—and the evening had hardly begun.

The Italian restaurant turned out to be very pretty, with pale green tablecloths, crystal glassware, and ornate table decorations. The maître d' showed us to a table by a window and handed us our menus.

Grant ordered a bottle of Chablis, and I nudged him and

asked if we could have a bottle of mineral water, too. I assumed Lauren must normally drink wine, and while I was happy to have a small glass, I needed water as well.

When it arrived, the water was sparkling. I liked my water still, just as nature provided it, but I didn't want to make a fuss, so I sipped at the slightly bitter bubbles and wondered what other compromises I was going to have to make as Lauren.

Grant turned out to be surprisingly good company. While we were waiting for our starters, he regaled me with humorous anecdotes involving awkward patients he had had to deal with, and I found myself gradually relaxing. By the time the main course arrived I was feeling almost light-headed with the unaccustomed alcohol, and discovered I was enjoying the evening a lot more than I had thought I would.

Halfway through the main course a couple entered the restaurant and sat at a far table, the woman with her back to me and the man, who was around Lauren's age with a shock of blond hair, facing in our direction. As my eyes roamed the restaurant behind Grant I realized the man was looking directly at me. My fork wobbled in my hand and I dropped my gaze immediately. Grant went on talking and I rested my fork on my plate, trying to appear interested in what he was saying, but when I glanced up again the man was still staring and making small eye signals in my direction.

Oh, please, no, I thought desperately as I tried to concentrate on Grant. Surely I couldn't be unlucky enough to have run into Lauren's "other man"?

chapter twelve

Throughout the remainder of the meal the man kept sneaking glances at me, until in the end the young woman who was with him turned around to see who was attracting her companion's attention. She scowled at me and I concentrated more wholeheartedly on my dessert, feeling myself blushing under her hostile scrutiny.

After coffee I needed to use the ladies' room. My passage would, of course, take me directly past the other couple's table, and I held off going until it became absolutely necessary, in the hope that they might finish their meals really quickly and leave the restaurant first.

They didn't.

As I passed their table the man rose to his feet and followed closely on my heels. No sooner had the outer door closed behind us than he grabbed me by the waist and pulled me to him.

"Oh God, Lauren!" he choked into my hair. "Why haven't you contacted me?" I tried to pull away from him, but he held me fast. "I thought you were dead. Why didn't you answer your mobile? I've been leaving message after message, frantic with worry."

"Please," I entreated, while struggling in vain to extract myself from his grasp. "I have no idea who you are."

He stepped back as if I'd slapped him. "What are you playing at, Lauren? Don't do this!"

At that moment the door opened behind him, and the young woman who had shared his table stood there glaring at me.

"How dare you make eyes at my husband all evening!" she said indignantly. "Don't you have a man of your own?"

Looking desperately from one to the other, I dived for the door marked "ladies," raced inside, and locked it behind me. Standing there trembling with my back to the door, I tried to collect myself. The woman was shouting at her husband now, telling him she'd had enough of his philandering ways. I decided I might as well use the toilet while I was in there. She hammered on the door once demanding I come out and face her, but when I didn't respond she must have walked off, because the man's voice came through the door a moment later, thin and wheedling.

"Lauren, come out. She's gone home without me. Please don't do this, I love you!"

"Go away," I said at last. "I don't know who you are."

"It's all out in the open now," he continued. "Felicity knows about us. You promised to tell your husband. You were going to leave him. Why have you changed your mind?"

"I've been in the hospital," I told him through the door. "I don't remember anything. I've lost my memory, so let's leave it at that. I'm staying with Grant and the children. They need me!"

"They don't need you as much as I do," he countered. "You don't care about the children anyway, you told me. You said they were driving you mad and that you would come away with me."

"No. I wouldn't leave the children. I don't believe I ever said that."

Not even Lauren would have wanted to leave the children, I thought angrily. This boyfriend of hers must have misunderstood her.

"You were looking at special homes for that retarded boy of yours," the man announced suddenly. "As soon as he was taken care of we were going away together. Open the door, Lauren!"

Angry now, I opened the door to face him.

"Don't call him that! And how dare you suggest such a thing! Lauren would never have put Teddy in a home!"

He stared at me, his mouth dropping open, presumably stunned at my use of Lauren's name in the third person. "Have you really lost your memory?"

"Yes, it appears she has," said a voice behind us.

Grant was standing in the open doorway, glowering at the other man, then shooting accusing looks at me. He reached around the young man, grabbed my arm, and pulled me out of the door.

It was almost midnight when Grant parked the Mercedes in the garage and strode around to open my door. We had barely spoken on the way home, but as he helped me out of the car, he suddenly slid his arms around my waist and crushed me against him.

"Tell me it's over, for good, and I'll say nothing more about it," he murmured. "I still love you, Lauren."

I pulled away from him, afraid he'd go back on his word not to touch me.

"What happened to my mobile phone, Grant?" I demanded. "Did you take it while I was lying unconscious in the hospital? I didn't even know I had a phone, and all the time you've been watching his calls come in, knowing he was worried sick about me!"

"He had no right to be worried about you. You are *my* wife."

"No wonder you were so suspicious of me. You've known all week that some other man existed. What sort of game have you been playing?"

Grant gripped the tops of my arms with iron fingers. "It is not a game, Lauren. It is my life, the kids' lives. What did you expect me to do? Was I supposed to give you your phone and say, 'Oh, by the way, your lover has been ringing you?' Would you have had me reminding you he was waiting for you to leave us?"

I shook my head and he loosened his grip. "He said Lauren was planning to put Teddy into a care facility. Is that true?" I asked.

"Stop talking about yourself in the third person. You're so melodramatic, Lauren. And no, of course we would never have put one of our children in a home. You might not be the most maternal woman on the planet, but I don't believe you ever wanted that."

We both turned as Karen opened the garage door. "Are you two going to shout at each other all night, or is there any chance I can go to bed without worrying about you?"

"I'm going to bed right now," I said, stomping past Grant toward the house. He tried to make a grab for me, but I shook him off.

"Don't go, Lauren. We can't leave it like this. I told you I wouldn't hold it against you as long as you promise the affair is over. Tell me you don't love anyone else."

I looked at Grant with a pang of guilt at how much he must be hurting, but then I thought of Dan again and realized I couldn't promise any such thing. How could I ever consider making a commitment to Grant when I loved Dan with all my heart and soul?

We stared at each other desperately for a second and then I shook my head. "I'm sorry, Grant. I can't think about this now. I'm going to bed. Good night."

I woke up soon after twelve and opened my eyes gingerly, unsure for a brief second which world I was in. Until now, no matter how busy I'd been the previous day in either of my alternate bodies, I had awakened refreshed in the body that had been resting in my absence. Today, however, I felt completely washed out.

It was a struggle to get out of bed. My mind kept returning to Grant and how hurt he'd looked. I shook the memory away and, after showering and making myself a late lunch, I meandered around the flat looking with new eyes at everything I'd seen from Lauren's perspective half a day ago. The flat seemed so quiet—not quite the comfortable silence I'd grown used to and taken for granted since moving out of Stephen's place, but the hush of a void that seemed suddenly unfillable. Today, everything about my life seemed shallow and insular. I knew it wasn't, of course: I had my job, Clara and my other friends, Frankie, and now Dan. Perhaps it was Frankie's absence that was making me feel morose, I thought, as I picked up her favorite squeaky toy and stared at it forlornly.

Shoving the plastic bone to one side, I grabbed the phone and dialed my parents' number. Mum answered on the second ring.

"Hi, Mum."

"How are you, darling?"

"I'm a lot better, thanks. I've had a couple of days off work but I'll go back in on Monday."

"I'm glad to hear you're being sensible. Are you sure you don't want your dad and me to come up?"

I pictured her looking at her diary, wondering if she could fit a visit in between the craft fair and the village jam-making competition. "No, I'm fine. Feeling sorry for myself, that's all."

We chatted for a few minutes before she bid me good-bye. "I'd better go, Jessica; your father's waiting for his lunch. We're a bit late, what with one thing and another."

"Okay, Mum, give my love to Dad. Take care."

As I replaced the receiver, I felt a bitter desolation envelope me. Even my parents seemed to have more going on in their lives than I would normally have, if it weren't for my other life as Lauren.

The temptation to sit hugging my knees in misery was overwhelming. I told myself I was being silly. The last week had been such an emotional and physical whirlwind that I was bound to be feeling insecure and somewhat drained.

Dragging bedding out of the cupboard, I decided to put clean sheets on the bed. There was plenty to keep me busy, I told myself severely, even without Frankie or the legal work I normally brought home at weekends. After pummeling my pillow energetically and fighting to get the duvet into its cover for ten minutes I felt decidedly better.

My next task was to take the car to the supermarket and load up with a week's supply of groceries. It took me only half an hour to fill my cart, pay, and have everything loaded into the back of my little car. I'd added six bottles of Guinness for Dan and his father to my purchases, and these I placed carefully on the backseat before heading in the direction of Dan's house.

As I drew up to his driveway I was disappointed to see that Dan's car wasn't there.

I rang on the doorbell anyway, and waited while Patrick shuffled down the hall to answer the door. When I saw him again in the daylight I was struck by how like Dan he looked. He was thinner and slower, and his hair was gray, but the facial structure was the same, and he was still good-looking even for a man in his seventies. The most telling feature, though, was his eyes—a penetrating blue with a mischievous twinkle that probably accounted for him having been married several times.

"Well, hello there," he said with a grin when he saw who it was. "You'd better come in, so you had."

I followed the old man down the hall to the living room, where the television set was booming away. He went over and switched it off.

"Take a seat, lass, Dan won't be long. He's dashed out to buy dog food. Your Frankie has an appetite on her and no mistake."

"I'm sorry. I've just been to buy some myself. I'll give Dan some of that to make up for what Frankie's eaten."

Patrick laughed wheezily and lowered himself into his chair. "I'm only pulling your leg, lass. He had to go shopping anyway."

I held out the Guinness. "I thought you might like these."

The old man's eyes lit up as he focused on the beer. "Now, I wouldn't say no to one of those. There's glasses in the sideboard over there. Be a darlin' and fetch me one out, would you?"

I watched while he took a deep pull of the dark beer, closing his eyes as he savored the taste of the rich liquid, the froth leaving a white mustache on his upper lip. "Are you sure you wouldn't like one for yourself?" he offered.

I shook my head, smiling. "No, I'm okay, Mr. Brennan, thank you."

"I told you to call me Pat," he said.

"Do you think Dan will be long?" I asked.

"Now, what if he is? You and I will have the time for a nice chat, so we will. I think Dan rates you somewhat highly, so I'll tell you all about him while we're waiting. Aye, there are plenty more saucy stories to tell about that boy, so there are."

Patrick's stories proved to be highly entertaining.

"Did I tell you about the time he dated twins?" he asked with a snort of laughter.

I shook my head, wondering if I should listen while Dan wasn't there to tell his version of the story.

"They were completely identical, and pretty girls—well proportioned, if you know what I mean. Well, he didn't know they were twins. He met the first girl in one of the clubs while he was working on securing an account for Brennan's Bandits. He went out with her for about two weeks before realizing that the reason she was so vague about what they'd done or talked about on each previous date was because the girls were taking turns with him; sharing him, like they apparently shared all their other possessions."

"I would have thought most men wouldn't have minded," I ventured with a smile.

"Aye, but he didn't like the dishonesty . . . If he'd known from the outset he'd have been in heaven, that's for sure, but he didn't appreciate being taken for a fool."

I thought about the secret I was keeping from Dan and quavered inside. "What did he do when he found out?"

"He ended it. Told them he wasn't prepared to two-time either of them. He's an old-fashioned guy at heart is my Dan; a one-woman man." Pat turned twinkling eyes on me and gave a theatrical shrug. "I can't for the life of me think where he gets that from."

I listened to more stories, including one about how Dan had

once been pursued by a female weight lifter at the wedding of a friend and how he'd used the bridegroom's car as a getaway vehicle.

"He was always being pursued by some female or other," Patrick said as he took a satisfying pull at his beer. "He just didn't seem ready to be pinned down by any of them."

By the time we heard Dan's key in the lock and the scrabbling of the dogs' claws on the wood block flooring in the hall, Pat and I were laughing together like old friends. We both looked up when Dan appeared at the living room door. He gazed from his father's rosy cheeks to the empty beer bottles on the hearth and raised an eyebrow questioningly. By then I was sipping at a mug of tea I'd made in his kitchen, and I put the mug down guiltily and rose to greet him.

"I'm sorry to have left Frankie with you for so long," I said. I ruffled Frankie's silky head as she tried to leap up into my arms. "Your dad and I have been having a chat."

Dan groaned. "What's he been telling you?"

"All sorts of things," I said with a grin. "You seem to have had a very interesting life."

"Don't you believe the half of it," he said, kissing me on the cheek. "And the other half you should take with a pinch of salt." I sat down again as he helped himself to one of the bottles of Guinness, not bothering with a glass. "Did you bring these?"

"She knows the way to a man's heart does that one," Pat said happily. "Now, if the two of you will excuse me, I'm going upstairs to have my afternoon nap. If you go out, take the dogs; they'll only get bored and wake me up, so they will."

We watched the old man make his way unsteadily from the room, then Dan came over and pulled me back to my feet, encompassing me in a bear hug.

"I was beginning to think you'd abandoned your dog and left the country," he murmured into my hair. "You sure slept late!"

"I am sorry, but I did need the sleep, and I've managed to do my weekly shop as well."

"Glad to be of service," he said, laughing.

He held me at arm's length and seemed to study my face minutely before reaching out and drawing me toward him. I thought of Grant squeezing my arms the previous night, how he'd asked me to promise I wasn't seeing another man, and I felt a tremor of apprehension run through me.

"What is it?" Dan asked, frowning. "That's the second time you've looked frightened when I've touched you."

"It's nothing," I lied. "I'm a bit cold, that's all."

Leaning into him, I rested my head on his shoulder.

He held me and stroked my hair, and I relaxed in his warm embrace.

"What would you like to do?" he asked. "Stay here, go to your place, or walk the dogs?"

"Let's walk on the Downs," I suggested. "Before it gets dark. I'd like to go back to the spot where we met."

The Downs seemed different in the dull light of late afternoon. The dogs bounded around us like a couple of puppies as we strolled hand in hand along the well-trodden paths. The air was cooling fast, and I pulled up the collar of my winter coat and thrust the hand that Dan wasn't holding deep into my pocket. As the light began to fade we headed back to Dan's car, but not before I'd recognized the place where he had first come across me huddled with the dogs the week before.

"I want you to remember this place always," I said, lifting my cold face to his. "This is a special place where our two souls met for the first time."

"You romantic thing, you!" he exclaimed, taking my face between his hands and kissing me on the lips. I felt my body thrill at his touch and I snuggled into him.

"Do you believe that two souls might recognize each other?" I asked, my voice muffled in his jacket. "I mean, without their bodies? Do you believe in life after death?"

"My goodness, Jessica, this is a bit deep, isn't it?"

"I know. I think about it, that's all. I just wondered what you believe?"

"My father was brought up a devout Catholic, but the church didn't approve of him divorcing. It wasn't just the once, either. He made quite a habit of it and they cast him out. He taught me to believe in God in my own way and not to listen to rules made by mere mortals in God's name."

"So you do believe there is a divine Creator? Someone or something with a plan for us all?"

I felt him shrug. "Yeah, I guess so."

"I sometimes wonder what his plan is for me," I said, pulling out of his embrace and taking his hand again. "Come on, it's getting dark. We ought to go back to the cars."

He strode along beside me, the dogs at our heels. When we arrived at the parking lot, he pulled me around to face him and looked deep into my eyes.

"Do you know, I reckon we were destined to meet and fall in love. I think God sent that lightning to make sure I didn't miss you."

I smiled up at him, then dropped my gaze. "What if He sent it for a different reason? Some big plan we don't yet understand?"

Dan looked thoughtful for a moment, his eyes taking on a faraway stare.

"I don't have the answers, Jessica, but I do know you were

heaven-sent to me. If there is a bigger plan, then you being here with me is definitely part of it. You heard from Dad what my love life has been like until now. I took girls out for all the wrong reasons, dumped them, got dumped myself sometimes, never made a commitment. I'm thirty, Jessica. I don't want to live like that anymore. I want you."

"You've only known me a week."

"I knew you were 'the One' within a minute of meeting you."

I laughed and he threw his arms around me, crushing me to him.

"There, it's your laugh. It sends tingles right through me. I told you I couldn't bear it if I never heard that sound again. No one else has a laugh like yours."

"Come on," I said, kissing his cheek. "Let's go back to my flat."

He opened the rear door of his car to let the dogs jump inside, while I fished in the pockets of my coat for my own car keys. I glanced up to find him grinning at me through the fading light. "Now, there's an offer that is definitely heaven-sent."

I woke up at eight-thirty on Sunday morning, having sneaked an extra hour with Dan the night before because of the hour change. Dan had stayed for a couple of wonderful, passionate hours, but had been happy enough to leave just before nine and go home to get his father's supper. I'd gotten myself ready for bed and prepared myself for the turmoil of family life I was about to reenter.

Grant was sitting in the kitchen, fully dressed and drinking orange juice when I appeared downstairs ready for the day ahead. He ignored me and carried on reading the Sunday paper that he had spread out on the breakfast bar. I could hear the children in the playroom and slipped past him to say good morning to the brood.

"You look remarkably fresh, considering your late night," Karen commented. She was eating a croissant and had a cup of coffee on the playroom table next to her.

The thought crossed my mind that it was having spent time with Dan that had refreshed me. When I'd arrived back as Jessica the previous day I'd felt terrible—until I'd spent a while by myself and then with Dan.

The children were clustered around the table drawing busily. "The others saw that fantastic picture Teddy did of you," Karen said through a mouthful of flaky crumbs. "They're competing to see if they can do anything as good."

I went to each of the children in turn, resting my hand on the tops of their heads as they bent over their pictures.

The feel of their glossy hair beneath my fingers made me feel warm inside.

"It is amazing, isn't it?" I commented, sitting on a low chair next to them and watching the children draw. "Teddy is only four and he's definitely gifted."

"Mozart was a musical genius at the age of four," Karen said. "I don't think age has anything to do with it. If you've got it, you've got it."

My mind turned to what Lauren's lover had told me the previous night about Teddy being put into a home, and my stomach lurched at the thought.

"Do you know which school Grant and I were thinking of sending the boys to? The girls go to a private girls' school, don't they? Grant has showed me where it is so I'll be able to take them tomorrow."

"Yeah, they had their half-term break a week earlier than the local schools," Karen said, licking flakes of croissant off her lips. "I'm not sure what they, er—you'd—settled on for the boys. At the moment the twins go to a small independent school with a nursery attached. I assumed they'd stay on through the main school. You'll have to ask Grant about it."

"I don't think he's speaking to me."

"Oh." She sipped her coffee, looking thoughtful. "Well, you are bound to have begun trying to find somewhere suitable by now if the boys aren't staying on there. You are usually very organized. Why don't you try going through your desk? It's where you would normally keep information about things like this."

"I don't think I realized before how talented Teddy is," I said, glad to follow Karen's lead in continuing the pretense that I'd merely lost my memory. "I think Grant and I should find somewhere that specializes in art."

She nodded. "I agree. This picture of you is unbelievably accurate." She peered into my face. "He's made the eyes an unusual color, though; an interesting mixture of blue over green."

I blushed, even though she knew the truth. It was difficult keeping the lie going when Karen knew everything I said was an invention. I felt rather as if I were an inexperienced actress in a play who was frantically ad-libbing while Karen had my actual lines in front of her.

"When are we leaving?" Sophie asked suddenly, looking up from her picture.

"Leaving?"

"She means leaving here, for church," Karen explained. "Remember, I told you the family go to church every Sunday, to the ten o'clock service."

I glanced at Lauren's expensive watch and realized it was past nine. "I don't know . . . what time do we usually leave?"

Grant appeared in the playroom doorway. "We leave at half past nine. On the dot, so please make sure the children are ready, Lauren."

His voice was cool, and he was obviously still very upset by everything that had happened the previous night. I turned to face him. "Anything else I should know?"

"The Sunday roast should be in the oven before we go. There's a joint of pork in the fridge. I took it out of the freezer last night. I had a feeling you might not remember we had a roast lunch on Sundays."

"At least you believe me at last."

"I don't have much of a choice, do I?"

"Not really," I said, turning my back on him. He was right; he didn't have much choice after hearing me talking to my supposed lover last night.

"I'll start the lunch while you are out," Karen whispered as Grant disappeared into the hall. "You go and get ready for church. And put a blouse or something over those bruises on your upper arms or you'll have all the old dears gossiping for weeks."

I gazed down in surprise at the tops of my arms where Grant had shaken me in agitation last night during our heated argument in the garage. I hadn't realized he'd done it so hard.

Back in the bedroom, I surveyed the bruises more carefully in the dressing table mirror. There was a small blue circle on each side where Grant's thumb had dug into my flesh. After rummaging through Lauren's dressing room I changed out of the slacks and sleeveless top I'd put on earlier, into a smart designer skirt, blouse, and jacket, then surveyed myself critically in the mirror. The singed hair was hardly noticeable, but there was a dark shadow near the scalp where Lauren's highlights were beginning to grow out. I ran my finger down the center part and wondered how often Lauren had her roots retouched.

Another thought struck me then. Karen's hair was brown, not blond like her sister's. Was it possible that Lauren wasn't a natural blonde? The thought excited me. I hadn't adjusted to being blond very well, and if Lauren wasn't a true blonde then I could grow it out and feel more like my real self. I remembered thinking that in the picture of Lauren on her wedding day her hair had been a lot fairer than it was now. Perhaps she'd had it bleached for the big day.

I was still thinking about my hair when I wandered into the dressing room and opened Lauren's desk. There was a drawer where I'd noticed a pile of glossy magazines, and I leafed through them, wondering how I should wear my hair once it had been returned to its natural color.

"Are you ready, Lauren? It's time we were going," Grant shouted up the stairs.

I jumped guiltily. Not only had I allowed Karen to start the lunch for me, I had also neglected to check that the children were clean and tidy; or that they had eaten sufficient breakfast or been to the toilet. Grant might have thought Lauren wasn't a particularly maternal person, but she must normally work a lot harder than I was managing in her stead. I admitted to myself with a pang of inadequacy that if Karen hadn't arrived when she had, the children wouldn't have had breakfast on time all week.

I was about to stuff the magazines hastily back into the drawer when a letter fell loose from inside one and drifted to the floor. Bending to retrieve it, my gaze alighted on the heading at the top and my breath felt as if it had frozen solid in my chest. Running my eyes over the typed print, I felt a mixture of anger and fear.

The letter was from a home in Kent for brain-damaged children, inviting Mrs. Richardson to an informal inspection of their facilities with a view to placing her son Edward in their care.

chapter thirteen

The church was some degrees warmer than the one I had been dragged to as a child. The vicar, rather than being a stuffy, self-opinionated old man, was a woman in her thirties who seemed friendly and approachable. The service appeared to be tailored for families, and the children sat quietly in the long wooden pews, with the exception of Teddy, who wandered about in the aisle without attracting any signs of disapproval from the rest of the congregation. Grant, who had been sitting for a while with his son on his lap, whispered that Teddy always did this. If we tried to stop him he would scream, shout, and throw himself on the floor. I had yet to witness that side of our child's behavior, although having seen one of his nightmares I had a good idea what one of Teddy's tantrums might be like.

At one point in the service the congregation was given the opportunity to pray quietly, and I scuffled down onto the hard kneeler, squeezed my eyes closed, and let my thoughts wander. In that moment of quiet contemplation, I found myself wondering if the omnipotent forces of the universe thought I was doing a good job of being Lauren. To my own surprise, I realized as I sat in that quiet place that it mattered to me very much that I was.

"I wish You would send a sign that I'm doing the right thing," I prayed dreamily. "There has to be some point to all this, doesn't there?"

A warm hand touched my arm and I opened my eyes to find Teddy smiling at me. Because I was kneeling, our faces were at the same level, and I found myself gazing directly into his sea-green eyes. Sophie and Toby also had those mesmerizing green-gray eyes inherited from their father, along with variations of his reddish brown hair color. Only Nicole had her mother's blue ones and the light mouse-brown hair that I suspected lay beneath my own highlighted locks.

I grinned back at Teddy, peeking through my folded fingertips at the rest of the congregation, who appeared to be silently conversing, eyes closed with God. Feeling like an outsider, I returned my gaze to Teddy, who had wriggled in next to me and rested his head against my shoulder. In a moment of spontaneity I kissed the top of his carroty curls and mouthed a silent thank-you toward the ceiling. It seemed that Teddy had accepted me for who I was, even though he appeared to know that I was not his mother, and this was certainly as much of an answer from on high as I could reasonably expect. After all, I told myself with an inward chuckle, He couldn't be expected to send a lightning bolt every day.

Prayers over, I slid back onto the hard wooden seat. Teddy climbed onto my lap and sat there quietly with his ball hugged to him. I thought of the letter in Lauren's desk and vowed it wouldn't happen. Teddy wasn't going to any special home—I'd make sure of that.

After the service we trooped through to the newly built

redbrick church hall. The architects had obviously been tasked with making it match the church itself, which was a large Victorian monstrosity, but inside the hall it was spacious and airy, with a window into a small kitchen through which two middle-aged ladies were serving coffee and trays of orange squash.

"Can I have a cookie, Mummy?" Toby asked, eyeing the selection on the plate.

"Just one, or you'll spoil your lunch."

I noticed Sophie slipping two cookies into her hand, and Nicole, who had been watching her older sister, followed suit. I was about to say something when I realized that in the scale of things one more cookie really didn't matter. They hadn't heard me say anything to Toby, so it wasn't a case of making my point. I took another cookie off the plate for Toby, telling him that since he'd been a good boy he could have the extra one, then watched as he ran off to join his sisters at the activity table.

Scanning the room through the mass of smartly dressed churchgoers, I spotted Teddy standing near the door and I squeezed apologetically past elbows and coffee cups to get to him.

"Would you like a cookie?" I asked, holding out a custard cream.

He shook his head. "A' will spoil my lunch."

"I don't think one or two cookies will hurt; it's still a couple of hours before we eat."

He pulled at my skirt and I crouched down beside him so we were on eye level again.

"Other Mummy dun't let me," he whispered conspiratorially.

"I don't think she'd mind you having one," I whispered back. "But thank you for telling me, Teddy."

He took the cookie and I realized with a sigh that although

he liked me and had accepted me for who I was, he was still loyal to his real mother, and that of course was how it should be. Lauren had brought the children up a certain way and, as I'd seen when talking to Karen a couple of days ago, by making too many changes it was indicating to Teddy that I didn't approve of the way Lauren had done things. With the other children my deviation from their mother's way of doing things didn't matter—they thought their mother had lost her memory and was making the changes herself. I reminded myself I must be more careful in my dealings with Teddy.

I stood up, still thinking things through as I pushed my way back to the serving window, where I was handed a cup of coffee. This parenting business was more complicated than I'd realized a week ago, I thought, taking a sip of the warm, bitter liquid. It required tact, diplomacy, finely honed organizational skills, and bucketloads of patience. Whatever decisions Lauren had been facing in the weeks or months before her death, I knew I was in no position to judge her.

"Hello, Lauren. We heard you've been ill. Are you better now?"

I turned to see a woman of indiscriminate age at my elbow. She was short and plump with dark wiry hair. Her somber blue skirt suit looked as if it had shrunk several sizes and was stretched across her broad frame.

"Yes, thank you. I'm much better."

I searched the hall for a glimpse of Grant but couldn't see him. He'd said on the way to the church that he would let me know who everyone was, but I could tell he was still in a bad mood from our encounter with Lauren's boyfriend the evening before. He had lost himself in the crowd as soon as the service was over and left me to struggle on my own.

"I notice you've allowed the children to have cookies today."

I stared at the woman in astonishment. She must have been scrutinizing my every move.

"And," she continued in a critical voice, "I hear from Nicole that you have allowed them to acquire pets."

"Yes," I stammered, wondering who this opinionated woman was. "A rabbit and a guinea pig. The girls adore them."

The woman lowered her voice an octave. "They may adore them, Lauren, but you must be careful. The devil works in devious ways. I hear Nicole has named her pet Ginny after one of the Harry Potter characters?"

"Yes."

"I thought we'd discussed those books and decided they were dangerous. Witchcraft and wizardry are strictly banned by the Bible. They are the devil's tools and as such should not be permitted to corrupt the innocent minds of children."

"They're only harmless stories," I protested. "Thousands of children have read them."

"Exactly!" she said. "The devil has entered the minds of thousands of innocents, laying them open to sin."

I turned away from her, hoping to bring the conversation to a close, but she rested a viselike hand on my arm, making my cup rattle in its saucer.

"Come back to our prayer group, Lauren. I can see you are sorely in need of salvation."

"I'm sorry, I simply don't have the time."

"You had plenty of time four years ago when you needed help," she hissed. "God isn't only there for when you're in trouble, you know. You should thank him every day of the twins' lives for His guidance and intervention there."

I stared at her, shocked, slowly registering what she must

mean. That's what Grant had meant when he had said that the boys hadn't been his idea, I thought, appalled. Karen had been right when she'd said she'd thought Grant and Lauren must have decided to end the pregnancy, but someone from the church—this woman—had intervened. Maybe it hadn't taken much persuasion for Lauren to keep the babies: It was no small thing to even consider getting rid of them, and if this woman had threatened her with God's displeasure she might easily have capitulated.

Much as I had grown fond of the twins, and was heartily glad of Lauren's decision to keep them, I felt a sudden anger toward this meddling stranger who seemed to think she had a right to inflict her ideals onto others. She had forced something upon Lauren when she was at her most vulnerable, and the family had suffered because of it.

I must have looked as angry as I felt because the woman wrenched her hand away as if my proximity were suddenly abhorrent to her, and the sudden movement sent my cup slipping from the saucer and crashing to the floor.

The hall fell instantly quiet and I felt every eye upon us.

"What happened to 'judge not lest you be judged'?" I said into the silence. "You knew nothing about this family and what it could cope with and what it couldn't, but you pressured her with your opinions, didn't you?"

The woman's eyes shot open. She looked appalled by my outburst and shrank from me as if Satan himself were staring at her. "Her? Who are you referring to, Lauren?"

"Didn't it ever occur to you that she might not have been able to take care of them?" I continued angrily. "That her whole family would suffer because of the decision you forced her into? She had a right to choose for herself, not to be bullied and threatened by someone professing to know what God intended for her! Who gave you the right to be her judge and jury?"

"Lauren!"

Grant had rushed over and was taking the empty saucer out of my hand, pulling at my elbow, trying to draw me toward the doorway. His normally pale face was suffused with red, and I saw now that the whole hall was staring wide-eyed at me.

"I helped you," the woman spat out suddenly. "Your soul was in jeopardy and I saved you."

Grant was beckoning the children over and nudging me toward the door. "Lauren isn't well yet, Dora. She's lost her memory, and this really isn't helping," he said as calmly as he could.

"She's got the devil inside her," the old woman muttered viciously.

"You're qualified to tell, are you?" I flung back. "Do you think you have a direct line to God or something?"

"I know evil when I see it!"

"You should, you must see it in the mirror every morning!"

"Lauren!" Grant hissed. "Stop it. Come on, children, we're going."

I turned and let Grant hustle me out the door, the children following with confused looks on their faces. As soon as we'd rounded the corner of the church hall, Grant burst out with great guffaws of laughter. I looked at him askance, my hands shaking as I pulled up short to face him.

"How can you laugh?"

"That's the funniest thing I've seen in years," he said between gasps for breath. "Every Sunday you come home fuming and upset after Dora gets her hooks into you, and at last you've put the horrible old bag in her place."

"We'll never be able to go back," I said as we walked toward the car, all the fight draining out of me. "I'll never live it down."

"Most of the congregation have been dying to pluck up the courage to tell her where to go for years," he went on as he unlocked the car. "She tells everyone what they should or shouldn't do, frightens the youngsters with her fire-and-brimstone stories. You'll be a hero, Lauren. You just wait and see."

I sat in silence on the way home from church, wondering just what damage my outburst might have done to the children. I knew my reaction to Dora had been rather hotheaded but I believed everyone had the right to make their own decisions, not be beaten about the head by Bible thumpers who made no effort to understand other people's frailties.

Staring out of the car window at the passing scenery, I attempted to justify my outburst. Every circumstance was different, I could see. Having lived Lauren's life for a whole week now, I was coming to understand that every parent possessed different capabilities. I shouldn't for a moment condemn Lauren for thinking of terminating her pregnancy, or for having an affair, or even for thinking of putting Teddy in a home, just because I wouldn't have contemplated doing any of those things myself. The power that ruled the universe might do the judging one day, but it certainly wasn't my place to do so, nor was it Dora's.

The car had stopped and the children were bundling out talking excitedly now that the tension had eased. I followed them into the house more slowly, furious with myself for my appalling lack of control.

Delicious smells of roast pork filled the air and I sniffed appreciatively. It seemed Karen had been doing my job for me remarkably well. How I was going to manage when she went home

I didn't know. The kitchen was cluttered with pans and potato peels, the sink full of vegetables and the counter covered with flour where she was working on producing pastry for an apple pie. Karen glanced up at me with the rolling pin in her hand and grinned.

"I hear you've been making trouble again."

"How could you possibly know that already?"

"The vicar rang. She said she's coming around this afternoon for a chat." Karen attacked the pastry again. "She said you had angry words with one of the other parishioners."

"You could say that," I sighed, tying an apron over Lauren's designer outfit and taking a peeler and knife from the cutlery drawer. "I made a complete spectacle of myself."

"Grant seems amused by it. He came in chuckling to himself, which is an improvement on the mood he left in earlier."

I smiled as I pulled a bag of cooking apples toward me. "I thought he'd be really angry with me. I mean, the family have been going to that church for years, and I only went once and look what happened!"

Karen went over to the kettle and flicked the on switch with floury hands. "I'll make us both a drink and you can tell me all about it. What would you prefer—coffee or tea?"

"Either will do. I don't mind which."

By the time I'd finished talking about what had happened that morning, I had a pile of peeled, sliced apple in front of me and Karen was smiling.

"Lauren told me . . . sorry, you told me a couple of years ago, that Dora was the one who persuaded you to go ahead with the pregnancy. I thought at the time that Lauren should have made her own mind up, but she never listened to me."

I glanced over my shoulder in case the children were nearby.

"We'll have to try to stop referring to Lauren in the third party," I said quietly. "I keep doing it—I even did it in the church hall and the whole village must have noticed. Grant actually covered for me, telling them I'd lost my memory, but I don't want the children to hear us talking about her as if it's not me."

"Sorry . . . it's so difficult now that I know."

"Tell me about it. The entire congregation of St. Martin's has seen me in a different light after today."

We giggled together like the sisters we were supposed to be.

"I'd like to know the real you," she said as she pressed down the fluted edges of the pie.

"This is the real me. That's why Lauren keeps getting into trouble."

"No, I mean you in your own body, your own surroundings. Is there any way I can meet Jessica?"

"I'm not sure," I said, thinking hard about all the possibilities. "When I went last time Jessica was asleep. The time changed during my journey. If you were with me and went through the time change, too, wouldn't that make us time travelers? I'm not sure that was ever intended."

"Was any of this intended?" she asked, opening the oven and sliding the finished pie inside. "You becoming Lauren and everything? Couldn't it have just been a mistake after all?"

"I hope not. I prefer to think of this experience as a journey. I'm following a predestined path, as the pawn in a grand universal plan."

"Bloody hell."

I giggled again, but then sobered as a thought entered my head.

"If I didn't go with you and you went on your own, then time might not change for you—after all, it doesn't seem to be your destiny that's being altered, it's mine. What if the time only changed for me because I couldn't exist in two places at the same time?"

She stared at me. "You mean I could drive over there now and you could be there as Jessica?"

"Oh, I don't know," I said, suddenly weary of trying to work out stuff that was way beyond a mere human's understanding.

"Why don't you try it and see? After all, Jessica has Sunday, too; it's just that I experience Sunday twice as the two different people."

"I wasn't going to go today," she said hastily. "I want to go and I don't. I mean, I do believe you aren't Lauren, and I do want to meet Jessica." She broke off, not really knowing what she meant. "I'm just not ready to go today."

"Just as well, because I've remembered I'm spending the day with a friend. I wouldn't be in."

We started laughing again at the weirdness of what we were saying. She came over and encompassed me in a great bear hug.

"You're bearing up very well. Not everyone could cope with something as phenomenal as this without going nuts. Aw!" she added with a sudden look of horror. "I hope I'm not being stupid by believing you, I don't want to find myself on 'hidden camera TV!' "

"You have no idea what a relief it is that you do believe me," I said, meaning every word. "And that you've so readily accepted me for who I am."

We listened to the sounds of the children playing in the next room. Sophie and Nicole were giggling about something and Toby was *brrming* his truck.

"Without you this family would be in mourning now, but

instead the children are the happiest I've seen for a long time. Who you are is all right."

"Grant isn't happy, though," I said, rubbing my hands over the bruises on my arms. "I can't make him happy, Karen, because I don't love him."

"At least you're not leaving him. If that young man last night was telling the truth, Lauren would have been gone soon anyway."

"There's something else I need to talk to you about," I began, lowering my voice another octave. "I found a letter in the desk upstairs. It seems . . . I . . . was going to put Teddy in a home before I left."

"No!" Karen went white. "She . . . you . . . wouldn't have done that. I don't believe it."

"It's true. I can show you the letter if you like."

"Shit, Lauren. Shit, shit, shit."

"I have asked you to mind your language in front of the children," Grant said from behind us.

We both started guiltily. I wondered how long he'd been standing there.

"The children are all in the playroom," Karen said hastily, turning away to check the roast, presumably so she wouldn't have to meet his gaze. "They won't have heard me."

"It's just as well," he said smoothly. "We don't want the boys to come out with words like that when they go back to nursery school tomorrow."

"Speaking of school," I said, watching him carefully for any sign that he'd overheard me telling Karen about finding the letter, "what are we doing about their next school? Did we have any particular plans for them?"

"They have until next July where they are now," Grant said guardedly. "You were looking into various possibilities for next year. I think we have their names down for one or two places."

"Both boys are to go to the same place then?"

"As far as I know. You were having a meeting with the head at the nursery sometime next week, I believe."

"Did . . . do I . . . have a diary?"

"It'll be in your desk, sweetheart."

Narrowing my eyes, I watched him suspiciously. He wasn't "sweethearting" me for nothing.

"Don't look at me like that, Lauren! I'm proud of you, that's all. It was very entertaining having you put Dora in her place earlier. It made me remember the spunky girl I married."

"Apparently the vicar is coming to see me this afternoon. I hope she sees things the same way."

Grant was saved from having to respond by Karen's call for help getting dinner ready, and for the next ten minutes we were absorbed in straining vegetables, setting the dining room table, and rounding up the children for the meal.

"You know," Grant said, looking down the long mahogany table to where I was sitting with Teddy on one side of me and Nicole on the other, "it's so nice to sit down together as a family. We missed you last weekend while you were in hospital, didn't we, children?"

They nodded dutifully as I wiped some of Teddy's food from his chin and then smiled around at them all. I felt so at home with this family, it was as if this was where I truly belonged.

Except that I was missing Dan, and Frankie, and I didn't love the man who was smiling benevolently at us all as if we were his prize possessions. I caught Karen's eye and she must have guessed what I was thinking because she gave me a sad little smile. This was her sister's family, after all, and I was an imposter.

It took almost as long to clear up after the meal as it had for Karen to prepare it. I made her sit down with a cup of tea and put her feet up while I scraped plates and loaded the dishwasher. Grant took the roasting pan into the utility room and I was pleased to note that it seemed to be his task to scrub it clean.

Because of the time change it seemed to start growing dark remarkably early. Karen had just finished helping me to sort out the girls' uniforms and their knapsacks for the morning, and I was thinking of drawing the curtains, when there was a knock at the front door.

"That'll be the Reverend Louise Penny," Karen said with a smirk.

"Oh no! I'd forgotten about her."

"Lauren!" Grant yelled from his office. "The vicar's here."

I could see that no one else was going to answer the door, so I left Karen checking on the children and went through to the hall, clicked on the light, and paused for a moment to collect my breath before opening it.

"Good afternoon, Reverend," I said formally, taking in the vicar's smart blue skirt and blouse with the white clerical collar just visible beneath her coat. I stepped back to let her enter. "Would you like to come through to the sitting room?"

"Thank you, Lauren," she said, following me through the hall. "And please, call me Louise, we're friends, remember?"

I nodded vaguely and indicated a chair, taking her coat and laying it across the arm of the sofa. When she was seated, I sat in a chair opposite her, my hands clasped in my lap.

"About this morning . . ." I began.

She held up a hand. "Don't worry about this morning. I've known for a long time your feelings about the twins. Dora had no right to start in on you in the first place, and I'm sorry your feelings of frustration and helplessness came out like that."

"I shouldn't have lost my temper so easily."

"With everything you've got to worry about right now, I'm hardly surprised."

I stared at her. She was a round-faced woman with short dark hair, no makeup, and plain features, yet there was a kindness in her expression that made it all too easy to talk to her. What things had Lauren been worrying about that she had confided to this woman? I wondered.

She leaned forward and patted my knee. "Have you come to a decision yet? Do you want to talk it through again?"

"Er . . . which decision are we talking about?"

"Come on, Lauren. We've been going over this for the last two months. I know this morning Grant said you've lost your memory, but it's not true, is it? You are obviously under a lot of strain. But are you going to leave Grant and the children, or have you been thinking about what I said?"

I shook my head. "I'm not leaving."

The beaming smile that lit up her face made me want to smile in return.

"I'm so glad, Lauren, so very glad. You have made the right choice, I assure you." She looked worried suddenly. "And the young man? You're letting him go?"

"I don't plan to see him again."

"Splendid. You are being so brave. Last time we spoke I felt sure you had decided on the other path, and I have prayed for you, Grant, and the children three times every day. I wanted the family to stay together so much."

Karen poked her head around the sitting room door. "Would you like a cup of tea?"

"That would be lovely," Louise said, the smile back in place on her face.

I nodded too and Karen tactfully withdrew.

"I hoped that as you were being so sensible about not being unfaithful with the young man that you might come to this decision, but I hardly dared believe it. I'm so, so happy for you, Lauren."

"I'm staying for the sake of the children," I whispered, afraid that Grant might be eavesdropping. "Is that the right thing, do you think?"

"Keeping the family together is the right thing," she said, nodding. "Leaving would have been the easy way out. You would have been giving in to your passions as far as the young man was concerned and neglecting your responsibilities as a mother. Many mothers want to run away sometimes, I'm sure—especially if they have the added burden of a brain-damaged child to care for. Your decision is the tough one, the one that requires true grit and strength of character, but it is the one God has guided you toward. He will not abandon you."

I wished I could tell her how hard and how ingeniously God—whoever He, She, or It was—had apparently worked to answer her three-times-a-day prayer sessions to keep the family together. Perhaps, I thought, this woman's prayers were super-powered or something, but they seemed to have been answered, and if that were the case it was probably her fault I was here.

But Lauren wasn't here, and I was suddenly reminded of something that Dr. Chin had told me when I had been in the hospital after my lightning strike as Jessica. He'd said that the Chinese had once believed lightning to be unlucky, that it was thought to be a sign of God's disapproval. For Lauren it had certainly been unlucky, I thought with a shiver, because it had killed her and robbed her of her future, wherever she had decided that might lie.

Karen arrived with a tray bearing tea and cookies. I asked her if she'd care to join us, but she said she ought to go and make sandwiches for the children's tea. I glanced at my watch and realized the day was rapidly disappearing.

Louise must have noticed my time check because she drank her tea down quickly and rose to her feet.

"Don't worry about this morning," she said as she pulled on her coat. "Many of my parishioners have wanted to tell Dora to mind her own business for a long time. No one will hold your outburst against you."

I followed her to the door and let her out into the dark front garden, watching as she walked along the driveway and climbed into her car.

The streetlights were coming on all along the road, and underneath one, parked a short distance from the house, was a motorbike, the dark figure of its helmeted rider turned in my direction. As the vicar's car trundled off down the road, I looked to see if the motorcyclist was still there. The figure remained motionless.

I felt the fine hair stand up on the back of my neck. I knew he was watching me, and I also knew with chilling certainty that underneath those black leathers and that dark anonymous helmet there was a young man with a shock of blond hair.

. . . . *chapter fourteen*

On Sunday morning I awoke at nine, stretched, and lay listening to the silence of the flat. Frankie was lying at the foot of my bed, peering at me reproachfully through one half-open eye.

"Come on then," I told her, sliding out of bed and slipping my dressing gown over my pajamas. "Out you go for a run."

After showering and dressing in black jeans and a white T-shirt with a chunky patterned sweater on top, I ate a quick breakfast of toast and marmalade, gave Frankie her meal, then took her for a brisk walk in the icy morning air.

Dan arrived at ten-fifteen, just as I was screwing the lid onto a vacuum flask of steaming coffee. He looked gorgeous in a pair of blue jeans, nubuck boots, and a tan open-necked sweater. The moment I saw him I knew we weren't going anywhere, not for a while anyway, and he must have seen the desire in my eyes because he grinned and pulled me toward him, fastening his mouth onto mine. The feel of his firm, warm body pressing against me had my senses pounding, and I kissed him with an intensity that took my breath away.

In the end we didn't leave the flat until after eleven o'clock, and I began to panic that we'd waste what was left of the day.

"Where first?" Dan asked as the car pulled out with Frankie sitting safely behind the barrier in the cargo area.

"Anywhere you like," I said, settling myself comfortably in the passenger seat. I was still glowing from having made love, and I really didn't care where we went as long as I was with him.

"There's a lovely place for walking in woods, with a lake, just down the A3," he suggested. "We could spend a couple of hours there, then stop in at a country pub for some lunch when we're hungry."

"Sounds perfect," I agreed, luxuriating in the sense of freedom our spontaneity invoked. Much as I liked the children, I was finding the constant routine of feeding, entertaining them, washing, and cleaning up both tiring and tedious. The fact that Dan and I had an unplanned day of leisure before us was like a salve to my battered senses.

It wasn't long before we were turning into a small parking lot and climbing out to stretch our legs. Frankie pranced around our ankles, getting in the way as we gathered up the thermos and car rug, then we headed off hand in hand down a leafy woodland path.

Dan's hand was warm and comforting in mine, and I kept stealing sideways glances at him as we walked, unable to keep my eyes off him. His profile was rugged and masculine and his body hard and toned. I knew he worked out at the gym a couple of times a week, and it showed. I shivered involuntarily with the sheer pleasure of being in his company.

A picture of Grant sprang into my mind, and I sighed. Grant was tall and lean and not the least bit like Dan, but there was a vulnerability about him that invoked my compassion. He was clearly devoted to Lauren, and although I found him overpossessive and a bit unpredictable, he had shown another, lighter side of his character after the incident at the church, which I had liked much better. I suppose it was understandable that he was confused, angry, and feeling insecure. I wondered what would happen if I stayed too long as Lauren. Could I keep him at arm's length indefinitely? Did I really want to? I feared it was bound to become increasingly difficult.

"What are you thinking?" Dan said suddenly.

I jumped guiltily as he stopped walking and turned to scrutinize me closely.

"I'm sorry, I was miles away," I stammered.

"There's no one else, is there, Jessica?" he asked uncertainly. "It's just that you seem to disappear every now and then. Where do you go?"

I wished I could tell him. Instead, I slid the thermos to the ground, wound my arms around his neck, and pulled his face down to mine. We kissed long and passionately until my lips were tingling and my heart was pounding in my chest.

"There's no one else," I told him when at last we surfaced for air. "There has never been anyone else like you."

He ran his hands up under my sweater and the touch of him on my bare skin sent more shivers exploding down my spine. We clung together, both reluctant to break the intense physical contact, but after a while we made our way to a fallen log, threw the rug over it, and sat side by side, our thighs and shoulders touching, our heads bent closely together.

I poured steaming coffee into a thermos cup and we shared it, sipping slowly while Frankie came and rested her head on my knee, looking inquiringly up at me.

"Yes, I love you, too," I told her fondly.

Dan stiffened at my side, and I realized what I had said. I glanced sideways at him and knew he was staring at me.

"I suppose we'd better see about some lunch," I said quickly, throwing the remains of the coffee into the leaves behind me. I screwed the cup onto the flask and stood up. "Ready?"

I watched as he slowly picked up the rug, shook it, and put it under his arm.

"Jessica?"

I looked expectantly at him. "Yes?"

He seemed suddenly tongue-tied, but then he smiled and held out his hand. "Come along then; we'd better get going before the pub stops serving."

That afternoon we went back to Dan's place for a late Sunday roast. It turned out that Dan had prepared everything before he'd left that morning, and Pat had put the oven on at the appointed hour so that by the time we walked through the door we were greeted by the tantalizing smell of roasting meat. Fortunately we'd only had a bowl of soup in the pub, so after putting some vegetables on to steam we sat down to a hearty meal with the old man.

"I couldn't leave him alone for the whole day," Dan whispered to me when we stood washing up in the kitchen after the meal. "I hope you don't mind."

"Of course not," I assured him, thinking that it wasn't that far removed from having children after all. "It was quite the right thing to do."

Later, he drove me home and we kissed again. I closed my eyes and wished I could kiss him all night and all day without stopping, but the evening was wearing on and I knew I had to leave him.

"I'll call you tomorrow evening," Dan said as I climbed out of his car in the space outside my flat.

"Okay," I replied, calling Frankie back from where she'd raced off into the darkness as soon as I'd opened the car door. "Thanks for a wonderful day."

As soon as he had gone, I fumbled the key into my front-door lock and raced through the dark sitting room to the kitchen, where I shook dog biscuits into Frankie's bowl. While she was eating I checked the time, gasped, then hurried into the bedroom, where I threw myself still fully clothed onto the bed. Closing my eyes, I willed myself to sleep, and almost immediately I was gone.

I awoke to find that Karen had roused the children, gotten them dressed, and given them breakfast. Glancing at the kitchen clock as I hurried into the kitchen, I found it was after half past eight.

"I'm glad you're up," Karen said. "I thought I was going to have to take them to school and nursery myself."

"You've been wonderful," I said, giving her a kiss on her rounded cheek. "Has Grant left for work?"

"An hour ago. He said he'd be home for dinner at six o'clock."

The girls, looking sweet in their green and red uniforms, were packing their school bags with cartons of apple juice and potato chips for break time, and I did the same for the boys, then hurried them all toward the garage.

"Who do I drop off first?"

"The girls. They have to be there in the next ten minutes. Registration is at ten to nine. Do you remember where to go?"

"Yes, Grant showed me."

"See you later."

"I'm going to be late back," I called out of the car window as I drove out of the garage. "I checked the diary and I'm having the meeting with the boys' headmistress this morning."

"Good luck!"

Once at the girls' school, Sophie and Nicole seemed to find it quite amusing that I didn't know where I normally dropped them off.

"You go into the playground and park over there, then you walk us to the door," Sophie explained. "And you come here again to collect us at four o'clock."

I hooked their bags over their shoulders, kissed them both good-bye at the door, and watched as they mingled with the other green-and-red-clad girls, before returning to the car to find Toby and Teddy fighting over a picture book that Lauren kept in the car for them.

"I've got to learn my letters," Toby was saying importantly to his brother. "Mummy said I should know my alphabet."

"I want look at pictures!" Teddy was yelling.

They were pulling at the book so hard I could see it ripping down the binding.

"Boys!" I admonished, taking the book from both of them. "You'll break it and then neither of you will be able to have it."

I started the car and nosed it out of the school driveway into the winding road, checking my rearview mirror as I joined the main flow of traffic. A couple of cars behind me I could see a motorbike, and I felt my heart miss a beat. My eyes flicked up to the mirror again. It was the same bike that had been parked outside the Richardsons' house last night, I was sure of it.

When I came to the boys' nursery school I parked along the roadside and opened the curb-side doors to let the boys climb out. The motorbike had passed as I'd parked, but I saw it draw up to the side of the road a little way ahead. The helmeted head swiveled in my direction and I forced myself to look pointedly away as I shepherded the twins into school.

Once inside the old school building my attention was taken by the pressing needs of the moment: where to hang the boys' coats, which classroom to take them into, and where to put their break-time drinks. Everything was painted in bold colors: There were alphabet friezes running around the walls, gaily colored stacks of toy bins, bright rugs on the cracked linoleum flooring, and rows and rows of pegs, each with an identifying picture beside it.

"Good morning, Mrs. Richardson," said a smiling teacher, taking Toby's hand and guiding him toward a door on the right of the main room. "Toby, you are in here with Mrs. Wells, as usual."

I felt Teddy's grip tighten on my hand and I looked down to find him staring with open hostility at the teacher, who had now turned her attention to him.

"And you will be in with Miss Stevens today, Edward. Come along."

"No!" Teddy said, taking a step behind me. "Don't like that."

"Come on, Teddy," I cajoled. "You like it at nursery school, don't you? I'm sure there will be lots of coloring and drawing to do."

"Want go with Toby."

"You can't go with your brother, Edward," the teacher said sternly. "You have to work with Miss Stevens until you have learned to sit quietly and form your letters."

Teddy began to cry, and I crouched down beside him, still holding his hand.

"What's the matter?" I asked gently. "You were happy here before the vacation started, weren't you?"

He shook his head, his face crumpled with the effort of trying to stop himself crying. He still had his ball clutched in his free hand and he let go of my hand to cuddle it to his chest.

"Want go with Toby."

"It's best if you leave, Mrs. Richardson," the teacher said. "He'll calm down as soon as you've gone."

I straightened up, not happy about leaving Teddy like this, but not sure if I was making matters worse by lingering. I wondered if he was feeling insecure because he wanted his real mother to bring him to school. Perhaps if I went, I reasoned, as I walked to the door, he would forget about me and settle down.

But Teddy had other ideas about me leaving him, and I'd barely reached the outside door when he came flying after me, screaming at me not to go. My instinct was to go back to him, but the teacher caught him and held him as he thrashed and cried.

"Please leave, Mrs. Richardson," she said through gritted teeth. "I promise you he will be all right."

I left as quickly as I could, the sounds of Teddy's screams still ringing in my ears.

I made my way to a second door marked "School Office" at the side of the building, knocked and went in. A bespectacled secretary was sitting at a desk sorting through a pile of envelopes. She looked up when I entered and smiled thinly with brightly lipsticked lips.

"Ah, Mrs. Richardson, Miss Webb is expecting you. Please go through to her office."

I glanced around and saw a second door marked "Headmistress," knocked and went in.

The woman with steel-gray hair sitting behind the enormous desk glanced up and gave me an even thinner smile than her secretary had managed. I thought it looked more like a grimace than a greeting, and immediately I felt on my guard.

"Sit down, please, Mrs. Richardson."

It was definitely an order rather than an invitation, and I obeyed reluctantly. The visitor's chair was slightly lower than Miss Webb's, instantly putting me at a disadvantage. I stared at the whitewashed brick of the walls, where several charts and timetables hung in an immaculately straight line. The office was a severe workplace, reflecting, I suspected, the head's own character, with none of the cheerful color of the nursery itself.

Miss Webb leaned toward me, her elbows resting on the desk, her fingertips pressed together disapprovingly.

"Have you given careful consideration to the matter we discussed before half-term, Mrs. Richardson?"

"And what was that?" I hedged.

"Oh, come now," Miss Webb said condescendingly. "Let's not play games."

I felt my hackles rise at the tone of her voice and struggled to keep my voice level.

"I don't play games, Miss Webb, not where my children's welfare is concerned. I thought this meeting was to discuss whether the boys were to remain in this school?"

She stared at me, her jaw working above the velvet collar of her jacket.

"As we have already discussed, there are no issues with Toby. He seems a bright boy and I'm sure there will be no problem with him continuing into the lower prep class next September. Edward is the concern. He is, in my opinion, in need of specialist care. As I said before, I do not feel we have the facilities to help him. Have you found anywhere for him to go after Christmas?"

"After Christmas? Can't you keep him here until the end of the school year?"

Miss Webb sighed rather rudely, and I resisted the temptation to reach across the pretentious acre of leather-topped desk and grab her by her scrawny throat.

"Humor me, Miss Webb. Did you suggest to me that Teddy would be better off in residential care?"

"That is what we discussed at the beginning of last term. And I have also pointed out that we do not allow the use of a child's nickname in school."

I stood up, straightening my jacket. "I will of course have to discuss this with my husband. If he agrees with me, you will have half a term's notice for both boys in writing by the end of the week, Miss Webb."

She stood up, too, on the far side of her desk. "I'm sorry you feel that way, Mrs. Richardson. Toby has been doing well with us."

"It could just as easily have been Toby who was having problems if he had been born second. It's not the child you care about, Miss Webb, but your school's reputation. Toby will probably do well anywhere, and I don't believe this school has the right ethos for either of our boys. Good day to you."

I was so angry as I walked out of the school office that I forgot to check to see if the motorbike was still lurking. Unlocking the car door, I climbed in and started the engine, thinking of all the things I should have said to the stuck-up, self-opinionated Miss Webb.

It wasn't until the bike passed me a few moments later, then cruised in front of me as I drove toward home, that I remembered Lauren's other pressing problem. The motorcyclist was jabbing his gloved hand to the left and looking ahead, and I saw a turning a little farther on. Sighing, I indicated left and eased the Galaxy into the small dirt lot, pulling in next to a vehicle where a dog walker was attaching a leash to the collar of a chocolate Labrador, which was standing in an open hatchback. I thought of Bessie, then Frankie, and wished she were here with me now. She would have been a comfort to me and perhaps a deterrent to this complete stranger who probably thought he was going to be able to persuade me that I loved him.

Turning off the engine, I waited for the motorcyclist to park his bike and walk across to me. The dog walker locked her car and disappeared down a tree-lined track. I lowered the window as the man drew level with the car and watched as he pulled off his helmet. As I had guessed, it was the young man from the restaurant. He ran a hand through his blond hair and gazed beseechingly at me with his blue eyes.

"Lauren, please give me a few minutes. I need to talk to you."

"I'm sorry. I explained the other night that I don't remember you. There's no point in talking if you mean nothing to me."

"You loved me once, Lauren . . . enough to promise to leave your family for me. Don't you think you owe me a few minutes of your time?"

I hesitated, and he picked up on it immediately. "Only five minutes," he begged. "I promise I'll leave you alone afterward."

"Okay. Get in. But don't try anything. You've got five minutes."

As soon as he was in the car he tried to take my hand, but I pulled it away and turned sideways to face him.

"I don't even know your name."

"It's Jason."

"Look, Jason. Whatever went on with us before is over. I'm not the same person I was before the lightning strike. I can understand that you miss what we had, but the Lauren you knew is gone for good."

Before I could say any more, he leaned over, took my face between his hands, and kissed me full on the lips. I was so surprised that for a moment I stayed there, held captive by his kiss. His lips were soft and moist and he smelled of an aftershave I couldn't identify. Even his chin, rubbing against mine, was smooth, almost as if he had no need to shave. He reminded me of a boy I had once kissed in junior school.

Turning away so that he was obliged to pull back, I shook my head.

"It's no good, Jason. You can't rekindle a love that I don't recall ever existed. I don't know you. I don't love you."

He gazed wildly at me as if such a thing were beyond his comprehension. "I don't believe you. You don't love your husband, I know you don't."

I lowered my eyes and he seized on the silent admission as if it were a lifeline. He grabbed me by the tops of my arms and shook me, just as Grant had done.

"Look at me and tell me you're in love with someone else, Lauren. Tell me that and I'll believe you."

I thought of Dan and a shiver ran through me. I loved Dan more than anyone in the world, and I hugged this realization to me, unaware of the dreamy look that crossed my features.

"I am in love with someone else, Jason," I said gently. "And I'm staying with Grant and the family. I'm sorry that you are hurting, but there's nothing I can do about my feelings. Think of the Lauren you knew as dead. I'm sure that if she was planning to leave the children for you, she must have loved you very much, but that isn't me. Grieve for her, Jason, because that Lauren no longer exists."

He watched me for another moment, the hurt reflecting deep in his eyes, then he turned abruptly from me, opened the door, and strode away across the car park.

Closing my eyes, I rested my head on the steering wheel, my hands gripped together in my lap. I heard the bike engine revving and the screech of tires on the hard-packed earth, and I knew I had hurt a virtual stranger more deeply than I had thought it possible to hurt anyone. By the time I reached home I felt exhausted. Karen took one look at me as I teetered silently into the immaculate kitchen and hurriedly put the kettle on.

"You look like shit, Lauren," she said as she rummaged in the cupboard for tea bags. "What the hell happened?"

I told her about Miss Webb and how I'd have to start looking for a new nursery school for both the boys, and then I told her about Jason.

"No wonder you look like you've just crawled out from a train wreck," she said, forcing a mug of tea between my clasped hands. "I'm so sorry, Jessica. Lauren does seem to have left you with a few major problems."

We both turned sharply at the clattering sound of a vacuum cleaner hose being dropped on the white-tiled floor behind us, and found Elsie standing in the kitchen doorway. She was frowning at us, and I could see from the jerkiness of her movements as she crossed the kitchen that she'd heard Karen refer to me as Jessica.

"Is everything all right, Elsie?" I asked sweetly. "It's wonderful to have you back with us after the weekend. I'm sorry everywhere was such a mess, but I'm still having trouble remembering where everything goes."

"That's all right, Mrs. Richardson," she muttered, watching me carefully as if she thought I might metamorphose into some sort of monster before her very eyes.

"I really must stop calling you by that silly nickname," Karen said loudly as Elsie crossed to the cupboard and put the vacuum away. "Mother should never have given you that second name, should she? See how confusing it is?"

"I don't mind if you call me Lauren or Jessica," I replied equally loudly. "Sisters can get away with anything. But don't mind if I start calling you by your middle name."

We laughed the moment away, and when Elsie crossed back with the polish and a duster she seemed more at ease.

As soon as we heard her moving about upstairs again, I hissed at Karen, "You've got to try to call me Lauren. I don't want to end up locked away in a mental institution, or, worse still, in a science lab with doctors cutting bits off me."

"I know, I'm sorry," she said sheepishly. "The trouble is, you don't seem like Lauren at all now that I know who you really are. I've accepted that my sister is probably dead and it's really hard seeing you walking about looking like her, let alone having to use her name for you."

I sipped at my tea and frowned. "I'm not happy about it, either. I don't want to look like her, Karen. I was thinking of having my hair dyed back to Lauren's natural color. If her roots are anything to go by, her hair is the same color as yours and Nicole's, isn't it?"

Karen nodded. "I suppose so. I haven't seen her natural coloring since we were both kids."

"Would it help you if I didn't look so much like her?"

Karen smiled. "It would be interesting. But it will make it harder still to remember to call you by her name."

I spent the rest of the day calling local schools for appointments to discuss Toby and Teddy's special needs, practicing Lauren's signature, checking her diary for forthcoming events, and making a hair appointment for the following day. I also did another two loads of laundry and put away piles of clothing in the children's rooms, for what I hoped were the right owners.

By the time I went out for the school pickup I was trembling with exhaustion. I'd had no idea that having a family entailed so much work. It worried me that Karen was carrying a large part of the workload and that she'd be gone next week, and I thanked my lucky stars that Grant employed Elsie. But next week was still going to be a struggle, especially getting up in time for school.

As I pulled the car out of the garage and across the drive, I glanced along the street and my heart sank further. The motorbike was back, parked by the junction of the next turning: the black-helmeted head staring toward me. Jason was obviously not going to be put off by a few home truths.

"Go away!" I muttered, thumping the steering wheel with the palm of my hands. "Leave me alone, you stupid man."

I accelerated away, but a glance in my rearview mirror told me that he was following me at a distance. He stayed with me all the way to the nursery school, where he parked a little way along the road, and he was still sitting there when I came out holding the boys by their hands and strapped them into their car seats.

Driving on to the girls' school, I realized I was spending more time looking in the mirror than at the road in front of me, and I forced myself to ignore him. I parked in the playground again, as the girls had instructed me, but to my dismay the motorbike followed me right into the school grounds. Climbing out of the car to wait with the other mothers, I kept glancing across until one of them asked if I knew him.

I shook my head. "He's nothing to do with me."

As soon as Sophie and Nicole arrived, I hurried them to the car, glancing over my shoulder to see if he was still watching.

"Did you have a good day?" I asked the girls with false enthusiasm as they fastened their safety belts.

"I told my class about Ginny," Nicole said happily. "The teacher said I could bring her in to show everyone. Can I, Mummy?"

I clambered into the driver's seat and put my own belt on. "I don't see why not."

"Mummy," Sophie said suddenly, her voice anxious, "isn't that the man you were talking to in the park?"

I looked over to where Jason was sitting astride his bike, his helmet in his hands. He was staring openly at me now, his expression grim.

I felt a tremor of fear run through me as I realized that Lauren's lovesick beau was not going to take no for an answer. As if I didn't have enough on my plate, it seemed that I now had a stalker.

chapter fifteen

By the time we arrived home, my hands were shaking so much that I couldn't get Teddy's safety belt undone. Jason had not only taken off his helmet so the children could identify him, but he'd also followed us home again and had taken up his previous position a short way up the road. I hoped he wouldn't be stupid enough to still be there when Grant came home from work.

Karen peered out of the window when I told her about him, but she said she couldn't see him from there. I busied myself making the children drinks and biscuits to keep them going until the meal was ready, then spent the next hour in the kitchen while Karen supervised the girls' homework.

"How will I do this next week?" I asked her as I turned down the heat under the pans of potatoes and vegetables and turned the chops under the grill. I paused to wipe a wisp of blond hair out of my eyes. "I can't be cooking the dinner and helping with homework at the same time. How did Lauren do it?"

"Sshh," she said, holding a finger up to her lips. "You're

talking about yourself in the third person again. How do you expect me to remember when you keep doing it?"

Shrugging despondently, I tested the potatoes with a fork. "I think they're ready."

"Shall I mash them?"

"Yes please. What homework did the girls have today? Was there much?"

"Sophie has spellings to learn, and a history sheet. Nicole only had some sums, and we've got to listen to both of them read out loud after tea."

Between us we managed to have the meal dished up and on the table in the dining room just as I heard Grant coming in from where he'd parked his car in the garage.

"Go and wash your hands!" I called to the children. "Tea's ready."

Grant came over and gave me a peck on the cheek. His face was slightly flushed, as if he'd had the heat turned up in his car—or was he angry because he'd spotted Jason parked in the road? I held my breath, expecting some sort of outburst, but none came.

"What's for dinner?"

"Pork chops."

"We had pork yesterday, Lauren," he groaned. "Your memory might be addled, but surely you have some common sense left?"

It was tempting to tell him that I'd actually had roast beef the previous day, with Dan and Patrick, but I resisted the impulse and avoided his gaze. Karen had indeed made a lovely roast pork lunch for us all in this family's yesterday, but that seemed so long ago to me, and so much had happened since then.

My pulse quickened at the thought of Dan and how happy we had been the day before. I missed him while I was here, and I felt suddenly drained of emotion and heartily fed up with the whole situation.

"Mummy?"

I looked down to see Teddy staring up at me, his eyes troubled.

"What, Teddy?"

"Don't be sad, Mummy."

His troubled expression was an echo of my own, and I made an effort to smile down at him. "I won't be sad. Not when I'm here with you. Come along, let's go and eat."

"You eating with us?" Karen asked Grant somewhat sharply as we all sat down at the table.

He looked at her, a surprised expression on his face. "Of course."

"Oh, it's just that I thought I heard you complain that you didn't want pork two days running."

"Don't be ridiculous, Karen," he said, picking up his knife and fork. "You know perfectly well that I didn't mean I wasn't having any."

"Lauren's been working really hard in the kitchen," Karen continued. "There's not much left in the freezer. She could have made sandwiches, I suppose. It would have been less trouble."

Grant laid his knife and fork back down and stared bewilderedly at Karen. Then he seemed to understand what she was inferring and forced a smile. "This is very nice, Lauren. Thank you."

Karen picked up her own cutlery with a satisfied grin and gave me a wink across the table. I smiled back, realizing as I listened to the children's chatter and watched the family interact, that I wasn't sad anymore. Karen might be confrontational;

Grant might be used to having his own way; this whole family might be very hard work, but I was beginning to think it might be worth every second of it to be here. To be Lauren.

Monday morning was cold and dark. I walked Frankie briskly around the block, then gave her breakfast, which she wolfed down while I had a quick shower and donned one of my skirts and blouses and a warm coat for work. Arriving at the office at ten o'clock on the dot, I was feeling rather pleased with myself for my punctuality when Stephen walked in with a scowl on his face that would have soured milk.

"Good morning, Stephen," I said chirpily. "Would you like some coffee before you start?"

He turned and glowered at me. "You," he said, handing me his heavy overcoat, "can call me Mr. Armitage."

I gawked at him, not knowing what to say. Clara cleared her throat behind me and I turned to hang his coat on the stand to hide my confusion.

"I'll have that coffee, then you can come in to take notes. And hurry up, I haven't got all day."

Clara raised her eyebrows as I poured a cup of coffee from the percolator and followed him into his office, closing the door behind me. Stephen was pacing up and down behind his desk.

"What's the matter?" I asked him. "Has something happened?"

"The matter is that we have a huge workload to get through, Jessica. I'd appreciate it if you would stop talking and start working."

"Is it your mother?" I asked, remembering that his mother had suffered from angina when he and I had been together. "Is she all right?"

He turned on me, his eyes flashing angrily. "How my mother might be feeling is no concern of yours. You wanted to keep our relationship on a strictly work level, so I'd rather you didn't ask personal questions. Now, please take notes."

I felt the color rush to my face, but I sat down obediently in the chair and opened my notebook.

"I'm ready when you are, Mr. Armitage," I said coldly.

Stephen kept me so busy all morning taking notes, then typing forty pages of a lease, that I didn't even have time for a quick coffee or to speak to Clara. By lunchtime I was gasping for a drink, and when I glanced at my watch I found it was after two o'clock.

"I have to go home and take Frankie out for a walk," I said at last.

"I need you to work through lunch today," Stephen said calmly.

"I'm entitled to a lunch break," I insisted.

"I've checked your contract," he said smoothly. "It says that your breaks are at your boss's discretion."

Biting my lip, I picked up my pen again, but then thought better of toeing the line for this man who had once meant something to me, and who had never taken my feelings into consideration even when we had been a couple. I pictured Frankie desperately watching the door, waiting for me to come home and let her out, and I pushed back my chair noisily.

"I'm going for my lunch now, Mr. Armitage. I'll be back in half an hour."

"I've told you, I need you to work."

"Rubbish! You are being petty-minded and childish. If it was just me, I'd put up with it, but I won't have Frankie peeing on the carpet because you've decided to make me suffer."

"If you walk out of that door, you needn't come back, Miss Taylor."

"I'll be back here in thirty minutes," I said, walking toward the door. "Otherwise I'll sue you for unfair dismissal."

My blood boiling, I grabbed my coat and stalked out of the office. Clara's chair was empty, and I presumed she'd already gone for her lunch. Hurrying home with quick, angry strides, I let myself into the flat and crouched to cuddle Frankie, who was, as always, delighted to see me. While she ran madly around the lawn outside, I put the kettle on for a cup of tea and rummaged in the fridge for something to eat. Stephen hadn't even allowed me out of his office when the sandwich girl had arrived, so I'd been unable to buy anything for my lunch.

As soon as I'd eaten and drunk my tea, I took Frankie for a walk, then headed back to the office, hoping that Stephen had had a chance to cool off.

When I got there I walked up the stone steps and pushed the front door to Chisleworth & Partners. It was locked. Ringing the bell, I waited impatiently while Clara came to the door. She opened it and stared at me nervously.

"I can't let you in, Jessica. Mr. Armitage has sacked you! He said if anyone lets you in he'll sack them as well."

"What!" I said, aghast. "He can't do that! He has to give me proper notice at least."

"He says you slapped him, Jessica. What did you do that for?"

"I didn't touch him!" I cried indignantly. "You didn't hear any slapping sounds, did you?"

"He says it was after I'd gone to lunch. He said you were taking it badly that he didn't like your new boyfriend—that you flew into a rage and hit him!"

"He's lying," I said stonily. "You don't believe him, do you, Clara?"

She shrugged. "I don't know what to believe. You have been acting strangely since that lightning strike, and anyway . . ." She paused and wouldn't meet my eyes. "I can't afford to lose my job."

"I'll take him to a tribunal," I fumed. "I've worked here since I left college!"

"Mr. Armitage said to tell you that it's instant dismissal for physical assault. He doesn't have to give you notice. And Jessica"—she lowered her voice—"he says he won't give you a reference, so don't bother to ask. I'm really sorry."

I stared at her frightened eyes and shrugged. "I'm sorry too, Clara. Good-bye."

Turning on my heel, I walked down the steps onto the pavement and strode back down the street the way I'd come.

As soon as I reached the sanctuary of my flat, I sank down onto the sofa and put my head in my hands. This was Stephen's revenge for my choosing Dan over him. Even though he'd refused to make a commitment to me himself, he couldn't bear to let anyone else have me. I also feared that trying to fight a solicitor within the legal system would be a waste of time. My career could well be in ruins.

For a long time I sat there, feeling sorry for myself. Frankie came and rested her head on my knee, staring up at me with big, soulful eyes. I didn't know what to do. I didn't even have a solicitor. Stephen had always handled things like the exchange of contracts for my flat and the drawing up of my will, and I couldn't very well get him to sue himself.

Stroking Frankie's silky ears, I gazed into space. I'd not only lost my job, I'd lost a friend, too. At this moment I wasn't sure my friendship with Clara could ever recover from her shutting the door in my face like that. And even if I forgave her, I thought unhappily, why would she want to socialize with an out-of-work nobody who had started having lengthy, unexplained fainting fits?

The afternoon faded into evening. The room darkened around me and I couldn't be bothered to turn on the lights. I stared through the gloom at the phone, longing to call Dan and pour my heart out to him.

The phone rang, crashing through the silence, making Frankie and me jump. I snatched it up, wondering if it might be Stephen ringing to apologize for his behavior. It wasn't, it was Dan, and I breathed a sigh of relief, my wretchedness dissipating instantly at the sound of his voice.

"How are you today?" he asked. "Everything okay?"

His concern acted like a balm to my shattered nerves and, incredibly, I felt myself smiling.

"Something awful happened today."

"Oh dear. That doesn't sound good. Do you want to come out for a drink this evening and talk about it?"

I turned on the table lamp and looked at the clock. It was half past five.

"That would be great, Dan. Where shall I meet you?"

"I'll come and collect you at, say, eight o'clock?"

"Nine would be better, if you don't mind," I said, thinking quickly.

"No classes with your friend Clara then?"

I remembered my lie with a guilty pang. "No. I'm not going to any more of those."

"See you at nine then. Bye."

As soon as I'd replaced the handset I grabbed Frankie and took her for another walk. It was strange how wintry it seemed, now that the clocks had changed, and I was shivering by the time we'd made our way home through the dark, despite my coat. I wished I still had my sheepskin jacket, but that had been consigned to the dustbin.

I fed Frankie and got myself ready for my date with Dan, having another quick shower and refreshing my makeup. Then I laid out the shoes I was going to wear, next to my handbag, and climbed fully clothed into bed as the hand of the bedside clock arrived at ten to seven. I fell asleep almost immediately, and in no time at all I found myself waking up in Lauren's double bed.

Karen was delighted to see me when I appeared downstairs dressed and ready to see to the children, and I was guiltily relieved to find that Grant had already left for work.

"I have been wondering how you were going to get the children to school when I go home next week," she said, putting down the cornflakes box and kissing me on the cheek. "How did you manage this?"

"Jessica is going out at nine o'clock. I reckoned I should be back from the school run by then. I've simply got to climb out of bed and I'm ready to go. I don't think anyone will miss Lauren this morning if I go back to bed for a couple of hours."

"Bloody hell," Karen said. "You're sailing close to the proverbial wind, aren't you?"

"I'll go back to bed until twelve; that'll give me three hours with my friend. Then I'll have to get up because Lauren has a hair appointment at one o'clock, and I'm being shown around a school at two-thirty."

"Have you scheduled lunch into your plans, or are you going on a crash diet?"

"I'll have a sandwich when I get up, don't worry," I said with a grin.

"Which 'get up' is that?" she asked sarcastically.

"Here," I said. "But I haven't eaten yet in my other world, so I'm hoping drinks with Dan will turn into dinner."

She rolled her eyes heavenward, then fixed her gaze on me with renewed interest.

"Dan? Is he your boyfriend?"

"I only met him last weekend," I said, unable to prevent the dreamy tone creeping into my voice. "But he's everything I've ever imagined in my wildest dreams. He's wonderful."

"This is so weird," Karen said, pouring cereal into four bowls. "You've got a jealous husband to deal with, a jilted lover who appears to be stalking you, and all the time you're in love with this Dan fellow. How can you cope with all this at once?"

"I don't have a choice, Karen. My other life is as important to me as this one, more so in fact, because that's who I really am. It isn't real to you because you don't know me as Jessica, but I'm there just as often as I'm here."

She shook her head. "I can't help feeling you're going to come apart at some point, Lauren. You're like a juggler with all your balls in the air at the same time."

"I'll manage," I promised her, changing the subject quickly. "Are the children awake yet?"

"I've just woken them. The girls are putting their uniforms on but the twins need a bit of help—they'll wear whatever you put out for them."

I hurried upstairs and looked in on the boys, who were fighting over who was going to wear what.

"Come on, guys," I urged. "Your cornflakes will get soggy."

I helped Teddy struggle into a pair of gray trousers and a blue sweatshirt. By the time he was ready Toby had already run downstairs, having dressed himself at lightning speed, and was sitting at the breakfast bar wolfing down his cereal.

I braided Sophie's long hair and was handing out drinks cartons and cereal bars for their breaks when Nicole produced a slip of paper from her blazer pocket.

"It's about our class play," she said. "You've got to fill it in to say if you and Daddy are coming or not." She looked up at me with an imploring expression. "Please can you come this time, Mummy? All the other mums and dads are coming."

"Of course," I said, smiling at her. "What part are you playing?"

"I'm a lamb," she informed me importantly. "I'm going to be given to the baby Jesus as a present."

I found a pen and started filling in the form, pausing to look at Karen. "Would you like to come, too?"

"When is it?"

I scanned the letter. "The second of December."

She grinned at me. "It's a ways off, but yeah, I can probably get away from work early. I'd like to see our Nicole performing. Put me down as a yes."

I filled the form in quickly and put it in Nicole's blazer pocket.

"You will really come, won't you?" she asked anxiously.

"I promise," I said, smiling.

As I drove the children to their respective schools and nursery I scanned the traffic anxiously for signs of the motorbike, but was relieved that, for the moment at least, Jason seemed to have given up on the idea of following me about.

Teddy clung to me again when I took him in, and I had to leave him crying, which left me with a leaden feeling in my stomach all the way home. I wondered how Lauren had stood it.

As I parked the car in the garage, I hoped that the school I would be looking at later turned out to be suitable. I didn't want to leave him at that nursery school any longer than was necessary.

I arrived home at about two minutes to nine, called a greeting to Karen, and bounded upstairs to my bedroom. Elsie was emerging with a can of polish and a duster in her hand.

"Miss Harper told me you weren't feeling all that well and that you'd be wanting a lie down, so I've done your room for you, Mrs. Richardson."

"Thank you, Elsie," I said, realizing after a moment's confusion that Harper was Karen's surname. I remembered her using it at the farm. My maiden name, I thought with a jolt. How little I really knew about this woman whose life I was living.

Closing the curtains, and without bothering to undress, I kicked off my shoes and climbed into bed. Several deep breaths later I felt myself drifting off to sleep. My last thought as my soul disconnected from Lauren was that this must be part of the big plan; otherwise how would I be able to send myself to sleep as easily as this and slip away like a ghost in the night?

Rousing to the sounds of pounding on the front door and Frankie's excited barking, I sat up in bed and swung my legs around until my feet touched the floor. Slipping my feet into the shoes I'd left by the bed, I scooped up my bag and coat, made my way through the sitting room, and grabbed Frankie's collar as I opened the door, to find Dan standing silhouetted against the dark night.

"I thought something had happened to you!" he gasped, stepping forward and enveloping me in a big hug. "I've been knocking for ten minutes!"

"I'm sorry. I lay down on the bed for a moment. I must have dropped off."

He pushed me backward into the flat and closed the door on the cold night air. He was eyeing me suspiciously. "You sleep like the dead, Jessica. Are you sure you're all right?"

"I'm fine, honestly. A bit hungry maybe . . . have you eaten yet?"

He shook his head. "I thought we might grab a bite in the pub."

"Great," I said, opening the door again. "Let's go."

I could see he was suspicious, but he remained quiet as he drove up onto the Downs and parked outside a busy pub. When he turned the engine off, he sat quietly, making no attempt to get out of the car.

"Tell me the truth, Jessica," he said, swiveling to look into my eyes in the gloomy light seeping from the pub window. "Did you pass out again?"

I hesitated, not sure how much to tell him. In the end I nodded. "I suppose I might have. I lay on the bed as soon as I was ready, and I didn't wake until I heard you hammering on the door. It's difficult to tell really."

"I want you to go back to the doctor," he said, taking my hand and squeezing it gently. "Something isn't right here, and I think you should be thoroughly checked out."

"I will," I promised. "I'll book an appointment with my doctor first thing tomorrow morning." I realized with a pang of guilt that not only was I lying to him, I also had no intention of keeping that other appointment that I, or rather Lauren, had made with the counselor in my other life.

He leaned over and kissed me. "I care about you, you know. I don't want anything to happen to you."

"It won't," I told him, thinking about his mother. "If there's anything wrong it's bound to be due to the lightning strike. I was fine before that. I expect my body needs time to recover, that's all."

"I hope so," he said firmly. "I don't want to lose you."

"And I don't want to be lost," I said with a reassuring smile. "I care for you, too, Dan. Very much."

We made our way into the warm, noisy atmosphere of the pub and found ourselves a table for two in one corner. Dan went to order drinks while I looked at the bar menu, though I found it hard to concentrate. Dan had said he cared for me, but if he thought there was something really wrong with me would he still stick around? I dreaded to think what he would say if he knew the truth about my shared existence with Lauren.

Dan arrived back at the table with our drinks and I sipped at my water while he studied the menu. When we'd made our choices I went up to the bar and ordered our meals, then returned and sat with my hand resting on his.

"Tell me about this terrible day of yours," he said, putting his glass of lager down. "It sounded as if it must have been pretty bad."

"Stephen sacked me," I said bluntly. "He made up some story about me hitting him and cited instant dismissal."

Dan looked suitably horrified. "No!"

I nodded grimly. "He kept me working all morning and half the afternoon without a break, and when I insisted on being allowed half an hour to walk Frankie, he told me that if I left I couldn't come back. I didn't really believe him. I thought he was jealous because of you, and just letting off steam."

"You're not going to let him get away with it, are you?"

"I could go to a tribunal, but Stephen knows all the solicitors hereabouts. He'd make sure I didn't get a fair hearing."

"You've got to do something. He's behaving like a spoiled child. It seems to me that he wanted you back solely because he didn't want anyone else to have you. And now, because you've rejected him, he's punishing you."

"I know. I've been going over it all afternoon. I thought I might go to the Citizens Advice Bureau tomorrow and see if they can help."

He squeezed my hand reassuringly. "I'm so sorry, Jessica, this is my fault. If he hadn't found me at your flat you'd still have your job now."

I smiled at him. "I'd rather have you."

Our food arrived and we ate quickly, knowing that all we really wanted was to be cuddled in each other's arms. As soon as we'd finished, I invited him back to the flat, and we only just made it in through the front door before our lips met hungrily and we were tugging at each other's clothes as we bundled toward the bedroom.

Later, lying snug together under my duvet, Dan rested his chin on my shoulder and stroked my hair.

"You're beautiful, Jessica, did you know that?"

"Would you still want me if I was old and covered in stretch marks?"

"I would," he said. "I love the person you are inside."

Thrilling at his words, I kissed him gently. "Do you know what you just said?"

"I do, and it's true. I love you, Jessica," he murmured into my hair.

"I love you too, Dan," I whispered as I rested my head against his chest. "I've loved you since the first moment I set eyes on you up on the Downs."

chapter sixteen

Dan had left at midnight, which was just as well, I thought, as I climbed out of Lauren's bed and headed for the bathroom. The last thing I'd wanted was for him to leave, but my eyes had strayed to the bedside clock and I'd been aware that Lauren's day was ticking by.

He'd seen me looking and thought I was tired. We'd held each other passionately, not really wanting to part, but then he'd groped about for his discarded clothes and begun to dress.

As soon as he was gone, I'd patted Frankie good night and slid back under the covers, closed my eyes, and let Jessica sleep.

Lauren looked pretty good, I decided, peering into her mirror. I brushed her blond hair off her shoulders and swiveled to look at the burns, which had miraculously all but healed in the week and a half since the accident. All that was now visible of the massive electrical shock that had killed her was a slight reddening of the skin.

"Karen!" I called as I walked through the kitchen a few

minutes later, carrying the requisite bundle of laundry, which I shoved into the machine. "Karen, where are you?" Elsie had finished for the morning and the house was silent. I wandered back into the kitchen to make myself the sandwich I'd promised Karen I'd eat before going out. Opening the fridge, I found a note propped against a pack of cheddar:

Lauren, I'm going to visit Jessica in Epsom. Back later.

Love Karen

I folded the note up, put it in the pocket of Lauren's jacket, and tried to think. Had I given her proper instructions? Would she be in any danger? My mind was in turmoil as I automatically buttered bread, sliced tomatoes, and grated the cheese. Perched at the breakfast bar, my mouth was almost too dry to eat, but I chewed on the sandwich halfheartedly, knowing that Lauren must eat before she . . . before I . . . went out.

Later, sitting in the hairdresser's, I listened to the mindless chatter of the girl who did Lauren's hair. She had been surprised at my request to dye my highlighted locks back to their natural color, and had persuaded me to go for lowlights instead of a solid dye.

"It will give you time to get used to the changeover," she said as she wrapped strands of my hair in silver foil. "It will certainly cover this singed area better, and if you like it you can go darker later on."

The whole process took a lot longer than I had anticipated, and as soon as the last blast of the hair dryer fell silent I shot over to the desk to pay.

"You look lovely," the receptionist said admiringly. "I'm sure your husband will like it."

"Thank you," I murmured, knowing full well that Grant would probably hate it. But I hadn't done it for him, I'd done it for me and for Karen, and from the moment I'd looked into the mirror at my newly blow-dried locks I knew I had made the right decision.

Arriving at the local infant school five minutes late, I flew through the door to find a matronly looking woman waiting for me in her office. She introduced herself as Mrs. Hoskins, the headmistress.

"Please sit down and tell me about your boys," she said, opening a file, which I assumed had the contents of our phone call within its covers.

I told her about Toby's cleverness, and Teddy's delayed entry into the world and how he struggled with things the rest of us took for granted. "But," I continued, taking a rolled-up sheet of paper from my bag, "look at how artistic he is."

I spread the drawing of myself on her desk and she studied it carefully.

"Your son certainly shows a flare for art," she said, sitting back. "We do have a special-needs unit attached to the school here, but it might be best for Teddy to integrate with the rest of the class and still have help from the special-needs teachers where necessary. I'm assuming Teddy has been assessed by an educational psychologist?"

Feeling myself color, I nodded quickly. I couldn't very well tell the headmistress that I had no idea whether my child had been assessed or not, but if that was the criterion for getting Teddy a place in her school, I would have to pretend that I knew he had.

She smiled. "If you could just send us a copy of the report, it would enable us to give Teddy the support where he most needs it."

"Yes, of course. I'll get it to you as soon as possible."

"Toby, of course, will have no problem getting on. We have a very high percentage of bright children here. Would you like to see the unit for yourself?"

I nodded again and accompanied her on a tour of the school, following her through the mainstream classrooms and the special-needs unit, where several children were receiving one-to-one instruction. The atmosphere was one of warmth and calm. The teachers seemed dedicated and kind, the children happy.

"Could I put both the boys' names down?" I asked as we returned to her office twenty minutes later. "I think this environment will suit them perfectly."

"Of course," she said, smiling. "You live in our catchment area, so there should be no problem."

"How soon could they start?"

Mrs. Hoskins looked again at her notes, which included the twins' date of birth. "They can start next term if you like. If you could fill in these forms and return them to me in the next few days, with the psychologist's report, I will send you confirmation of their places."

I wanted to race around the desk and hug her, but I smiled broadly instead.

"Thank you so much," I said, holding out my hand. "I'll be in touch as soon as I've spoken to my husband."

Glancing at my watch, I hurried back to the car and set off for the school pickups. The boys finished at three-thirty and I was late. Driving as quickly as the speed limit allowed, I glanced in my rearview mirror then turned into the road where the nursery school was situated. My heart gave a jolt as I spotted the bike parked a hundred yards from the nursery-school entrance. Jason was lying in wait in the one place he could be certain I would show up.

As I climbed out of the car, he removed his helmet again and sat staring at me, a look of longing on his face. I hurried into the building and stood with the other mums waiting for our children to emerge.

Teddy seemed happy enough when I spotted him among the throng of children piling out of the door, and I hoped the teachers were telling me the truth when they said he'd stopped crying the moment I'd left him that morning.

Both boys rushed up to me, and Teddy threw his arms around my waist. I gently detached him, held them both by their hands, and walked them to where I'd parked. Jason was still there, watching me, and I had the horrible feeling he was going to follow me to the girls' school, as he had done the day before.

Once the girls were collected I drove back home, with half my mind occupied by how Karen might be getting on and the other half wondering if the bike was still following me. The children chatted about what they'd done in school and I tried to remember to make the right noises in the right places.

To my enormous relief, Karen was waiting for us when we walked through the door. The delicious smells emanating from the kitchen told me she'd started dinner, and I asked the girls to go out and feed their pets before we ate to give us a minute alone together.

The two girls went off clutching carrots and greens, led by Sophie, who held a torch, while the boys stayed in the playroom to unwind and watch TV.

"What happened?" I begged Karen as soon as we were alone.

"Should I tell you?" she asked. "After all, today hasn't happened for you yet. Won't I be changing the laws of physics if I tell you what you're going to do and say tomorrow?"

"You saw me then?"

She nodded. "I saw you, and we talked. I love your little dog, too. You must miss her while you're here."

"What time did you get there . . . did the time change or anything?"

She shook her head as she stirred the Bolognese sauce and checked to make sure the spaghetti wasn't burning.

"I don't think I should tell you too much about it, but no, the time didn't change. You were there today, wide awake, while Lauren was awake here."

"Wow!"

"Time must change only for you," she went on calmly, as if discussing the most natural thing in the world. "So you can cope with being in two places at the same time. For the rest of us Tuesday is Tuesday. It's only you who hasn't experienced Jessica's Tuesday yet."

I realized that Karen was more relaxed now that she'd actually met me as Jessica. It was as if she'd come to terms with the strange reality of the situation. She'd had the ultimate proof and was taking it in stride.

"I can hardly believe it," I breathed, shaking my head, wishing I could be as levelheaded as Karen. "Jessica was there today, but I haven't experienced it yet."

"I wouldn't think about it too much if I were you," she said, draining the spaghetti into the colander over the sink. "You'll drive yourself crazy. But I can assure you that it works, whatever this thing is that happens to enable you to be in two places at the same time."

"Did we get along?" I asked, ignoring her advice to limit the conversation. "Did you recognize me?"

We fell silent as the girls came back indoors and went to join their brothers watching television, then Karen gave a little laugh.

"It took me a little while to adjust to your appearance, but once we got talking I would have known you anywhere. You're exactly the same person, you say and do the same things, even though your voice and looks are different." She paused, reached out a hand, and patted my hair. "I like this very much by the way. Less like Lauren and much easier for me to cope with."

"Thanks, but tell me more about what you thought of the real me."

"I knew you were, you know . . . you, in exactly the same way that last week I suspected you couldn't be Lauren. You and my sister are such different people. I'm surprised Grant hasn't sussed it out really."

"I wish Jason would suss it out," I said quietly. "He was waiting for me when I got to the nursery school again. He followed me and watched me while I collected the girls. He gives me the creeps, Karen."

We called the children in to have their tea, then I supervised their homework and listened to the girls read. After their baths I read to the boys, and by seven o'clock Grant was home. We ate the remains of the spaghetti Bolognese with Karen in the dining room while he told us about the rigors of his day at the practice.

After clearing away the food and moving the laundry from the washer to the dryer, I joined Grant in the living room to fill him in on what had happened with my appointment at the school.

He stared at me as if noticing my hair for the first time. "You've done something to your hair," he said accusingly.

"Do you like it?" I asked. "I had lowlights instead of highlights for a change, since it covers the singed section."

"It's different," he said noncommittally. "You don't look like you."

"Actually, it looks more like the real me, because it's closer to my natural coloring," I said.

Grant frowned, and I remembered Karen's assertion that over the years he had modeled Lauren to his own liking, but I hurried on, telling him about the school I'd visited.

"We're in the catchment area, so there's no problem with getting the boys in. We need to have Teddy assessed, though."

"He's been assessed, Lauren. That's why you've been looking at alternative schools. The report is in the safe. Here," he said, scribbling a number on the pad by the phone.

"This is the combination. You can send it on to the headmistress tomorrow."

"Thank you, Grant," I said in relief. "It's perfect for Teddy, as there's a special-needs unit attached to the school, but he will still mix with the other children." I took a deep breath. "And I think Toby will do very well there, too. It seems a friendly and caring environment."

"Toby's not going there. We've had his name down at several good schools locally. It wouldn't be fair to educate the girls privately and send Toby to a state school."

"He's bright," I said. "He'll do well anywhere."

"No," Grant replied, rising to his feet and pacing across the powder-blue carpet. "I won't have Toby sent there."

"But Grant! We can't use the state system just for our special-needs child and not also send his brother."

"I won't have it," Grant said stubbornly. "You can send Teddy there if you want, I agree it sounds right for him, but Toby stays at the nursery school and goes to one of the private schools we've already chosen."

"Can we afford to put three children through private school?"

Grant rolled his eyes. "I keep forgetting the amnesia. My parents have made provision to educate the children, Lauren. They've been paying into the fund for years and the school fees will never be a problem. In fact, there will be money to spare if Teddy isn't educated privately, too."

I stared at Grant, irritated by his stubborn insistence that Toby couldn't go to the same school as his brother, especially when he hadn't even seen the place. I didn't want to let the pompous Miss Webb have the satisfaction of keeping Toby, but then I remembered the children were Grant's. They weren't really mine, and I was new at this parenting thing. Did I have the right to change what their father wanted for them? I wondered.

Remembering that we had to continue to live together in some sort of harmony, I decided for the sake of peace between us that I wouldn't press the point. "Is that your final decision about Toby then?"

"Absolutely. Fill in the forms for Teddy. Toby stays put."

As I went up to bed I peeked into each of the children's rooms. Toby was asleep on his back, his mouth open. Teddy was curled up, clutching his ball. The girls were both on their sides, their long hair spilling over their pillows. I stood watching them for a while, wondering again how Lauren could ever have contemplated leaving them. They were lovely children and I felt so, so lucky to be given the chance to be a part of their lives.

On Tuesday morning I walked to the Citizens Advice Bureau, with Frankie trotting at my heels, to ask about representation for a tribunal for unfair dismissal. Now that I'd had a chance to cool off and think things through in a rational manner, I'd decided there was no way I was going to let Stephen get away with it. It appeared that without witnesses to the supposed assault, Stephen's case rested on pretty shaky ground. I walked home again, determined to fight him all the way. It wasn't that I wanted my job back, in fact the thought of working for him again after this was impossible, but I wanted justice, and I wanted a good reference so I could look around for something else.

After a short shopping trip, I went home to await Karen's visit. I knew that although she had been reluctant to tell me much about it yesterday, I would find out exactly what went on in person today.

At twelve o'clock I heard a tentative knock at the front door. Frankie raced me to the door, barking wildly, and I opened it to find Karen standing on the step looking nervous and apprehensive.

"Karen!" I cried, taking her arm and drawing her into the sitting room. "I've been waiting for you."

She stared at me incredulously. "But I didn't tell anyone I was coming."

"Come in and sit down," I said, taking her shaggy jacket as she stood watching my every move. "How was the journey?"

She ignored my question and spluttered, "How did you know I was coming? I haven't even told Lauren; I left her asleep upstairs. You are Jessica, aren't you?"

"You told me when you got back," I explained, restraining

Frankie, who was trying to claim our attention by jumping up against Karen's trousers. "Please don't look so worried, Karen. It's me, Jessica . . . Lauren . . . your new sister."

Karen sank heavily onto the couch, and Frankie rested her head against Karen's ample calves, gazing up at her with adoring eyes.

"Frankie likes you," I commented, trying to put her at ease.

"This is so weird," she said. "I wanted to see you for myself, but I wasn't sure if it would be safe . . . Have I done the right thing?"

"It's quite safe, Karen. Lauren experiences each day first, that's all. You left me a note propped in the fridge telling me you were coming here. When you get home this afternoon you tell Lauren . . . me . . . a bit about your visit, that you've been here today, so I . . . Jessica . . . knew you were coming by here today."

Karen rubbed a hand over her eyes as if trying to dispel a nightmare.

"Bloody hell."

I grinned at her. "Fancy a cup of tea?"

She nodded, still looking shell-shocked.

It didn't take long to make two mugs of tea in my small kitchen, and I walked back into the sitting room and handed one to Karen, who, it seemed, couldn't take her eyes off me.

"You're as pretty as Lauren, but in a different way," she said at last. "I can see why you don't want to be blond; your hair is a lovely color."

"Thanks. By the time you get home, Lauren will have been to the hairdresser and had lowlights put in."

Sipping at my tea, I couldn't help smiling at her bemused expression. She must have felt she was sitting drinking tea with a complete stranger, whereas I felt completely at home with this woman who'd believed until only a few days ago that I was her sister.

"Would you like to see around the flat?" I asked, more to break the tension than from any desire to show her my possessions.

"Yes, I'd like that. I want to know the real person who's masquerading as my sister."

"I'm sorry, Karen, I know this must be difficult for you, but you must believe that I never asked for any of this."

"How do you do it?" she asked as she followed me into the bedroom and then peeked into my tiny bathroom."How do you cope with being dropped into the life of a mother of four, in that huge house that's so different to everything you have here?"

I shrugged. "No choice. It's where I wake up in the mornings. I just do the best I can."

I watched as her shoulders relaxed slightly, and then she smiled.

"I'm sorry if you think I'm giving you a hard time. This is all so strange. Once I suspected you weren't my sister, I had to accept your explanation of what happened to her, but seeing you in the body of a complete stranger is really freaky. I don't know what I was expecting to find by coming here, but I don't think I expected to find you. On the way over here in the car I thought about all the things I was going to ask you, but when you opened the door I was struck dumb. I can't get my head around it at all."

"Don't try," I said, smiling back. "We'll both go mad if we think about it too much. How about having some lunch? I went out and bought some oven fries this morning. I know how much you like them!"

She laughed then and followed me into the kitchen, where I put the oven on and sprinkled some fries onto a baking tray.

"I thought you'd appreciate this, since it's the meal that gave my identity away," I chuckled. "Sophie obviously realized that as I'd lost my memory she could pull a fast one and tell me that I gave them all oven fries, ketchup, and ice cream every day!"

"I definitely thought that something very odd was going on," Karen admitted. "Lauren never let them have fries as a main meal; I expect they were only in the freezer as a standby. I just didn't know at that point how strange things were going to become!"

Karen stayed for over an hour, then glanced at her wristwatch.

I ought to be getting back. Lauren might be worrying about me."

"I was worrying about you," I said. "But you got home before me and started the dinner."

"I'm thinking of doing spaghetti Bolognese," she said. "Do I change my mind on the way home?"

"No," I laughed. "You make a delicious Bolognese sauce. But I won't tell you any more about what happens later. It isn't a good idea to tell someone what's going to happen in the future."

"I'll obey the same rule when I get home then," she said. "I won't tell you too much about what happened today, because as Lauren you won't have had Jessica's version of today."

"Right then," I said, shaking my head with a confused smile. "I'll see you later."

I waved from the door as she walked back up the courtyard steps and disappeared around the corner, then I pulled on a coat and took Frankie for another walk. I had only been back in the flat ten minutes and was pulling off my shoes when the doorbell rang. I answered it to find Dan standing there.

"Would you care to join Dad and me for some tea?" he asked.

I glanced at my watch; clock-watching had become a necessity of late.

"It's a bit early for tea, but I'd love to come over. How is your father?"

"He's great, but he gets lonely when I'm at work all day, even when I leave Bessie there to keep him company. I thought we might cook another meal together at my place and share it with the old man. Do you like cooking?"

"I don't dislike it," I said, thinking guiltily of the oven fries I'd served my guest at lunchtime. "What did you have in mind?"

"I stopped off and bought some minced beef on the way over here. Do you like spaghetti Bolognese?"

I nearly laughed, but stopped myself in time. "That would be lovely," I said, struggling to keep my expression neutral. "Do you need me to bring anything or have you got it all?"

"I forgot to buy any black pepper, if you've got some."

I nodded and headed for the kitchen, remembering only at the last minute that I hadn't cleared away the lunch things. Dan followed me in and stood staring at the used mugs and plates I'd carelessly heaped onto the drying rack before taking Frankie for her walk.

"You've had company then?"

"Er . . . yes, an old friend dropped by for lunch."

"Oh."

He looked horribly suspicious and doubtful, and I realized that he might think it had been Stephen.

"It was a female friend named Karen."

"Oh, well, it's none of my business anyway."

I could feel his eyes boring into the back of my head as I rummaged in the kitchen cupboard for the pepper mill, and I felt myself flush guiltily. I hoped he wouldn't probe too deeply about Karen, because as Jessica I had no way of knowing her, and I didn't want to start lying to him again if I could help it. I couldn't very well tell him she was my sister when he knew I didn't have one.

"Do you mind if I change quickly? I've been out walking Frankie and I could do with a brush-up."

"Go ahead," he said, taking the pepper mill from me and settling himself onto the sofa. "There's no rush."

When I'd changed into a clean pair of jeans and T-shirt and reapplied my makeup, I returned to find him leaning back on the sofa, eyes closed.

"Hard day?" I asked him, perching next to him and resting my hand on his knee.

He opened his eyes and smiled.

"I can't get anything done. Since I met you all I think about is you. I can hardly wait to come over and see you, and work has suddenly become a chore."

"If it's any consolation, I feel the same way," I said, returning the smile. "I was hoping to see you today, but I didn't want you to feel suffocated."

He shook his head. "Not possible. I told you, I'm besotted with you, Jessica. I was worried you might be the one feeling stifled."

He fidgeted with the zipper on one of the cushions, breaking eye contact with me, then said suddenly, "I don't know what's got into me. You have no idea how incredibly jealous I felt when I saw you'd had someone here for lunch. I've never been that way before! My previous girlfriends complained I wasn't demonstrative enough, that I didn't show them I cared about them."

"And did you?"

"Not really, nothing like this, though I suppose I thought I cared at the time."

I leaned toward him until our faces were nearly touching, and breathed in the scent of him.

"We're so lucky," I whispered. "Most people never experience anything like this in their whole lives. It's a mixture of liking and accepting each other, faults and all . . . and," I giggled, "the sex isn't bad, either."

He leaned a little closer still, so that our noses were only a hair's breadth apart. I could feel his breath caressing my skin.

"I love you, Jessica Taylor," he murmured. "I understand we haven't known each other long, but I know without a doubt that I want to be with you, have lots of children with you, and grow old and wrinkly together."

I gazed at him, slightly taken aback. "You don't beat around the bush, do you? And you want children?"

"Lots," he repeated with a grin. "To make up for all the brothers and sisters out there that I never got to know."

I pulled back even further and watched his expression carefully. "And after what happened to your mother, what would you do if there was something wrong with one of our children? Would you run a mile, or stay the course?"

"Any child of ours would be perfect," he said firmly.

"But if it wasn't? What then?"

He frowned as he considered his answer. "If we love each other enough we could cope with anything, Jessica. With you at my side I would stay forever, no matter what problems we had to face."

I almost told him then, but something still held me back. My problem sounded so far-fetched, even to my own ears, that I couldn't bring myself to say anything. Instead I leaned toward him again and traced the outline of his lips with the tip of my tongue. He put his arms around me, pulling me close, and we clung together, lost in each other's embrace.

On Wednesday morning the weather broke, and I awoke to the sound of rain lashing at Lauren's bedroom windows. After dressing hurriedly I helped Karen prepare the children for school. I was late, and since Karen had been expecting me to be up in time this morning, everyone was behind and consequently in bad moods.

"I haven't got long; Dan thinks I'm having a nap after dinner," I whispered to Karen as I hurried the boys to get their shoes on.

"Mum, I want to see Blackie before we go to school," Sophie wailed as I tried to brush her long hair into a ponytail.

"It's too wet. I'll feed the animals when I get home," I promised. "And you can see her this evening."

"But you said I could take Ginny to school to show to my class," Nicole whined, catching her sister's mood. "Everyone is waiting to see her."

"You can take her tomorrow," I said, handing her one of the raincoats Karen had found in the under-stairs cupboard. "Come on, we're going to be late."

"Not going," Teddy said, as I helped him tie his laces. "Don't want go!"

"Teddy is a baby, Teddy is a baby!" Toby chanted.

"Stop it, Toby. You're not helping your brother, are you?" I said crossly.

"He doesn't like the rain, so he is a baby, isn't he?" Toby said, trying to stare me down.

"You should be kind to your brother, Toby. Tell him he doesn't have to worry about a bit of rain."

"You're all going to be late to school at this rate," Karen said unnecessarily. "The traffic's always worse when it's raining."

I took Teddy's hand and started walking toward the garage, but he resisted, pulling against me.

"Won't go, won't go!" he shouted. I turned, trying to get a better grip on his hand, when his foot shot out and caught me directly on the shin.

"Ouch! Teddy, that hurt!"

He stared at me, his lower lip trembling, then he flung his arms around my waist and buried his head in my coat.

"Don't catch fire, Mummy," he sobbed. "Don't go 'way."

"Oh, Teddy," I said, crouching down and putting my arms around his shaking shoulders. "I'm not going to get hurt again. There's no lightning, it's just rain."

I held him against me until his sobs had subsided, then wiped his smeary face with a tissue. "I promise nothing will happen to me. Come and look out of the window. See? Just big raindrops, no thunder, no lightning. It's quite safe."

He stared at me, sticking out his bottom lip in a doubtful pout. We both looked up as Sophie stuck her head in from the garage and called that we were going to be late if we didn't hurry up.

"We're coming, Sophie," I called back. I got to my feet and ruffled Teddy's hair. "Will you be all right now?"

He nodded dubiously, and clung tightly to my hand as we walked to the car.

"See, Teddy? We don't even have to go outside."

After making sure all the children had their seat belts fastened, I drove out into the gray morning with a sigh. As Karen had predicted, our late start and the weather meant that the traffic was twice as heavy as usual. I wouldn't be back by nine now, and Dan would be worried that I was sleeping for so long. I hoped to goodness that he had the good sense to leave me be.

chapter seventeen

Dan was sitting on a chair watching me when I woke up at half past nine that evening in his bed, where I'd gone more than two hours earlier on the pretext of needing a nap. Predictably, Teddy had cried even more desperately when I'd left him at nursery school. It was only when I had promised him he could leave at the end of the term, and that Daddy and I had found a lovely school for him nearby, that he'd eventually relinquished his grip on my clothing.

The traffic had been slow on the way back; the only good thing was that the rain seemed to have kept Jason at home, since there was no sign of him or his bike. As soon as I got in, I had to race down the garden in the torrential rain to feed the animals, before hurrying upstairs to lie down.

For an awful moment, as I lay there panting, my heart pounding from the rushing about, my hair damp from the rain, I thought I wasn't going to be able to sleep. But the ability to swap from one body to another was still with me, and it wasn't long before I felt myself begin to drift.

"Jessica?" Dan said as I began to stir. "You've been asleep for a long time. I was beginning to think you were going to be here for the night."

"I'm sorry, Dan," I said, sitting up. "I must have been more tired than I thought."

I got up and crossed to the hand mirror he kept on the windowsill and straightened my tousled hair. When I looked up he was still watching me.

"Are you going to tell me what's going on?"

"What do you mean?"

"There's something wrong with you, isn't there? The fainting at the office the other day, the collapse while I was with you at the flat. This ability of yours to sleep so soundly. What is it, Jessica?"

I felt myself grow hot under his scrutiny.

"It's nothing, just a residual tiredness from the lightning strike."

He came and stood behind me and pulled my arm around so I was facing him.

"That's not the whole truth, is it?"

I tried to avoid his gaze, but he cupped my face in his hands and stared directly into my eyes.

"Tell me the truth, Jessica . . . please."

"I'm so sorry, Dan," I stammered. "I love you, and I don't want to lose you."

"Tell me!"

"I . . . I can't."

He dropped his hands to his sides and walked to the other side of the room. I could see the frustration in his every move, but I didn't know what to tell him. He stared at me, then came back toward me and tried again.

"Tell me, Jessica. Nothing can be worse than what I'm imagining."

"It was the lightning strike," I said in a hoarse whisper. "It . . . did something to me."

"What?" he cried. "You've said that once before. Is it those turns you were having? Is it something that . . . can't be fixed?"

I turned and stared out of the window at the dark night. I could feel him standing behind me, but he didn't touch me.

"I asked you once if you believed in life after death," I said quietly. "I asked if you thought you would know a soul even if it wasn't in a body you recognized."

"What are you talking about?" he asked.

He sounded desperate, and I wanted more than anything in the world to hold him and tell him that everything was all right. The trouble was, I admitted to myself at last, it wasn't all right. It never could be all right. I had been living in the ridiculous hope that I could juggle being two people at once. I had lied to him, and to Lauren's family. I was, although unwittingly, a fraud, and I wasn't good enough for someone as wonderful as Dan.

"I'm not who you think I am," I said at last. "Since the lightning strike I have been living the lives of two people. I'm Jessica some of the time, but when I sleep my life force transfers to a woman called Lauren. She's the mother of four children, Dan. And the friend I had over for lunch today was her sister . . . my sister."

Dan was standing with his mouth open. I knew I was hurting him terribly. After what had happened to his mother he would have no choice but to think I was crazy, and the knowledge was as painful to me as having a stake driven through my heart.

"You need help," he said shakily. "There are doctors who can help you, Jessica."

"No. No one can help. I didn't want to hurt you, Dan. I'm sorry I didn't tell you everything before, but I knew you wouldn't understand. No one can do anything to help me."

Dan laid a hand tentatively on my shoulder and I rubbed the side of my face on the back of his hand, closing my eyes at the feel of his skin, warm on mine for what I feared might be the last time.

I felt the tears starting, but I choked them silently away, turning to look up at him in what I dreaded would be our final moments together.

His face was gray and hollow. I could see the sorrow etched deeply into his being, and knew that I was responsible for hurting the person I had come to love most in all the world.

"If it's some sort of dual personality disorder," he whispered fearfully, "there are places you can go . . ."

"I told you, it's not a disorder, it's real. I really am living as two different people."

"No, Jessica! That isn't possible. You must talk to someone about this . . ."

"Good-bye, Dan," I murmured as I slipped out from under the deadweight of his hand and made my way to the door. "Tell your father I think he's great . . . and Dan?"

"Yes?"

"Look after Frankie for me."

I wasn't sure what prompted me to ask him to look after Frankie for me. It was a gut feeling . . . something I couldn't quite put my finger on—a sixth sense that she would be better off with him, for tonight at least. During the long walk home the rain started. It began as a whisper of moisture against my skin, increasing gradually until I had to wipe droplets from my eyelashes. I hardly felt the cold; I was too numb already. By the time

I reached my flat, my clothes were soaked through and my feet were squelching inside my shoes. Without even bothering to dry off or turn on the lights, I closed the front door behind me, kicked off my sodden shoes, and flopped down onto the couch, burying my head in my arms.

It was still raining heavily when I awoke at midday in Lauren's bed; I could hear it lashing against the bedroom window. Consciousness as Lauren was hardly more appealing than how I'd felt as Jessica, and before I'd even opened my eyes I began to sob uncontrollably, hugging the frilled pillow to me and curling my racked body into a fetal position around it.

After a while, I heard a knock on the bedroom door and Karen's voice asking if I was all right.

I sat up and wiped my nose on the back of my hand, sniffing loudly.

"You can come in," I called in a nasal croak, sitting up with the pillow still clutched in my arms.

"What on earth's happened?" she said, taking one look at me and hurrying across the room to perch on the edge of the bed.

"I told Dan the truth about what's happening to me, and he thinks I'm insane," I sniffled, the tears flowing freely again. "I mean he would, wouldn't he? No one in their right mind would believe such a story. I wouldn't have believed it myself if it hadn't happened to me."

"I believe it," Karen said, putting her arm around my shaking shoulders. "Did you give him a chance to absorb what you told him, or did you just drop it on him from a great height and run away?"

I squinted at her through swollen eyelids. "Okay, I ran away, but he didn't come after me, did he?"

"How do you know he isn't banging on the door of your flat right now?"

"It won't make any difference," I wailed, breaking into a fresh torrent of sobs. "I can't do this anymore. I can't be two people. It's not fair to anyone, least of all me!"

"I know, I know," Karen said soothingly. "I wondered how long you'd be able to keep it up, but Lauren, think of the children. They need you! What would happen to this family without you? Grant can hardly cope with the children on his own. Without you their lives would be in the hands of a long succession of nannies. The children love you, Lauren. I've seen how happy everyone has been since you arrived."

"But I'm an imposter! I'm not their real mother. I'm lying to them and to Grant and to everyone I meet while I'm in her body."

"Would you rather they had no mother at all?"

"You could look after them. They love you."

"They love me as an auntie. I'm not cut out to be a mum. I like being here, helping, but my life is in London. I love my job, Lauren, and I love Jen. Can you see Grant allowing me and my partner to move in here?"

She paused as I smiled through my tears, sniffing loudly. "Probably not."

Sensing a moment of weakness, she gave me a squeeze. "Please, Lauren, I know I'm asking an awful lot of you. And I don't know what you're going to do about Dan, but Lauren has to stay." She set her lips in a firm line. "Come on, get up. I thought we might go out together and look for a swing set for the garden, as you suggested."

"I can't go out looking like this," I exclaimed, throwing down the pillow and walking over to the bathroom, where I peered in the mirror. "My face is all puffed up."

"It's raining; no one will notice," she said. "Come on, I've put all the clean laundry away while you've been over in Epsom, and I've put a chicken casserole in the oven for later, so you've got time to come out with me."

It took twenty minutes to make Lauren's face look respectable enough to go out, then Karen and I headed off to the farm where we'd taken the children the previous week. I'd noticed then that they were selling play equipment, and we headed back there to order a huge multi-swing gym. In the converted barn restaurant we ate a late lunch, which I toyed with listlessly, hardly tasting the food. Karen tried to jolly me along, and together we chose the equipment we wanted. Later, Karen watched anxiously under the shelter of the huge barn roof while I tapped Lauren's pin numbers into the credit card machine.

"I'm glad they're willing to deliver it," she said as we ran through the rain back to the car. "We'd never have gotten it into your van."

I smiled wanly, glad she'd made me come out of the house. "I hope Grant will be able to put it together when it arrives," I said as I started the engine. "I'm hopeless at those self-assembly things."

Looking in the mirror, ready to reverse, I let out a long slow whistle of breath.

"Don't look now," I told Karen. "But there's my stalker."

Jason was standing astride his powerful bike, watching us, his blond hair plastered to his head as rivulets of water ran down his face.

"He must be mad to be out in weather like this on a bike," Karen exclaimed, swiveling her head to stare at him. "What does he think he's going to achieve by hounding you?"

"I don't know," I said grimly as I nosed the car through the puddles and out of the parking lot onto the tarmac access road. "But he must have followed us from home. We probably didn't notice him because of the rain."

As I swept the car up the road, the bike came zooming past, throwing up flumes of spray.

"Bloody hell!" Karen shrieked as the bike stopped suddenly in front of us.

I floored the brakes, the wheels screaming for traction on the wet surface. The car spun sideways, narrowly missing the bike, but ended up with the passenger wheels half up a grassy bank. Karen lowered her window and yelled obscenities at Jason, who was sitting staring at us a little way off.

"Bugger off, you idiot!" Karen shouted. "Or I'll report you to the police."

Jason calmly gunned the bike toward us, and stopped only when its front wheel was rammed up against the driver's door. He rapped on the window until I reluctantly wound it down.

"This is doing no good," I said wearily as the rain splashed onto my face and arm through the open window. "Leave me alone, Jason."

He stared at me with his wild blue eyes and I shuddered at the desperation I saw there.

"I'm never giving you up," he hissed. "I know you love me. You're only staying with them out of a misplaced sense of duty."

"No, I'm staying because I want to."

"You don't know the half of it, though," he said coldly. "What do you think I came to talk to you about that day in the park? You tried telling me it was too risky meeting me with the children there, but I knew there was no risk at all."

I stared at him, dreading what he might be about to say.

He thrust his wet head through the open window. "I came to tell you Grant knew about us," he said. "That bastard husband of yours had found out about me. And do you know what he did about it?"

I sat rigidly, waiting for him to tell me, while the rain hammered down on the windshield and trickled down Jason's face.

"He tried to pay me off, Lauren. He thinks money can solve everything. He knew about us, but he thought I'd go away like a good little boy if he paid me enough of his precious money."

Gasping, I clutched at my throat, which seemed to be constricting painfully. I could barely breathe. So Grant had known all along! No wonder he'd been skeptical about Lauren's memory loss! He must have thought Jason had told me he'd found out about us and that I'd used the lightning strike to fake a lost memory to avoid the consequences of his wrath. And no wonder he'd taken my mobile phone and ignored Jason's pleading messages, I thought numbly.

Jason was still hovering over me, his presence a horrible reminder of Lauren's indiscretions and Grant's overbearing possessiveness.

Karen leaned across from the passenger side and glared at him. "No matter what you say, she's staying with her family, get it? She's made her choice, and you're not it. Now get lost."

"You told me something that day in the park, too," Jason pressed on, ignoring Karen's comment. "You told me why you'd decided to come away with me as soon as the time was right."

I peered up at him, the rain cold on my face through the open window. Something in his eyes reminded me suddenly of Dan. He was looking at me in that same sorrowful way that

Dan had looked at me last night, full of love and pity and desperation.

"Tell me," I said at last.

"He hit you," he said, raising his voice against the roar of the rain, watching my reaction with piercing eyes. "Before I could warn you that Grant had found out about us, you told me you already knew. He'd knocked you about badly, Lauren! You said he'd done it before. I begged you to come away with me there and then, but you refused to leave the retarded boy with him. You were afraid he'd take out his anger and frustration on him. You were going to find a new nanny for the other kids and put the boy safely out of harm's way in a home. When they were settled, we were going to start a new life. You promised, Lauren. You said you loved me."

I sat dumbly, trying to assimilate everything he'd told me. I remembered the bruises I'd seen on Lauren's ribs when I had stood in the shower that first time in the hospital. I'd believed they were the result of vigorous CPR, but now I wondered if they had been the result of Grant's anger. There had been the bruising to my arms, too, when he'd held me tightly after we'd met Jason in the restaurant. It would also explain why Lauren had been looking at special homes without her husband's knowledge, I thought grimly.

"I'm not leaving the children, Jason," I said quietly.

He leaned swiftly in at the window and kissed me full on the mouth. When I didn't respond, he stood back, stared at me for what seemed like an eternity, then backed away from the car, revving his engine wildly. For an awful moment I thought he was going to come at us again and ram the car with his bike, but then he backed the bike up and turned the wheel away from us.

"If I can't have you, he's not having you either!" he shouted.

We watched, struck dumb as Jason gunned the bike and zoomed away, the sound of the bike quickly fading into the mist and rain.

The honking of a horn behind us made us both jump, and I realized we were partially blocking the access-road. Shaking, I pulled the steering wheel around until the car screeched and skidded off the bank, then I waved my thanks at the other driver for waiting, and headed back onto the main road.

"Was that a death threat?" I asked Karen fearfully as we headed for home, my voice trembling and my mouth dry. "Would he rather see me dead than living with Grant?"

Karen frowned, obviously worried. "The ranting of a jilted lover, certainly. But we have to hope he wouldn't really do anything."

"Should we call the police, do you think?"

"I don't think there's much they could do. He hasn't hurt you, has he? And I don't believe he would. I think he's just besotted with you."

Dan's words came back to me, telling me that he was besotted with me, Jessica. Poor Jason, I thought. Poor Dan. Back at the house we made tea and drank it quietly, not sure what to say to each other while the rain pelted relentlessly down outside. It was nearly time for the school pickup, and I asked Karen if she'd mind coming with me, just in case Jason returned for another attempt to win his lover back.

"What am I going to do about Grant?" I asked as we drove through the rain once more. "Lauren was obviously scared for herself and Teddy."

"Jason might have been making it up," Karen cautioned. "He would have said anything to win you back."

"No." I shook my head. "It all makes sense. Grant is so controlling. He would never have let Lauren leave him, and he definitely knew about Jason, that's why he was so reluctant to believe in the memory loss. He probably couldn't believe his luck that just as his world was about to fall apart he was miraculously handed another chance. Lauren couldn't remember the affair, or the fact that he'd hit her. And it explains why he didn't know about the home for Teddy; Lauren was probably organizing that in secret."

It was pitch dark by the time we got to the boys' school and parked outside. If Jason had been lurking somewhere about we wouldn't have been able to see him anyway.

Toby and Teddy came out together. We listened to them chattering excitedly about having had to spend both break times indoors, but my thoughts were elsewhere. The girls were in gloomier moods, since they had both been given double homework, but I soon cheered up Nicole by reminding her that she could take Ginny to school in the morning.

As soon as we walked into the house we could detect the delicious smell of Karen's casserole cooking in the oven, and the children clamored to be fed at once. Hurrying into the kitchen, I paused only to tie an apron around my waist, and was about to serve up the food when I heard the front doorbell ring.

"Can you get it?" I called to Karen as I placed the ovenproof dish on the counter and removed the lid. I grabbed a soup ladle and had begun to dish the chicken portions onto plates when Karen came into the kitchen, her eyes wide and staring, her face ashen.

I froze.

"What?"

Behind her, two uniformed figures appeared, their navy blue coats slick with rain, flat caps twisting in their hands.

"What's happened?"

"It's Grant," Karen said tonelessly. "He's been involved in a traffic accident."

"I'm very sorry, Mrs. Richardson." One of the police officers stepped toward me. "Your husband's car was involved in a multiple collision and he has been taken to St. Matthew's Accident and Emergency by ambulance."

"Is he all right?"

"The doctors were working on him when we left."

I gripped the ladle tightly as I stared at their solemn faces, unaware of the gravy pooling on the counter beside me. "What happened?"

"It seems from initial witness reports that a motorbike jumped a red light at the crossroads. The driver behind your husband's Mercedes says your husband swerved to avoid it and collided with a container truck coming in the other direction. The bike's momentum apparently carried it right on and it skidded into both vehicles. In these wet conditions there was nothing either Mr. Richardson or the truck driver could have done."

"What are you saying?"

The police officer looked decidedly ill at ease. "I'm afraid the motorcyclist didn't make it."

"You mean he's dead?" I grabbed the corner of the kitchen counter for support, my mind whirling frantically. Had the motorcyclist been Jason? Had he done it on purpose?

The officer nodded. "I'm afraid so."

Coming to my senses, I propped the ladle in the casserole dish, untied the apron, and threw it on the counter. "Can I go and see my husband?"

The police officers exchanged glances. "We've got instructions to take you to the hospital right away, if you're ready, Mrs. Richardson."

"Mummy, what's happening?"

I looked down to see Sophie staring up at me, her eyes wide with fear.

"It's Daddy. He's in the hospital. I'm going to see him now."

"Can I come?"

I glanced down at her, then up at Karen. "Can you give the children their dinner and then bring them along later?"

Karen nodded and I turned my attention back to Sophie. "Auntie Karen will bring you and Nicole and the boys to the hospital when you've eaten." I turned to follow the officers into the hall, grabbing my coat and bag from the banisters as I went. "Be a good girl and help Auntie Karen," I called back to Sophie from the hall. "I'll see you later."

My first view of the entrance to the emergency unit at St. Matthew's Hospital was through a haze of teeming rain. Lights shone out onto the tarmac from the double doors, illuminating the bouncing drops and sending them skyward in a fine spray. The police car pulled up at the entrance, turned off the windshield wipers, and killed the engine. I thanked both officers, who followed me as I scrambled out into the dark night and hurried toward the lighted entrance. Once inside, the police officers removed their hats and stood quietly against the far wall while I gave a woman at the reception desk my name.

Recognition passed over her face when I told her I'd come to visit my husband, who had been brought in from a traffic accident. She asked me to take a seat on one of the waiting room chairs among a group of anxious and resigned-looking patients while she rang for a member of staff.

It seemed that I had only just sat down when a uniformed nurse arrived to escort me through the double doors into the inner sanctum of the emergency room. I eyed the row of curtained cubicles apprehensively, but she led me past them to an open area where several medics were working on a patient lying on a stretcher, surrounded by carts overflowing with machinery, wires, and hospital equipment.

"I'll fetch a doctor to come and speak to you," she said as she scurried toward the group.

I waited anxiously, running the strap of my bag nervously through my fingers, watching as the nurse tapped one of the doctors on the shoulder and motioned toward where I was standing. I couldn't see Grant and assumed he had been separated off into a side room or taken up to a ward.

The doctor looked around at the nurse's whispered words and I recognized him at once. It was Dr. Shakir, who had attended me when I'd been in the hospital myself less than two weeks before. He hurried across to greet me, his hand outstretched.

"I'm sorry to have to meet you again under such difficult circumstances, Mrs. Richardson."

"Where is my husband? Is he all right?" I asked, realizing through the numbness in my brain that it was a pretty foolish question. But I still wasn't sure where Grant had been taken or how badly he was injured.

"Your husband has been in a very bad accident," Dr. Shakir explained. He turned to indicate the patient behind him on the stretcher, and I realized with a sickening jolt that the patient who was warranting all the attention must be Grant. I tried to look past Dr. Shakir but the other medical staff blocked my view.

The doctor took my elbow and guided me smoothly back out

into the corridor, where he waved me down onto a chair and perched on the corner of another one beside me.

"Can I see him?" I fixed frightened eyes on the doctor. "How bad is he?"

"We are trying to get him stabilized, so we can take him to the operating room."

I breathed out a sigh of relief. "So it's fixable? Has he broken something?"

Dr. Shakir's expression became infinitely sympathetic. "Mrs. Richardson . . . Lauren, wasn't it? Apart from multiple cuts and contusions to his head and body, your husband suffered severe crush injuries when he was trapped under the truck. The fire brigade freed him as swiftly as possible, but, as with many crush injuries, there are complications."

I felt my mouth go dry and I glanced past him to where a blue curtain obscured my view through the low window to the emergency room. "Will he be all right?"

"At this stage it is difficult to say. Your husband is presenting with severe hypovolemia—that is, decreased blood volume—due, we believe, to the possible hemorrhaging of internal injuries sustained in the accident. He hasn't long come in and we are at present in the throes of assessing him while administering intravenous fluids. We have ordered an emergency full-body MRI scan to locate the source of the bleeding . . . but"—Dr. Shakir avoided my anxious gaze—"there is a danger that a combination of the shock and dehydration may result in acute renal failure."

I looked at him blankly, not willing to understand what he was saying. Taking a deep breath, I asked the question again. "You mean you don't know where he's hurt?"

"We believe Mr. Richardson has multiple internal injuries,

but until we have the scan and we have him stabilized, we can't risk opening him up."

"Is it very serious?"

"Your husband is fighting for his life."

My whole body seemed to deflate. For a moment the room swam woozily before me, and then I raised my head and looked the doctor in the eye. "Can I see him?"

Dr. Shakir rose to his feet and waved me back toward the emergency room. As I approached the bed, the other nurses and doctors stood back and I could see Grant at last, although I hardly recognized him, surrounded as he was by tubes, wires, and catheters all connected in turn to bags of fluid, oxygen, blood, drainage tubes, and rhythmically beeping machinery. His head was dotted with heavy gauze dressings and I wondered how bad the cuts and contusions were.

"The head wounds are minor"—Dr. Shakir was at my elbow and seemed to be reading my thoughts—"in comparison to his other injuries."

"Can he hear me?" I crept closer to the bed and stared down at this man whom I had only known for such a short time, yet who had played such a significant part in my life as Lauren and in the lives of the children. I tried not to think of my bruised ribs and Grant's duplicity in allowing me to believe all had been well between us before the lightning strike. Taking one of his bloody hands in mine, I squeezed it gently, remembering how he had been there for me when I had come around in hospital that first time, confused and in denial about what was happening.

"Grant," I whispered, bending low so he could hear me, "Grant, you have to fight. The children need you."

Grant's eyes flickered open and he squinted up at me. "Lauren? Is that you?"

His voice was thin and rasping, as if the strain of speaking was almost too much for him. The beeping of the machines increased in intensity with the effort and the medics clustered around, checking his pulse, drawing blood, and checking his drainage bags.

"I'm here, Grant," I told him, still holding his hand, although I stepped back slightly to allow Dr. Shakir to examine him again.

"We can't wait for the MRI. I think we'll have to risk opening him up." Dr. Shakir was shaking his head.

"We have an elevated creatinine reading," one of the nurses reported urgently. "He's going into renal failure."

"I think we're losing him," another nurse exclaimed. "Stand by with the crash cart."

The medics pushed me away and I stood back, my hands shaking and my eyes wide with fear, watching as Grant fought for breath. I vowed to repay the favor and be there for him for as long as he needed me.

He opened his eyes again, and this time he seemed to focus clearly on my face. I stepped closer again. "Can you forgive me?" he whispered.

"You did what you thought was right." I felt tears brimming in my eyes and blinked them back.

"I would never have harmed the children," he said, so quietly I had to make myself a space in the press of bodies around him and lean close to hear him.

"I know, Grant. You are a good father. I never doubted it."

He smiled faintly, though his face had drained of blood and his eyes had taken on a dull, almost lifeless depth. His voice was no more than a labored exhale. "You know I love you, Lauren, don't you?"

I leaned even closer and pressed Lauren's lips briefly to his forehead. "I know."

Grant's eyes closed and the machine beside him gave several jerky fluttering beeps, culminating in a long, flat, unbroken tone.

The medics and nurses leapt into action and I was pulled away and hustled out into the corridor, only vaguely aware of the escalating activity around his bed and the shouts of "clear" from one of the medics. For several minutes all was pandemonium and then I was suddenly aware that the room had gone quiet. The feverish activity around Grant's strecter had ceased and everyone was standing very still.

The machine emitted a long, low wail, and I held my hand to my mouth, realizing that the children's father was dead.

The evening passed in a daze. Karen had brought the children to the hospital and I had taken Sophie to see her father's body, believing she was old enough to understand and to say good-bye.

The younger children didn't really comprehend the enormity of what had befallen them, and the necessity of continuing with their normal bedtime routine gave me a reason to leave the hospital with them and Karen and return to Grant's family home without him, despite the fact that my heart was weeping for his children.

After getting the younger children to bed, Sophie cried herself to sleep on my lap. Eventually, Karen and I tucked her up in her bed without undressing her in case she woke again, then we sat in the lounge and stared at each other, too shocked by what had happened to speak.

At length, we drew the curtains against the outside world and Karen poured us each a large brandy. I sipped at it hesitantly, not used to the burning sensation as the unaccustomed alcohol trickled down my throat.

"Do you think Jason did it on purpose?" I asked at last.

Karen nodded. "It looks like it. The police said witnesses reported the motorbike sped across the path of Grant's car at the junction, giving him no chance whatsoever. In wet conditions like this he could never have avoided the crash. It's fortunate the truck driver wasn't hurt, too."

"Jason can't have meant to kill himself as well, surely?"

"He seemed pretty desperate to me. That's what he must have meant about no one having you if he couldn't. He wasn't threatening you, he was planning to get rid of Grant, even if it meant killing himself."

"Why didn't you say any of this to the police?"

Karen shrugged. "What would have been the point of that? I didn't want to implicate you. It's better that the police think Jason was a stranger. The children need you more than ever now, and we can't risk anyone thinking you were involved in any way."

"What if this is my fault?" I asked, taking a large mouthful of the brandy and choking as it stung my throat. I wiped a hand over my eyes and looked beseechingly at Karen. "I know I didn't choose any of this but if I hadn't taken Lauren's place, she would probably have gone off with Jason, and Grant would still be alive."

"We don't know for sure that she would really have gone with him," Karen said gently.

"The vicar believed Lauren was going to leave the family," I reminded her. "That's why she prayed so hard for the family to stay together."

"You have to assume that her prayers were answered then,"

Karen pointed out. "The powers that be may or may not have known the journey would end like this, but they still set you on it, didn't they?"

I shook my head. "I still feel this hasn't worked out as it should. Both the children's parents are dead now, aren't they? That can't have been intended."

"We'll probably never know whether any of this was intended," Karen said, shaking her head. "Maybe, after all, it's to do with that stuff you said you'd looked up about the relativity of space and time, and the lightning being the catalyst to set it all in motion. But whether any of this was planned, or whether it was some huge accident of nature, the outcome is that you are still here. The children believe you are their mother and they love you."

"Except Teddy. He knows I'm not."

"You can't have everything. And he loves you anyway. You're doing the best you can, Lauren. The children will learn to cope."

"I hope you're right," I whispered, taking another swig of brandy. "I really hope you are right."

I was sure I wouldn't sleep that night, but as soon as Lauren's head touched the pillow I awoke to find that I was lying cold and stiff and miserable on the couch in my flat. I stretched out my cramped limbs and looked at the sitting room clock. It was ten o'clock in the morning on the last day of Grant's life.

Putting my head in my hands, I wondered if there was any way I could warn Grant about what Jason was intending, but then realized that although from my perspective I hadn't experienced my Wednesday yet, Lauren had already had hers. The accident had already taken place in Grant's and Lauren's lives and there was nothing I could do to change those terrible events, no matter how much I might wish to do so.

For a moment I sat in absolute dejection. My life as Lauren had been turned upside down, and in this consciousness—as Jessica—I had driven away the man I loved with all my heart and soul.

Dragging myself to the bathroom, I began to run a bath, but the boiler must have blown out in the night because there was no hot water coming from the taps. I stared out of the high window at the rain pelting down outside. My clothes were damp and soggy from last night's long walk home in the rain, and my hair hung in stringy clumps. The flat was so silent that even the ticking of the clock made my nerves quiver.

A flash of lightning lit the gray sky outside the window, and I listened for the thunder, counting automatically in my head. Three seconds. The storm must be several miles away.

Walking back to the sitting room, I looked at the mat in front of the door. No sign of a note there from Dan. So Karen had been wrong; he hadn't been banging on my door in the night. But she had been right about one thing, I thought, as I replayed the previous night's events in my mind. I'd been so sure of his reaction that I hadn't really given Dan a chance to come to grips with what I was telling him. I'd just blurted it out and run away.

I realized that I owed it to him to try to explain what had been happening to me in a more rational manner, and to give him a chance to talk to me about it.

Picking up my car keys, I ran outside through the pelting rain and climbed into my car. I knew I looked a wreck, but I needed to talk to Dan urgently before he left for work.

It only took me a few minutes to get to his place, and I parked the car, then ran up the drive and hammered on the door.

After a few minutes I figured I must have missed him, and I didn't want to risk dragging his father out of bed to answer the door, so I went back to the car and sat there with my newly wetted hair dripping onto my jeans, and tried to think.

If Dan had gone to work after what had happened between us I would have been very surprised. If he wasn't at home, I reasoned he could be out walking with the dogs, despite the rain, thinking things over. If that were the case, I thought I knew where he might have gone.

Ramming the car into reverse, I turned and drove back the way I had come, out of Epsom and up toward the Downs. I parked in the same lot I'd parked in almost two weeks ago, shaking my head at the realization of how much had happened to me in such a short space of time. Locking the car and wrapping my arms around my shivering body, I headed towards the spot where I had first met Dan. The rain was bitterly cold and I was wet through to the bone already. I knew without needing a mirror that my lips would be a deep purple color by now, as deep as the ominous-looking sky. The trees on the horizon, which had been so beautiful in their autumn regalia only a week ago, looked sad and bedraggled under the onslaught of the pounding rain, and the beaten-down grass resembled the gray sheen of a rolling ocean.

After following the chalk path for a few minutes I glanced up to see a small shape hurtling toward me.

"Frankie!"

She barked in delight and tried to jump up at me, and in another moment Bessie had joined her. I knelt to pet and hug both the soggy dogs against me, and as I did so I glanced up through the gray mist of rain to see Dan standing a short way off, watching silently.

Slowly, I rose to my feet, my eyes locked on his.

Frankie stared anxiously from me to him, then ran back with

Bessie in her wake to stand with Dan. Dan bent and clipped the dogs' leashes to their collars, then he straightened up and gazed sorrowfully at me. I felt his eyes boring into mine and then he started to walk toward me.

Lightning flashed suddenly with a tremendous cracking sound and my whole world lit up around me. It felt as if the heavens had opened and sent shards of white-hot glass slicing into my body. The rain ceased to exist and I was standing in a golden glow of light. I could feel my hair standing on end and hear a high-pitched ringing in my ears. Very slowly I saw Dan reach out his hand to me, a look of desperate horror on his face. The two dogs were howling, but somehow it sounded very faint and far away. For one blissful moment I felt totally connected to Dan, and then the ringing in my ears became a roaring sound and my world went blank.

I sat up in bed with a jolt. Sweat was pouring off me and my whole body was shaking uncontrollably. Reaching over to the bedside cabinet, I flicked on the light and realized it was only eleven-thirty at night. I'd been in bed no more than an hour and a half, yet I felt as if I'd been in the deepest of sleeps. I gazed around at the familiar room with the door leading off to the en suite bathroom. Nothing seemed out of the ordinary, yet I felt strangely disconcerted.

Climbing out of bed, I drew my negligee closely around me and tiptoed out onto the landing. At the door of each of the children's rooms I paused and peeped inside. Sophie was curled up, a damp tissue balled in her fist. Her peaceful face was still wet with tears. Grant, of course! No wonder I felt so disoriented. The children's father had been killed in a terrible collision with—that motorcyclist. How could I have forgotten something so terrible?

Nicole, looking so like me, was on her back snoring with her mouth slightly open. I tiptoed in and straightened her covers, then wandered on to the next room, where the twins were sleeping in adjacent beds.

Toby was smiling in his sleep, and I brushed a lock of hair from his forehead, then turned to gaze at Teddy. My special child was curled around his precious ball, his breathing shallow, even, and peaceful. I touched the back of my hand to his pink cheek and thrilled at the comforting warmth of his little body.

I loved the children so much it almost hurt to breathe, yet when I thought of Grant I felt nothing but regret for a wasted life and sorrow for the children that they would have to grow up without him.

I turned to walk back to my bedroom just as the spare-room door opened and Karen stuck her tousled head into the landing.

"Oh, it's only you," she said. "I wondered who that was walking about. I thought you were asleep."

"I had the weirdest dream," I told her, frowning. "It seemed so real at the time, but now I can't remember what happened."

"Lauren?" my sister said sharply, looking at me strangely. "Is that you?"

I stood stock still, staring at her uncertainly, and then I smiled and threw my arms round her neck. "I dreamed," I whispered in a fascinated voice. "Lauren dreamed, and I'm still here in the middle of the night."

"Jessica?"

"Yes," I nodded. "I'm here."

Karen let out a cry that was half sigh, half groan. "I thought for a moment there that you'd gone, that it was Lauren here on her own—the real Lauren, I mean."

I shook my head, still puzzling over some incident that I couldn't remember. "Something bad has happened," I said.

"It's been a terrible night," Karen agreed. "Will you be all right? Do you want me to stay with you for the rest of the night?"

"No, I'll be fine. I just wanted to make sure everything was as it should be. I needed to make sure I was really here. I've got this really weird feeling."

"You mean because you haven't flitted off to be somewhere else?"

I shook my head. "It's not just that . . . I don't remember . . . it was something about Jessica, but the dream is fading, and the more I try to capture it the more it eludes me."

"Go back to bed," Karen said, guiding me to my room. "Everything will seem clearer in the morning."

"I'm afraid to sleep," I murmured as I padded over to the big bed and pulled the covers over me. "What if I'm not here in the morning?"

"You silly thing," she smiled. "Of course you'll be here, Lauren. This is where you belong."

epilogue

The next morning I awoke to find I was still Lauren: the new Lauren with her dark blond hair and hazel eyes. Karen and I decided to take the three younger children to school, since they hadn't seemed to understand the enormity of what had befallen the family and there seemed no point in upsetting their routine. Nicole took Ginny in a straw-filled box, her eyes shining with pride as she went toward her classroom.

We kept Sophie at home, where she stayed snuggled in bed with her rabbit in a box next to her. I looked in on her every so often to find her tearfully hugging her pet. I sat with her for a while, listening as she talked about her father and reassuring her I would be there for her always, then hoping and praying that I was right.

I was anxious because I hadn't felt or experienced anything as Jessica in the night. I waited until the house was quiet, then dialed the number of my flat. The phone rang and rang unanswered and I slammed the phone down, knowing she couldn't answer because I was here, but I was worried all the same.

Next I rang my parents' number in Somerset. My heart lurched at the sound of my father's voice as he answered the phone.

"Hello?"

"Mr. Taylor?"

"Yes."

"Hello, this is Lauren Richardson. I'm a friend of Jessica's. I'm having trouble reaching her; I was wondering, have you heard from her at all?"

The sob at the end of the line confirmed my worst fears, and I slumped down in the living room chair, my legs unable to support me.

"I'm very sorry to have to tell you," he said at last, in a shuddering voice that was barely under control. "Our daughter died yesterday. She was out on the Downs when she was struck by lightning, and it caused her heart to stop."

I dropped the phone with a wail of anguish and buried my face in my hands. Karen came running in, took one look at me, and picked up the receiver. I heard her asking questions and making sympathetic noises into the phone, and then she hung up and gathered me into her arms.

Karen stayed for a few days after Grant's funeral, while we recovered from the shock of what had happened to Grant and to Jessica, but her work was calling her, and at the end of the weekend she bade us a tearful good-bye.

We hugged in the doorway. "Make sure you come and visit more often," I said. "Come as many weekends as you can. We'll see you again on the day of Nicole's concert, of course, and then you must persuade your partner Jen to come with you and spend Christmas with us."

The house seemed empty without her. I roamed from room to

room, searching for something that was missing, but I knew that what I was looking for wasn't here. The children ate and played and did their homework, and I cooked and cleared up, sorted their endless laundry into piles, and pretended that my heart wasn't breaking.

Teddy had taken to following me around the house, as if he felt sure that if he let me out of his sight I'd vanish or something. I teased him about it, but he simply gazed at me knowingly, keeping our silent secret. He was happier at nursery school now, with the knowledge that he would soon be leaving, and I had honored Grant's wish that we should leave Toby where he was, despite my personal feelings on the matter.

On the Monday morning two weeks after Grant's fatal accident, the day dawned crisp and bright. After depositing the children at their schools, I decided to go for a drive. I needed time to think and to get my new life in order.

I didn't really know where I was heading when I set out, but after an hour or so of driving I realized that, like a homing pigeon, I was coming close to the Epsom Downs.

The car seemed to find the lot all by itself, and I parked and climbed out, breathing in the fresh November air. It was quite chilly, so I slipped a cashmere jacket over my new jeans, then headed off up the familiar chalk track, marveling at the stunning scenery around me.

I'd not gone far when a small black terrier came bounding toward me.

"Frankie!"

I bent to gather her into my arms, stroking her silky head ecstatically as she barked wildly and jumped up, licking my face. Tears trickled down my cheeks as I thought how much the children would love her, and then the tears turned to laughter as she bounded and leapt around me with such exuberance that it was hard to resist her joyful mood.

"I'm sorry, is Frankie bothering you?" a male voice asked nearby, making me jump.

Glancing up over her head, I saw Dan looking at me, and my heart gave a surge of joy.

"Not at all," I said, blushing to the roots of my light brown hair. "I think she's very sweet."

He was looking at me strangely, almost as if he recognized me, and I stood up, desperately resisting the urge to throw myself into his arms.

"She doesn't often behave like this," he said, and we both laughed suddenly as the small dog capered around me. "She belongs to a friend who died recently. Frankie only ever acted like this for her."

"I'm sorry . . . about your friend, I mean. My husband died recently, too, so I know how you must be feeling."

He came closer and gazed into my eyes with his deep mischievous blue ones, and I felt a tingle run right through me.

"There's something about your laugh . . ." He broke off, sounding puzzled.

I smiled widely, unable to contain myself, wondering if he'd remember what I'd told him on our last evening together. "My name is Lauren."

He paled and took a step back.

"I'm Dan," he said hesitantly. "Look, I know this must seem like a weird question, but do you have any children?"

"I have four of them," I said proudly. "And I love them to bits."

He swallowed hard, as if he were trying not to choke on something.

"Are you all right?" I asked lightly.

"Yes," he managed at last. He was still looking at me oddly, but then he seemed to pull himself together. "I know we've only just met, but perhaps we could go for a coffee or something? I think I need a drink."

I gazed at him, wondering if I would ever be able to tell him the whole truth. In my mind's eye I saw him pushing Teddy on the swing and kicking a football with Toby while the girls and Frankie raced around him excitedly, vying for attention.

"You look more like a Guinness man to me," I said with a smile. "But coffee will do very well."

"There's a good pub up by the grandstand. Perhaps we could go there and scrap the coffee. How about a glass of wine?"

He was looking at me in that strange way again, as if he were testing me.

I shook my head. "I'll stick with the coffee thanks, or water. I don't drink alcohol."

Dan laughed incredulously, then took my hand in his, calling to the dogs as he did so. A thrill ran through me at his touch, almost like a spark of electricity. I smiled into his eyes and together we walked back toward the cars, with Frankie trotting happily at our heels.

about the author

Melanie Rose was an avid reader from an early age and found herself looking at the world around her and wondering "what if?" She began writing as a teenager, progressing to short stories and articles for magazines and newspapers. She trained as a nursery nurse and later became a play therapist on the children's ward at the Royal Marsden Hospital, continuing to write in her spare time.

Her first novel was voted one of the favorite reads of the year by listeners of Britain Radio 4's *Open Book* program.

She now lives in Surrey with her husband and four sons, who, along with many of the children she has cared for, provide much inspiration for her books.

For further information about Melanie please visit www.melanierose.co.uk.